Ghetto Comedies by Israel Zangwill

Israel Zangwill was born in London on 21st January 1864, to a family of Jewish immigrants from the Russian Empire.

Zangwill was initially educated in Plymouth and Bristol. At age 9 he was enrolled in the Jews' Free School in Spitalfields in east London. Zangwill excelled here. He began to teach part-time at the school and eventually full time. Whilst teaching he also studied with the University of London and by 1884 had earned his BA with triple honours in philosophy, history, and the sciences.

His writing earned him the sobriquet "the Dickens of the Ghetto" primarily based on his much lauded novel 'Children of the Ghetto: A Study of a Peculiar People' in 1892 and its glimpse of the poverty-stricken life in London's Jewish quarter.

As a writer he was keen to reflect on his political and social outlooks. His simulation of Yiddish sentence structure in English aroused great interest. His mystery work, 'The Big Bow Mystery' (1892) was the first locked room mystery novel.

Zangwill was also involved with narrowly focused Jewish issues as an assimilationist, an early Zionist, and later a territorialist. In the early 1890s he had joined the Lovers of Zion movement in England. In 1897 he joined Theodor Herzl (considered the father of modern political Zionism) in founding the World Zionist Organization.

Zangwill quit the established philosophy of Zionism when his plan for a homeland in Uganda was rejected and founded his own organisation; the Jewish Territorialist Organization. Its stated goal was to create a Jewish homeland in whatever territory in the world could be found for them.

Amongst the challenges in his life he found time to write poetry. He had translated a medieval Jewish poet in 1903 and his volume 'Blind Children' in 1908 shows his promise in this new endeavour.

'The Melting Pot' in 1909 made Zangwill's name as an admired playwright. When the play opened in Washington D.C., former President Theodore Roosevelt leaned over the edge of his box and shouted, "That's a great play, Mr. Zangwill, that's a great play."

Israel Zangwill died on 1st August 1926 in Midhurst, West Sussex.

Index of Contents
NOTE
THE MODEL OF SORROWS
ANGLICIZATION
THE JEWISH TRINITY
THE SABBATH QUESTION IN SUDMINSTER
THE RED MARK
THE BEARER OF BURDENS

THE LUFTMENSCH
THE TUG OF LOVE
THE YIDDISH 'HAMLET'
THE CONVERTS
HOLY WEDLOCK
ELIJAH'S GOBLET
THE HIRELINGS
SAMOOBORONA
ISRAEL ZANGWILL – A SHORT BIOGRAPHY
ISRAEL ZANGWILL – A CONCISE BIBLIOGRAPHY

NOTE

Simultaneously with the publication of these 'Ghetto Comedies' a fresh edition of my 'Ghetto Tragedies' is issued, with the original title restored. In the old definition a comedy could be distinguished from a tragedy by its happy ending. Dante's Hell and Purgatory could thus appertain to a 'comedy.' This is a crude conception of the distinction between Tragedy and Comedy, which I have ventured to disregard, particularly in the last of these otherwise unassuming stories.

I.Z.
SHOTTERMILL, April, 1907.

CHAPTER I

HOW I FOUND THE MODEL

I cannot pretend that my ambition to paint the Man of Sorrows had any religious inspiration, though I fear my dear old dad at the Parsonage at first took it as a sign of awakening grace. And yet, as an artist, I have always been loath to draw a line between the spiritual and the beautiful; for I have ever held that the beautiful has in it the same infinite element as forms the essence of religion. But I cannot explain very intelligibly what I mean, for my brush is the only instrument through which I can speak. And if I am here paradoxically proposing to use my pen to explain what my brush failed to make clear, it is because the criticism with which my picture of the Man of Sorrows has been assailed drives me to this attempt at verbal elucidation. My picture, let us suppose, is half-articulate; perhaps my pen can manage to say the other half, especially as this other half mainly consists of things told me and things seen.

And in the first place, let me explain that the conception of the picture which now hangs in its gilded frame is far from the conception with which I started—was, in fact, the ultimate stage of an evolution—for I began with nothing deeper in my mind than to image a realistic Christ, the Christ who sat in the synagogue of Jerusalem, or walked about the shores of Galilee. As a painter in love with the modern, it seemed to me that, despite the innumerable representations of Him by the masters of all nations, few, if any, had sought their inspiration in reality. Each nation had unconsciously given Him its own national type, and though there was a subtle truth in this, for what each nation worshipped was truly the God made over again in its own highest image, this was not the truth after which I was seeking.

I started by rejecting the blonde, beardless type which Da Vinci and others have imposed upon the world, for Christ, to begin with, must be a Jew. And even when, in the course of my researches for a Jewish model, I became aware that there were blonde types, too, these seemed to me essentially Teutonic. A characteristic of the Oriental face, as I figured it, was a sombre majesty, as of the rabbis of Rembrandt, the very antithesis of the ruddy gods of Walhalla. The characteristic Jewish face must suggest more of the Arab than of the Goth.

I do not know if the lay reader understands how momentous to the artist is his model, how dependent he is on the accident of finding his creation already anticipated, or at least shadowed forth, in Nature. To me, as a realist, it was particularly necessary to find in Nature the original, without which no artist can ever produce those subtle nuances which give the full sense of life. After which, if I say, that my aim is not to copy, but to interpret and transfigure, I suppose I shall again seem to be self-contradictory. But that, again, must be put down to my fumbling pen-strokes.

Perhaps I ought to have gone to Palestine in search of the ideal model, but then my father's failing health kept me within a brief railway run of the Parsonage. Besides, I understood that the dispersion of the Jews everywhere made it possible to find Jewish types anywhere, and especially in London, to which flowed all the streams of the Exile. But long days of hunting in the Jewish quarter left me despairing. I could find types of all the Apostles, but never of the Master.

Running down one week-end to Brighton to recuperate, I joined the Church Parade on the lawns. It was a sunny morning in early November, and I admired the three great even stretches of grass, sea, and sky, making up a picture that was unspoiled even by the stuccoed boarding-houses. The parasols fluttered amid the vast crowd of promenaders like a swarm of brilliant butterflies. I noted with amusement that the Church Parade was guarded by beadles from the intrusion of the ill-dressed, and the spectacle of over-dressed Jews paradoxically partaking in it reminded me of the object of my search. In vain my eye roved among these; their figures were strangely lacking in the dignity and beauty which I had found among the poorest. Suddenly I came upon a sight that made my heart leap. There, squatting oddly enough on the pavement-curb of a street opposite the lawns, sat a frowsy, gaberdined Jew. Vividly set between the tiny green cockle-shell hat on his head and the long uncombed black beard was the face of my desire. The head was bowed towards the earth; it did not even turn towards the gay crowd, as if the mere spectacle was beadle-barred. I was about to accost this strange creature who sat there so immovably, when a venerable Royal Academician who resides at Hove came towards me with hearty hand outstretched, and bore me along in the stream of his conversation and geniality. I looked back yearningly; it was as if the Academy was dragging me away from true Art.

'I think, if you don't mind, I'll get that old chap's address,' I said.

He looked back and shook his head in laughing reproof.

'Another study in dirt and ugliness! Oh, you youngsters!'

My heart grew hot against his smug satisfaction with his own conventional patterns and prettinesses.

'Behind that ugliness and dirt I see the Christ,' I retorted. 'I certainly did not see Him in the Church Parade.'

'Have you gone on the religious lay now?' he asked, with a burst of his bluff laughter.

'No, but I'm going,' I said, and turned back.

I stood, pretending to watch the gay parasols, but furtively studying my Jew. Yes, in that odd figure, so strangely seated on the pavement, I had chanced on the very features, the haunting sadness and mystery of which I had been so long in quest. I wondered at the simplicity with which he was able to maintain a pose so essentially undignified. I told myself I beheld the East squatted broodingly as on a divan, while the West paraded with parasol and Prayer-Book. I wondered that the beadles were unobservant of him. Were they content with his abstention from the holy ground of the Church Parade, and the less sacred seats on the promenade without, or would they, if their eyes drew towards him, move him on from further profaning those frigidly respectable windows and stuccoed portals?

At last I said: 'Good-morning.' And he rose hurriedly and began to move away uncomplainingly, as one used to being hounded from everywhere.

'Guten Morgen,' I said in German, with a happy inspiration, for in my futile search in London I had found that a corrupt German called Yiddish usually proved a means of communication.

He paused, as if reassured. 'Gut' Morgen,' he murmured; and then I saw that his stature was kingly, like that of the sons of Anak, and his manner a strange blend of majesty and humility.

'Pardon me,' I went on, in my scrupulously worst German, 'may I ask you a question?'

He made a curious movement of acquiescence, compounded of a shrug and a slight uplifting of his palms.

'Are you in need of work?'

'And why do you wish to know?' he replied, answering, as I had already found was the Jewish way, one question by another.

'I thought I could find you some,' I said.

'Have you scrolls of the Law for me to write?' he replied incredulously. 'You are not even a Jew.'

'Still, there may be something,' I replied. 'Let us walk along.'

I felt that the beadle's eye was at last drawn to us both, and I hurried my model down a side-street. I noticed he hobbled as if footsore. He did not understand what I wanted, but he understood a pound a week, for he was starving, and when I said he must leave Brighton for London, he replied, awe-struck: 'It is the finger of God.' For in London were his wife and children.

His name was Israel Quarriar, his country Russia.

The picture was begun on Monday morning. Israel Quarriar's presence dignified the studio. It was thrilling and stimulating to see his noble figure and tragic face, the head drooped humbly, the beard like a prophet's.

'It is the finger of God,' I, too, murmured, and fell to work, exalted.

I worked, for the most part, in rapt silence—perhaps the model's silence was contagious—but gradually through the days I grew to communion with his shy soul, and piecemeal I learnt his sufferings. I give his story, so far as I can, in his own words, which I often paused to take down, when they were characteristic.

CHAPTER II

THE MODEL'S STORY

I came here because Russia had grown intolerable to me. All my life, and during the lives of my parents, we Quarriars had been innkeepers, and thereby earned our bread. But Russia took away our livelihood for herself, and created a monopoly. Thus we were left destitute. So what could I do with a large family? Of London and America I had long heard as places where they have compassion on foreigners. They are not countries like Russia, where Truth exists not. Secondly, my children also worried me greatly. They are females, all the five, and a female in Russia, however beautiful, good and clever she be, if she have no dowry, has to accept any offer of marriage, however uncongenial the man may be. These things conspired to drive me from Russia. So I turned everything into money, and realized three hundred and fifty roubles. People had told me that the whole journey to London should cost us two hundred roubles, so I concluded I should have one hundred and fifty roubles with which to begin life in the new country. It was very bitter to me to leave my Fatherland, but as the moujik says: 'Necessity brings everything.' So we parted from our friends with many tears: little had we thought we should be so broken up in our old age. But what else could I do in such a wretched country? As the moujik says: 'If the goat doesn't want to go to market it is compelled to go.' So I started for London. We travelled to Isota on the Austrian frontier. As we sat at the railway-station there, wondering how we were going to smuggle ourselves across the frontier, in came a benevolent-looking Jew with a long venerable beard, two very long ear-locks, and a girdle round his waist, washed his hands ostentatiously at the station tap, prayed aloud the Asher Yotzer with great fervour, and on finishing his prayer looked everyone expectantly in the eyes, and all responded 'Amen.' Then he drew up his coat-sleeve with great deliberation, extended his hand, gave me an effusive 'Shalom Aleichem' and asked me how it went with me. Soon he began to talk about the frontier. Said he: 'As you see me, an Ish kosher (a ritually correct man), I will do you a kindness, not for money, but for the sake of the Mitzvah (good deed).' I began to smell a rat, and thought to myself, How comes it that you know I want the frontier? Your kindness is suspicious, for, as the moujik says: 'The devil has guests.' But if we need the thief, we cut him down even from the gallows.

Such a necessary rascal proved Elzas Kazelia. I asked him how much he wanted to smuggle me across. He answered thus: 'I see that you are a clever respectable man, so look upon my beard and ear-locks, and you will understand that you will receive fair treatment from me. I want to earn a Mitzvah (good deed) and a little money thereby.'

Then he cautioned me not to leave the station and go out into the street, because in the street were to be found Jews without beards, who would inform on me and give me up to the police. 'The world does not contain a sea of Kazelias,' said he. (Would that it did not contain even that one!)

Then he continued: 'Shake out your money on the table, and we will see how much you have, and I will change it for you.'

'Oh,' said I, 'I want first to find out the rate of exchange.'

When Kazelia heard this, he gave a great spring and shrieked 'Hoi, hoi! On account of Jews like you, the Messhiach (Messiah) can't come, and the Redemption of Israel is delayed. If you go out into the street, you will find a Jew without a beard, who will charge you more, and even take all your money away. I swear to you, as I should wish to see Messhiach Ben David, that I want to earn no money. I only desire your good, and so to lay up a little Mitzvah in heaven.'

Thereupon I changed my money with him. Afterwards I found that he had swindled me to the extent of fifteen roubles. Elzas Kazelia is like to the Russian forest robber, who waylays even the peasant.

We began to talk further about the frontier. He wanted eighty roubles, and swore by his kosher Yiddishkeit (ritually pure Judaism) that the affair would cost him seventy-five.

Thereupon I became sorely troubled, because I had understood it would only cost us twenty roubles for all of us, and so I told him. Said he: 'If you seek others with short beards, they will take twice as much from you.' But I went out into the street to seek a second murderer. The second promised to do it cheaper, said that Kazelia was a robber, and promised to meet me at the railway station.

Immediately I left, Elzas Kazelia, the kosher Jew, went to the police, and informed them that I and my family were running away from Russia, and were going to London; and we were at once arrested, and thrown bag and baggage into a filthy cell, lighted only by an iron grating in the door. No food or drink was allowed us, as though we were the greatest criminals. Such is Russian humanity, to starve innocent people. The little provender we had in a bag scarcely kept us from fainting with hunger. On the second day Kazelia sent two Jews with beards. Suddenly I heard the door unlock, and they appeared saying: 'We have come to do you a favour, but not for nothing. If your life and the lives of your family are dear to you, we advise you to give the police seventy roubles, and we want ten roubles for our kindness, and you must employ Kazelia to take you over the frontier for eighty roubles, otherwise the police will not be bribed. If you refuse, you are lost.'

Well, how could I answer? How could one give away the last kopeck and arrive penniless in a strange land? Every rouble taken from us was like a piece of our life. So my people and I began to weep and to beg for pity. 'Have compassion,' we cried. Answered they: 'In a frontier town compassion dwells not. Give money. That will bring compassion.' And they slammed the door, and we were locked in once more. Tears and cries helped nothing. My children wept agonizedly. Oh, truth, truth! Russia, Russia! How scurvily you handle the guiltless! For an enlightened land to be thus!

'Father, father,' the children said, 'give away everything so that we die not in this cell of fear and hunger.'

But even had I wished, I could do nothing from behind barred doors. Our shouting was useless. At last I attracted a warder who was watching in the corridor. 'Bring me a Jew,' I cried; 'I wish to tell him of our plight.' And he answered: 'Hold your peace if you don't want your teeth knocked out. Recognise that you are a prisoner. You know well what is required of you.'

Yes, I thought, my money or my life.

On the third day our sufferings became almost insupportable, and the Russian cold seized on our bodies, and our strength began to fail. We looked upon the cell as our tomb, and on Kazelia as the Angel of Death. Here, it seemed, we were to die of hunger. We lost hope of seeing the sun. For well we know Russia. Who seeks Truth finds Death more easily. As the Russian proverb says, 'If you want to know Truth, you will know Death.'

At length the warder seemed to take pity on our cries, and brought again the two Jews. 'For the last time we tell you. Give us money, and we will do you a kindness. We have been seized with compassion for your family.'

So I said no more, but gave them all they asked, and Elzas Kazelia came and said to me rebukingly: 'It is a characteristic of the Jew never to part with his money unless chastised.' I said to Elzas Kazelia: 'I thought you were an honourable, pious Jew. How could you treat a poor family so?'

He answered me: 'An honourable, pious Jew must also make a little money.'

Thereupon he conducted us from the prison, and sent for a conveyance. No sooner had we seated ourselves than he demanded six roubles. Well, what could I do? I had fallen among thieves, and must part with my money. We drove to a small room, and remained there two hours, for which we had to pay three roubles, as the preparations for our crossing were apparently incomplete. When we finally got to the frontier—in this case a shallow river—they warned us not even to sneeze, for if the soldiers heard we should be shot without more ado. I had to strip in order to wade through the water, and several men carried over my family. My two bundles, with all my belongings, consisting of clothes and household treasures, remained, however, on the Russian side. Suddenly a wild disorder arose. 'The soldiers! The soldiers! Hide! Hide! In the bushes! In the bushes!'

When all was still again—though no soldiers became visible—the men went back for the baggage, but brought back only one bundle. The other, worth over a hundred roubles, had disappeared. Wailing helped nothing. Kazelia said: 'Hold your peace. Here, too, dangers lurk.'

I understood the game, but felt completely helpless in his hands. He drove us to his house, and our remaining bundle was deposited there. Later, when I walked into the town, I went to the Rabbi and complained. Said he: 'What can I do with such murderers? You must reconcile yourself to the loss.'

I went back to my family at Kazelia's house, and he cautioned me against going into the street. On my way I had met a man who said he would charge twenty-eight roubles each for our journey to London. So Kazelia was evidently afraid I might yet fall into honester hands.

Then we began to talk with him of London, for it is better to deal with the devil you know than the devil you don't know. Said he: 'It will cost you thirty-three roubles each.' I said: 'I have had an offer of twenty-eight roubles, but you I will give thirty.' 'Hoi, hoi!' shrieked he. 'On a Jew a lesson is lost. It is just as at the frontier: you wouldn't give eighty roubles, and it cost you double. You want the same again. One daren't do a Jew a favour.'

So I held my peace, and accepted his terms. But I saw I should be twenty-five roubles short of what was required to finish the journey. Said Kazelia: 'I can do you a favour: I can borrow twenty-five roubles on your luggage at the railway, and when you get to London you can repay.' And he took the bundle, and conveyed it to the railway. What he did there I know not. He came back, and told me he had done me a turn. (This time it seemed a good one.) He then took envelopes, and placed in each the amount I was to pay at each stage of the journey. So at last we took train and rode off. And at each place I paid the dues from its particular envelope. The children were offered food by our fellow-passengers, though they could only take it when it was kosher, and this enabled us to keep our pride. There was one kind Jewess from Lemberg with a heart of gold and delicious rings of sausages.

When we arrived at Leipsic they told me the amount was twelve marks short. So we missed our train, not knowing what to do, as I had now no money whatever but what was in the envelopes. The officials ordered us from the station. So we went out and walked about Leipsic; we attracted the suspicion of the police, and they wanted to arrest us. But we pleaded our innocence, and they let us go. So we retired into a narrow dark street, and sat down by a blank wall, and told each other not to murmur. We sat together through the whole rainy night, the rain mingling with our tears.

When day broke I thought of a plan. I took twelve marks from the envelope containing the ship's money, and ran back to the station, and took tickets to Rotterdam, and so got to the end of our overland journey. When we got to the ship, they led us all into a shed like cattle. One of the Kazelia conspirators—for his arm reaches over Europe—called us into his office, and said: 'How much money have you?' I shook out the money from the envelopes on the table. Said he: 'The amount is twelve marks short.' He had had advices, he said, from Kazelia that I would bring a certain amount, and I didn't have it.

'Here you can stay to-night. To-morrow you go back.' So he played on my ignorance, for I was paying at every stage in excess of the legal fares. But I knew not what powers he had. Every official was a possible disaster. We hardly lived till the day.

Then I began to beg him to take my Tallis and Tephillin (praying-shawl and phylacteries) for the twelve marks. Said he: 'I have no use for them; you must go back.' With difficulty I got his permission to go out into the town, and I took my Tallis and Tephillin, and went into a Shool (synagogue), and I begged someone to buy them. But a good man came up, and would not permit the sale. He took out twelve marks and gave them to me. I begged him to give me his address that I might be able to repay him. Said he: 'I desire neither thanks nor money.' Thus was I able to replace the amount lacking.

We embarked without a bit of bread or a farthing in money. We arrived in London at nine o'clock in the morning, penniless and without luggage, whereas I had calculated to have at least one hundred and fifty roubles and my household stuff. I had a friend's address, and we all went to look for him, but found that he had left London for America. We walked about all day till eight o'clock at night. The children could scarcely drag along from hunger and weariness. At last we sat down on the steps of a house in Wellclose Square. I looked about, and saw a building which I took to be a Shool (synagogue), as there were Hebrew posters stuck outside. I approached it. An old Jew with a long grey beard came to meet me, and began to speak with me. I understood soon what sort of a person he was, and turned away. This Meshummad (converted Jew) persisted, tempting me sorely with offers of food and drink for the family, and further help. I said: 'I want nothing of you, nor do I desire your acquaintance.'

'I went back to my family. The children sat crying for food. They attracted the attention of a man, Baruch Zezangski (25, Ship Alley), and he went away, returning with bread and fish. When the children saw this, they rejoiced exceedingly, and seized the man's hand to kiss it. Meanwhile darkness fell, and there was nowhere to pass the night. So I begged the man to find me a lodging for the night. He led us to a cellar in Ship Alley. It was pitch black. They say there is a hell. This may or may not be, but more of a hell than the night we passed in this cellar one does not require. Every vile thing in the world seemed to have taken up its abode therein. We sat the whole night sweeping the vermin from us. After a year of horror—as it seemed—came the dawn. In the morning entered the landlord, and demanded a shilling. I had not a farthing, but I had a leather bag which I gave him for the night's lodging. I begged him to let me a room in the house. So he let me a small back room upstairs, the size of a table, at three and sixpence a week. He relied on our collecting his rent from the kind-hearted.

We entered the empty room with joy, and sat down on the floor. We remained the whole day without bread. The children managed to get a crust now and again from other lodgers, but all day long they cried for food, and at night they cried because they had nothing to sleep on. I asked our landlord if he knew of any work we could do. He said he would see what could be done. Next day he went out, and returned with a heap of linen to be washed. The family set to work at once, but I am sure my wife washed the things less with water than with tears. Oh, Kazelia! We washed the whole week, the landlord each day bringing bread and washing. At the end of the week he said: 'You have worked out your rent, and have nothing to pay.' I should think not indeed!

My eldest daughter was fortunate enough to get a place at a tailor's for four shillings a week, and the others sought washing and scrubbing. So each day we had bread, and at the end of the week rent. Bread and water alone formed our sustenance. But we were very grateful all the same. When the holidays came on, my daughter fell out of work. I heard a word 'slack.' I inquired, 'What is the meaning of the word "slack"?' Then my daughter told me that it means schlecht (bad). There is nothing to be earned. Now, what should I do? I had no means of living. The children cried for bread and something to sleep on. Still we lived somehow till Rosh Hashanah (New Year), hoping it would indeed be a New Year.

It was Erev Yomtov (the day before the holiday), and no washing was to be had. We struggled as before death. The landlord of the house came in. He said to me: 'Aren't you ashamed? Can't you see your children have scarcely strength to live? Why have you not compassion on your little ones? Go to the Charity Board. There you will receive help.' Believe me, I would rather have died. But the little ones were starving, and their cries wrung me. So I went to a Charity Board. I said, weeping: 'My children are perishing for a morsel of bread. I can no longer look upon their sufferings.' And the Board answered: 'After Yomtov we will send you back to Russia.' 'But meanwhile,' I answered, 'the children want food.' Whereupon one of the Board struck a bell, and in came a stalwart Angel of Death, who seized me by the arm so that it ached all day, and thrust me through the door. I went out, my eyes blinded with tears, so that I could not see where I went. It was long before I found my way back to Ship Alley. My wife and daughters already thought I had drowned myself for trouble. Such was our plight the Eve of the Day of Atonement, and not a morsel of bread to 'take in' the fast with! But just at the worst a woman from next door came in, and engaged one of my daughters to look after a little child during the fast (while she was in the synagogue) at a wage of tenpence, paid in advance. With joy we expended it all on bread, and then we prayed that the Day of Atonement should endure long, so that we could fast long, and have no need to buy food; for as the moujik says, 'If one had no mouth, one could wear a golden coat.'

I went to the Jews' Free School, which was turned into a synagogue, and passed the whole day in tearful supplication. When I came home at night my wife sat and wept. I asked her why she wept. She answered: 'Why have you led me to such a land, where even prayer costs money—at least, for women? The whole day I went from one Shool to another, but they would not let me in. At last I went to the Shool of the "Sons of the Soul," where pray the pious Jews, with beards and ear-locks, and even there I was not allowed in. The heathen policeman begged for me, and said to them: "Shame on you not to let the poor woman in." The Gabbai (treasurer) answered: "If one hasn't money, one sits at home."' And my wife said to him, weeping: 'My tears be on your head,' and went home, and remained home the whole day weeping. With a woman Yom Kippur is a wonder-working day. She thought that her prayers might be heard, that God would consider her plight if she wept out her heart to Him in the Shool. But she was frustrated, and this was perhaps the greatest blow of all to her. Moreover, she was oppressed by her own brethren, and this was indeed bitter. If it had been the Gentile, she would have consoled herself with the thought, 'We are in exile.' When the fast was over, we had nothing but a little bread left to break our fast on, or to prepare for the next day's fast. Nevertheless we sorrowfully slept. But the wretched day came again, and the elder children went out into the street to seek Parnosoh (employment), and found scrubbing, that brought in nine-pence. We bought bread, and continued to live further. Likewise we obtained three shillings worth of washing to do, and were as rich as Rothschild. When Succoth (Tabernacles) came, again no money, no bread, and I went about the streets the whole day to seek for work. When I was asked what handicraftsman I was, of course I had to say I had no trade, for, foolishly enough, among the Jews in my part of Russia a trade is held in contempt, and when they wish to hold one up to scorn, they say to him: 'Anybody can see you are a descendant of a handicraftsman.'

I could write Holy Scrolls, indeed, and keep an inn, but what availed these accomplishments? As I found I could obtain no work, I went into the Shool of the 'Sons of the Soul.' I seated myself next a man, and we began to speak. I told him of my plight. Said he: 'I will give you advice. Call on our Rabbi. He is a very fine man.'

I did so. As I entered, he sat in company with another man, holding his Lulov and Esrog (palm and citron). 'What do you want?' I couldn't answer him, my heart was so oppressed, but suddenly my tears gushed forth. It seemed to me help was at hand. I felt assured of sympathy, if of nothing else. I told him we were perishing for want of bread, and asked him to give me advice. He answered nothing. He turned to the man, and spoke concerning the Tabernacle and the Citron. He took no further notice of me, but left me standing.

So I understood he was no better than Elzas Kazelia. And this is a Rabbi! As I saw I might as well have talked to the wall, I left the room without a word from him. As the moujik would say: 'Sad and bitter is the poor man's lot. It is better to lie in the dark tomb and not to see the sunlit world than to be a poor man and be compelled to beg for money.'

I came home, where my family was waiting patiently for my return with bread. I said: 'Good Yomtov,' weeping, for they looked scarcely alive, having been without a morsel of food that day.

So we tried to sleep, but hunger would not permit it, but demanded his due. 'Hunger, you old fool, why don't you let us sleep?' But he refused to be talked over. So we passed the night. When day came the little children began to cry: 'Father, let us go. We will beg bread in the streets. We die of hunger. Don't hold us back.'

When the mother heard them speak of begging in the streets, she swooned, whereupon arose a great clamour among the children. When at length we brought her to, she reproached us bitterly for restoring her to life. 'I would rather have died than hear you speak of begging in the streets—rather see my children die of hunger before my eyes.' This speech of the mother caused them to forget their hunger, and they sat and wept together. On hearing the weeping, a man from next door, Gershon Katcol, came in to see what was the matter. He looked around, and his heart went out to us. So he went away, and returned speedily with bread and fish and tea and sugar, and went away again, returning with five shillings. He said: 'This I lend you.' Later he came back with a man, Nathan Beck, who inquired into our story, and took away the three little ones to stay with him. Afterwards, when I called to see them in his house in St. George's Road, they hid themselves from me, being afraid I should want them to return to endure again the pangs of hunger. It was bitter to think that a stranger should have the care of my children, and that they should shun me as one shuns a forest-robber.

After Yomtov I went to Grunbach, the shipping agent, to see whether my luggage had arrived, as I had understood from Kazelia that it would get here in a month's time. I showed my pawn-ticket, and inquired concerning it. Said he: 'Your luggage won't come to London, only to Rotterdam. If you like, I will write a letter to inquire if it is at Rotterdam, and how much money is due to redeem it.' I told him I had borrowed twenty-five roubles on it. Whereupon he calculated that it would cost me £4 6s., including freight to redeem it. But I told him to write and ask. Some days later a letter came from Rotterdam stating the cost at eighty-three roubles (£8 13s.), irrespective of freight dues. When I heard this, I was astounded, and I immediately wrote to Kazelia: 'Why do you behave like a forest-robber, giving me only twenty-five roubles where you got eighty-three?' Answered he: 'Shame on you to write such a letter! Haven't you been in my house, and seen what an honourable Jew I am? Shame on you! To such men as you one can't do a favour. Do you think there are a sea of Kazelias in the world? You are all thick-headed. You can't read a letter. I only took fifty-four roubles on the luggage; I had to recoup myself because I lost money through sending you to London. I calculated my loss, and only took what was due to me.' I showed the letter to Grunbach, and he wrote again to Rotterdam, and they answered that they knew nothing of a Kazelia. I must pay the £8 13s. if I wanted my bundle. Well, what was to be done? The weather grew colder. Hunger we had become inured to. But how could we pass the winter nights on the bare boards? I wrote again to Kazelia, but received no answer whatever. Day and night I went about asking advice concerning the luggage. Nobody could help me.

And as I stood thus in the middle of the sea, word came to me of a Landsmann (countryman) I had once helped to escape from the Russian army, in the days when I was happy and had still my inn. They said he had a great business in jewellery on a great highroad in front of the sea in a great town called Brighton. So I started off at once to talk to him—two days' journey, they said—for I knew he would help; and if not he, who? I would come to him as his Sabbath guest; he would surely fall upon my neck. The first night I slept in a barn with another tramp, who pointed me the way; but because I stopped to earn sixpence by chopping wood, lo! when Sabbath came I was still twelve miles away, and durst not profane the Sabbath by walking. So I lingered that Friday night in a village, thanking God I had at least the money for a bed, though it was sinful even to touch my money. And all next day, I know not why, the street-boys called me a Goy (heathen) and a fox—'Goy-Fox, Goy-Fox!'—and they let off fireworks in my face. So I had to wander in the woods around, keeping within the Sabbath radius, and when the three stars appeared in the sky I started for Brighton. But so footsore was I, I came there only at midnight, and could not search. And I sat down on a bench; it was very cold, but I was so tired. But the policeman came and drove me away—he was God's messenger, for I should perchance have died—and a drunken female with a painted face told him to let me be, and gave me a shilling. How could I refuse? I slept again in a bed. And on the Sunday morning I started out, and walked all down in front of the sea; but my heart grew sick, for I saw the shops were shut. At last I saw a jewellery shop and my Landsmann's name over it. It sparkled with gold and diamonds, and little bills were spread over it—'Great sale! Great sale!' Then I went joyfully to the door, but lo! it was bolted. So I knocked and knocked, and at last a woman came from above, and told me he lived in that road in Hove, where I found indeed my redeemer, but not my Landsmann. It was a great house, with steps up and steps down. I went down to a great door, and there came out a beautiful heathen female with a shining white cap on her head and a shining white apron, and she drove me away.

'Goy-Fox was yesterday,' she shouted with wrath and slammed the door on my heart; and I sat down on the pavement without, and I became a pillar of salt, all frozen tears. But when I looked up, I saw the Angel of the Lord.

CHAPTER III

THE PICTURE EVOLVES

Such was my model's simple narrative, the homely realism of which appealed to me on my most imaginative side, for through all its sordid details stood revealed to me the tragedy of the Wandering Jew. Was it Heine or another who said 'The people of Christ is the Christ of peoples'? At any rate, such was the idea that began to take possession of me as I painted away at the sorrow-haunted face of my much-tried model—to paint, not the Christ that I had started out to paint, but the Christ incarnated in a race, suffering—and who knew that He did not suffer over again?—in its Passion. Yes, Israel Quarriar could still be my model, but after another conception altogether.

It was an idea that called for no change in what I had already done. For I had worked mainly upon the head, and now that I purposed to clothe the figure in its native gaberdine, there would be little to re-draw. And so I fell to work with renewed intensity, feeling even safer now that I was painting and interpreting a real thing than when I was trying to reconstruct retrospectively the sacred figure that had walked in Galilee.

And no sooner had I fallen to work on this new conception than I found everywhere how old it was. It appeared even to have Scriptural warrant, for from a brief report of a historical-theological lecture by a Protestant German Professor I gleaned that many of the passages in the Prophets which had been interpreted as pointing to a coming Messiah, really applied to Israel, the people. Israel it was whom Isaiah, in that famous fifty-third chapter, had described as 'despised and rejected of men: a man of sorrows.' Israel it was who bore the sins of the world. 'He was oppressed and he was afflicted, yet he opened not his mouth; he is brought as a lamb to the slaughter.' Yes, Israel was the Man of Sorrows. And in this view the German Professor, I found, was only re-echoing Rabbinic opinion. My model proved a mine of lore upon this as upon so many other points. Even the Jewish expectation of the Messiah, he had never shared, he said—that the Messhiach would come riding upon a white ass. Israel would be redeemed by itself, though his neighbours would have called the sentiment 'epicurean.'

'Whoever saves me is my Messhiach,' he declared suddenly, and plucked at my hand to kiss it.

'Now, you shock me,' I said, pushing him away.

'No, no,' he said; 'I agree with the word of the moujik: "the good people are God."'

'Then I suppose you are what is called a Zionist,' I said.

'Yes,' he replied; 'now that you have saved me, I see that God works only through men. As for the Messhiach on the white ass, they do not really believe it, but they won't let another believe otherwise. For my own part, when I say the prayer, "Blessed be Thou who restorest the dead to life," I always mean it of you.'

Such Oriental hyperbolic gratitude would have satisfied the greediest benefactor, and was infinitely in excess of what he owed me. He seemed unconscious that he was doing work, journeying punctually long miles to my studio in any and every weather. It is true that I early helped him to redeem his household gods, but could I do less for a man who had still no bed to sleep in?

My recovery of the Rotterdam bundle served to unveil further complications. The agents at the East End charged him three shillings and sixpence per letter, and conducted the business with a fine legal delay. But it was not till Kazelia was eulogized by one of these gentry as a very fine man that both the model and I grew suspicious that the long chain of roguery reached even unto London, and that the confederates on this side were playing for time, so that the option should expire, and the railway sell the unredeemed luggage, which they would doubtless buy in cheap, making another profit.

Ultimately Quarriar told me his second daughter—for the eldest was blind of one eye—was prepared to journey alone to Rotterdam, as the safest way of redeeming the goods. Admiring her pluck, I added her fare to the expenses.

One fine morning Israel appeared, transfigured with happiness.

'When does man rejoice most?' he cried. 'When he loses and finds again.'

'Ah, then you have got your bedding at last,' I cried, now accustomed to his methods of expression. 'I hope you slept well.'

'We could not sleep for blessing you,' he replied unexpectedly. 'As the Psalmist says, "All my bones praise the Lord!"'

Not that the matter had gone smoothly even now. The Kazelia gang at Rotterdam denied all knowledge of the luggage, sent the girl to the railway, where the dues had now mounted to £10 6s. Again the cup was dashed from her lips, for I had only given her £9. But she went to the Rabbi, and offered if he supplied the balance to repledge the Sabbath silver candlesticks that were the one family heirloom in the bundle, and therewith repay him instantly. While she was pleading with him, in came a noble Jew, paid the balance, lodged her and fed her, and saw her safely on board with the long-lost treasures.

CHAPTER IV

I BECOME A SORTER

As the weeks went by, my satisfaction with the progress I was making was largely tempered by the knowledge that after the completion of my picture my model would be thrown again on the pavement, and several times I fancied I detected him gazing at it sadly as if watching its advancing stages with a sort of hopeless fear. My anxiety about him and his family grew from day to day, but I could not see any possible way of helping him. He was touchingly faithful, anxious to please, and uncomplaining either of cold or hunger. Once I gave him a few shillings to purchase a second-hand pair of top-boots, which were necessary for the picture, and these he was able to procure in the Ghetto Sunday market for a minute sum, and he conscientiously returned me the balance—about two-thirds.

I happened to have sold an English landscape to Sir Asher Aaronsberg, the famous philanthropist and picture-buyer of Middleton, then up in town in connection with his Parliamentary duties, and knowing how indefatigably he was in touch with the London Jewish charities, I inquired whether some committee could not do anything to assist Quarriar. Sir Asher was not very encouraging. The man knew no trade. However, if he would make application on the form enclosed and answer the questions, he would see what could be done. I saw that the details were duly filled in—the ages and sex of his five children, etc.

But the committee came to the conclusion that the only thing they could do was to repatriate the man. 'Return to Russia!' cried Israel in horror.

Occasionally I inquired if any plan for the future had occurred to him. But he never raised the subject of his difficulties of his own accord, and his very silence, born, as it seemed to me, of the majestic dignity of the man, was infinitely pathetic. Now and again came a fitful gleam of light. His second daughter would be given a week's work for a few shillings by his landlord, a working master-tailor in a small way, from whom he now rented two tiny rooms on the top floor. But that was only when there was an extra spasm of activity. His half-blind daughter would do a little washing, and the landlord would allow her the use of the backyard.

At last one day I found he had an idea, and an idea, moreover, that was carefully worked out in all its details. The scheme was certainly a novel and surprising one to me, but it showed how the art of forcing a livelihood amid impossible circumstances had been cultivated among these people, forced for centuries to exist under impossible conditions.

Briefly his scheme was this. In the innumerable tailors' workshops of his district great piles of cuttings of every kind and quality of cloth accumulated, and for the purchase of these cuttings a certain competition existed among a class of people, known as piece-sorters. The sale of these cuttings by weight and for cash brought the master-tailors a pleasant little revenue, which was the more prized as it was a sort of perquisite. The masters were able to command payment for their cuttings in advance, and the sorter would call to collect them week by week as they accumulated, till the amount he had advanced was exhausted. Quarriar would set up as a piece-sorter, and thus be able to employ his daughters too. The whole family would find occupation in sorting out their purchases, and each quality and size would be readily saleable as raw material, to be woven again into the cheaper woollen materials. Through the recommendation of his countrymen, there were several tailors who had readily agreed to give him the preference. His own landlord in particular had promised to befriend him, and even now was allowing his cuttings to accumulate at some inconvenience, since he might have had ready money for them. Moreover, his friends had introduced him to a very respectable and honest sorter, who would take him into partnership, teach him, and allow his daughters to partake in the sorting, if he could put down twenty pounds! His friends would jointly advance him eight on the security of his silver candlesticks, if only he could raise the other twelve.

This promising scheme took an incubus off my mind, and I hastened, somewhat revengefully, to acquaint the professional philanthropist, who had been so barren of ideas, with my intention to set up Quarriar as a piece-sorter.

'Ah,' Sir Asher replied, unmoved. 'Then you had better employ my man Conn; he does a good deal of this sort of work for me. He will find Quarriar a partner and professor.'

'But Quarriar has already found a partner.' I explained the scheme.

'The partner will cheat him. Twenty pounds is ridiculous. Five pounds is quite enough. Take my advice, and let it all go through Conn. If I wanted my portrait painted, you wouldn't advise me to go to an amateur. By the way, here are the five pounds, but please don't tell Conn I gave them. I don't believe the money'll do any good, and Conn will lose his respect for me.'

My interest in piece-sorting—an occupation I had never even heard of before—had grown abnormally, and I had gone into the figures and quantities—so many hundredweights, purchased at fifteen shillings, sorted into lots, and sold at various prices—with as thorough-going an eagerness as if my own livelihood were to depend upon it.

I confess I was now rather bewildered by so serious a difference of estimate as to the cost of a partnership, but I was inclined to set down Sir Asher's scepticism to that pessimism which is the penalty of professional philanthropy.

On the other hand, I felt that whether the partnership was to cost five pounds or twenty, Quarriar's future would be safer from Kazelias under the auspices of Sir Asher and his Conn. So I handed the latter the five pounds, and bade him find Quarriar a guide, philosopher, and partner.

With the advent of Conn, all my troubles began, and the picture passed into its third and last stage.

I soon elicited that Quarriar and his friends were rather sorry Conn had been introduced into the matter. He was alleged to favour some people at the expense of others, and to be not at all popular among the people amid whom he worked. And altogether it was abundantly clear that Quarriar would rather have gone on with the scheme in his own way without official interference.

Later, Sir Asher wrote to me direct that the partner put forward by the Quarriar faction was a shady customer; Conn had selected his own man, but even so there was little hope Quarriar's future would be thus provided for.

There seemed, moreover, a note of suspicion of Quarriar sounding underneath, but I found comfort in the reflection that to Sir Asher my model was nothing more than the usual applicant for assistance, whereas to me who had lived for months in daily contact with him he was something infinitely more human.

Spring was now nearing; I finished my picture early in March—after four months' strenuous labour—shook hands with my model, and received his blessing. I was somewhat put out at learning that Conn had not yet given him the five pounds necessary to start him, as I had been hoping he might begin his new calling immediately the sittings ended. I gave him a small present to help tide over the time of waiting.

But that tragic face on my own canvas remained to haunt me, to ask the question of his future, and few days elapsed ere I found myself starting out to visit him at his home. He lived near Ratcliffe Highway, a district which I found had none of that boisterous marine romance with which I had associated it.

The house was a narrow building of at least the sixteenth century, with the number marked up in chalk on the rusty little door. I happened to have stumbled on the Jewish Passover. Quarriar was called down, evidently astonished and unprepared for my appearance at his humble abode, but he expressed pleasure, and led me up the narrow, steep stairway, whose ceiling almost touched my head as I climbed up after him. On the first floor the landlord, in festal raiment, intercepted us, introduced himself in English (which he spoke with pretentious inaccuracy), and, barring my further ascent, took possession of me, and led the way to his best parlour, as if it were entirely unbecoming for his tenant to receive a gentleman in his attic.

He was a strapping young fellow, full of acuteness and vigour—a marked contrast to Quarriar's drooping, dignified figure standing silently near by, and radiating poverty and suffering all the more in the little old panelled room, elegant with a big carved walnut cabinet, and gay with chromos and stuffed birds. Effusively the master-tailor painted himself as the champion of the poor fellow, and protested against this outside partnership that was being imposed on him by the notorious Conn. He himself, though he could scarcely afford it, was keeping his cuttings for him, in spite of tempting offers from other quarters, even of a shilling a sack. But of course he didn't see why an outsider foisted upon him by a philanthropic factotum should benefit by this goodness of his. He discoursed to me in moved terms of the sorrows and privations of his tenants in their two tiny rooms upstairs. And all the while Quarriar preserved his attitude of drooping dignity, saying no syllable except under special appeal.

The landlord produced a goblet of rum and shrub for the benefit of the high-born visitor, and we all clinked glasses, the young master-tailor beaming at me unctuously as he set down his glass.

'I love company,' he cried, with no apparent consciousness of impudent familiarity.

I returned, however, to my central interest in life—the piece-sorting. It occurred to me afterwards that possibly I ought not to have insisted on such a secular subject on a Jewish holiday, but, after all, the landlord had broached it, and both men now entered most cordially into the discussion. The landlord started repeating his lament—what a pity it would be if Quarriar were really forced to accept Conn's partner—when Quarriar timidly blurted out that he had already signed the deed of partnership, though he had not yet received the promised capital from Conn, nor spoken over matters with the partner provided. The landlord seemed astonished and angry at learning this, pricking up his ears curiously at the word 'signed,' and giving Quarriar a look of horror.

'Signed!' he cried in Yiddish. 'What hast thou signed?'

At this point the landlord's wife joined us in the parlour, with a pretty child in her arms and another shy one clinging to her skirts, completing the picture of felicity and prosperity, and throwing into greater shadow the attic to which I shortly afterwards climbed my way up the steep, airless stairs. I was hardly prepared for the depressing spectacle that awaited me at their summit. It was not so much the shabby, fusty rooms, devoid of everything save a couple of mattresses, a rickety wooden table, a chair or two, and a heap of Passover cakes, as the unloveliness of the three women who stood there, awkward and flushing before their important visitor. The wife-and-mother was dwarfed and black-wigged, the daughters were squat, with tallow-coloured round faces, vaguely suggestive of Caucasian peasants, while the sightless eye of the elder lent a final touch of ugliness.

How little my academic friends know me who imagine I am allured by the ugly! It is only that sometimes I see through it a beauty that they are blind to. But here I confess I saw nothing but the ghastly misery and squalor, and I was oppressed almost to sickness as much by the scene as by the atmosphere.

'May I open a window?' I could not help inquiring.

The genial landlord, who had followed in my footsteps, rushed to anticipate me, and when I could breathe more freely, I found something of the tragedy that had been swallowed in the sordidness. My eye fell again on the figure of my host standing in his drooping majesty, the droop being now necessary to avoid striking the ceiling with his kingly head.

Surely a pretty wife and graceful daughters would have detracted from the splendour of the tragedy. Israel stood there, surrounded by all that was mean, yet losing nothing of his regal dignity—indeed the Man of Sorrows.

Ere I left I suddenly remembered to ask after the three younger children. They were still with their kind benefactor, the father told me.

'I suppose you will resume possession of them when you make your fortune by the piece-sorting?' I said.

'God grant it,' he replied. 'My bowels yearn for that day.'

Against my intention I slipped into his hand the final seven pounds I was prepared to pay. 'If your partnership scheme fails, try again alone,' I said.

His blessings pursued me down the steep staircase. His womankind remained shy and dumb.

When I got home I found a telegram from the Parsonage. My father was dangerously ill. I left everything and hastened to help nurse him. My picture was not sent in to any Exhibition—I could not let it go without seeing it again, without a last touch or two. When, some months later, I returned to town, my first thought—inspired by the sight of my picture—was how Quarrier was faring. I left the studio and telephoned to Sir Asher Aaronsberg at the London office of his great Middleton business.

'That!' His contempt penetrated even through the wires. 'Smashed up long ago. Just as I expected.'

And the sneer of the professional philanthropist vibrated triumphantly. I was much upset, but ere I could recover my composure Sir Asher was cut off. In the evening I received a note saying Quarrier was a rogue, who had to flee from Russia for illicit sale of spirits. He had only two, at most three, elderly daughters; the three younger girls were a myth. For a moment I was staggered; then all my faith in Israel returned. Those three children a figment of the imagination! Impossible! Why, I remembered countless little anecdotes about these very children, told me with the most evident fatherly pride. He had even repeated the quaint remarks the youngest had made on her return home from her first morning at the English school. Impossible that these things could have been invented on the spur of the moment. No; I could not possibly doubt the genuineness of my model's spontaneous talk, especially as in those days he had had no reason for expecting anything from me, and he had most certainly not demanded anything.

And then I remembered that tragic passage describing how these three little ones, sheltered and fed by a kindly soul, hid themselves when their father came to see them, fearing to be reclaimed by him to hunger and cold. If Quarriar could invent such things, he was indeed a poet, for in the whole literature of starvation I could recall no better touch.

I went to Sir Asher. He said that Quarriar, challenged by Conn to produce these children, had refused to do so, or to answer any further questions. I found myself approving of his conduct. 'A man ought not to be insulted by such absurd charges,' I said. Sir Asher merely smiled and took up his usual unshakable position behind his impregnable wall of official distrust and pessimism.

I wrote to Quarriar to call on me without delay. He came immediately, his head bowed, his features care-worn and full of infinite suffering. Yes, it was true; the piece-sorting had failed. For a few weeks all had gone well. He had bought cuttings himself, had given the partner thrust upon him by Conn various sums for the same purpose. They had worked together, sorting in a cellar rented for the purpose, of which his partner kept the key. So smoothly had things gone that he had felt encouraged to invest even the reserve seven pounds I had given him, but when the cellar was full of their common stock, and his own suspicions had been lulled by the regular division of the profits—seventeen shillings per week for each—one morning, on arriving at the cellar to start the day's work, he found the place locked, and when he called at the partner's house for an explanation, the man laughed in his face. Everything in the cellar now belonged to him, he claimed, insisting that Quarriar had eaten up the original capital and his share of the profits besides.

'Besides, it never was your money,' was the rogue's ultimate argument. 'Why shouldn't I profit, too, by the Christian's simplicity?'

Conn blindly believed his own man, for the transactions had not been recorded in writing, and it was only a case of Quarriar's word against the partner's. It was the latter who in his venomous craft had told Conn the younger children did not exist. But, thank Heaven! his quiver was not empty of them. He had blissfully taken them home when prosperity began, but now that he was again face to face with starvation, they had returned to his hospitable countryman, Nathan Beck.

'You are sure you could absolutely produce the little ones?'

He looked grieved at my distrusting him. My faith in his probity was, he said with dignity, the one thing he valued in this world. I dismissed him with a little to tide him over the next week, thoroughly determined that the man's good name should be cleared. The crocodile partner must disgorge, and the eyes of my benevolent friend and of Conn must be finally opened to the injustice they had unwittingly sanctioned. Again I wrote to my friend. As usual, Sir Asher replied kindly and without a trace of impatience. Would I get some intelligible written statement from Quarriar as to what had taken place?

So, at my request, Quarriar sent me a statement in quaint English—probably the landlord's—alleging specifically that the partner had detained goods and money belonging to Quarriar to the amount of £7 9s. 5d., and had assaulted him into the bargain. When the partner was threatened with police-court proceedings, he had defied Quarriar with the remark that Mr. Conn would bear out his honesty. Quarriar could give as references, to show that he was an honest man and had made a true statement as to the number of his children, seven Russians (named) who would attest that the partner provided by Conn was well known as a swindler. Though he was starving, Quarriar refused to have anything further to say to Conn. Quarriar further referred to his landlord, who would willingly testify to his honesty. But being afraid of Conn, and not inclined to commit himself in writing, the landlord would give his version verbally.

Against this statement my philanthropic friend had to set another as made by the partner. Quarriar, according to this, had received the five pounds direct from Conn, and had handed over niggardly sums to the partner for the purchase of goods, to wit, two separate sums of one pound each (of which he returned to Quarriar thirty-three shillings from sales), while Quarriar only gave him as his share of the profits for the whole of the five weeks the sum of seventeen shillings, instead of the minimum of ten shillings each week that had been arranged.

The partner insisted further that he had never handled any money (of which Quarriar had always retained full control), and that all the goods in the cellar at the time of the quarrel were only of the value of ten shillings, to which he was entitled, as Quarriar still owed him thirty-three shillings. Moreover, he was willing to repeat in Quarriar's presence the lies the latter had tried to persuade him to tell. As to the children, he challenged Quarriar to produce them.

In vain I attempted to grapple with these conflicting documents. My head was in a whirl. It seemed to me that no judicial bench, however eminent, could, from the bare materials presented, probe to the bottom of this matter. The arithmetic of both parties was hopelessly beyond me. The names of the witnesses introduced showed that there must be two camps, and that certainly Quarriar was solidly encamped amid his advisers.

The whole business was taking on a most painful complexion, and I was torn by conflicting emotions and swayed alternately by suspicion and confidence.

How sift the false from the true amid all this tangled mass? And yet mere curiosity would not leave me content to go to my grave not knowing whether my model was apostle or Ananias. I, too, must then become a rag-sorter, dabbling amid dirty fragments. Was there a black rag, and was there a white, or were both rags parti-coloured? To take only the one point of the children, it would seem a very simple matter to determine whether a man has five daughters or two; and yet the more I looked into it, the more I saw the complexity. Even if three little girls were produced for my inspection, it was utterly impossible for me to tell whether they really were the model's. Nor was it open to me to repeat the device of Solomon and have them hacked in two to see whose heart would be moved.

And then, if Israel's story was false here, what of the rest? Was Kazelia also a myth? Did the second daughter ever go to Hamburg? Was the landlord's detaining me in the parlour a ruse to gain time for the attics to be emptied of any comforts? Where were the silver candlesticks? These and other questions surged up torturingly. But I remembered the footsore figure on the Brighton pavement; I remembered the months he had practically lived with me, the countless conversations, and as the Man of Sorrows rose reproachful before me from my own canvas, with his noble bowed head, my faith in his dignity and probity returned unbroken.

I called on Sir Asher—I had to go to the House of Commons to find him—and his practical mind quickly suggested the best course in the circumstances. He appointed a date for all parties—himself, myself, Conn, the two partners, and any witnesses they might care to bring—to appear at his office. But, above all, Quarriar must bring the three children with him.

On getting back to my studio, I found Quarriar waiting for me. He was come to pour out his heart to me, and to complain that all sorts of underhand inquiries were being directed against him, so that he scarcely dared to draw breath, so thick was the air with treachery. He was afraid that his very friends, who were anxious not to offend Conn and Sir Asher, might turn against him. Even his landlord had threatened to kick him out, as he had been unable to pay his rent the last week or two.

I told him he might expect a letter asking him to attend at Sir Asher's office, that I should be there, and he should have an opportunity of facing his swindling partner. He welcomed it joyfully, and enthusiastically promised to obey the call and bring the children. I emptied my purse into his hand— there were three or four pounds—and he promised me that quite apart from the old tangle, he could now as an expert set up as a piece-sorter himself. And so his kingly figure passed out of my sight.

The next document sent me in this cause célèbre was a letter from Conn to announce that he had made all arrangements for the great meeting.

'Sir Asher's private room in his office will be placed at the disposal of the inquiry. The original application form filled up by Quarriar clearly condemns him. The partner will be there, and I have arranged for Quarriar's landlord to appear if you think it necessary. I may add that I have very good reason to believe that Quarriar does not mean to appear. I fancy he is trying to wriggle out of the appointment.'

I at once wrote a short note to Quarriar reminding him of the absolute necessity of appearing with the children, who should be even kept away from school.

I reproduce the exact reply:

'DEAR SIR,

'Referring to your welcome letter, I gratify you very much for the trouble you have taken for me. But I'm sorry to tell you that I refuse to go before the committee according you arranged to, as I received a letter without any name threatening me that I should not dare to call for the committee to tell the truth for I will be put into mischief and trouble. It is stated also that the same gentleman does not require the truth. He helps only those he likes to. So I will not call and wish you my dear gentleman not to trouble to come. Therefore if you wish to assist me in somehow is very good and I will certainly gratify you and if not I will have to do without it, and will have to trust the Almighty. So kindly do not trouble about it as I do not wish to enter a risk, I remain your humble and grateful servant,

'ISRAEL QUARRIAR.

'P.S.—Last Wednesday a man called on my landlord and asked him some secrets about me, and told him at last that I shall have to state according I will be commanded to and not as I wish. I enclose you herewith the same letter I received, it is written in Jewish. Please not to show it to anyone but to tear it at once as I would not trust it to any other one. I would certainly call at the office and follow your advice. But my life is dearer. So you should not trouble to come. I fear already I gratify you for kind help till now, in the future you may do as you wish.'

CHAPTER V

This letter seemed decisive. I did not trouble Mr. Conn to English the Yiddish epistle. My imagination saw too clearly Quarrier himself dictating its luridly romantic phraseology. Such counter-plots, coils, treasons, and stratagems in so simple a matter! How Quarrier could even think them plausible I could not at first imagine; and with my anger was mingled a flush of resentment at his low estimate of my intellect.

After-reflection instructed me that he wrote as a Russian to whom apparently nothing mediæval was strange. But at the moment I had only the sense of outrage and trickery. All these months I had been fed upon lies. Day after day I had been swathed with them as with feathers. I had so pledged my reputation as a reader of character that he would appear with his three younger children, bear every test, and be triumphantly vindicated. And in that moment of hot anger and wounded pride I had almost slashed through my canvas and mutilated beyond redemption that kingly head. But it looked at me sadly with its sweet majesty, and I stayed my hand, almost persuaded to have faith in it still. I began multiplying excuses for Quarrier, figuring him as misled by his neighbours, more skilled than he in playing upon philanthropic heart-strings; he had been told, doubtless, that two daughters made no impression upon the flinty heart of bureaucratic charity, that in order to soften it one must 'increase and multiply.' He had got himself into a network of falsehood from which, though his better nature recoiled, he had been unable to disentangle himself. But then I remembered how even in Russia he had pursued an illegal calling, how he had helped a friend to evade military service, and again I took up my knife. But the face preserved its reproachful dignity, seemed almost to turn the other cheek. Illegal calling! No; it was the law that was illegal—the cruel, impossible law, that in taking away all means of livelihood had contorted the Jew's conscience. It was the country that was illegal—the cruel country whose frontiers could only be crossed by bribery and deceit—the country that had made him cunning like all weak creatures in the struggle for survival. And so, gradually softer thoughts came to me, and less unmingled feelings. I could not doubt the general accuracy of his melancholy wanderings between Russia and Rotterdam, between London and Brighton. And were he spotless as the dove, that only made surer the blackness of Kazelia and the partner—his brethren in Israel and in the Exile.

And so the new Man of Sorrows shaped himself to my vision. And, taking my brush, I added a touch here and a touch there till there came into that face of sorrows a look of craft and guile. And as I stood back from my work, I was startled to see how nearly I had come to a photographic representation of my model; for those lines of guile had indeed been there, though I had eliminated them in my confident misrepresentation. Now that I had exaggerated them, I had idealized, so to speak, in the reverse direction. And the more I pondered upon this new face, the more I saw that this return to a truer homeliness and a more real realism did but enable me to achieve a subtler beauty. For surely here at last was the true tragedy of the people of Christ—to have persisted sublimely, and to be as sordidly perverted; to be king and knave in one; to survive for two thousand years the loss of a fatherland and the pressure of persecution, only to wear on its soul the yellow badge which had defaced its garments.

For to suffer two thousand years for an idea is a privilege that has been accorded only to Israel—'the soldier of God.' That were no tragedy, but an heroic epic, even as the prophet Isaiah had prefigured. The true tragedy, the saddest sorrow, lay in the martyrdom of an Israel unworthy of his sufferings. And this was the Israel—the high tragedian in the comedy sock—that I tried humbly to typify in my Man of Sorrows.

ANGLICIZATION

'English, all English, that's my dream.'
CECIL RHODES.

I

Even in his provincial days at Sudminster Solomon Cohen had distinguished himself by his Anglican mispronunciation of Hebrew and his insistence on a minister who spoke English and looked like a Christian clergyman; and he had set a precedent in the congregation by docking the 'e' of his patronymic. There are many ways of concealing from the Briton your shame in being related through a pedigree of three thousand years to Aaron, the High Priest of Israel, and Cohn is one of the simplest and most effective. Once, taken to task by a pietist, Solomon defended himself by the quibble that Hebrew has no vowels. But even this would not account for the whittling away of his 'Solomon.' 'S. Cohn' was the insignium over his clothing establishment. Not that he was anxious to deny his Jewishness—was not the shop closed on Saturdays?—he was merely anxious not to obtrude it. 'When we are in England, we are in England,' he would say, with his Talmudic sing-song.

S. Cohn was indeed a personage in the seaport of Sudminster, and his name had been printed on voting papers, and, what is more, he had at last become a Town Councillor. Really the citizens liked his stanch adherence to his ancient faith, evidenced so tangibly by his Sabbath shutters: even the Christian clothiers bore him goodwill, not suspecting that S. Cohn's Saturday losses were more than counterbalanced by the general impression that a man who sacrificed business to religion would deal more fairly by you than his fellows. And his person, too, had the rotundity which the ratepayer demands.

But twin with his Town Councillor's pride was his pride in being Gabbai (treasurer) of the little synagogue tucked away in a back street: in which for four generations prayer had ebbed and flowed as regularly as the tides of the sea, with whose careless rovers the worshippers did such lucrative business. The synagogue, not the sea, was the poetry of these eager traffickers: here they wore phylacteries and waved palm-branches and did other picturesque things, which in their utter ignorance of Catholic or other ritual they deemed unintelligible to the heathen and a barrier from mankind. Very imposing was Solomon Cohn in his official pew under the reading platform, for there is nothing which so enhances a man's dignity in the synagogue as the consideration of his Christian townsmen. That is one of the earliest stages of Anglicization.

II

Mrs. Cohn was a pale image of Mr. Cohn, seeing things through his gold spectacles, and walking humbly in the shadow of his greatness. She had dutifully borne him many children, and sat on the ground for such as died. Her figure refused the Jewess's tradition of opulence, and remained slender as though repressed. Her work was manifold and unceasing, for besides her domestic and shop-womanly duties she was necessarily a philanthropist, fettered with Jewish charities as the Gabbai's wife, tangled with Christian charities as the consort of the Town Councillor. In speech she was literally his echo, catching up his mistakes, indeed, admonished by him of her slips in speaking the Councillor's English. He had had the start of her by five years, for she had been brought from Poland to marry him, through the good offices of a friend of hers who saw in her little dowry the nucleus of a thriving shop in a thriving port.

And from this initial inferiority she never recovered—five milestones behind on the road of Anglicization! It was enough to keep down a more assertive personality than poor Hannah's. The mere danger of slipping back unconsciously to the banned Yiddish put a curb upon her tongue. Her large, dark eyes had a dog-like look, and they were set pathetically in a sallow face that suggested ill-health, yet immense staying power.

That S. Cohn was a bit of a bully can scarcely be denied. It is difficult to combine the offices of Gabbai and Town Councillor without a self-satisfaction that may easily degenerate into dissatisfaction with others. Least endurable was S. Cohn in his religious rigidity, and he could never understand that pietistic exercises in which he found pleasure did not inevitably produce ecstasy in his son and heir. And when Simon was discovered reading 'The Pirates of Pechili,' dexterously concealed in his prayer-book, the boy received a strapping that made his mother wince. Simon's breakfast lay only at the end of a long volume of prayers; and, having ascertained by careful experiment the minimum of time his father would accept for the gabbling of these empty Oriental sounds, he had fallen back on penny numbers to while away the hungry minutes. The quartering and burning of these tales in an avenging fireplace was not the least of the reasons why the whipped youth wept, and it needed several pieces of cake, maternally smuggled into his maw while the father's back was turned, to choke his sobs.

III

With the daughters—and there were three before the son and heir—there was less of religious friction, since women have not the pious privileges and burdens of the sterner sex. When the eldest, Deborah, was married, her husband received, by way of compensation, the goodwill of the Sudminster business, while S. Cohn migrated to the metropolis, in the ambition of making 'S. Cohn's trouserings' a household word. He did, indeed, achieve considerable fame in the Holloway Road.

Gradually he came to live away from his business, and in the most fashionable street of Highbury. But he was never to recover his exalted posts. The London parish had older inhabitants, the local synagogue richer members. The cry for Anglicization was common property. From pioneer, S. Cohn found himself outmoded. The minister, indeed, was only too English—and especially his wife. One would almost have thought from their deportment that they considered themselves the superiors instead of the slaves of the congregation. S. Cohn had been accustomed to a series of clergymen, who must needs be taught painfully to parrot 'Our Sovereign Lady Queen Victoria, the Prince of Wales, the Princess of Wales, and all the Royal Family'—the indispensable atom of English in the service—so that he, the expert, had held his breath while they groped and stumbled along the precipitous pass. Now the whilom Gabbai and Town Councillor found himself almost patronized—as a poor provincial—by this mincing, genteel clerical couple. He retorted by animadverting upon the preacher's heterodoxy.

An urban unconcern met the profound views so often impressed on Simon with a strap. 'We are not in Poland now,' said the preacher, shrugging his shoulders.

'In Poland!' S. Cohn's blood boiled. To be twitted with Poland, after decades of Anglicization! He, who employed a host of Anglo-Saxon clerks, counter-jumpers, and packers! 'And where did your father come from?' he retorted hotly.

He had almost a mind to change his synagogue, but there was no other within such easy walking distance—an important Sabbatic consideration—and besides, the others were reported to be even worse. Dread rumours came of a younger generation that craved almost openly for organs in the synagogue and women's voices in the choir, nay, of even more flagitious spirits—devotional dynamitards—whose dream was a service all English, that could be understood instead of chanted! Dark mutterings against the ancient Rabbis were in the very air of these wealthier quarters of London.

'Oh, shameless ignorance of the new age,' S. Cohn was wont to complain, 'that does not know the limits of Anglicization!'

IV

That Simon should enter his father's business was as inevitable as that the business should prosper in spite of Simon.

His career had been settled ere his father became aware that Highbury aspired even to law and medicine, and the idea that Simon's education was finished was not lightly to be dislodged. Simon's education consisted of the knowledge conveyed in seaport schools for the sons of tradesmen, while a long course of penny dreadfuls had given him a peculiar and extensive acquaintance with the ways of the world. Carefully curtained away in a secret compartment, lay his elementary Hebrew lore. It did not enter into his conception of the perfect Englishman. Ah, how he rejoiced in this wider horizon of London, so thickly starred with music-halls, billiard-rooms, and restaurants! 'We are emancipated now,' was his cry: 'we have too much intellect to keep all those old laws;' and he swallowed the forbidden oyster in a fine spiritual glow, which somehow or other would not extend to bacon. That stuck more in his throat, and so was only taken in self-defence, to avoid the suspicions of a convivial company.

As he sat at his father's side in the synagogue—a demure son of the Covenant—this young Englishman lurked beneath his praying-shawl, even as beneath his prayer-book had lurked 'The Pirates of Pechili.'

In this hidden life Mrs. S. Cohn was not an aider or abettor, except in so far as frequent gifts from her own pocket-money might be considered the equivalent of the surreptitious cake of childhood. She would have shared in her husband's horror had she seen Simon banqueting on unrighteousness, and her apoplexy would have been original, not derivative. For her, indeed, London had proved narrowing rather than widening. She became part of a parish instead of part of a town, and of a Ghetto in a parish at that! The vast background of London was practically a mirage—the London suburb was farther from London than the provincial town. No longer did the currents of civic life tingle through her; she sank entirely to family affairs, excluded even from the ladies' committee. Her lord's life, too, shrank, though his business extended—the which, uneasily suspected, did but increase his irritability. He had now the pomp and pose of his late offices minus any visible reason: a Sir Oracle without a shrine, an abdomen without authority.

Even the two new sons-in-law whom his ability to clothe them had soon procured in London, listened impatiently, once they had safely passed under the Canopy and were ensconced in plush parlours of their own. Home and shop became his only realm, and his autocratic tendencies grew the stronger by compression. He read 'the largest circulation,' and his wife became an echo of its opinions. These opinions, never nebulous, became sharp as illuminated sky-signs when the Boer War began.

'The impertinent rascals!' cried S. Cohn furiously. 'They have invaded our territory.'

'Is it possible?' ejaculated Mrs. Cohn. 'This comes of our kindness to them after Majuba!'

V

A darkness began to overhang the destinies of Britain. Three defeats in one week!

'It is humiliating,' said S. Cohn, clenching his fist.

'It makes a miserable Christmas,' said Mrs. Cohn gloomily. Although her spouse still set his face against the Christmas pudding which had invaded so many Anglo-Jewish homes, the festival, with its shop-window flamboyance, entered far more vividly into his consciousness than the Jewish holidays, which produced no impression on the life of the streets.

The darkness grew denser. Young men began to enlist for the front: the City formed a new regiment of Imperial Volunteers. S. Cohn gave his foreign houses large orders for khaki trouserings. He sent out several parcels of clothing to the seat of war, and had the same duly recorded in his favourite Christian newspaper, whence it was copied into his favourite Jewish weekly, which was, if possible, still more chauvinist, and had a full-page portrait of Sir Asher Aaronsberg, M.P. for Middleton, who was equipping a local corps at his own expense. Gradually S. Cohn became aware that the military fever of which he read in both his organs was infecting his clothing emporium—that his own counter-jumpers were in heats of adventurous resolve. The military microbes must have lain thick in the khaki they handled. At any rate, S. Cohn, always quick to catch the contagion of the correct thing, announced that he would present a bonus to all who went out to fight for their country, and that he would keep their places open for their return. The Saturday this patriotic offer was recorded in his newspaper—'On inquiry at S. Cohn's, the great clothing purveyor of the Holloway Road, our representative was informed that no less than five of the young men were taking advantage of their employer's enthusiasm for England and the Empire'—the already puffed-up Solomon had the honour of being called to read in the Law, and first as befitted the sons of Aaron. It was a man restored almost to his provincial pride who recited the ancient benediction; 'Blessed art Thou, O Lord our God, who hast chosen us from among all peoples and given to us His law.'

But there was a drop of vinegar in the cup.

'And why wasn't Simon in synagogue?' he inquired of his wife, as she came down the gallery stairs to meet her lord in the lobby, where the congregants loitered to chat.

'Do I know?' murmured Mrs. Cohn, flushing beneath her veil.

'When I left the house he said he was coming on.'

'He didn't know you were to be "called up."'

'It isn't that, Hannah,' he grumbled. 'Think of the beautiful war-sermon he missed. In these dark days we should be thinking of our country, not of our pleasures.' And he drew her angrily without, where the brightly-dressed worshippers, lingeringly exchanging eulogiums on the 'Rule Britannia' sermon, made an Oriental splotch of colour on the wintry pavement.

At lunch the reprobate appeared, looking downcast.

'Where have you been?' thundered S. Cohn, who, never growing older, imagined Simon likewise stationary.

'I went out for a walk—it was a fine morning.'

'And where did you go?'

'Oh, don't bother!'

'But I shall bother. Where did you go?'

He grew sullen. 'It doesn't matter—they won't have me.'

'Who won't have you?'

'The War Office.'

'Thank God!' broke from Mrs. Cohn.

'Eh?' Mr. Cohn looked blankly from one to the other.

'It is nothing—he went to see the enlisting and all that. Your soup is getting cold.'

But S. Cohn had taken off his gold spectacles and was polishing them with his serviette—always a sign of a stormy meal.

'It seems to me something has been going on behind my back,' he said, looking from mother to son.

'Well, I didn't want to annoy you with Simon's madcap ideas,' Hannah murmured. 'But it's all over now, thank God!'

'Oh, he'd better know,' said Simon sulkily, 'especially as I am not going to be choked off. It's all stuff what the doctor says. I'm as strong as a horse. And, what's more, I'm one of the few applicants who can ride one.'

'Hannah, will you explain to me what this Meshuggas (madness) is?' cried S. Cohn, lapsing into a non-Anglicism.

'I've got to go to the front, just like other young men!'

'What!' shrieked S. Cohn. 'Enlist! You, that I brought up as a gentleman!'

'It's gentlemen that's going—the City Imperial Volunteers!'

'The volunteers! But that's my own clerks.'

'No; there are gentlemen among them. Read your paper.'

'But not rich Jews.'

'Oh, yes. I saw several chaps from Bayswater.'

'We Jews of this favoured country,' put in Hannah eagerly, 'grateful to the noble people who have given us every right, every liberty, must—'

S. Cohn was taken aback by this half-unconscious quotation from the war-sermon of the morning. 'Yes, we must subscribe and all that,' he interrupted.

'We must fight,' said Simon.

'You fight!' His father laughed half-hysterically. 'Why, you'd shoot yourself with your own gun!' He had not been so upset since the day the minister had disregarded his erudition.

'Oh, would I, though?' And Simon pursed his lips and nodded meaningly.

'As sure as to-day is the Holy Sabbath. And you'd be stuck on your own bayonet, like an obstinate pig.'

Simon got up and left the table and the room.

Hannah kept back her tears before the servant. 'There!' she said. 'And now he's turned sulky and won't eat.'

'Didn't I say an obstinate pig? He's always been like that from a baby. But his stomach always surrenders.' He resumed his meal with a wronged air, keeping his spectacles on the table, for frequent nervous polishing.

Of a sudden the door reopened and a soldier presented himself—gun on shoulder. For a moment S. Cohn, devoid of his glasses, stared without recognition. Wild hereditary tremors ran through him, born of the Russian persecution, and he had a vague nightmare sense of the Chappers, the Jewish man-gatherers who collected the tribute of young Jews for the Little Father. But as Simon began to loom through the red fog, 'A gun on the Sabbath!' he cried. It was as if the bullet had gone through all his conceptions of life and of Simon.

Hannah snatched at the side-issue. 'I read in Josephus—Simon's prize for Hebrew, you know—that the Jews fought against the Romans on Sabbath.'

'Yes; but they fought for themselves—for our Holy Temple.'

'But it's for ourselves now,' said Simon. 'Didn't you always say we are English?'

S. Cohn opened his mouth in angry retort. Then he discovered he had no retort, only anger. And this made him angrier, and his mouth remained open, quite terrifyingly for poor Mrs. Cohn.

'What is the use of arguing with him?' she said imploringly. 'The War Office has been sensible enough to refuse him.'

'We shall see,' said Simon. 'I am going to peg away at 'em again, and if I don't get into the Mounted Infantry, I'm a Dutchman—and of the Boer variety.'

He seemed any kind of man save a Jew to the puzzled father. 'Hannah, you must have known of this— these clothes,' S. Cohn spluttered.

'They don't cost anything,' she murmured. 'The child amuses himself. He will never really be called out.'

'If he is, I'll stop his supplies.'

'Oh,' said Simon airily, 'the Government will attend to that.'

'Indeed!' And S. Cohn's face grew black. 'But remember—you may go, but you shall never come back.'

'Oh, Solomon! How can you utter such an awful omen?'

Simon laughed. 'Don't bother, mother. He's bound to take me back. Isn't it in the papers that he promised?'

S. Cohn went from black to green.

VII

Simon got his way. The authorities reconsidered their decision. But the father would not reconsider his. Ignorant of his boy's graceless existence, he fumed at the first fine thing in the boy's life. ''Tis a wise father that knows his own child.

Mere emulation of his Christian comrades, and the fun of the thing, had long ago induced the lad to add volunteering to his other dissipations. But, once in it, the love of arms seized him, and when the call for serious fighters came, some new passion that surprised even himself leapt to his breast—the first call upon an idealism, choked, rather than fed, by a misunderstood Judaism. Anglicization had done its work; from his schooldays he had felt himself a descendant, not of Judas Maccabæus, but of Nelson and Wellington; and now that his brethren were being mowed down by a kopje-guarded foe, his whole soul rose in venomous sympathy. And, mixed with this genuine instinct of devotion to the great cause of country, were stirrings of anticipated adventure, gorgeous visions of charges, forlorn hopes, picked-up shells, redoubts stormed; heritages of 'The Pirates of Pechili,' and all the military romances that his prayer-book had masked.

He looked every inch an Anglo-Saxon, in his khaki uniform and his great slouch hat, with his bayonet and his bandolier.

The night before he sailed for South Africa there was a service in St. Paul's Cathedral, for which each volunteer had two tickets. Simon sent his to his father. 'The Lord Mayor will attend in state. I dare say you'll like to see the show,' he wrote flippantly.

'He'll become a Christian next,' said S. Cohn, tearing the cards in twain.

Later, Mrs. Cohn pieced them together. It was the last chance of seeing her boy.

VIII

Unfortunately the Cathedral service fell on a Friday night, when S. Cohn, the Emporium closed, was wont to absorb the Sabbath peace. He would sit, after high tea, of which cold fried fish was the prime ingredient, dozing over the Jewish weekly. He still approved platonically of its bellicose sentiments. This January night, the Sabbath arriving early in the afternoon, he was snoring before seven, and Mrs. Cohn slipped out, risking his wrath. Her religion forced her to make the long journey on foot; but, hurrying, she arrived at St. Paul's before the doors were opened. And throughout the long walk was a morbid sense of one wasted ticket. She almost stopped at a friend's house to offer the exciting spectacle, but dread of a religious rebuff carried her past. With Christians she was not intimate enough to invite companionship. Besides, would not everybody ask why she was going without her husband?

She inquired for the door mentioned on her ticket, and soon found herself one of a crowd of parents on the steps. A very genteel crowd, she noted with pleasure. Her boy would be in good company. The scraps of conversation she caught dealt with a world of alien things—how little she was Anglicized, she thought, after all those years! And when she was borne forward into the Cathedral, her heart beat with a sense of dim, remote glories. To have lived so long in London and never to have entered here! She was awed and soothed by the solemn vistas, the perspectives of pillars and arches, the great nave, the white robes of the choir vaguely stirring a sense of angels, the overarching dome, defined by a fiery rim, but otherwise suggesting dim, skyey space.

Suddenly she realized that she was sitting among the men. But it did not seem to matter. The building kept one's thoughts religious. Around the waiting congregation, the human sea outside the Cathedral rumoured, and whenever the door was opened to admit some dignitary the roar of cheering was heard like a salvo saluting his entry. The Lord Mayor and the Aldermen passed along the aisle, preceded by mace-bearers; and mingled with this dazzle of gilded grandeur and robes, was a regretful memory of the days when, as a Town Councillor's consort, she had at least touched the hem of this unknown historic English life. The skirl of bagpipes shrilled from without—that exotic, half-barbarous sound now coming intimately into her life. And then, a little later, the wild cheers swept into the Cathedral like a furious wind, and the thrill of the marching soldiers passed into the air, and the congregation jumped up on the chairs and craned towards the right aisle to stare at the khaki couples. How she looked for Simon!

The volunteers filed on, filed on—beardless youths mostly, a few with a touch of thought in the face, many with the honest nullity of the clerk and the shopman, some with the prizefighter's jaw, but every face set and serious. Ah! at last, there was her Simon—manlier, handsomer than them all! But he did not see her: he marched on stiffly; he was already sucked up into this strange life. Her heart grew heavy.

But it lightened again when the organ pealed out. The newspapers the next day found fault with the plain music, with the responses all in monotone, but to her it was divine. Only the words of the opening hymn, which she read in the 'Form of Prayer,' discomforted her:

'Fight the good fight with all thy might, Christ is thy Strength and Christ thy Right'

But the bulk of the liturgy surprised her, so strangely like was it to the Jewish. The ninety-first Psalm! Did they, then, pray the Jewish prayers in Christian churches? 'For He shall give His angels charge over thee: to keep thee in all thy ways.' Ah! how she prayed that for Simon!

As the ecclesiastical voice droned on, unintelligibly, inaudibly, in echoing, vaulted space, she studied the hymns and verses, with their insistent Old Testament savour, culminating in the farewell blessing:

'The Lord bless you and keep you. The Lord make His face to shine upon you and be gracious unto you. The Lord lift up the light of His countenance upon you and give you peace.'

How often she had heard it in Hebrew from the priests as they blessed the other tribes! Her husband himself had chanted it, with uplifted palms and curiously grouped fingers. But never before had she felt its beauty: she had never even understood its words till she read the English of them in the gilt-edged Prayer-Book that marked rising wealth. Surely there had been some monstrous mistake in conceiving the two creeds as at daggers drawn, and though she only pretended to kneel with the others, she felt her knees sinking in surrender to the larger life around her.

As the volunteers filed out and the cheers came in, she wormed her way nearer to the aisle, scrambling even over backs of chairs in the general mellay. This time Simon saw her. He stretched out his martial arm and blew her a kiss. Oh, delicious tears, full of heartbreak and exaltation! This was their farewell.

She passed out into the roaring crowd, with a fantastic dream-sense of a night-sky and a great stone building, dark with age and solemnity, and unreal figures perched on railings and points of vantage, and hurrahing hordes that fused themselves with the procession and became part of its marching. She yearned forwards to vague glories, aware of a poor past. She ran with the crowd. How they cheered her boy! Her boy! She saw him carried off on the shoulders of Christian citizens. Yes; he was a hero. She was the mother of a hero.

IX

The first news she got from him was posted at St. Vincent. He wrote to her alone, with a jocose hope that his father would be satisfied with his sufferings on the voyage. Not only had the sea been rough, but he had suffered diabolically from the inoculation against enteric fever, which, even after he had got his sea-legs, kept him to his berth and gave him a 'Day of Atonement' thirst.

'Ah!' growled S. Cohn; 'he sees what a fool he's been, and he'll take the next boat back.'

'But that would be desertion.'

'Well, he didn't mind deserting the business.'

Mr. Cohn's bewilderment increased with every letter. The boy was sleeping in sodden trenches, sometimes without blankets; and instead of grumbling at that, his one grievance was that the regiment was not getting to the front. Heat and frost, hurricane and dust-storm—nothing came amiss. And he described himself as stronger than ever, and poured scorn on the medical wiseacre who had tried to refuse him.

'All the same,' sighed Hannah, 'I do hope they will just be used to guard the lines of communication.' She was full of war-knowledge acquired with painful eagerness, prattled of Basuto ponies and Mauser bullets, pontoons and pom-poms, knew the exact position of the armies, and marked her war-map with coloured pins.

Simon, too, had developed quite a literary talent under the pressure of so much vivid new life, and from his cheery letters she learned much that was not in the papers, especially in those tense days when the C.I.V.'S did at last get to the front—and remained there: tales of horses mercifully shot, and sheep mercilessly poisoned, and oxen dropping dead as they dragged the convoys; tales of muddle and accident, tales of British soldiers slain by their own protective cannon as they lay behind ant-heaps facing the enemy, and British officers culled under the very eyes of the polo-match; tales of hospital and camp, of shirts turned sable and putties worn to rags, and all the hidden miseries of uncleanliness and insanitation that underlie the glories of war. There were tales, too, of quarter-rations; but these she did not read to her husband, lest the mention of 'bully-beef' should remind him of how his son must be eating forbidden food. Once, even, two fat pigs were captured at a hungry moment for the battalion. But there came a day when S. Cohn seized those letters and read them first. He began to speak of his boy at the war—nay, to read the letters to enthralled groups in the synagogue lobby—groups that swallowed without reproach the tripha meat cooked in Simon's mess-tin.

It was like being Gabbai over again.

Moreover, Simon's view of the Boer was so strictly orthodox as to give almost religious satisfaction to the proud parent. 'A canting hypocrite, a psalm-singer and devil-dodger, he has no civilization worth the name, and his customs are filthy. Since the great trek he has acquired, from long intercourse with his Kaffir slaves, many of the native's savage traits. In short, a born liar, credulous and barbarous, crassly ignorant and inconceivably stubborn.'

'Crassly ignorant and inconceivably stubborn,' repeated S. Cohn, pausing impressively. 'Haven't I always said that? The boy only bears out what I knew without going there. But hear further! "Is it to be wondered at that the Boer farmer, hidden in the vast undulations of the endless veldt, with his wife, his children and his slaves, should lose all sense of proportion, ignorant of the outside world, his sole knowledge filtering through Jo-burgh?"'

As S. Cohn made another dramatic pause, it was suddenly borne in on his wife with a stab of insight that he was reading a description of himself—nay, of herself, of her whole race, hidden in the great world, awaiting some vague future of glory that never came. The important voice of her husband broke again upon her reflections:

'"He has held many nights of supplication to his fetish, and is still unconvinced that his God of Battles is asleep."' The reader chuckled, and a broad smile overspread the synagogue lobby. '"They are brave—oh, yes, but it is not what we mean by it—they are good fighters, because they have Dutch blood at the back of them, and a profound contempt for us. Their whole life has been spent on the open veldt (we are always fighting them on somebody's farm, who knows every inch of the ground), and they never risk anything except in the trap sort of manoeuvres. The brave rush of our Tommies is unknown to them, and their slim nature would only see the idiocy of walking into a death-trap, cool as in a play. Were there ever two races less alike?"' wound up the youthful philosopher in his tent. '"I really do not see how they are to live together after the war."'

'That's easy enough,' S. Cohn had already commented to his wife as oracularly as if she did not read the same morning paper. 'Intermarriage! In a generation or two there will be one fine Anglo-African race. That's the solution—mark my words. And you can tell the boy as much—only don't say I told you to write to him.'

'Father says I'm to tell you intermarriage is the solution,' Mrs. Cohn wrote obediently. 'He really is getting much softer towards you.'

'Tell father that's nonsense,' Simon wrote back. 'The worst individuals we have to deal with come from a Boer mother and an English father, deposited here by the first Transvaal war.'

S. Cohn snorted angrily at the message. 'That was because there were two Governments—he forgets there will be only one United Empire now.'

He was not appeased till Private Cohn was promoted, and sent home a thrilling adventure, which the proud reader was persuaded by the lobby to forward to the communal organ. The organ asked for a photograph to boot. Then S. Cohn felt not only Gabbai, but town councillor again.

This wonderful letter, of which S. Cohn distributed printed copies to the staff of the Emporium with a bean-feast air, ran:

'We go out every day—I am speaking of my own squadron—each officer taking his turn with twenty to fifty men, and sweep round the farms a few miles out; and we seldom come back without seeing Boers hanging round on the chance of a snipe at our flanks, or waiting to put up a trap if we go too far. The local commando fell on our cattle-guard the other day—a hundred and fifty to our twenty-five—and we suffered; it was a horrible bit of country. There was a young chap, Winstay—rather a pal of mine—he had a narrow squeak, knocked over by a shot in his breast. I managed to get him safe back to camp—Heaven knows how!—and they made me a lance-corporal, and the beggar says I saved his life; but it was really through carrying a fat letter from his sister—not even his sweetheart. We chaff him at missing such a romantic chance. He got off with a flesh wound, but there is a great blot of red ink on the letter. You may imagine we were not anxious to let our comrades go unavenged. My superiors being sick or otherwise occupied, I was allowed to make a night-march with thirty-five men on a farm nine miles away—just to get square. It was a nasty piece of work, as we were within a few miles of the Boer laager, three hundred strong. There was moonlight, too—it was like a dream, that strange, silent ride, with only the stumble of a horse breaking the regular thud of the hoofs. We surrounded the farm in absolute silence, dismounting some thousand yards away, and fixing bayonets. I told the men I wanted no shots—that would have brought down the commando—but cold steel and silence. We crept up and swept the farm—it was weird, but, alas! they were out on the loot. The men were furious, but we live in hopes.'

The end was a trifle disappointing, but S. Cohn, too, lived in hopes—of some monstrous and memorable butchery. Even his wife had got used to the firing-line, now that neither shot nor shell could harm her boy. 'For He shall give His angels charge over thee.' She had come to think her secret daily repetition of the ninety-first Psalm talismanic.

When Simon sent home the box which had held the chocolates presented by the Queen, a Boer bullet, and other curios, S. Cohn displayed them in his window, and the crowd and the business they brought him put him more and more in sympathy with Simon and the Empire. In conversation he deprecated the non-militarism of the Jew: 'If I were only a younger man myself, sir....'

The night Mafeking was relieved, the Emporium was decorated with bunting from roof to basement, and a great illuminated window revealed nothing but stacks of khaki trouserings.

So that, although the good man still sulked over Simon to his wife, she was not deceived; and, the time drawing nigh for Simon's return, she began to look happily forward to a truly reunited family.

In her wildest anxiety it never occurred to her that it was her husband who would die. Yet this is what the irony of fate brought to pass. In the unending campaign which death wages with life, S. Cohn was slain, and Simon returned unscratched from the war to recite the Kaddish in his memory.

X

Simon came back bronzed and a man. The shock of finding his father buried had supplied the last transforming touch; and, somewhat to his mother's surprise, he settled down contentedly to the business he had inherited. And now that he had practically unlimited money to spend, he did not seem to be spending it, but to be keeping better hours than when dodging his father's eye. His only absences from home he accounted for as visits to Winstay, his pal of the campaign, with whom he had got chummier than ever since the affair of the cattle-guard. Winstay, he said, was of good English family, with an old house in Harrow—fortunately on the London and North Western Railway, so that he could easily get a breath of country air on Saturday and Sunday afternoons. He seemed to have forgotten (although the Emporium was still closed on Saturdays) that riding was forbidden, and his mother did not remind him of it. The life that had been risked for the larger cause, she vaguely felt as enfranchised from the limitations of the smaller.

Nearly two months after Simon's return, a special military service was held at the Great Synagogue on the feast of Chanukah—the commemoration of the heroic days of Judas Maccabæus—and the Jewish C.I.V.'s were among the soldiers invited. Mrs. Cohn, too, got a ticket for the imposing ceremony which was fixed for a Sunday afternoon.

As they sat at the midday meal on the exciting day, Mrs. Cohn said suddenly: 'Guess who paid me a visit yesterday.'

'Goodness knows,' said Simon.

'Mr. Sugarman.' And she smiled nervously.

'Sugarman?' repeated Simon blankly.

'The—the—er—the matrimonial agent.'

'What impudence! Before your year of mourning is up!'

Mrs. Cohn's sallow face became one flame. 'Not me! You!' she blurted.

'Me! Well, of all the cheek!' And Simon's flush matched his mother's.

'Oh, it's not so unreasonable,' she murmured deprecatingly. 'I suppose he thought you would be looking for a wife before long; and naturally,' she added, her voice growing bolder, 'I should like to see you settled before I follow your father. After all, you are no ordinary match. Sugarman says there isn't a girl in Bayswater, even, who would refuse you.'

'The very reason for refusing them,' cried Simon hotly. 'What a ghastly idea, that your wife would just as soon have married any other fellow with the same income!'

Mrs. Cohn cowered under his scorn, yet felt vaguely exalted by it, as by the organ in St. Paul's, and strange tears of shame came to complicate her emotions further. She remembered how she had been exported from Poland to marry the unseen S. Cohn. Ah! how this new young generation was snapping asunder the ancient coils! how the new and diviner sap ran in its veins!

'I shall only marry a girl I love, mother. And it's not likely to be one of these Jewish girls, I tell you frankly.'

She trembled. 'One of which Jewish girls?' she faltered.

'Oh, any sort. They don't appeal to me.'

Her face grew sallower. 'I am glad your father isn't alive to hear that,' she breathed.

'But father said intermarriage is the solution,' retorted Simon.

Mrs. Cohn was struck dumb. 'He was thinking how to make the Boers English,' she said at last.

'And didn't he say the Jews must be English, too?'

'Aren't there plenty of Jewish girls who are English?' she murmured miserably.

'You mean, who don't care a pin about the old customs? Then where's the difference?' retorted Simon.

The meal finished in uncomfortable silence, and Simon went off to don his khaki regimentals and join in the synagogue parade.

Mrs. Cohn's heart was heavy as she dressed for the same spectacle. Her brain was busy piecing it all together. Yes, she understood it all now—those sedulous Saturday and Sunday afternoons at Harrow. She lived at Harrow, then, this Christian, this grateful sister of the rescued Winstay: it was she who had steadied his life; hers were those 'fat letters,' faintly aromatic. It must be very wonderful, this strange passion, luring her son from his people with its forbidden glamour. How Highbury would be scandalized, robbed of so eligible a bridegroom! The sons-in-law she had enriched would reproach her for the shame imported into the family—they who had cleaved to the Faith! And—more formidable than all the rest—she heard the tongue of her cast-off seaport, to whose reverence or disesteem she still instinctively referred all her triumphs and failures.

Yet, on the other hand, surged her hero-son's scorn at the union by contract consecrated by the generations! But surely a compromise could be found. He should have love—this strange English thing—but could he not find a Jewess? Ah, happy inspiration! he should marry a quite poor Jewess—he had money enough, thank Heaven! That would show him he was not making a match, that he was truly in love.

But this strange girl at Harrow—he would never be happy with her! No, no; there were limits to Anglicization.

XI

It was not till she was seated in the ancient synagogue, relieved from the squeeze of entry in the wake of soldiers and the exhilaration of hearing 'See the Conquering Hero comes' pealing, she knew not whence, that she woke to the full strangeness of it all, and to the consciousness that she was actually sitting among the men—just as in St. Paul's. And what men! Everywhere the scarlet and grey of uniforms, the glister of gold lace—the familiar decorous lines of devout top-hats broken by glittering helmets, bear-skins, white nodding plumes, busbies, red caps a-cock, glengarries, all the colour of the British army, mixed with the feathered jauntiness of the Colonies and the khaki sombreros of the C.I.V.'s! Coldstream Guards, Scots Guards, Dragoon Guards, Lancers, Hussars, Artillery, Engineers, King's Royal Rifles, all the corps that had for the first time come clearly into her consciousness in her tardy absorption into English realities, Jews seemed to be among them all. And without conscription—oh, what would poor Solomon have thought of that?

The Great Synagogue itself struck a note of modern English gaiety, as of an hotel dining-room, freshly gilded, divested of its historic mellowness, the electric light replacing the ancient candles and flooding the winter afternoon with white resplendence. The pulpit—yes, the pulpit—was swathed in the Union Jack; and looking towards the box of the Parnass and Gabbai, she saw it was occupied by officers with gold sashes. Somebody whispered that he with the medalled breast was a Christian Knight and Commander of the Bath—'a great honour for the synagogue!' What! were Christians coming to Jewish services, even as she had gone to Christian? Why, here was actually a white cross on an officer's sleeve.

And before these alien eyes, the cantor, intoning his Hebrew chant on the steps of the Ark, lit the great many-branched Chanukah candlestick. Truly, the world was changing under her eyes.

And when the Chief Rabbi went toward the Ark in his turn, she saw that he wore a strange scarlet and white gown (military, too, she imagined in her ignorance), and—oh, even rarer sight!—he was followed by a helmeted soldier, who drew the curtain revealing the ornate Scrolls of the Law.

And amid it all a sound broke forth that sent a sweetness through her blood. An organ! An organ in the Synagogue! Ah! here indeed was Anglicization.

It was thin and reedy even to her ears, compared with that divine resonance in St. Paul's: a tinkling apology, timidly disconnected from the congregational singing, and hovering meekly on the borders of the service—she read afterwards that it was only a harmonium—yet it brought a strange exaltation, and there was an uplifting even to tears in the glittering uniforms and nodding plumes. Simon's eyes met his mother's, and a flash of the old childish love passed between them.

There was a sermon—the text taken with dual appropriateness from the Book of Maccabees. Fully one in ten of the Jewish volunteers, said the preacher, had gone forth to drive out the bold invader of the Queen's dominions. Their beloved country had no more devoted citizens than the children of Israel who had settled under her flag. They had been gratified, but not surprised, to see in the Jewish press the names of more than seven hundred Jews serving Queen and country. Many more had gone unrecorded, so that they had proportionally contributed more soldiers—from Colonel to bugler-boy—than their mere numbers would warrant. So at one in spirit and ideals were the Englishman and the Jew whose Scriptures he had imbibed, that it was no accident that the Anglophobes of Europe were also Anti-Semites.

And then the congregation rose, while the preacher behind the folds of the Union Jack read out the names of the Jews who had died for England in the far-off veldt. Every head was bent as the names rose on the hushed air of the synagogue. It went on and on, this list, reeking with each bloody historic field, recalling every regiment, British or colonial; on and on in the reverent silence, till a black pall seemed to descend, inch by inch, overspreading the synagogue. She had never dreamed so many of her brethren had died out there. Ah! surely they were knit now, these races: their friendship sealed in blood!

As the soldiers filed out of synagogue, she squeezed towards Simon and seized his hand for an instant, whispering passionately: 'My lamb, marry her—we are all English alike.'

Nor did she ever know that she had said these words in Yiddish!

XII

Now came an enchanting season of confidences; the mother, caught up in the glow of this strange love, learning to see the girl through the boy's eyes, though the only aid to his eloquence was the photograph of a plump little blonde with bewitching dimples. The time was not ripe yet for bringing Lucy and her together, he explained. In fact, he hadn't actually proposed. His mother understood he was waiting for the year of mourning to be up.

'But how will you be married?' she once asked.

'Oh, there's the registrar,' he said carelessly.

'But can't you make her a proselyte?' she ventured timidly.

He coloured. 'It would be absurd to suddenly start talking religion to her.'

'But she knows you're a Jew.'

'Oh, I dare say. I never hid it from her brother, so why shouldn't she know? But her father's a bit of a crank, so I rather avoid the subject.'

'A crank? About Jews?'

'Well, old Winstay has got it into his noddle that the Jews are responsible for the war—and that they leave the fighting to the English. It's rather sickening: even in South Africa we are not treated as we should be, considering—'

Her dark eye lost its pathetic humility. 'But how can he say that, when you yourself—when you saved his—'

'Well, I suppose just because he knows I was fighting, he doesn't think of me as a Jew. It's a bit illogical, I know.' And he smiled ruefully. 'But, then, logic is not the old boy's strong point.'

'He seemed such a nice old man,' said Mrs. Cohn, as she recalled the photograph of the white-haired cherub writing with a quill at a property desk.

'Oh, off his hobby-horse he's a dear old boy. That's why I don't help him into the saddle.'

'But how can he be ignorant that we've sent seven hundred at least to the war?' she persisted. 'Why, the paper had all their photographs!'

'What paper?' said Simon, laughing. 'Do you suppose he reads the Jewish what's-a-name, like you? Why, he's never heard of it!'

'Then you ought to show him a copy.'

'Oh, mother!' and he laughed again. 'That would only prove to him there are too many Jews everywhere.'

A cloud began to spread over Mrs. Cohn's hard-won content. But apparently it only shadowed her own horizon. Simon was as happily full of his Lucy as ever.

Nevertheless, there came a Sunday evening when Simon returned from Harrow earlier than his wont, and Hannah's dog-like eye noted that the cloud had at last reached his brow.

'You have had a quarrel?' she cried.

'Only with the old boy.'

'But what about?'

'The old driveller has just joined some League of Londoners for the suppression of the immigrant alien.'

'But you should have told him we all agree there should be decentralization,' said Mrs. Cohn, quoting her favourite Jewish organ.

'It isn't that—it's the old fellow's vanity that's hurt. You see, he composed the "Appeal to the Briton," and gloated over it so conceitedly that I couldn't help pointing out the horrible contradictions.'

'But Lucy—' his mother began anxiously.

'Lucy's a brick. I don't know what my life would have been without the little darling. But listen, mother.' And he drew out a portentous prospectus. 'They say aliens should not be admitted unless they produce a certificate of industrial capacity, and in the same breath they accuse them of taking the work away from the British workman. Now this isn't a Jewish question, and I didn't raise it as such—just a piece of muddle—and even as an Englishman I can't see how we can exclude Outlanders here after fighting for the Outland—'

'But Lucy—' his mother interrupted.

His vehement self-assertion passed into an affectionate smile.

'Lucy was dimpling all over her face. She knows the old boy's vanity. Of course she couldn't side with me openly.'

'But what will happen? Will you go there again?'

The cloud returned to his brow. 'Oh, well, we'll see.'

A letter from Lucy saved him the trouble of deciding the point.

'DEAR SILLY OLD SIM,' it ran,

'Father has been going on dreadfully, so you had better wait a few Sundays till he has cooled down. After all, you yourself admit there is a grievance of congestion and high rents in the East End. And it is only natural—isn't it?—that after shedding our blood and treasure for the Empire we should not be in a mood to see our country overrun by dirty aliens.'

'Dirty!' muttered Simon, as he read. 'Has she seen the Christian slums—Flower and Dean Street?' And his handsome Oriental brow grew duskier with anger. It did not clear till he came to:

'Let us meet at the Crystal Palace next Saturday, dear quarrelsome person. Three o'clock, in the Pompeian Room. I have got an aunt at Sydenham, and I can go in to tea after the concert and hear all about the missionary work in the South Sea Islands.'

XIII

Ensued a new phase in the relation of Simon and Lucy. Once they had met in freedom, neither felt inclined to revert to the restricted courtship of the drawing-room. Even though their chat was merely of books and music and pictures, it was delicious to make their own atmosphere, untroubled by the flippancy of the brother or the earnestness of the father. In the presence of Lucy's artistic knowledge Simon was at once abashed and stimulated. She moved in a delicate world of symphonies and silver-point drawings of whose very existence he had been unaware, and reverence quickened the sense of romance which their secret meetings had already enhanced.

Once or twice he spoke of resuming his visits to Harrow, but the longer he delayed the more difficult the conciliatory visit grew.

'Father is now deeper in the League than ever,' she told him. 'He has joined the committee, and the prospectus has gone forth in all its glorious self-contradiction.'

'But, considering I am the son of an alien, and I have fought for—'

'There, there! quarrelsome person,' she interrupted laughingly. 'No, no, no, you had better not come till you can forget your remote genealogy. You see, even now father doesn't quite realize you are a Jew. He thinks you have a strain of Jewish blood, but are in every other respect a decent Christian body.'

'Christian!' cried Simon in horror.

'Why not? You fought side by side with my brother; you ate ham with us.'

Simon blushed hotly. 'But, Lucy, you don't think religion is ham?'

'What, then? Merely Shem?' she laughed.

Simon laughed too. How clever she was! 'But you know I never could believe in the Trinity and all that. And, what's more, I don't believe you do yourself.'

'It isn't exactly what one believes. I was baptized into the Church of England—I feel myself a member. Really, Sim, you are a dreadfully argumentative and quarrelsome person.'

'I'll never quarrel with you, Lucy,' he said half entreatingly; for somehow he felt a shiver of cold at the word 'baptized,' as though himself plunged into the font.

In this wise did both glide away from any deep issue or decision till the summer itself glided away. Mrs. Cohn, anxiously following the courtship through Sim's love-smitten eyes, her suggestion that the girl be brought to see her received with equal postponement, began to fret for the great thing to come to pass. One cannot be always heroically stiffened to receive the cavalry of communal criticism. Waiting weakens the backbone. But she concealed from her boy these flaccid relapses.

'You said you'd bring her to see me when she returned from the seaside,' she ventured to remind him.

'So I did; but now her father is dragging her away to Scotland.'

'You ought to get married the moment she gets back.'

'I can't expect her to rush things—with her father to square. Still, you are not wrong, mother. It's high time we came to a definite understanding between ourselves at least.'

'What!' gasped Mrs. Cohn. 'Aren't you engaged?'

'Oh, in a way, of course. But we've never said so in so many words.'

For fear this should be the 'English' way, Mrs. Cohn forbore to remark that the definiteness of the Sugarman method was not without compensations. She merely applauded Simon's more sensible mood.

But Mrs. Cohn was fated to a further season of fret. Day after day the 'fat letters' arrived with the Scottish postmark and the faint perfume that always stirred her own wistful sense of lost romance—something far-off and delicious, with the sweetness of roses and the salt of tears. And still the lover, floating in his golden mist, vouchsafed her no definite news.

One night she found him restive beyond his wont. She knew the reason. For two days there had been no scented letter, and she saw how he started at every creak of the garden-gate, as he waited for the last post. When at length a step was heard crunching on the gravel, he rushed from the room, and Mrs. Cohn heard the hall-door open. Her ear, disappointed of the rat-tat, morbidly followed every sound; but it seemed a long time before her boy's returning footstep reached her. The strange, slow drag of it worked upon her nerves, and her heart grew sick with premonition.

He held out the letter towards her. His face was white. 'She cannot marry me, because I am a Jew,' he said tonelessly.

'Cannot marry you!' she whispered huskily. 'Oh, but this must not be! I will go to the father; I will explain! You saved his son—he owes you his daughter.'

He waved her hopelessly back to her seat—for she had started up. 'It isn't the father, it's herself. Now that I won't let her drift any longer, she can't bring herself to it. She's honest, anyway, my little Lucy. She won't fall back on the old Jew-baiter.'

'But how dare she—how dare she think herself above you!' Her dog-like eyes were blazing yet once again.

'Why are you Jews surprised?' he said bitterly. 'You've held yourself aloof from the others long enough, God knows. Yet you wonder they've got their prejudices, too.'

And, suddenly laying his head on the table, he broke into sobs—sobs that tore at his mother's heart, that were charged with memories of his ancient tears, of the days of paternal wrath and the rending of 'The Pirates of Pechili.' And, again, as in the days when his boyish treasures were changed to ashes, she stole towards him, with an involuntary furtive look to see if S. Cohn's back was turned, and laid her hands upon his heaving shoulders. But he shook her off! 'Why didn't a Boer bullet strike me down?' Then with a swift pang of remorse he raised his contorted face and drew hers close against it—their love the one thing saved from Anglicization.

THE JEWISH TRINITY

I

With the Christian Mayoress of Middleton to take in to dinner at Sir Asher Aaronsberg's, Leopold Barstein as a Jewish native of that thriving British centre, should have felt proud and happy. But Barstein was young and a sculptor, fresh from the Paris schools and Salon triumphs. He had long parted company with Jews and Judaism, and to his ardent irreverence even the Christian glories of Middleton seemed unspeakably parochial. In Paris he had danced at night on the Boule Miche out of sheer joy of life, and joined in choruses over midnight bocks; and London itself now seemed drab and joyless, though many a gay circle welcomed the wit and high spirits and even the physical graces of this fortunate young man who seemed to shed a blonde radiance all around him. The factories of Middleton, which had manufactured Sir Asher Aaronsberg, ex-M.P., and nearly all his wealthy guests, were to his artistic eye an outrage upon a beautiful planet, and he was still in that crude phase of juvenile revolt in which one speaks one's thoughts of the mess humanity has made of its world. But, unfortunately, the Mayoress of Middleton was deafish, so that he could not even shock her with his epigrams. It was extremely disconcerting to have his bland blasphemies met with an equally bland smile. On his other hand sat Mrs. Samuels, the buxom and highly charitable relict of 'The People's Clothier,' whose ugly pictorial posters had overshadowed Barstein's youth. Little wonder that the artist's glance frequently wandered across the great shining table towards a girl who, if they had not been so plaguily intent on honouring his fame, might have now been replacing the Mayoress at his side. True, the girl was merely a Jewess, and he disliked the breed. But Mabel Aaronsberg was unexpected. She had a statuesque purity of outline and complexion; seemed, indeed, worthy of being a creation of his own. How the tedious old manufacturer could have produced this marmoreal prodigy provided a problem for the sculptor, as he almost silently ate his way through the long and exquisite menu.

Not that Sir Asher himself was unpicturesque. Indeed, he was the very picture of the bluff and burly Briton, white-bearded like Father Christmas. But he did not seem to lead to yonder vision of poetry and purity. Lady Aaronsberg, who might have supplied the missing link, was dead—before even arriving at ladyship, alas!—and when she was alive Barstein had not enjoyed the privilege of moving in these high municipal circles. This he owed entirely to his foreign fame, and to his invitation by the Corporation to help in the organization of a local Art Exhibition.

'I do admire Sir Asher,' the Mayoress broke in suddenly upon his reflections; 'he seems to me exactly like your patriarchs.'

A Palestinian patriarch was the last person Sir Asher, with his hovering lackeys, would have recalled to the sculptor, who, in so far as the patriarchs ever crossed his mind, conceived them as resembling Rembrandt's Rabbis. But he replied blandly: 'Our patriarchs were polygamists.'

'Exactly,' assented the deaf Mayoress.

Barstein, disconcerted, yearned to repeat his statement in a shout, but neither the pitch nor the proposition seemed suitable to the dinner-table. The Mayoress added ecstatically: 'You can imagine him sitting at the door of his tent, talking with the angels.'

This time Barstein did shout, but with laughter. All eyes turned a bit enviously in his direction. 'You're having all the fun down there,' called out Sir Asher benevolently; and the bluff Briton—even to the northerly burr—was so vividly stamped upon Barstein's mind that he wondered the more that the Mayoress could see him as anything but the prosy, provincial, whilom Member of Parliament he so transparently was. 'A mere literary illusion,' he thought. 'She has read the Bible, and now reads Sir Asher into it. As well see a Saxon pirate or a Norman jongleur in a modern Londoner.'

As if to confirm Barstein's vision of the bluff and burly Briton, Sir Asher was soon heard over the clatter of conversation protesting vehemently against the views of Tom Fuller, the degenerate son of a Tory squire.

'Give Ireland Home Rule?' he was crying passionately. 'Oh, my dear Mr. Fuller, it would be the beginning of the end of our Empire!'

'But the Irish have as much right to govern themselves as we have!' the young Englishman maintained.

'They would not so much govern themselves as misgovern the Protestant minority,' cried Sir Asher, becoming almost epigrammatic in his excitement. 'Home Rule simply means the triumph of Roman Catholicism.'

It occurred to the cynical Barstein that even the defeat of Roman Catholicism meant no victory for Judaism, but he stayed his tongue with a salted almond. Let the Briton make the running. This the young gentleman proceeded to do at a great pace.

'Then how about Home Rule for India? There's no Catholic majority there!'

'Give up India!' Sir Asher opened horrified eyes. This heresy was new to him. 'Give up the brightest jewel in the British crown! And let the Russian bear come and swallow it up! No, no! A thousand times no!' Sir Asher even gestured with his fork in his patriotic fervour, forgetting he was not on the platform.

'So I imagine the patriarchs to have talked!' said the Mayoress, admiringly observing his animation. Whereat the sculptor laughed once more. He was amused, too, at the completeness with which the lion of Judah had endued himself with the skin of the British lion. To a cosmopolitan artist this bourgeois patriotism was peculiarly irritating. But soon his eyes wandered again towards Miss Aaronsberg, and he forgot trivialities.

II

The end of the meal was punctuated, not by the rising of the ladies, but by the host's assumption of a black cap, which popped up from his coat-tail pocket. With his head thus orientally equipped for prayer, Sir Asher suddenly changed into a Rembrandtesque figure, his white beard hiding the society shirtfront; and as he began intoning the grace in Hebrew, the startled Barstein felt that the Mayoress had at least a superficial justification. There came to him a touch of new and artistic interest in this prosy, provincial ex-M.P., who, environed by powdered footmen, sat at the end of his glittering dinner-table uttering the language of the ancient prophets; and he respected at least the sturdiness with which Miss Aaronsberg's father wore his faith, like a phylactery, on his forehead. It said much for his character that these fellow-citizens of his had once elected him as their Member, despite his unpopular creed and race, and were now willing to sit at his table under this tedious benediction. Sir Asher did not even let them off with the shorter form of grace invented by a wise Rabbi for these difficult occasions, yet so far as was visible it was only the Jewish guests—comically distinguished by serviettes shamefacedly dabbed on their heads—who fidgeted under the pious torrent. These were no doubt fearful of boring the Christians whose precious society the Jew enjoyed on a parlous tenure. In the host's son Julius a superadded intellectual impatience was traceable. He had brought back from Oxford a contempt for his father's creed which was patent to every Jew save Sir Asher. Barstein, observing all this uneasiness, became curiously angry with his fellow-Jews, despite that he had scrupulously forborne to cover his own head with his serviette; a racial pride he had not known latent in him surged up through all his cosmopolitanism, and he maliciously trusted that the brave Sir Asher would pray his longest. He himself had been a tolerable Hebraist in his forcedly pious boyhood, and though he had neither prayed nor heard any Hebrew prayers for many a year, his new artistic interest led him to listen to the grace, and to disentangle the meaning from the obscuring layers of verbal association and from the peculiar chant enlivened by occasional snatches of melody with which it was intoned.

How he had hated this grace as a boy—this pious task-work that almost spoilt the anticipation of meals! But to-night, after so long an interval, he could look at it without prejudice, and with artistic aloofness render to himself a true impression of its spiritual value.

'We thank Thee, O Lord our God, because Thou didst give as an heritage unto our fathers a desirable, good, and ample land, and because Thou didst bring us forth, O Lord our God, from the land of Egypt, and didst deliver us from the house of bondage—'

Barstein heard no more for the moment; the paradox of this retrospective gratitude was too absorbing. What! Sir Asher was thankful because over three thousand years ago his ancestors had obtained—not without hard fighting for it—a land which had already been lost again for eighteen centuries. What a marvellous long memory for a race to have!

Delivered from the house of bondage, forsooth! Sir Asher, himself—and here a musing smile crossed the artist's lips—had never even known a house of bondage, unless, indeed, the House of Commons (from which he had been delivered by the Radical reaction) might be so regarded, and his own house was, as he was fond of saying, Liberty Hall. But that the Russian Jew should still rejoice in the redemption from Egypt! O miracle of pious patience! O sublime that grazed the ridiculous!

But Sir Asher was still praying on:

'Have mercy, O Lord our God, upon Israel Thy people, upon Jerusalem Thy city, upon Zion the abiding place of Thy glory, upon the kingdom of the house of David, Thine anointed....'

Barstein lost himself in a fresh reverie. Here was indeed the Palestinian patriarch. Not with the corporation of Middleton, nor the lobbies of Westminster, not with his colossal business, not even with the glories of the British Empire, was Sir Asher's true heart. He had but caught phrases from the environment. To his deepest self he was not even a Briton. 'Have mercy, O Lord, upon Israel Thy people.' Despite all his outward pomp and prosperity, he felt himself one of that dispersed and maltreated band of brothers who had for eighteen centuries resisted alike the storm of persecution and the sunshine of tolerance, and whose one consolation in the long exile was the dream of Zion. The artist in Barstein began to thrill. What more fascinating than to catch sight of the dreamer beneath the manufacturer, the Hebrew visionary behind the English M.P.!

This palatial dwelling-place with its liveried lackeys was, then, no fort of Philistinism in which an artist must needs asphyxiate, but a very citadel of the spirit. A new respect for his host began to steal upon him. Involuntarily he sought the face of the daughter; the secret of her beauty was, after all, not so mysterious. Old Asher had a soul, and 'the soul is form and doth the body make.'

Unconscious of the effect he was producing on the sensitive artist, the Rembrandtesque figure prayed on: 'And rebuild Jerusalem, the holy city, speedily and in our days....'

It was the climax of the romance that had so strangely stolen over the British dinner-table. Rebuild Jerusalem to-day! Did Jews really conceive it as a contemporary possibility? Barstein went hot and cold. The idea was absolutely novel to him; evidently as a boy he had not understood his own prayers or his own people. All his imagination was inflamed. He conjured up a Zion built up by such virile hands as Sir Asher's, and peopled by such beautiful mothers as his daughter: the great Empire that would spring from the unity and liberty of a race which even under dispersion and oppression was one of the most potent peoples on the planet. And thus, when the ladies at last rose, he was in so deep a reverie that he almost forgot to rise too, and when he did rise, he accompanied the ladies outside the door. It was only Miss Aaronsberg's tactful 'Don't you want to smoke?' that saved him.

'Almost as long a grace as the dinner!' Tom Fuller murmured to him as he returned to the table. 'Do the Jews say that after every meal?'

'They're supposed to,' Barstein replied, a little jarred as he picked up a cigar.

'No wonder they beat the Christians,' observed the young Radical, who evidently took original views. 'So much time for digestion would enable any race to survive in this age of quick lunches. In America, now they should rule the roast. Literally,' he added, with a laugh.

'It's a beautiful grace,' said Barstein rebukingly. 'The glamour of Zion thrown over the prose of diet.'

'You're not a Jew?' said Tom, with a sudden suspicion.

'Yes, I am,' the artist replied with a dignity that surprised himself.

'I should never have taken you for one!' said Tom ingenuously.

Despite himself, Barstein felt a thrill of satisfaction. 'But why?' he asked himself instantly. 'To feel complimented at not being taken for a Jew—what does it mean? Is there a core of anti-Semitism in my nature? Has our race reached self-contempt?'

'I beg your pardon,' Tom went on. 'I didn't mean to be irreverent. I appreciate the picturesqueness of it all—hearing the very language of the Bible, and all that. And I do sympathize with your desire for Jewish Home Rule.'

'My desire?' murmured the artist, taken aback. Sir Asher here interrupted them by pressing his '48 port upon both, and directing the artist's attention in particular to the pictures that hung around the stately dining-room. There was a Gainsborough, a Reynolds, a Landseer. He drew Barstein round the walls.

'I am very fond of the English school,' he said. His cap was back in his coat-tail, and he had become again the bluff and burly Briton.

'You don't patronize the Italians at all?' asked the artist.

'No,' said Sir Asher. He lowered his voice. 'Between you and I,' said he—it was his main fault of grammar—'in Italian art one is never safe from the Madonna, not to mention her Son.' It was a fresh reminder of the Palestinian patriarch. Sir Asher never discussed theology except with those who agreed with him. Nor did he ever, whether in private or in public, breathe an unfriendly word against his Christian fellow-citizens. All were sons of the same Father, as he would frequently say from the platform. But in his heart of hearts he cherished a contempt, softened by stupefaction, for the arithmetical incapacity of Trinitarians.

Christianity under any other aspect did not exist for him. It was a blunder impossible to a race with a genius for calculation. 'How can three be one?' he would demand witheringly of his cronies. The question was in his eye now as he summed up Italian art to the sculptor, and a faint smile twitching about his lips invited his fellow-Jew to share with him his feeling of spiritual and intellectual superiority to the poor blind Christians at his table, as well as to Christendom generally.

But the artist refused to come up on the pedestal. 'Surely the Madonna was a very beautiful conception,' he said.

Sir Asher looked startled. 'Ah yes, you are an artist,' he remembered. 'You think only of the beautiful outside. But how can there be three-in-one or one-in-three?'

Barstein did not reply, and Sir Asher added in a low scornful tone: 'Neither confounding the persons, nor dividing the substance.'

III

A sudden commission recalled Barstein to town before he could even pay his after-dinner call. But the seed sown in his soul that evening was not to be stifled. This seed was nothing less than the idea of a national revival of his people. He hunted up his old prayer-books, and made many discoveries as his modern consciousness depolarized page upon page that had never in boyhood been anything to him but a series of syllables to be gabbled off as rapidly as possible, when their meaning was not still further overlaid by being sung slowly to a tune. 'I might as well have turned a prayer-wheel,' he said regretfully, as he perceived with what iron tenacity the race beaten down by the Roman Empire and by every power that had reigned since, had preserved its aspiration for its old territory. And this mystery of race and blood, this beauty of unforgetting aspiration, was all physically incarnate in Mabel Aaronsberg.

He did not move one inch out of his way to see her, because he saw her all day long. She appeared all over his studio in countless designs in clay. But from this image of the beauty of the race, his deepening insight drove him to interpret the tragedy also, and he sought out from the slums and small synagogues of the East End strange forlorn figures, with ragged curls and wistful eyes. It was from one of these figures that he learnt to his astonishment that the dream of Zion, whereof he imagined himself the sole dreamer, was shared by myriads, and had even materialized into a national movement.

He joined the movement, and it led him into strange conventicles. He was put on a committee which met in a little back-room, and which at first treated him and his arguments with deference, soon with familiarity, and occasionally with contempt. Hucksters and cigar-makers held forth much more eloquently on their ideals than he could, with far greater command of Talmudic quotation, while their knowledge of how to run their local organization was naturally superior. But throughout all the mean surroundings, the petty wrangles, and the grotesque jealousies that tarnished the movement he retained his inner exaltation. He had at last found himself and found his art. He fell to work upon a great Michel-angelesque figure of the awakening genius of his people, blowing the trumpet of resurrection. It was sent for exhibition to a Zionist Congress, where it caused a furore, and where the artist met other artists who had long been working under the very inspiration which was so novel to him, and whose work was all around him in plaque and picture, in bust and book, and even postcard. Some of them were setting out for Palestine to start a School of Arts and Crafts.

Barstein began to think of joining them. Meantime the Bohemian circles which he had adorned with his gaiety and good-fellowship had been wondering what had become of him. His new work in the Exhibitions supplied a sort of answer, and the few who chanced to meet him reported dolefully that he was a changed man. Gone was the light-hearted and light-footed dancer of the Paris pavement. Silent the licentious wit of the neo-Pagan. This was a new being with brooding brow and pained eyes that lit up only when they beheld his dream. Never had Bohemia known such a transformation.

IV

But a change came over the spirit of the dream. Before he could seriously plan out his journey to Palestine, he met Mabel Aaronsberg in the flesh. She was staying in town for the season in charge of an aunt, and the meeting occurred in one of the galleries of the newer art, in front of Mabel's own self in marble. She praised the Psyche without in the least recognising herself, and Barstein, albeit disconcerted, could not but admit how far his statue was from the breathing beauty of the original.

After this the Jewish borderland of Bohemia, where writers and painters are courted, began to see Barstein again. But, unfortunately, this was not Mabel's circle, and Barstein was reduced to getting himself invited to that Jewish Bayswater, his loathing for which had not been overcome even by his new-found nationalism. Here, amid hundreds of talking and dancing shadows, with which some shadowy self of his own danced and talked, he occasionally had a magic hour of reality—with Mabel.

One could not be real and not talk of the national dream. Mabel, who took most of her opinions from her brother Julius, was frankly puzzled, though her marmoreal gift of beautiful silence saved her lover from premature shocks. She had, indeed, scarcely heard of such things. Zionism was something in the East End. Nobody in her class ever mentioned it. But, then, Barstein was a sculptor and strange, and, besides, he did not look at all like a Jew, so it didn't sound so horrible in his mouth. His lithe figure stood out almost Anglo-Saxon amid the crowds of hulking undersized young men, and though his manners were not so good as a Christian's—she never forgot his blunder at her father's dinner-party—still, he looked up to one with almost a Christian's adoration, instead of sizing one up with an Oriental's calculation. These other London Jews thought her provincial, she knew, whereas Barstein had one day informed her she was universal. Julius, too, had admired Barstein's sculpture, the modern note in which had been hailed by the Oxford elect. But what most fascinated Mabel was the constant eulogy of her lover's work in the Christian papers; and when at last the formal proposal came, it found her fearful only of her father's disapproval.

'He's so orthodox,' she murmured, as they sat in a rose-garlanded niche at a great Jewish Charity Ball, lapped around by waltz-music and the sweetness of love confessed.

'Well, I'm not so wicked as I was,' he smiled.

'But you smoke on the Sabbath, Leo—you told me.'

'And you told me your brother Julius does the same.'

'Yes, but father doesn't know. If Julius wants to smoke on Friday evening, he always goes to his own room.'

'And I shan't smoke in your father's.'

'No—but you'll tell him. You're so outspoken.'

'Well, I won't tell him—unless he asks me.'

She looked sad. 'He won't ask you—he'll never get as far.'

He smiled confidently. 'You're not very encouraging, dear; what's the matter with me?'

'Everything. You're an artist, with all sorts of queer notions. And you're not so'—she blushed and hesitated—'not so rich—'

He pressed her fingers. 'Yes, I am; I'm the richest man here.'

A little delighted laugh broke from her lips, though they went on: 'But you told me your profits are small—marble is so dear.'

'So is celibacy. I shall economize dreadfully by marrying.'

She pouted; his flippancy seemed inadequate to the situation, and he seemed scarcely to realize that she was an heiress. But he continued to laugh away her fears. She was so beautiful and he was so strong—what could stand between them? Certainly not the Palestinian patriarch with whose inmost psychology he had, fortunately, become in such cordial sympathy.

But Mabel's pessimism was not to be banished even by the supper champagne. They had secured a little table for two, and were recklessly absorbed in themselves.

'At the worst, we can elope to Palestine,' he said at last, gaily serious.

Mabel shuddered. 'Live entirely among Jews!' she cried.

The radiance died suddenly out of his face; it was as if she had thrust the knife she was wielding through his heart. Her silent reception of his nationalist rhapsodies he had always taken for agreement.

Nor might Mabel have undeceived him had his ideas remained Platonic. Their irruption into the world of practical politics, into her own life, was, however, another pair of shoes. Since Barstein had brought Zionism to her consciousness, she had noted that distinguished Christians were quite sympathetic, but this was the one subject on which Christian opinion failed to impress Mabel. 'Zionism's all very well for Christians—they're in no danger of having to go to Palestine,' she had reflected shrewdly.

'And why couldn't you live entirely among Jews?' Barstein asked slowly.

Mabel drew a great breath, as if throwing off a suffocating weight. 'One couldn't breathe,' she explained.

'Aren't you living among Jews now?'

'Don't look so glum, silly. You don't want Jews as background as well as foreground. A great Ghetto!' And again she shuddered instinctively.

'Every other people is background as well as foreground. And you don't call France a Ghetto or Italy a Ghetto?' There was anti-Semitism, he felt—unconscious anti-Semitism—behind Mabel's instinctive repugnance to an aggregation of Jews. And he knew that her instinct would be shared by every Jew in that festive aggregation around him. His heart sank. Never—even in those East End back-rooms where the pitiful disproportion of his consumptive-looking collaborators to their great task was sometimes borne in dismally upon him—had he felt so black a despair as in this brilliant supper-room, surrounded by all that was strong and strenuous in the race—lawyers and soldiers, and men of affairs, whose united forces and finances could achieve almost anything they set their heart upon.

'Jews can't live off one another,' Mabel explained with an air of philosophy.

Barstein did not reply. He was asking himself with an artist's analytical curiosity whence came this suicidal anti-Semitism. Was it the self-contempt natural to a race that had not the strength to build and fend for itself? No, alas! it did not even spring from so comparatively noble a source. It was merely a part of their general imitation of their neighbours—Jews, reflecting everything, had reflected even the dislike for the Jew; only since the individual could not dislike himself, he applied the dislike to the race. And this unconscious assumption of the prevailing point of view was quickened by the fact that the Jewish firstcomers were always aware of an existence on sufferance, with their slowly-won privileges jeopardized if too many other Jews came in their wake. He consulted his own pre-Zionist psychology. 'Yes,' he decided. 'Every Jew who moves into our country, our city, our watering-place, our street even, seems to us an invader or an interloper. He draws attention to us, he accentuates our difference from the normal, he increases the chance of the renewal of Rishus (malice). And so we become anti-Semites ourselves. But by what a comical confusion of logic is it that we carry over the objection to Jewish aggregation even to an aggregation in Palestine, in our own land! Or is it only too logical? Is it that the rise of a Jewish autonomous power would be a standing reminder to our fellow-citizens that we others are not so radically British or German or French or American as we have vaunted ourselves? Are we afraid of being packed off to Palestine and is the fulfilment of the dream of eighteen centuries our deadliest dread?'

The thought forced from him a sardonic smile.

'And I feared you were like King Henry—never going to smile again.' Mabel smiled back in relief.

'We're such a ridiculous people,' he answered, his smile fading into sombreness. 'Neither fish, flesh, fowl, nor good red herring.'

'Well, finish your good white fowl,' laughed Mabel. She had felt her hold over him slipping, and her own apprehensions now vanished in the effort to banish his gloom.

But she had only started him on a new tack. 'Fowl!' he cried grimly. 'Kosher, of course, but with bits of fried Wurst to ape the scraps of bacon. And presently we shall be having water ices to simulate cream. We can't even preserve our dietary individuality. Truly said Feuerbach, "Der Mensch ist was er isst." In Palestine we shall at least dare to be true to our own gullets.' He laughed bitterly.

'You're not very romantic,' Mabel pouted. Indeed, this Barstein, whose mere ideal could so interrupt the rhapsodies due to her admissions of affection, was distinctly unsatisfactory. She touched his hand furtively under the tablecloth.

'After all, she is very young,' he thought, thrilling. And youth was plastic—he, the sculptor, could surely mould her. Besides, was she not Sir Asher's daughter? She must surely have inherited some of his love for Palestine and his people. It was this Philistine set that had spoiled her. Julius, too, that young Oxford prig—he reflected illogically—had no doubt been a baleful influence.

'Shall I give you some almond-pudding?' he replied tenderly.

Mabel laughed uneasily. 'I ask for romance, and you offer me almond-pudding. Oh, I should like to go to a Jewish party where there wasn't almond-pudding!'

'You shall—in Palestine,' he laughed back.

She pouted again. 'All roads lead to Palestine.'

'They do,' he said seriously. 'Without Palestine our past is a shipwreck and our future a quicksand.'

She looked frightened again. 'But what should we do there? We can't pray all day long.'

'Of course not,' he said eagerly. 'There's the new generation to train for its glorious future. I shall teach in the Arts and Crafts School. Bezalel, it's called; isn't that a beautiful name? It's from Bezalel, the first man mentioned in the Bible as filled with Divine wisdom and understanding in all manner of workmanship.'

She shook her head. 'You'll be excommunicated. The Palestine Rabbis always excommunicate everything and everybody.'

He laughed. 'What do you know about Palestine?'

'More than you think. Father gets endless letters from there with pressed flowers and citrons, and olive-wood boxes and paper-knives—a perennial shower. The letters are generally in the most killing English. And he won't let me laugh at them because he has a vague feeling that even Palestine spelling and grammar are holy.'

Barstein laughed again. 'We'll send all the Rabbis to Jericho.'

She smiled, but retorted: 'That's where they'll send you, you maker of graven images. Why, your very profession is forbidden.'

'I'll corner 'em with this very Bezalel text. The cutting of stones is just one of the arts which God says He had inspired Bezalel with. Besides, you forget my statue at the Bâle Congress.'

'Bâle isn't Palestine. There's nothing but superstition and squalor, and I'm sorry to say father's always bolstering it all up with his cheques.'

'Bravo, Sir Asher! Unconsciously he has been bolstering up the eventual Renaissance. Your father and his kind have kept the seed alive; we shall bring it to blossom.'

His prophetic assurance cast a fresh shade of apprehension over her marmoreal brow. But her face lightened with a sudden thought. 'Well, perhaps, after all, we shan't need to elope.'

'I never thought for a moment we should,' he answered as cheerfully. 'But, all the same, we can spend our honeymoon in Palestine.'

'Oh, I don't mind that,' said Mabel. 'Lots of Christians do that. There was a Cook's party went out from Middleton for last Easter.'

The lover was too pleased with her acquiescence in the Palestinian honeymoon to analyse the terms in which it was given. He looked into her eyes, and saw there the Shechinah—the Divine glory that once rested on Zion.

V

It was in this happier mood that Barstein ran down to Middleton to plead his suit verbally with Sir Asher Aaronsberg. Mabel had feared to commit their fates to a letter, whether from herself or her lover. A plump negative would be so difficult to fight against. A personal interview permitted one to sound the ground, to break the thing delicately, to reason, to explain, to charm away objections. It was clearly the man's duty to face the music.

Not that Barstein expected anything but the music of the Wedding March. He was glad that his original contempt for Sir Asher had been exchanged for sincere respect, and that the bluff Briton was a mere veneer. It was to the Palestinian patriarch that he would pour out his hopes and his dreams.

Alas! he found only the bluff Briton, and a Briton no longer genially, but bluntly, bluff.

'It is perfectly impossible.'

Barstein, bewildered, pleaded for enlightenment. Was he not pious enough, or not rich enough, too artistic or too low-born? Or did Sir Asher consider his past life improper or his future behaviour dubious? Let Sir Asher say.

But Sir Asher would not say. 'I am not bound to give my reasons. We are all proud of your work—it confers honour on our community. The Mayor alluded to it only yesterday.' He spoke in his best platform manner. 'But to receive you into my family—that is another matter.'

And all the talk advanced things no further.

'It would be an entirely unsuitable match.' Sir Asher caressed his long beard with an air of finality.

With a lover's impatience, Barstein had made the mistake of seeking Sir Asher in his counting-house, where the municipal magnate sat among his solidities. The mahogany furniture, the iron safes, the ledgers, the silent obsequious clerks and attendants through whom Barstein had had to penetrate, the factory buildings stretching around, with their sense of throbbing machinery and disciplined workers, all gave the burly Briton a background against which visions and emotions seemed as unreal as ghosts under gaslight. The artist felt all this solid life closing round him like the walls of a torture-chamber, squeezing out his confidence, his aspirations, his very life.

'Then you prefer to break your daughter's heart!' he cried desperately.

'Break my daughter's heart!' echoed Sir Asher in amaze. It was apparently a new aspect to him.

'You don't suppose she won't suffer dreadfully?' Barstein went on, perceiving his advantage.

'Break her heart!' repeated Sir Asher, startled out of his discreet reticence. 'I'd sooner break her heart than see her married to a Zionist!'

This time it was the sculptor's turn to gasp.

'To a what?' he cried.

'To a Zionist. You don't mean to deny you're a Zionist?' said Sir Asher sternly.

Barstein gazed at him in silence.

'Come, come,' said Sir Asher. 'You don't suppose I don't read the Jewish papers? I know all about your goings-on.'

The artist found his tongue. 'But—but,' he stammered, 'you yearn for Zion too.'

'Naturally. But I don't presume to force the hand of Providence.'

'How can any of us force Providence to do anything it doesn't want to? Surely it is through human agency that Providence always works. God helps those who help themselves.'

'Spare me your blasphemies. Perhaps you think you are the Messiah.'

'I can be an atom of Him. The whole Jewish people is its own Messiah—God working through it.'

'Take care, young man; you'll be talking Trinity next. And with these heathen notions you expect to marry my daughter! You must excuse me if I wish to hear no further.' His hand began to wander towards the row of electric bells on his desk.

'Then how do you suppose we shall ever get to Palestine?' inquired the irritated artist.

Sir Asher raised his eyes to the ceiling. 'In God's good time,' he said.

'And when will that be?'

'When we are either too good or too bad for our present sphere. To-day we are too neutral. Besides, there will be signs enough.'

'What signs?'

'Read your Bible. Mount Zion will be split by an earthquake, as the prophet—'

Barstein interrupted him with an impatient gesture. 'But why can't we go to Jerusalem and wait for the earthquake there?' he asked.

'Because we have a mission to the nations. We must live dispersed. We have to preach the unity of God.'

'I have never heard you preach it. You lowered your voice when you denounced the Trinity to me, lest the Christians should hear.'

'We have to preach silently, by our example. Merely by keeping our own religion we convert the world.'

'But who keeps it? Dispersion among Sunday-keeping peoples makes our very Sabbath an economic impossibility.'

'I have not found it so,' said Sir Asher crushingly. 'Indeed, the growth of the Saturday half-holiday since my young days is a remarkable instance of Judaizing.'

'So we have to remain dispersed to promote the week-end holiday?'

'To teach international truth,' Sir Asher corrected sharply; 'not narrow tribalism.'

'But we don't remain dispersed. Five millions are herded in the Russian Pale to begin with.'

'The Providence of God has long been scattering them to New York.'

'Yes, four hundred thousand in one square mile. A pretty scattering!'

Sir Asher flushed angrily. 'But they go to the Argentine too. I heard of a colony even in Paraguay.'

'Where they are preaching the Unity to the Indians.'

'I do not discuss religion with a mocker. We are in exile by God's decree—we must suffer.'

'Suffer!' The artist's glance wandered cynically round the snug solidities of Sir Asher's exile, but he forbore to be personal. 'Then if we must suffer, why did you subscribe so much to the fund for the Russian Jews?'

Sir Asher looked mollified at Barstein's acquaintance with his generosity. 'That I might suffer with them,' he replied, with a touch of humour.

'Then you are a Jewish patriot,' retorted Barstein.

The bluff British face grew clouded again.

'Heaven forbid. I only know of British patriots. You talk treason to your country, young man.'

'Treason—I!' The young man laughed bitterly.

'It is you Zionists that will undermine all the rights we have so painfully won in the West.'

'Oh, then you're not really a British patriot,' Barstein began.

'I will beg you to remember, sir, that I equipped a corps of volunteers for the Transvaal.'

'I dare say. But a corps of volunteers for Zion—that is blasphemy, narrow tribalism.'

'Zion's soil is holy; we want no volunteers there: we want saints and teachers. And what would your volunteers do in Zion? Fight the Sultan with his million soldiers? They couldn't even live in Palestine as men of peace. There is neither coal nor iron—hence no manufactures. Agriculture? It's largely stones and swamps. Not to mention it's too hot for Jews to work in the fields. They'd all starve. You've no right to play recklessly with human lives. Besides, even if Palestine were as fertile as England, Jews could never live off one another. And think how they'd quarrel!'

Sir Asher ended almost good-humouredly. His array of arguments seemed to him a row of steam-hammers.

'We can live off one another as easily as any other people. As for quarrelling, weren't you in Parliament? Party government makes quarrel the very basis of the Constitution.'

Sir Asher flushed again. A long lifetime of laying down the law had ill prepared him for repartee.

'A pretty mess we should make of Government!' he sneered.

'Why? We have given Ministers to every Cabinet in the world.'

'Yes—we're all right as long as we're under others. Sir Asher was recovering his serenity.

'All right so long as we're under others!' gasped the artist. 'Do you realize what you're saying, Sir Asher? The Boers against whom you equipped volunteers fought frenziedly for three years not to be under others! And we—the thought of Jewish autonomy makes us foam at the mouth. The idea of independence makes us turn in the graves we call our fatherlands.'

Sir Asher dismissed the subject with a Podsnappian wave of the hand. 'This is all a waste of breath. Fortunately the acquisition of Palestine is impossible.'

'Then why do you pray for it—"speedily and in our days"?'

Sir Asher glared at the bold questioner.

'That seems a worse waste of breath,' added Barstein drily.

'I said you were a mocker,' said Sir Asher severely. 'It is a Divine event I pray for—not the creation of a Ghetto.'

'A Ghetto!' Barstein groaned in sheer hopelessness. 'Yes, you're an anti-Semite too—like your daughter, like your son, like all of us. We're all anti-Semites.'

'I an anti-Semite! Ho! ho! ho!' Sir Asher's anger broke down in sheer amusement. 'I have made every allowance for your excitement,' he said, recovering his magisterial note. 'I was once in love myself. But when it comes to calling me an anti-Semite, it is obvious you are not in a fit state to continue this interview. Indeed, I no longer wonder that you think yourself the Messiah.'

'Even if I do, our tradition only makes the Messiah a man; somebody some day will have to win your belief. But what I said was that God acts through man.'

'Ah yes,' said Sir Asher good-humouredly. 'Three-in-one and one-in-three.'

'And why not?' said Barstein with a flash of angry intuition. 'Aren't you a trinity yourself?'

'Me?' Sir Asher was now quite sure of the sculptor's derangement.

'Yes—the Briton, the Jew, and the anti-Semite—three-in-one and one-in-three.'

Sir Asher touched one of the electric bells with a jerk. He was quite alarmed.

Barstein turned white with rage at his dismissal. Never would he marry into these triune tribes. 'And it's the same in every land where we're emancipated, as it is called,' he went on furiously. 'The Jew's a patriot everywhere, and a Jew everywhere and an anti-Semite everywhere. Passionate Hungarians, and true-born Italians, eagle-waving Americans, and loyal Frenchmen, imperial Germans, and double Dutchmen, we are dispersed to preach the Unity, and what we illustrate is the Jewish trinity. A delicious irony! Three-in-one and one-in-three.' He laughed; to Sir Asher his laugh sounded maniacal. The old gentleman was relieved to see his stalwart doorkeeper enter.

Barstein turned scornfully on his heel. 'Neither confounding the persons nor dividing the substance,' he ended grimly.

THE SABBATH QUESTION IN SUDMINSTER

I

There was a storm in Sudminster, not on the waters which washed its leading Jews their living, but in the breasts of these same marine storekeepers. For a competitor had appeared in their hive of industry—an alien immigrant, without roots or even relatives at Sudminster. And Simeon Samuels was equipped not only with capital and enterprise—the showy plate-glass front of his shop revealed an enticing miscellany—but with blasphemy and bravado. For he did not close on Friday eve, and he opened on Saturday morning as usual.

The rumour did not get round all Sudminster the first Friday night, but by the Sabbath morning the synagogue hummed with it. It set a clammy horror in the breasts of the congregants, distracted their prayers, gave an unreal tone to the cantor's roulades, brought a tremor of insecurity into the very foundations of their universe. For nearly three generations a congregation had been established in Sudminster—like every Jewish congregation, a camp in not friendly country—struggling at every sacrifice to keep the Holy Day despite the supplementary burden of Sunday closing, and the God of their fathers had not left unperformed His part of the contract. For 'the harvests' of profit were abundant, and if 'the latter and the former rain' of their unchanging supplication were mere dried metaphors to a people divorced from Palestine and the soil for eighteen centuries, the wine and the oil came in casks, and the corn in cakes. The poor were few and well provided for; even the mortgage on the synagogue was paid off. And now this Epicurean was come to trouble the snug security, to break the long chain of Sabbath observance which stretched from Sinai. What wonder if some of the worshippers, especially such as had passed his blatant shop-window on their return from synagogue on Friday evening, were literally surprised that the earth had not opened beneath him as it had opened beneath Korah.

'Even the man who gathered sticks on the Sabbath was stoned to death,' whispered the squat Solomon Barzinsky to the lanky Ephraim Mendel, marine-dealers both.

'Alas! that would not be permitted in this heathen country,' sighed Ephraim Mendel, hitching his praying-shawl more over his left shoulder. 'But at least his windows should be stoned.'

Solomon Barzinsky smiled, with a gleeful imagining of the shattering of the shameless plate-glass. 'Yes, and that wax-dummy of a sailor should be hung as an atonement for his—Holy, holy, holy is the Lord of Hosts; the whole earth is full of His glory.' The last phrase Solomon suddenly shouted in Hebrew, in antiphonal response to the cantor, and he rose three times on his toes, bowing his head piously. 'No wonder he can offer gold lace for the price of silver,' he concluded bitterly.

'He sells shoddy new reach-me-downs as pawned old clo,' complained Lazarus Levy, who had taken over S. Cohn's business, together with his daughter Deborah, 'and he charges the Sudminster donkey-heads more than the price we ask for 'em as new.'

Talk of the devil—! At this point Simeon Samuels stalked into the synagogue, late but serene.

Had the real horned Asmodeus walked in, the agitation could not have been greater. The first appearance in synagogue of a new settler was an event in itself; but that this Sabbath-breaker should appear at all was startling to a primitive community. Escorted by the obsequious and unruffled beadle to the seat he seemed already to have engaged—that high-priced seat facing the presidential pew that had remained vacant since the death of Tevele the pawnbroker—Simeon Samuels wrapped himself reverently in his praying-shawl, and became absorbed in the service. His glossy high hat bespoke an immaculate orthodoxy, his long black beard had a Rabbinic religiousness, his devotion was a rebuke to his gossiping neighbours.

A wave of uneasiness passed over the synagogue. Had he been the victim of a jealous libel? Even those whose own eyes had seen him behind his counter when he should have been consecrating the Sabbath-wine at his supper-table, wondered if they had been the dupe of some hallucination.

When, in accordance with hospitable etiquette, the new-comer was summoned canorously to the reading of the Law—'Shall stand Simeon, the son of Nehemiah'—and he arose and solemnly mounted the central platform, his familiarity with the due obeisances and osculations and benedictions seemed a withering reply to the libel. When he descended, and the Parnass proffered his presidential hand in pious congratulation upon the holy privilege, all the congregants who found themselves upon his line of return shot forth their arms with remorseful eagerness, and thus was Simeon Samuels switched on to the brotherhood of Sudminsterian Israel. Yet as his now trusting co-religionists passed his shop on their homeward walk—and many a pair of legs went considerably out of its way to do so—their eyes became again saucers of horror and amaze. The broad plate-glass glittered nakedly, unveiled by a single shutter; the waxen dummy of the sailor hitched devil-may-care breeches; the gold lace, ticketed with layers of erased figures, boasted brazenly of its cheapness; the procession of customers came and went, and the pavement, splashed with sunshine, remained imperturbably, perturbingly acquiescent.

II

On the Sunday night Solomon Barzinsky and Ephraim Mendel in pious black velvet caps, and their stout spouses in gold chains and diamond earrings, found themselves playing solo whist in the Parnass's parlour, and their religious grievance weighed upon the game. The Parnass, though at heart as outraged as they by the new departure, felt it always incumbent upon him to display his presidential impartiality and his dry humour. His authority, mainly based on his being the only retired shopkeeper in the community, was greatly strengthened by his slow manner of taking snuff at a crisis. 'My dear Mendel,' observed the wizened senior, flicking away the spilth with a blue handkerchief, 'Simeon Samuels has already paid his annual subscription—and you haven't!'

'My money is good,' Mendel replied, reddening.

'No wonder he can pay so quickly!' said Solomon Barzinsky, shuffling the cards savagely.

'How he makes his money is not the question,' said the Parnass weightily. 'He has paid it, and therefore if I were to expel him, as you suggest, he might go to Law.'

'Law!' retorted Solomon. 'Can't we prove he has broken the Law of Moses?'

'And suppose?' said the Parnass, picking up his cards placidly. 'Do we want to wash our dirty Talysim (praying-shawls) in public?'

'He is right, Solomon,' said Mrs. Barzinsky. 'We should become a laughing-stock among the heathen.'

'I don't believe he'd drag us to the Christian courts,' the little man persisted. 'I pass.'

The rubber continued cheerlessly. 'A man who keeps his shop open on Sabbath is capable of anything,' said the lanky Mendel, gloomily sweeping in his winnings.

The Parnass took snuff judicially. 'Besides, he may have a Christian partner who keeps all the Saturday profits,' he suggested.

'That would be just as forbidden,' said Barzinsky, as he dealt the cards.

'But your cousin David,' his wife reminded him, 'sells his groceries to a Christian at Passover.'

'That is permitted. It would not be reasonable to destroy hundreds of pounds of leaven. But Sabbath partnerships are not permitted.'

'Perhaps the question has never been raised,' said the Parnass.

'I am enough of a Lamdan (pundit) to answer it,' retorted Barzinsky.

'I prefer going to a specialist,' rejoined the Parnass.

Barzinsky threw down his cards. 'You can go to the devil!' he cried.

'For shame, Solomon!' said his wife. 'Don't disturb the game.'

'To Gehenna with the game! The shame is on a Parnass to talk like an Epikouros (Epicurean).'

The Parnass blew his nose elaborately. 'It stands in the Talmud: "For vain swearing noxious beasts came into the world." And if—'

'It stands in the Psalmist,' Barzinsky interrupted: '"The Law of Thy mouth is better to me than thousands of gold and silver."'

'It stands in the Perek,' the Parnass rejoined severely, 'that the wise man does not break in upon the speech of his fellow.'

'It stands in the Shulchan Aruch,' Barzinsky shrieked, 'that for the sanctification of the Sabbath—'

'It stands in the Talmud,' interposed Mendel, with unwonted animation in his long figure, 'that one must not even offer a nut to allure customers. From light to heavy, therefore, it may be deduced that—'

A still small voice broke in upon the storm. 'But Simeon Samuels hasn't a Christian partner,' said Mrs. Mendel.

There was an embarrassed pause.

'He has only his wife to help him,' she went on. 'I know, because I went to the shop Friday morning on pretence of asking for a cuckoo-clock.'

'But a marine-dealer doesn't sell clocks,' put in the Parnass's wife timidly. It was her first contribution to the conversation, for she was overpowered by her husband's greatness.

'Don't be silly, Hannah!' said the Parnass. 'That was just why Mrs. Mendel asked for it.'

'Yes, but unfortunately Simeon Samuels did have one,' Mrs. Mendel confessed; 'and I couldn't get out of buying it.'

There was a general laugh.

'Cut-throat competition, I call it,' snarled Solomon Barzinsky, recovering from his merriment.

'But you don't sell clocks,' said the Parnass.

'That's just it; he gets hold of our customers on pretence of selling them something else. The Talmudical prohibition cited by Mendel applies to that too.'

'So I wasn't so silly,' put in the Parnass's wife, feeling vaguely vindicated.

'Well, you saw his wife,' said the Parnass to Mendel's wife, disregarding his own. 'More than I've done, for she wasn't in synagogue. Perhaps she is the Christian partner.' His suggestion brought a new and holier horror over the card-table.

'No, no,' replied Mrs. Mendel reassuringly. 'I caught sight of her frying fish in the kitchen.'

This proof of her Jewishness passed unquestioned, and the new-born horror subsided.

'But in spite of the fish,' said Mr. Mendel, 'she served in the shop while he was at synagogue.'

'Yes,' hissed Barzinsky; 'and in spite of the synagogue he served in the shop. A greater mockery was never known!'

'Not at all, not at all,' said the Parnass judicially. 'If a man breaks one commandment, that's no reason he should break two.'

'But he does break two,' Solomon thundered, smiting the green cloth with his fist; 'for he steals my custom by opening when I'm closed.'

'Take care—you will break my plates,' said the Parnass. 'Take a sandwich.'

'Thank you—you've taken away my appetite.'

'I'm sorry—but the sandwiches would have done the same. I really can't expel a respectable seat-holder before I know that he is truly a sinner in Israel. As it is written, "Thou shalt inquire and make search and ask diligently." He may have only opened this once by way of a send-off. Every dog is allowed one bite.'

'At that rate, it would be permitted to eat a ham-sandwich—just for once,' said Solomon scathingly.

'Don't say I called you a dog,' the Parnass laughed.

'A mezaire!' announced the hostess hurriedly. 'After all, it's the Almighty's business, not ours.'

'No, it's our business,' Solomon insisted.

'Yes,' agreed the Parnass drily; 'it is your business.'

III

The week went by, with no lull in the storm, though the plate-glass window was unshaken by the gusts. It maintained its flaunting seductiveness, assisted, people observed, by Simeon Samuels' habit of lounging at his shop-door and sucking in the hesitating spectator. And it did not shutter itself on the Sabbath that succeeded.

The horror was tinged with consternation. The strange apathy of the pavement and the sky, the remissness of the volcanic fires and the celestial thunderbolts in face of this staring profanity, lent the cosmos an air almost of accessory after the fact. Never had the congregation seen Heaven so openly defied, and the consequences did not at all correspond with their deep if undefined forebodings. It is true a horse and carriage dashed into Peleg, the pawnbroker's, window down the street, frightened, Peleg maintained, by the oilskins fluttering outside Simeon Samuels' shop; but as the suffering was entirely limited to the nerves of Mrs. Peleg, who was pious, and to the innocent nose of the horse, this catastrophe was not quite what was expected. Solomon Barzinsky made himself the spokesman of the general dissatisfaction, and his remarks to the minister after the Sabbath service almost insinuated that the reverend gentleman had connived at a breach of contract.

The Rev. Elkan Gabriel quoted Scripture. 'The Lord is merciful and long-suffering, and will not at once awaken all His wrath.'

'But meantime the sinner makes a pretty penny!' quoth Solomon, unappeased. 'Saturday is pay-day, and the heathen haven't patience to wait till the three stars are out and our shops can open. It is your duty, Mr. Gabriel, to put a stop to this profanation.'

The minister hummed and ha'd. He was middle-aged, and shabby, with a German diploma and accent and a large family. It was the first time in his five years of office that one of his congregants had suggested such authoritativeness on his part. Elected by their vote, he was treated as their servant, his duties rigidly prescribed, his religious ideas curbed and corrected by theirs. What wonder if he could not suddenly rise to dictatorship? Even at home Mrs. Gabriel was a congregation in herself. But as the week went by he found Barzinsky was not the only man to egg him on to prophetic denunciation; the congregation at large treated him as responsible for the scandal, and if the seven marine-dealers were the bitterest, the pawnbrokers and the linen-drapers were none the less outraged.

'It is a profanation of the Name,' they said unanimously, 'and such a bad example to our poor!'

'He would not listen to me,' the poor minister would protest. 'You had much better talk to him yourself.'

'Me!' the button-holer would ejaculate. 'I would not lower myself. He'd think I was jealous of his success.'

Simeon Samuels seemed, indeed, a formidable person to tackle. Bland and aloof, he pursued his own affairs, meeting the congregation only in synagogue, and then more bland and aloof than ever.

At last the Minister received a presidential command to preach upon the subject forthwith.

'But there's no text suitable just yet,' he pleaded. 'We are still in Genesis.'

'Bah!' replied the Parnass impatiently, 'any text can be twisted to point any moral. You must preach next Sabbath.'

'But we are reading the Sedrah (weekly portion) about Joseph. How are you going to work Sabbath-keeping into that?'

'It is not my profession. I am a mere man-of-the-earth. But what's the use of a preacher if he can't make any text mean something else?'

'Well, of course, every text usually does,' said the preacher defensively. 'There is the hidden meaning and the plain meaning. But Joseph is merely historical narrative. The Sabbath, although mentioned in Genesis, chapter two, wasn't even formally ordained yet.'

'And what about Potiphar's wife?'

'That's the Seventh Commandment, not the Fourth.'

'Thank you for the information. Do you mean to say you can't jump from one Commandment to another?'

'Oh, well—' The minister meditated.

IV

'And Joseph was a goodly person, and well favoured. And it came to pass that his master's wife cast her eyes upon Joseph....'

The congregation looked startled. Really this was not a text which they wished their pastor to enlarge upon. There were things in the Bible that should be left in the obscurity of the Hebrew, especially when one's womenkind were within earshot. Uneasily their eyes lifted towards the bonnets behind the balcony-grating.

'But Joseph refused.'

Solomon Barzinsky coughed. Peleg the pawnbroker blew his nose like a protesting trumpet. The congregation's eyes returned from the balcony and converged upon the Parnass. He was taking snuff as usual.

'My brethren,' began the preacher impressively, 'temptation comes to us all—'

A sniff of indignant repudiation proceeded from many nostrils. A blush overspread many cheeks.

'But not always in the shape it came to Joseph. In this congregation, where, by the blessing of the Almighty, we are free from almost every form of wrong-doing, there is yet one temptation which has power to touch us—the temptation of unholy profit, the seduction of Sabbath-breaking.'

A great sigh of dual relief went up to the balcony, and Simeon Samuels became now the focus of every eye. His face was turned towards the preacher, wearing its wonted synagogue expression of reverential dignity.

'Oh, my brethren, that it could always be said of us: "And Joseph refused"!'

A genial warmth came back to every breast. Ah, now the cosmos was righting itself; Heaven was speaking through the mouth of its minister.

The Rev. Elkan Gabriel expanded under this warmth which radiated back to him. His stature grew, his eloquence poured forth, polysyllabic. As he ended, the congregation burst into a heartfelt 'Yosher Koach' ('May thy strength increase!').

The minister descended the Ark-steps, and stalked back solemnly to his seat. As he passed Simeon Samuels, that gentleman whipped out his hand and grasped the man of God's, and his neighbours testified that there was a look of contrite exaltation upon his goodly features.

V

The Sabbath came round again, but, alas! it brought no balm to the congregation; rather, was it a day of unrest. The plate-glass window still flashed in iniquitous effrontery; still the ungodly proprietor allured the stream of custom.

'He does not even refuse to take money,' Solomon Barzinsky exclaimed to Peleg the pawnbroker, as they passed the blasphemous window on their way from the Friday-evening service.

'Why, what would be the good of keeping open if you didn't take money?' naïvely inquired Peleg.

'Behemah (animal)!' replied Solomon impatiently. 'Don't you know it's forbidden to touch money on the Sabbath?'

'Of course, I know that. But if you open your shop—!'

'All the same, you might compromise. You might give the customers the things they need, as it is written, "Open thy hand to the needy!" but they could pay on Saturday night.'

'And if they didn't pay? If they drank their money away?' said the pawnbroker.

'True, but why couldn't they pay in advance?'

'How in advance?'

'They could deposit a sum of money with you, and draw against it.'

'Not with me!' Peleg made a grimace. 'All very well for your line, but in mine I should have to deposit a sum of money with them. I don't suppose they'd bring their pledges on Friday night, and wait till Saturday night for the money. Besides, how could one remember? One would have to profane the Sabbath by writing!'

'Write! Heaven forbid!' ejaculated Solomon Barzinsky. 'But you could have a system of marking the amounts against their names in your register. A pin could be stuck in to represent a pound, or a stamp stuck on to indicate a crown. There are lots of ways. One could always give one's self a device,' he concluded in Yiddish.

'But it is written in Job, "He disappointeth the devices of the crafty, so that their hands cannot perform their enterprise." Have a little of Job's patience, and trust the Lord to confound the sinner. We shall yet see Simeon Samuels in the Bankruptcy Court.'

'I hope not, the rogue! I'd like to see him ruined!'

'That's what I mean. Leave him to the Lord.'

'The Lord is too long-suffering,' said Solomon. 'Ah, our Parnass has caught us up. Good Shabbos (Sabbath), Parnass. This is a fine scandal for a God-fearing congregation. I congratulate you.'

'Is he open again?' gasped the Parnass, hurled from his judicial calm.

'Is my eye open?' witheringly retorted Barzinsky. 'A fat lot of good your preacher does.'

'It was you who would elect him instead of Rochinsky,' the Parnass reminded him. Barzinsky was taken aback.

'Well, we don't want foreigners, do we?' he murmured.

'And you caught an Englishman in Simeon Samuels,' chuckled the Parnass, in whose breast the defeat of his candidate had never ceased to rankle.

'Not he. An Englishman plays fair,' retorted Barzinsky. He seriously considered himself a Briton, regarding his naturalization papers as retrospective. 'We are just passing the Reverend Gabriel's house,' he went on. 'Let us wait a moment; he'll come along, and we'll give him a piece of our minds.'

'I can't keep my family waiting for Kiddush' (home service), said Peleg.

'Come home, father; I'm hungry,' put in Peleg junior, who with various Barzinsky boys had been trailing in the parental wake.

'Silence, impudent face!' snapped Barzinsky. 'If I was your father—Ah, here comes the minister. Good Shabbos (Sabbath), Mr. Gabriel. I congratulate you on the effect of your last sermon.'

An exultant light leapt into the minister's eye. 'Is he shut?'

'Is your mouth shut?' Solomon replied scathingly. 'I doubt if he'll even come to Shool (synagogue) to-morrow.'

The ministerial mouth remained open in a fishy gasp, but no words came from it.

'I'm afraid you'll have to use stronger language, Mr. Gabriel,' said the Parnass soothingly.

'But if he is not there to hear it.'

'Oh, don't listen to Barzinsky. He'll be there right enough. Just give it to him hot!'

'Your sermon was too general,' added Peleg, who had lingered, though his son had not. 'You might have meant any of us.'

'But we must not shame our brother in public,' urged the minister. 'It is written in the Talmud that he who does so has no share in the world to come.'

'Well, you shamed us all,' retorted Barzinsky. 'A stranger would imagine we were a congregation of Sabbath-breakers.'

'But there wasn't any stranger,' said the minister.

'There was Simeon Samuels,' the Parnass reminded him. 'Perhaps your sermon against Sabbath-breaking made him fancy he was just one of a crowd, and that you have therefore only hardened him—'

'But you told me to preach against Sabbath-breaking,' said the poor minister.

'Against the Sabbath-breaker,' corrected the Parnass.

'You didn't single him out,' added Barzinsky; 'you didn't even make it clear that Joseph wasn't myself.'

'I said Joseph was a goodly person and well-favoured,' retorted the goaded minister.

The Parnass took snuff, and his sneeze sounded like a guffaw.

'Well, well,' he said more kindly, 'you must try again to-morrow.'

'I didn't undertake to preach every Saturday,' grumbled the minister, growing bolder.

'As long as Simeon Samuels keeps open, you can't shut,' said Solomon angrily.

'It's a duel between you,' added Peleg.

'And Simeon actually comes into to-morrow's Sedrah' (portion), Barzinsky remembered exultantly. '"And took from them Simeon, and bound him before their eyes." There's your very text. You'll pick out Simeon from among us, and bind him to keep the Sabbath.'

'Or you can say Satan has taken Simeon and bound him,' added the Parnass. 'You have a choice—yourself or Satan.'

'Perhaps you had better preach yourself, then,' said the minister sullenly. 'I still can't see what that text has to do with Sabbath-breaking.'

'It has as much to do with Sabbath-breaking as Potiphar's wife,' shrieked Solomon Barzinsky.

VI

'"And Jacob their father said unto them, Me have ye bereaved. Joseph is not, and Simeon is not, and ye will take Benjamin."'

As the word 'Simeon' came hissing from the preacher's lips, a veritable thrill passed through the synagogue. Even Simeon Samuels seemed shaken, for he readjusted his praying-shawl with a nervous movement.

'My brethren, these words of Israel, the great forefather of our tribes, are still ringing in our ears. To-day more than ever is Israel crying. Joseph is not—our Holy Land is lost. Simeon is not—our Holy Temple is razed to the ground. One thing only is left us—one blessing with which the almighty father has blessed us—our Holy Sabbath. And ye will take Benjamin.' The pathos of his accents melted every heart. Tears rolled down many a feminine cheek. Simeon Samuels was seen to blow his nose softly.

Thus successfully launched, the Rev. Elkan Gabriel proceeded to draw a tender picture of the love between Israel and his Benjamin, Sabbath—the one consolation of his exile, and he skilfully worked in the subsequent verse: 'If mischief befall him by the way on which ye go, then shall ye bring down my grey hairs with sorrow to the grave.' Yes, it would be the destruction of Israel, he urged, if the Sabbath decayed. Woe to those sons of Israel who dared to endanger Benjamin. 'From Reuben and Simeon down to Gad and Asher, his life shall be required at their hands.' Oh, it was a red-hot-cannon-ball-firing sermon, and Solomon Barzinsky could not resist leaning across and whispering to the Parnass: 'Wasn't I right in refusing to vote for Rochinsky?' This reminder of his candidate's defeat was wormwood to the Parnass, spoiling all his satisfaction in the sermon. He rebuked the talker with a noisy 'Shaa' (silence).

The congregation shrank delicately from looking at the sinner; it would be too painful to watch his wriggles. His neighbours stared pointedly every other way. Thus, the only record of his deportment under fire came from Yankele, the poor glazier's boy, who said that he kept looking from face to face, as if to mark the effect on the congregation, stroking his beard placidly the while. But as to his behaviour after the guns were still, there was no dubiety, for everybody saw him approach the Parnass in the exodus from synagogue, and many heard him say in hearty accents: 'I really must congratulate you, Mr. President, on your selection of your minister.'

'You touched his heart so,' shrieked Solomon Barzinsky an hour later to the Reverend Elkan Gabriel, 'that he went straight from Shool (synagogue) to his shop.' Solomon had rushed out the first thing after breakfast, risking the digestion of his Sabbath fish, to call upon the unsuccessful minister.

'That is not my fault,' said the preacher, crestfallen.

'Yes, it is—if you had only stuck to my text. But no! You must set yourself up over all our heads.'

'You told me to get in Simeon, and I obeyed.'

'Yes, you got him in. But what did you call him? The Holy Temple! A fine thing, upon my soul!'

'It was only an—an—analogy,' stammered the poor minister.

'An apology! Oh, so you apologized to him, too! Better and better.'

'No, no, I mean a comparison.'

'A comparison! You never compared me to the Holy Temple. And I'm Solomon—Solomon who built it.'

'Solomon was wise,' murmured the minister.

'Oh, and I'm silly. If I were you, Mr. Gabriel, I'd remember my place and who I owed it to. But for me, Rochinsky would have stood in your shoes—'

'Rochinsky is lucky.'

'Oh, indeed! So this is your gratitude. Very well. Either Simeon Samuels shuts up shop or you do. That's final. Don't forget you were only elected for three years.' And the little man flung out.

The Parnass, meeting his minister later in the street, took a similar view.

'You really must preach again next Sabbath,' he said. 'The congregation is terribly wrought up. There may even be a riot. If Simeon Samuels keeps open next Sabbath, I can't answer that they won't go and break his windows.'

'Then they will break the Sabbath.'

'Oh, they may wait till the Sabbath is out.'

'They'll be too busy opening their own shops.'

'Don't argue. You must preach his shop shut.'

'Very well,' said the Reverend Gabriel sullenly.

'That's right. A man with a family must rise to great occasions. Do you think I'd be where I am now if I hadn't had the courage to buy a bankrupt stock that I didn't see my way to paying for? It's a fight between you and Simeon Samuels.'

'May his name be blotted out!' impatiently cried the minister in the Hebrew imprecation.

'No, no,' replied the Parnass, smiling. 'His name must not be blotted out—it must be mentioned, and—unmistakably.'

'It is against the Talmud. To shame a man is equivalent to murder,' the minister persisted.

'Yet it is written in Leviticus: "Thou shalt in any wise rebuke thy neighbour, and not suffer sin upon him."' And the Parnass took a triumphant pinch.

VIII

'Simeon and Levi are brethren ... into their assembly be not thou united: in their self-will they digged down a wall.'

The Parnass applauded mentally. The text, from Jacob's blessing, was ingeniously expurgated to meet the case. The wall, he perceived at once, was the Sabbath—the Jews' one last protection against the outer world, the one last dyke against the waves of heathendom. Nor did his complacency diminish when his intuition proved correct, and the preacher thundered against the self-will—ay, and the self-seeking—that undermined Israel's last fortification. What did they seek under the wall? Did they think their delving spades would come upon a hidden store of gold, upon an ancient treasure-chest? Nay, it was a coffin they would strike—a coffin of dead bones and living serpents.

A cold wave of horror traversed the synagogue; a little shriek came from the gallery.

'I don't think I ever enjoyed a sermon so much,' said the pawnbroker to the Parnass.

'Oh, he's improving,' said the Parnass, still swollen with satisfaction.

But as that worthy elder emerged from the synagogue, placidly snuffing himself, he found an excited gentleman waiting him in the lobby. It was Lazarus Levy, whom his wife Deborah, daughter of S. Cohn (now of Highbury), was vainly endeavouring to pacify.

'Either that Reverend Gabriel goes, Mr. Parnass, or I resign my membership.'

'What is it, Mr. Levy—what is the matter?'

'Everybody knows I've been a good Jew all my life, and though Saturday is so good for the clothing business, I've striven with all my might to do my duty by the Almighty.'

'Of course, of course; everybody knows that.'

'And yet to-day I'm pointed out as a sinner in Israel; I'm coupled with that Simeon Samuels. Simeon and Levy are brothers in their iniquity—with their assembly be not united. A pretty libel, indeed!'

The Parnass's complacency collapsed like an air-ball at a pin-prick. 'Oh, nonsense, everybody knows he couldn't mean you.'

'I don't know so much. There are always people ready to think one has just been discovered keeping a back-door open or something. I shouldn't be at all surprised to get a letter from my father-in-law in London—you know how pious old Cohn is! As for Simeon, he kept looking at me as if I was his long-lost brother. Ah, there comes our precious minister.... Look here, Mr. Gabriel, I'll have the law on you. Simeon's no brother of mine—'

The sudden appearance of Simeon through the other swing-door cut the speaker short. 'Good Shabbos,' said the shameless sinner. 'Ah, Mr. Gabriel, that was a very fine sermon.' He stroked his beard. 'I quite agree with you. To dig down a public wall is indefensible. Nobody has the right to make more than a private hole in it, where it blocks out his own prospect. So please do not bracket me with Mr. Levy again. Good Shabbos!' And, waving his hand pleasantly, he left them to their consternation.

IX

'What an impudent face!' said the Gabbai (treasurer), who witnessed the episode.

'And our minister says I'm that man's brother! exclaimed Mr. Levy.

'Hush! Enough!' said the Parnass, with a tactful inspiration. 'You shall read the Haphtorah (prophetic section) next Shabbos.'

'And Mr. Gabriel must explain he didn't mean me,' he stipulated, mollified by the magnificent Mitzvah (pious privilege).

'You always try to drive a hard bargain,' grumbled the Parnass. 'That's a question for Mr. Gabriel.'

The reverend gentleman had a happy thought. 'Wait till we come to the text: "Wherefore Levi hath no part nor inheritance with his brethren."'

'You're a gentleman, Mr. Gabriel,' ejaculated S. Cohn's son-in-law, clutching at his hand.

'And if he doesn't close to-day after your splendid sermon,' added the Gabbai, 'you must call and talk to him face to face.'

The minister made a wry face. 'But that's not in my duties.'

'Pardon me, Mr. Gabriel,' put in the Parnass, 'you have to call upon the afflicted and the bereaved. And Simeon Samuels is spiritually afflicted, and has lost his Sabbath.'

'But he doesn't want comforting.'

'Well, Solomon Barzinsky does,' said the Parnass. 'Go to him instead, then, for I'm past soothing him. Choose!'

'I'll go to Simeon Samuels,' said the preacher gloomily.

X

'It is most kind of you to call,' said Simeon Samuels as he wheeled the parlour armchair towards his reverend guest. 'My wife will be so sorry to have missed you. We have both been looking forward so much to your visit.'

'You knew I was coming?' said the minister, a whit startled.

'I naturally expected a pastoral visit sooner or later.'

'I'm afraid it is later,' murmured the minister, subsiding into the chair.

'Better late than never,' cried Simeon Samuels heartily, as he produced a bottle from the sideboard. 'Do you take it with hot water?'

'Thank you—not at all. I am only staying a moment.'

'Ah!' He stroked his beard. 'You are busy?'

'Terribly busy,' said the Rev. Elkan Gabriel.

'Even on Sunday?'

'Rather! It's my day for secretarial work, as there's no school.'

'Poor Mr. Gabriel. I at least have Sunday to myself. But you have to work Saturday and Sunday too. It's really too bad.'

'Eh,' said the minister blankly.

'Oh, of course I know you must work on the Sabbath.'

'I work on—on Shabbos!' The minister flushed to the temples.

'Oh, I'm not blaming you. One must live. In an ideal world of course you'd preach and pray and sing and recite the Law for nothing so that Heaven might perhaps overlook your hard labour, but as things are you must take your wages.'

[Illustration: "I work on—on Shabbos!"]

The minister had risen agitatedly. 'I earn my wages for the rest of my work—the Sabbath work I throw in,' he said hotly.

'Oh come, Mr. Gabriel, that quibble is not worthy of you. But far be it from me to judge a fellow-man.'

'Far be it indeed!' The attempted turning of his sabre-point gave him vigour for the lunge. 'You—you whose shop stands brazenly open every Saturday!'

'My dear Mr. Gabriel, I couldn't break the Fourth Commandment.'

'What!'

'Would you have me break the Fourth Commandment?'

'I do not understand.'

'And yet you hold a Rabbinic diploma, I am told. Does not the Fourth Commandment run: "Six days shalt thou labour and do all thy work"? If I were to close on Saturday I should only be working five days a week, since in this heathen country Sunday closing is compulsory.'

'But you don't keep the other half of the Commandment,' said the bewildered minister. '"And on the seventh is the Sabbath."'

'Yes, I do—after my six days the seventh is my Sabbath. I only sinned once, if you will have it so, the first time I shifted the Sabbath to Sunday, since when my Sabbath has arrived regularly on Sundays.'

'But you did sin once!' said the minister, catching at that straw.

'Granted, but as to get right again would now make a second sin, it seems more pious to let things be. Not that I really admit the first sin, for let me ask you, sir, which is nearer to the spirit of the Commandment—to work six days and keep a day of rest—merely changing the day once in one's whole lifetime—or to work five days and keep two days of rest?'

The minister, taken aback, knew not how to meet this novel defence. He had come heavily armed against all the usual arguments as to the necessity of earning one's bread. He was prepared to prove that even from a material point of view you really gained more in the long run, as it is written in the Conclusion-of-Sabbath Service: 'Blessed shalt thou be in the city, and blessed shalt thou be in the field.'

Simeon Samuels pursued his advantage.

'My co-religionists in Sudminster seem to have put all the stress upon the resting half of the Commandment, forgetting the working half of it. I do my best to meet their views—as you say, one should not dig down a wall—by attending their Sabbath service on a day most inconvenient to me. But no sacrifice is too great to achieve prayerful communion with one's brethren.'

'But if your views were to prevail there would be an end of Judaism!' the minister burst forth.

'Then Heaven forbid they should prevail!' said Simeon Samuels fervently. 'It is your duty to put the opposition doctrine as strongly as possible from the pulpit.' Then, as the minister rose in angry obfuscation, 'You are sure you won't have some whisky?' he added.

'No, I will take nothing from a house of sin. And if you show yourself next Sabbath I will preach at you again.'

'So that is your idea of religion—to drive me from the synagogue. You are more likely to drive away the rest of the congregation, sick of always hearing the same sermon. As for me, you forget how I enjoy your eloquence, devoted though it is to the destruction of Judaism.'

'Me!' The minister became ungrammatical in his indignation.

'Yes, you. To mix up religion with the almanac. People who find that your Sabbath wall shuts them out of all public life and all professions, just go outside it altogether, and think themselves outside the gates of Judaism. If my father—peace be upon him—hadn't had your narrow notions, I should have gone to the Bar instead of being condemned to shop-keeping.'

'You are a very good devil's advocate now,' retorted the minister.

Simeon Samuels stroked his beard. 'Thank you. And I congratulate your client.'

'You are an Epikouros (Epicurean), and I am wasting my time.'

'And mine too.'

The minister strode into the shop. At the street-door he turned.

'Then you persist in setting a bad example?'

'A bad example! To whom? To your godly congregation? Considering every other shop in the town is open on Shabbos, one more or less can't upset them.'

'When it is the only Jewish shop! Are you aware, sir, that every other Jew in Sudminster closes rigorously on the Sabbath?'

'I ascertained that before I settled here,' said Simeon Samuels quietly.

XI

The report of the pastor's collapse produced an emergency meeting of the leading sheep. The mid-day dinner-hour was chosen as the slackest. A babble of suggestions filled the Parnass's parlour. Solomon Barzinsky kept sternly repeating his Delenda est Carthago: 'He must be expelled from the congregation.'

'He should be expelled from the town altogether,' said Mendel. 'As it is written: "And remove Satan from before and behind us."'

'Since when have we owned Sudminster?' sneered the Parnass. 'You might as well talk of expelling the Mayor and the Corporation.'

'I didn't mean by Act of Parliament,' said Mendel. 'We could make his life a torture.'

'And meantime he makes yours a torture. No, no, the only way is to appeal to his soul—'

'May it be an atonement for us all!' interrupted Peleg the pawnbroker.

'We must beg him not to destroy religion,' repeated the Parnass.

'I thought Mr. Gabriel had done that,' said the Gabbai.

'He is only a minister. He has no worldly tact.'

'Then, why don't you go?' said Solomon Barzinsky.

'I have too much worldly tact. The President's visit might seem like an appeal to authority. It would set up his bristles. Besides, there wouldn't be me left to appeal to. The congregation must keep some trump up its sleeve. No, a mere plain member must go, a simple brother in Israel, to talk to him, heart to heart. You, Barzinsky, are the very man.'

'No, no, I'm not such a simple brother as all that. I'm in the same line, and he might take it for trade jealousy.'

'Then Peleg must go.'

'No, no, I'm not worthy to be the Sheliach Tzibbur!' (envoy of the congregation).

The Parnass reassured him as to his merits. 'The congregation could not have a worthier envoy.'

'But I can't leave my business.'

'You, with your fine grown-up daughters!' cried Barzinsky.

'Don't beshrew them—I will go at once.'

'And these gentlemen must await you here,' said the President, tapping his snuffbox incongruously at the 'here,' 'in order to continue the sitting if you fail.'

'I can't wait more than a quarter of an hour,' grumbled various voices in various keys.

Peleg departed nervously, upborne by the congregational esteem. He returned without even his own. Instead he carried a bulky barometer.

'You must buy this for the synagogue, gentlemen,' he said. 'It will do to hang in the lobby.'

The Parnass was the only one left in command of his breath.

'Buy a barometer!' he gasped.

'Well, it isn't any good to me,' retorted Peleg angrily.

'Then why did you buy it?' cried the Gabbai.

'It was the cheapest article I could get off with.'

'But you didn't go to buy,' said the Parnass.

'I know that—but you come into the shop—naturally he takes you for a customer—he looks so dignified; he strokes his beard—you can't look a fool, you must—'

'Be one,' snapped the Parnass. 'And then you come to us to share the expenses!'

'Well, what do I want with a barometer?'

'It'll do to tell you there's a storm when the chimney-pots are blowing down,' suggested the Parnass crushingly.

'Put it in your window—you'll make a profit out of it,' said Mendel.

'Not while Simeon Samuels is selling them cheaper, as with his Sabbath profits he can well afford to do!'

'Oh, he said he'd stick to his Sabbath profit, did he?' inquired the Parnass.

'We never touched on that,' said Peleg miserably. 'I couldn't manage to work the Sabbath into the conversation.'

'This is terrible.' Barzinsky's fist smote the table. 'I'll go—let him suspect my motives or not. The Almighty knows they are pure.'

'Bravo! Well spoken!' There was a burst of applause. Several marine-dealers shot out their hands and grasped Barzinsky's in admiration.

'Do not await me, gentlemen,' he said importantly. 'Go in peace.'

XII

'Good afternoon, Mr. Samuels,' said Solomon Barzinsky.

'Good afternoon, sir. What can I do for you?'

'You—you don't know me? I am a fellow-Jew.'

'That's as plain as the nose on your face.'

'You don't remember me from Shool? Mr. Barzinsky! I had the rolling-up of the Scroll the time you had the elevation of it.'

'Ah, indeed. At these solemn moments I scarcely notice people. But I am very glad to find you patronizing my humble establishment.'

'I don't want a barometer,' said Solomon hurriedly.

'That is fortunate, as I have just sold my last. But in the way of waterproofs, we have a new pattern, very seasonable.'

'No, no; I didn't come for a waterproof.'

'These oilskins—'

'I didn't come to buy anything.'

'Ah, you wish to sell me something.'

'Not that either. The fact is, I've come to beg of you, as one Jew to another—'

'A Schnorrer!' interrupted Simeon Samuels. 'Oh, Lord, I ought to have recognised you by that synagogue beginning.'

'Me, a Schnorrer!' The little man swelled skywards. 'Me, Solomon Barzinsky, whose shop stood in Sudminster twenty years before you poked your nose in—'

'I beg your pardon. There! you see I'm a beggar, too.' And Simeon Samuels laughed mirthlessly. 'Well, you've come to beg of me.' And his fingers caressed his patriarchal beard.

'I don't come on my own account only,' Barzinsky stammered.

'I understand. You want a contribution to the Passover Cake Fund. My time is precious, so is yours. What is the Parnass giving?'

'I'm not begging for money. I represent the congregation.'

'Dear me, why didn't you come to the point quicker? The congregation wishes to beg my acceptance of office. Well, it's very good of you all, especially as I'm such a recent addition. But I really feel a diffidence. You see, my views of the Sabbath clash with those of the congregation.'

'They do!' cried Barzinsky, leaping at his opportunity.

'Yes, I am for a much stricter observance than appears general here. Scarcely one of you carries his handkerchief tied round his loins like my poor old father, peace be upon him! You all carry the burden of it impiously in a pocket.'

'I never noticed your handkerchief round your waist!' cried the bewildered Barzinsky.

'Perhaps not; I never had a cold; it remained furled.'

Simeon Samuels' superb insolence twitched Barzinsky's mouth agape. 'But you keep your shop open!' he cried at last.

'That would be still another point of clashing,' admitted Simeon Samuels blandly. 'Altogether, you will see the inadvisability of my accepting office.'

'Office!' echoed Barzinsky, meeting the other's ironic fence with crude thwacks. 'Do you think a God-fearing congregation would offer office to a Sabbath-breaker?'

'Ah, so that was at the back of it. I suspected something underhand in your offer. I was to be given office, was I, on condition of closing my shop on Saturday? No, Mr. Barzinsky. Go back and tell those who sent you that Simeon Samuels scorns stipulations, and that when you offer to make him Parnass unconditionally he may consider your offer, but not till then. Good-bye. You must jog along with your present apology for a Parnass.'

'You—you Elisha ben Abuyai!' And, consoled only by the aptness of his reference to the atheist of the Talmud, Barzinsky rushed off to tell the Parnass how Simeon Samuels had insulted them both.

XIII

The Parnass, however, was not to be drawn yet. He must keep himself in reserve, he still insisted. But perhaps, he admitted, Simeon Samuels resented mere private members or committeemen. Let the Gabbai go.

Accordingly the pompous treasurer of the synagogue strode into the notorious shop on the Sabbath itself, catching Simeon Samuels red-handed.

But nothing could be suaver than that gentleman's 'Good Shabbos. What can I do for you?'

'You can shut up your shop,' said the Gabbai brusquely.

'And how shall I pay your bill, then?'

'I'd rather give you a seat and all the honours for nothing than see this desecration.'

'You must have a goodly surplus, then.'

'We have enough.'

'That's strange. You're the first Gabbai I ever knew who was satisfied with his balance-sheet. Is it your excellent management, I wonder, or have you endowments?'

'That's not for me to say. I mean we have five or six hundred pounds in legacies.'

'Indeed! Soundly invested, I hope?'

'First-class. English Railway Debentures.'

'I see. Trustee stock.' Simeon Samuels stroked his beard. 'And so your whole congregation works on the Sabbath. A pretty confession!'

'What do you mean?'

'Runs railway trains, lights engine-fires, keeps porters and signal-men toiling, and pockets the profits!'

'Who does?'

'You, sir, in particular, as the financial representative of the congregation. How can any Jew hold industrial shares in a heathen country without being a partner in a Sabbath business—ay, and opening on the Day of Atonement itself? And it is you who have the audacity to complain of me! I, at least, do my own dirty work, not hide myself behind stocks and shares. Good Shabbos to you, Mr. Gabbai, and kindly mind your own business in future—your locomotives and your sidings and your stinking tunnels.'

XIV

The Parnass could no longer delay the diplomatic encounter. 'Twas vain to accuse the others of tactlessness, and shirk the exhibition of his own tact. He exhibited it most convincingly by not informing the others that he was about to put it to a trial.

Hence he refrained from improving a synagogue opportunity, but sneaked one week-day towards the shop. He lingered without, waiting to be invited within. Thus all appearance of his coming to rebuke would be removed. His mission should pop up from a casual conversation.

He peeped into the window, passed and repassed.

Simeon Samuels, aware of a fly hovering on the purlieus of his web, issued from its centre, as the Parnass turned his back on the shop and gazed musingly at the sky.

'Looks threatening for rain, sir,' observed Simeon Samuels, addressing the back. 'Our waterproofs— Bless my soul, but it surely isn't our Parnass!'

'Yes, I'm just strolling about. I seem to have stumbled on your establishment.'

'Lucky for me.'

'And a pleasure for me. I never knew you had such a nice display.'

'Won't you come inside, and see the stock?'

'Thank you, I must really get back home. And besides, as you say, it is threatening for rain.'

'I'll lend you a waterproof, or even sell you one cheap. Come in, sir—come in. Pray honour me.'

Congratulating himself on catching the spider, the fly followed him within.

A quarter of an hour passed, in which he must buzz about the stock. It seemed vastly difficult to veer round to the Sabbath through the web of conversation the spider wove round him. Simeon Samuels' conception of a marine-dealer's stock startled him by its comprehensiveness, and when he was asked to admire an Indian shawl, he couldn't help inquiring what it was doing there.

'Well,' explained Simeon Samuels, 'occasionally a captain or first mate will come back to England, home, and beauty, and will have neglected to buy foreign presents for his womenkind. I then remind him of the weakness of womenkind for such trophies of their menfolks' travel.'

'Excellent. I won't tell your competitors.'

'Oh, those cattle!' Simeon snapped his fingers. 'If they stole my idea, they'd not be able to carry it out. It's not easy to cajole a captain.'

'No, you're indeed a honeyed rascal,' thought the Parnass.

'I also do a brisk business in chutney,' went on Simeon. 'It's a thing women are especially fond of having brought back to them from India. And yet it's the last thing their menkind think of till I remind them of it on their return.'

'I certainly brought back none,' said the Parnass, smiling in spite of himself.

'You have been in India?'

'I have,' replied the Parnass, with a happy inspiration, 'and I brought back to my wife something more stimulating than chutney.'

'Indeed?'

'Yes, the story of the Beni-Israel, the black Jews, who, surrounded by all those millions of Hindoos, still keep their Sabbath.'

'Ah, poor niggers. Then you've been half round the world.'

'All round the world, for I went there and back by different routes. And it was most touching, wherever I went, to find everywhere a colony of Jews, and everywhere the Holy Sabbath kept sacred.'

'But on different days, of course,' said Simeon Samuels.

'Eh? Not at all! On the same day.'

'On the same day! How could that be? The day changes with every move east or west. When it's day here, it's night in Australia.'

Darkness began to cloud the presidential brow.

'Don't you try to make black white!' he said angrily.

'It's you that are trying to make white black,' retorted Simeon Samuels. 'Perhaps you don't know that I hail from Australia, and that by working on Saturday I escape profaning my native Australian Sabbath, while you, who have been all round the world, and have either lost or gained a day, according as you travelled east or west, are desecrating your original Sabbath either by working on Friday or smoking on Sunday.'

The Parnass felt his head going round—he didn't know whether east or west. He tried to clear it by a pinch of snuff, which he in vain strove to make judicial.

'Oh, and so, and so—atchew!—and so you're the saint and I'm the sinner!' he cried sarcastically.

'No, I don't profess to be a saint,' replied Simeon Samuels somewhat unexpectedly. 'But I do think the Saturday was meant for Palestine, not for the lands of the Exile, where another day of rest rules. When you were in India you probably noted that the Mohammedans keep Friday. A poor Jew in the bazaar is robbed of his Hindoo customers on Friday, of his Jews on Saturday, and his Christians on Sunday.'

'The Fourth Commandment is eternal!' said the Parnass with obstinate sublimity.

'But the Fifth says, "that thy days may be long in the land which the Lord thy God giveth thee." I believe this reward belongs to all the first five Commandments—not only to the Fifth—else an orphan would have no chance of long life. Keep the Sabbath in the land that the Lord giveth thee; not in England, which isn't thine.'

'Oho!' retorted the Parnass. 'Then at that rate in England you needn't honour your father and mother.'

'Not if you haven't got them!' rejoined Simeon Samuels. 'And if you haven't got a land, you can't keep its Sabbath. Perhaps you think we can keep the Jubilee also without a country.'

'The Sabbath is eternal,' repeated the Parnass doggedly. 'It has nothing to do with countries. Before we got to the Promised Land we kept the Sabbath in the wilderness.'

'Yes, and God sent a double dose of manna on the Friday. Do you mean to say He sends us here a double dose of profit?'

'He doesn't let us starve. We prospered well enough before you brought your wretched example—'

'Then my wretched example cannot lead the congregation away. I am glad of it. You do them much more harm by your way of Sabbath-breaking.'

'My way!'

'Yes, my dear old father—peace be upon him!—would have been scandalized to see the burden you carry on the Sabbath.'

'What burden do I carry?'

'Your snuff-box!'

The Parnass almost dropped it. 'That little thing!'

'I call it a cumbrous, not to say tasteless thing. But before the Almighty there is no great and no small. One who stands in such a high place in the synagogue must be especially mindful, and every unnecessary burden—'

'But snuff is necessary for me—I can't do without it.'

'Other Presidents have done without it. As it is written in Jeremiah: "And the wild asses did stand in the high places; they snuffed up the wind."'

The Parnass flushed like a beetroot. 'I'll teach you to know your place, sir.' He turned his back on the scoffer, and strode towards the door.

'But if you'd care for a smaller snuff-box,' said Simeon Samuels, 'I have an artistic assortment.'

XV

At the next meeting of the Synagogue Council a notice of motion stood upon the agenda in the name of the Parnass himself:

'That this Council views with the greatest reprobation the breach of the Fourth Commandment committed weekly by a member of the congregation, and calls upon him either to resign his seat, with the burial and other rights appertaining thereto, or to close his business on the Sabbath.'

When the resolution came up Mr. Solomon Barzinsky moved as an amendment that weekly be altered into 'twice a week,' since the member kept open on Friday night as well as Saturday.

The Parnass refused to accept the amendment. There was only one Sabbath a week, though it had two periods. 'And the evening and the morning were one day.'

Mr. Peleg supported the amendment. They must not leave Mr. Simeon Samuels a loophole of escape. It was also, he said, the duty of the Council to buy a barometer the rogue had foisted upon him.

After an animated discussion, mainly about the barometer, the President accepted the amendment, but produced a great impression by altering 'twice a week' into 'bi-weekly.'

A Mr. John Straumann, however, who prided himself on his style, and had even changed his name to John because Jacob grated on his delicate ear, refused to be impressed.

Committed bi-weekly by a member sounded almost jocose, he argued. 'Buy! buy!' it sounded like a butcher's cry.

Mr. Enoch, the kosher butcher, rose amid excitement, and asked if he had come there to be insulted!

'Sit down! sit down!' said the Parnass roughly. 'It's no matter how the resolution sounds. It will be in writing.'

'Then why not add,' sarcastically persisted the stylist, '"Committed bi-weekly by a member by buying and selling."'

'Order, order!' said the Parnass angrily. 'Those who are in favour of the resolution! Carried.'

'By a majority,' sneered the stylist, subsiding.

'Mr. Secretary'—the President turned to the poor Reverend-of-all-work—'you need not record this verbal discussion in the minutes.'

'By request,' said the stylist, reviving.

'But what's the use of the resolution if you don't mention the member's name?' suddenly inquired Ephraim Mendel, stretching his long, languid limbs.

'But there's only one Sabbath-breaker,' replied the Parnass.

'To-day, yes, but to-morrow there might be two.'

'It could hardly be to-morrow,' said the stylist. 'For that happens to be a Monday.'

Barzinsky bashed the table. 'Mr. President, are we here for business or are we not?'

'You may be here for business—I am here for religion,' retorted Straumann the stylist.

'You—you snub-nosed monkey, what do you mean?'

'Order, order, gentlemen,' said the Parnass.

'I will not order,' said Solomon Barzinsky excitedly. 'I did not come here to be insulted.'

'Insulted!' quoth Straumann. 'It's you that must apologize, you illiterate icthyosaurus! I appeal to the President.'

'You have both insulted me,' was that worthy's ruling. 'I give the word to Mr. Mendel.'

'But—' from both the combatants simultaneously.

'Order, order!' from a dozen throats.

'I said Simeon Samuels' name must be put in,' Mendel repeated.

'You should have said so before—the resolution is carried now,' said the President.

'And a fat lot of good it will do,' said Peleg. 'Gentlemen, if you knew him as well as I, if you had my barometer to read him by, you'd see that the only remedy is to put him in Cherem' (excommunication).

'If he can't get buried it is a kind of Cherem,' said the Gabbai.

'Assuredly,' added the Parnass. 'He will be frightened to think that if he dies suddenly—'

'And he is sure to take a sudden death,' put in Barzinsky with unction.

'He will not be buried among Jews,' wound up the Parnass.

'Hear, hear!' A murmur of satisfaction ran round the table. All felt that Simeon Samuels was cornered at last. It was resolved that the resolution be sent to him.

XVI

'Mr. Simeon Samuels requests me to say that he presents his compliments to the secretary of the Sudminster Hebrew Congregation, and begs to acknowledge the receipt of the Council's resolution. In reply I am to state that Mr. Samuels regrets that his views on the Sabbath question should differ from those of his fellow-worshippers, but he has not attempted to impress his views on the majority, and he regrets that in a free country like England they should have imported the tyranny of the lands of persecution from which they came. Fortunately such procedure is illegal. By the act of Charles I. the Sabbath is defined as the Sunday, and as a British subject Mr. Samuels takes his stand upon the British Constitution. Mr. Samuels has done his best to compromise with the congregation by attending the Sabbath service on the day most convenient to the majority. In regard to the veiled threat of the refusal of burial rights, Mr. Samuels desires me to say that he has no intention of dying in Sudminster, but merely of getting his living there. In any case, under his will, his body is to be deported to Jerusalem, where he has already acquired a burying-place.'

'Next year in Jerusalem!' cried Barzinsky fervently, when this was read to the next meeting.

'Order, order,' said the Parnass. 'I don't believe in his Jerusalem grave. They won't admit his dead body.'

'He relies on smuggling in alive,' said Barzinsky gloomily, 'as soon as he has made his pile.'

'That won't be very long at this rate,' added Ephraim Mendel.

'The sooner the better,' said the Gabbai impatiently. 'Let him go to Jericho.'

There was a burst of laughter, to the Gabbai's great astonishment.

'Order, order, gentlemen,' said the Parnass. 'Don't you see from this insolent letter how right I was? The rascal threatens to drag us to the Christian Courts, that's clear. All that about Jerusalem is only dust thrown into our eyes.'

'Grave-dust,' murmured Straumann.

'Order! He is a dangerous customer.'

'Shopkeeper,' corrected Straumann.

The Parnass glared, but took snuff silently.

'I don't wonder he laughed at us,' said Straumann, encouraged. 'Bi-weekly by a member. Ha! ha! ha!'

'Mr. President!' Barzinsky screamed. 'Will you throw that laughing hyena out, or shall I?'

Straumann froze to a statue of dignity. 'Let any animalcule try it on,' said he.

'Shut up, you children, I'll chuck you both out,' said Ephraim Mendel in conciliatory tones. 'The point is—what's to be done now, Mr. President?'

'Nothing—till the end of the year. When he offers his new subscription we refuse to take it. That can't be illegal.'

'We ought all to go to him in a friendly deputation,' said Straumann. 'These formal resolutions "Buy! buy!" put his back up. We'll go to him as brothers—all Israel are brethren, and blood is thicker than water.'

'Chutney is thicker than blood,' put in the Parnass mysteriously. 'He'll simply try to palm off his stock on the deputation.'

Ephraim Mendel and Solomon Barzinsky jumped up simultaneously. 'What a good idea,' said Ephraim. 'There you have hit it!' said Solomon. Their simultaneous popping-up had an air of finality—like the long and the short of it!

'You mean?' said the Parnass, befogged in his turn.

'I mean,' said Barzinsky, 'we could buy up his stock, me and the other marine-dealers between us, and he could clear out!'

'If he sold it reasonably,' added Mendel.

'Even unreasonably you must make a sacrifice for the Sabbath,' said the Parnass. 'Besides, divided among the lot of you, the loss would be little.'

'And you can buy in my barometer with the rest,' added Peleg.

'We could call a meeting of marine-dealers,' said Barzinsky, disregarding him. 'We could say to them we must sacrifice ourselves for our religion.'

'Tell that to the marine-dealers!' murmured Straumann.

'And that we must buy out the Sabbath-breaker at any cost.'

'Buy! buy!' said Straumann. 'If you'd only thought of that sort of "Buy! buy!" at the first!'

'Order, order!' said the Parnass.

'It would be more in order,' said Straumann, 'to appoint an executive sub-committee to deal with the question. I'm sick of it. And surely we as a Synagogue Council can't be in order in ordering some of our members to buy out another.'

'Hear, hear!' His suggestion found general approval. It took a long discussion, however, before the synagogue decided to wash its hands of responsibility, and give over to a sub-committee of three the task of ridding Sudminster of its plague-spot by any means that commended itself to them.

Solomon Barzinsky, Ephraim Mendel, and Peleg the pawnbroker were elected to constitute this Council of Three.

XVII

The glad news spread through the Sudminster Congregation that Simeon Samuels had at last been bought out—at a terrible loss to the martyred marine-dealers who had had to load themselves with chutney and other unheard-of and unsaleable stock. But they would get back their losses, it was felt, by the removal of his rivalry. Carts were drawn up before the dismantled plate-glass window carrying off its criminal contents, and Simeon Samuels stood stroking his beard amid the ruins.

Then the shop closed; the shutters that should have honoured the Sabbath now depressed the Tuesday. Simeon Samuels was seen to get into the London train. The demon that troubled their sanctity had been exorcised. A great peace reigned in every heart, almost like the Sabbath peace coming into the middle of the week.

'If they had only taken my advice earlier,' said Solomon Barzinsky to his wife, as he rolled his forkful of beef in the chutney.

'You can write to your father, Deborah,' said Lazarus Levy, 'that we no longer need the superior reach-me-downs.'

On the Wednesday strange new rumours began to circulate, and those who hastened to confirm them stood dumbfounded before great posters on all the shutters:

CLOSED FOR RE-STOCKING

THE OLD-FASHIONED STOCK OF THIS BUSINESS
HAVING BEEN SOLD OFF TO THE TRADE,

SIMEON SAMUELS

IS TAKING THE OPPORTUNITY

TO LAY IN THE BEST AND MOST UP-TO-DATE
LONDON AND CONTINENTAL GOODS
FOR HIS CUSTOMERS.
BARGAINS AND NOVELTIES IN EVERY DEPARTMENT.

RE-OPEN SATURDAY NEXT

XVIII

A hurried emergency meeting of the Executive Sub-Committee was called.

'He has swindled us,' said Solomon Barzinsky. 'This paper signed by him merely undertakes to shut up his shop. And he will plead he meant for a day or two.'

'And he agreed to leave the town,' wailed Peleg, 'but he meant to buy goods.'

'Well, we can have the law of him,' said Mendel. 'We paid him compensation for disturbance.'

'And can't he claim he was disturbed?' shrieked Barzinsky. 'His whole stock turned upside down!'

'Let him claim!' said Mendel. 'There is such a thing as obtaining money under false pretences.'

'And such a thing as becoming the laughing-stock of the heathen,' said Peleg. 'We must grin and bear it ourselves.'

'It's all very well for you to grin,' said Solomon tartly. 'We've got to bear it. You didn't take over any of his old rubbish.'

'Didn't I, indeed? What about the barometer?'

'Confound your barometer!' cried Ephraim Mendel. 'I'll have the law of him; I've made up my mind.'

'Well, you'll have to bear the cost, then,' said Peleg. 'It's none of my business.'

'Yes, it is,' shouted Mendel. 'As a member of the Sub-Committee you can't dissociate yourselves from us.'

'A nice idea that—I'm to be dragged into your law-suits!'

'Hush, leave off these squabbles!' said Solomon Barzinsky. 'The law is slow, and not even sure. The time has come for desperate measures. We must root out the plague-spot with our own hands.'

'Hear, hear,' said the rest of the Sub-Committee.

XIX

On the succeeding Sabbath Simeon Samuels was not the only figure in the synagogue absorbed in devotion. Solomon Barzinsky, Ephraim Mendel, and Peleg the pawnbroker were all rapt in equal piety, while the rest of the congregation was shaken with dreadful gossip about them. Their shops were open, too, it would seem.

Immediately after the service the Parnass arrested Solomon Barzinsky's exit, and asked him if the rumour were true.

'Perfectly true,' replied Solomon placidly. 'The Executive Sub-Committee passed the resolution to—'

'To break the Sabbath!' interrupted the Parnass.

'We had already sacrificed our money; there was nothing left but to sacrifice our deepest feelings—'

'But what for?'

'Why, to destroy his advantage, of course. Five-sixths of his Sabbath profits depend on the marine-dealers closing, and when he sees he's breaking the Sabbath in vain—'

'Rubbish! You are asked to stop a congregational infection, and you—'

'Vaccinate ourselves with the same stuff, to make sure the attack shall be light.'

'It's a hair of the dog that bit us,' said Mendel, who, with Peleg, had lingered to back up Barzinsky.

'Of the mad dog!' exclaimed the Parnass. 'And you're all raging mad.'

'It's the only sane way,' urged Peleg. 'When he sees his rivals open—'

'You!' The President turned on him. 'You are not even a marine-dealer. Why are you open?'

'How could I dissociate myself from the rest of the Sub-Committee?' inquired Peleg with righteous indignation.

'You are a set of sinners in Israel!' cried the Parnass, forgetting even to take snuff. 'This will split up the congregation.'

'The congregation through its Council gave the Committee full power to deal with the matter,' said Barzinsky with dignity.

'But then the other marine-dealers will open as well as the Committee!'

'I trust not,' replied Barzinsky fervently. 'Two of us are enough to cut down his takings.'

'But the whole lot of you would be still more efficacious. Oh, this is the destruction of our congregation, the death of our religion!'

'No, no, no,' said Solomon soothingly. 'You are mistaken. We are most careful not to touch money. We are going to trust our customers, and keep our accounts without pen or ink. We have invented a most ingenious system, which gives us far more work than writing, but we have determined to spare ourselves no trouble to keep the Sabbath from unnecessary desecration.'

'And once the customers don't pay up, your system will break down. No, no; I shall write to the Chief Rabbi.'

'We will explain our motives,' said Mendel.

'Your motives need no explanation. This scandal must cease.'

'And who are you to give orders?' shrieked Solomon Barzinsky. 'You're not speaking to a Schnorrer, mind you. My banking account is every bit as big as yours. For two pins I start an opposition Shool.'

'A Sunday Shool!' said the Parnass sarcastically.

'And why not? It would be better than sitting playing solo on Sundays. We are not in Palestine now.'

'Oh, Simeon Samuels has been talking to you, has he?'

'I don't need Simeon Samuels' wisdom. I'm an Englishman myself.'

XX

The desperate measures of the Sub-Committee were successful. The other marine-dealers hastened to associate themselves with the plan of campaign, and Simeon Samuels soon departed in search of a more pious seaport.

But, alas! homoeopathy was only half-vindicated. For the remedy proved worse than the disease, and the cutting-out of the original plague-spot left the other marine-stores still infected. The epidemic spread from them till it had overtaken half the shops of the congregation. Some had it in a mild form—only one shutter open, or a back door not closed—but in many it came out over the whole shop-window.

The one bright spot in the story of the Sudminster Sabbath is that the congregation of which the present esteemed Parnass is Solomon Barzinsky, Esq., J.P., managed to avert the threatened split, and that while in so many other orthodox synagogues the poor minister preaches on the Sabbath to empty benches, the Sudminster congregation still remains at the happy point of compromise acutely discovered by Simeon Samuels: of listening reverentially every Saturday morning to the unchanging principles of its minister-elect, the while its shops are engaged in supplying the wants of Christendom.

THE RED MARK

The curious episode in the London Ghetto the other winter, while the epidemic of small-pox was raging, escaped the attention of the reporters, though in the world of the Board-schools it is a vivid memory. But even the teachers and the committees, the inspectors and the Board members, have remained ignorant of the part little Bloomah Beckenstein played in it.

To explain how she came to be outside the school-gates instead of inside them, we must go back a little and explain her situation both outside and inside her school.

Bloomah was probably 'Blume,' which is German for a flower, but she had always been spelt 'Bloomah' in the school register, for even Board-school teachers are not necessarily familiar with foreign languages.

They might have been forgiven for not connecting Bloomah with blooms, for she was a sad-faced child, and even in her tenth year showed deep, dark circles round her eyes. But they were beautiful eyes, large, brown, and soft, shining with love and obedience.

Mrs. Beckenstein, however, found neither of these qualities in her youngest born, who seemed to her entirely sucked up by the school.

'In my days,' she would grumble, 'it used to be God Almighty first, your parents next, and school last. Now it's all a red mark first, your parents and God Almighty nowhere.'

The red mark was the symbol of punctuality, set opposite the child's name in the register. To gain it, she must be in her place at nine o'clock to the stroke. A moment after nine, and only the black mark was attainable. Twenty to ten, and the duck's egg of the absent was sorrowfully inscribed by the Recording Angel, who in Bloomah's case was a pale pupil-teacher with eyeglasses.

But it was the Banner which loomed largest on the school horizon, intensifying Bloomah's anxiety and her mother's grievance.

'I don't see nothing,' Mrs. Beckenstein iterated; 'no prize, no medal—nothing but a red mark and a banner.'

The Banner was indeed a novelty. It had not unfurled itself in Mrs. Beckenstein's young days, nor even in the young days of Bloomah's married brothers and sisters.

As the worthy matron would say: 'There's been Jack Beckenstein, there's been Joey Beckenstein, there's been Briny Beckenstein, there's been Benjy Beckenstein, there's been Ada Beckenstein, there's been Becky Beckenstein, God bless their hearts! and they all grew up scholards and prize-winners and a credit to their Queen and their religion without this meshuggas (madness) of a Banner.'

Vaguely Mrs. Beckenstein connected the degenerate innovation with the invasion of the school by 'furriners'—all these hordes of Russian, Polish, and Roumanian Jews flying from persecution, who were sweeping away the good old English families, of which she considered the Beckensteins a shining example. What did English people want with banners and such-like gewgaws?

The Banner was a class trophy of regularity and punctuality. It might be said metaphorically to be made of red marks; and, indeed, its ground-hue was purple.

The class that had scored the highest weekly average of red marks enjoyed its emblazoned splendours for the next week. It hung by a cord on the classroom wall, amid the dull, drab maps—a glorious sight with its oaken frame and its rich-coloured design in silk. Life moved to a chivalrous music, lessons went more easily, in presence of its proud pomp: 'twas like marching to a band instead of painfully plodding.

And the desire to keep it became a passion to the winners; the little girls strained every nerve never to be late or absent; but, alas! some mischance would occur to one or other, and it passed, in its purple and gold, to some strenuous and luckier class in another section of the building, turning to a funeral-banner as it disappeared dismally through the door of the cold and empty room.

Woe to the late-comer who imperilled the Banner. The black mark on the register was a snowflake compared with the black frown on all those childish foreheads. As for the absentee, the scowls that would meet her return not improbably operated to prolong her absence.

Only once had Bloomah's class won the trophy, and that was largely through a yellow fog which hit the other classes worse.

For Bloomah was the black sheep that spoilt the chances of the fold—the black sheep with the black marks. Perhaps those great rings round her eyes were the black marks incarnate, so morbidly did the poor child grieve over her sins of omission.

Yet these sins of omission were virtues of commission elsewhere; for if Bloomah's desk was vacant, it was only because Bloomah was slaving at something that her mother considered more important.

'The Beckenstein family first, the workshop second, and school nowhere,' Bloomah might have retorted on her mother.

At home she was the girl-of-all-work. In the living-rooms she did cooking and washing and sweeping; in the shop above, whenever a hand fell sick or work fell heavy, she was utilized to make buttonholes, school hours or no school hours.

Bloomah was likewise the errand-girl of the establishment, and the portress of goods to and from S. Cohn's Emporium in Holloway, and the watch-dog when Mrs. Beckenstein went shopping or pleasuring.

'Lock up the house!' the latter would cry, when Bloomah tearfully pleaded for that course. 'My things are much too valuable to be locked up. But I know you'd rather lose my jewellery than your precious Banner.'

When Mrs. Beckenstein had new grandchildren—and they came frequently—Bloomah would be summoned in hot haste to the new scene of service. Curt post-cards came on these occasions, thus conceived:

'DEAR MOTHER,
'A son. Send Bloomah.
'BRINY.'

Sometimes these messages were mournfully inverted:

'DEAR MOTHER,
'Poor little Rachie is gone. Send Bloomah to your heart-broken
'BECKY.'

Occasionally the post-card went the other way:

'DEAR BECKY,
'Send back Bloomah.
'Your loving mother.'

The care of her elder brother Daniel was also part of Bloomah's burden; and in the evenings she had to keep an eye on his street sports and comrades, for since he had shocked his parents by dumping down a new pair of boots on the table, he could not be trusted without supervision.

Not that he had stolen the boots—far worse! Beguiled by a card cunningly printed in Hebrew, he had attended the evening classes of the Meshummodim, those converted Jews who try to bribe their brethren from the faith, and who are the bugbear and execration of the Ghetto.

Daniel was thereafter looked upon at home as a lamb who had escaped from the lions' den, and must be the object of their vengeful pursuit, while on Bloomah devolved the duties of shepherd and sheep-dog.

It was in the midst of all these diverse duties that Bloomah tried to go to school by day, and do her home lessons by night. She did not murmur against her mother, though she often pleaded. She recognised that the poor woman was similarly distracted between domestic duties and turns at the machines upstairs.

Only it was hard for the child to dovetail the two halves of her life. At night she must sit up as late as her elders, poring over her school books, and in the morning it was a fierce rush to get through her share of the housework in time for the red mark. In Mrs. Beckenstein's language: 'Don't eat, don't sleep, boil nor bake, stew nor roast, nor fry, nor nothing.'

Her case was even worse than her mother imagined, for sometimes it was ten minutes to nine before Bloomah could sit down to her own breakfast, and then the steaming cup of tea served by her mother was a terrible hindrance; and if that good woman's head was turned, Bloomah would sneak towards the improvised sink—which consisted of two dirty buckets, the one holding the clean water being recognisable by the tin pot standing on its covering-board—where she would pour half her tea into the one bucket and fill up from the other.

When this stratagem was impossible, she almost scalded herself in her gulpy haste. Then how she snatched up her satchel and ran through rain, or snow, or fog, or scorching sunshine! Yet often she lost her breath without gaining her mark, and as she cowered tearfully under the angry eyes of the classroom, a stab at her heart was added to the stitch in her side.

It made her classmates only the angrier that, despite all her unpunctuality, she kept a high position in the class, even if she could never quite attain prize-rank.

But there came a week when Bloomah's family remained astonishingly quiet and self-sufficient, and it looked as if the Banner might once again adorn the dry, scholastic room and throw a halo of romance round the blackboard.

Then a curious calamity befell. A girl who had left the school for another at the end of the previous week, returned on the Thursday, explaining that her parents had decided to keep her in the old school. An indignant heart-cry broke through all the discipline:

'Teacher, don't have her!'

From Bloomah burst the peremptory command: 'Go back, Sarah!'

For the unlucky children felt that her interval would now be reckoned one of absence. And they were right. Sarah reduced the gross attendance by six, and the Banner was lost.

Yet to have been so near incited them to a fresh spurt. Again the tantalizing Thursday was reached before their hopes were dashed. This time the break-down was even crueller, for every pinafored pupil, not excluding Bloomah, was in her place, red-marked.

Upon this saintly company burst suddenly Bloomah's mother, who, ignoring the teacher, and pointing her finger dramatically at her daughter, cried:

'Bloomah Beckenstein, go home!'

Bloomah's face became one large red mark, at which all the other girls' eyes were directed. Tears of humiliation and distress dripped down her cheeks over the dark rings. If she were thus hauled off ere she had received two hours of secular instruction, her attendance would be cancelled.

The class was all in confusion. 'Fold arms!' cried the teacher sharply, and the girls sat up rigidly. Bloomah obeyed instinctively with the rest.

'Bloomah Beckenstein, do you want me to pull you out by your plait?'

'Mrs. Beckenstein, really you mustn't come here like that!' said the teacher in her most ladylike accents.

'Tell Bloomah that,' answered Mrs. Beckenstein, unimpressed. 'She's come here by runnin' away from home. There's nobody but her to see to things, for we are all broken in our bones from dancin' at a weddin' last night, and comin' home at four in the mornin', and pourin' cats and dogs. If you go to our house, please, teacher, you'll see my Benjy in bed; he's given up his day's work; he must have his sleep; he earns three pounds a week as head cutter at S. Cohn's—he can afford to be in bed, thank God! So now, then, Bloomah Beckenstein! Don't they teach you here: "Honour thy father and thy mother"?'

Poor Bloomah rose, feeling vaguely that fathers and mothers should not dishonour their children. With hanging head she moved to the door, and burst into a passion of tears as soon as she got outside.

After, if not in consequence of, this behaviour, Mrs. Beckenstein broke her leg, and lay for weeks with the limb cased in plaster-of-Paris. That finished the chances of the Banner for a long time. Between nursing and house management Bloomah could scarcely ever put in an attendance.

So heavily did her twin troubles weigh upon the sensitive child day and night that she walked almost with a limp, and dreamed of her name in the register with ominous rows of black ciphers; they stretched on and on to infinity—in vain did she turn page after page in the hope of a red mark; the little black eggs became larger and larger, till at last horrid horned insects began to creep from them and scramble all over her, and she woke with creeping flesh. Sometimes she lay swathed and choking in the coils of a Black Banner.

And, to add to these worries, the School Board officer hovered and buzzed around, threatening summonses.

But at last she was able to escape to her beloved school. The expected scowl of the room was changed to a sigh of relief; extremes meet, and her absence had been so prolonged that reproach was turned to welcome.

Bloomah remorsefully redoubled her exertions. The hope of the Banner flamed anew in every breast. But the other classes were no less keen; a fifth standard, in particular, kept the Banner for a full month, grimly holding it against all comers, came they ever so regularly and punctually.

Suddenly a new and melancholy factor entered into the competition. An epidemic of small-pox broke out in the East End, with its haphazard effects upon the varying classes. Red marks, and black marks, medals and prizes, all was luck and lottery. The pride of the fifth standard was laid low; one of its girls was attacked, two others were kept at home through parental panic. A disturbing insecurity as of an earthquake vibrated through the school. In Bloomah's class alone—as if inspired by her martial determination—the ranks stood firm, unwavering.

The epidemic spread. The Ghetto began to talk of special psalms in the little synagogues.

In this crisis which the epidemic produced the Banner seemed drifting steadily towards Bloomah and her mates. They started Monday morning with all hands on deck, so to speak; they sailed round Tuesday and Wednesday without a black mark in the school-log. The Thursday on which they had so often split was passed under full canvas, and if they could only get through Friday the trophy was theirs.

And Friday was the easiest day of all, inasmuch as, in view of the incoming Sabbath, it finished earlier. School did not break up between the two attendances; there was a mere dinner-interval in the playground at midday. Nobody could get away, and whoever scored the first mark was sure of the second.

Bloomah was up before dawn on the fateful winter morning; she could run no risks of being late. She polished off all her house-work, wondering anxiously if any of her classmates would oversleep herself, yet at heart confident that all were as eager as she. Still there was always that troublesome small-pox—! She breathed a prayer that God would keep all the little girls and send them the Banner.

As she sat at breakfast the postman brought a post-card for her mother. Bloomah's heart was in her mouth when Mrs. Beckenstein clucked her tongue in reading it. She felt sure that the epidemic had invaded one of those numerous family hearths.

Her mother handed her the card silently.

'DEAR MOTHER,
'I am rakked with neuraljia. Send Bloomah to fry the fish.
'BECKY.'

Bloomah turned white; this was scarcely less tragic.

'Poor Becky!' said her heedless parent.

'There's time after school,' she faltered.

'What!' shrieked Mrs. Beckenstein. 'And not give the fish time to get cold! It's that red mark again—sooner than lose it you'd see your own sister eat hot fish. Be off at once to her, you unnatural brat, or I'll bang the frying-pan about your head. That'll give you a red mark—yes, and a black mark, too! My poor Becky never persecuted me with Banners, and she's twice the scholard you are.'

'Why, she can't spell "neuralgia,"' said Bloomah resentfully.

'And who wants to spell a thing like that? It's bad enough to feel it. Wait till you have babies and neuralgy of your own, and you'll see how you'll spell.'

'She can't spell "racked" either,' put in Daniel.

His mother turned on him witheringly. 'She didn't go to school with the Meshummodim.'

Bloomah suddenly picked up her satchel.

'What's your books for? You don't fry fish with books.' Mrs. Beckenstein wrested it away from her, and dashed it on the floor. The pencil-case rolled one way, the thimble another.

'But I can get to school for the afternoon attendance.'

'Madness! With your sister in agony? Have you no feelings? Don't let me see your brazen face before the Sabbath!'

Bloomah crept out broken-hearted. On the way to Becky's her feet turned of themselves by long habit down the miry street in which the red-brick school-building rose in dreary importance. The sight of the great iron gate and the hurrying children caused her a throb of guilt. For a moment she stood wrestling with the temptation to enter.

It was but for the moment. She might rise to the heresy of hot fried fish in lieu of cold, but Becky's Sabbath altogether devoid of fried fish was a thought too sacrilegious for her childish brain.

From her earliest babyhood chunks of cold fried fish had been part of her conception of the Day of Rest. Visions and odours of her mother frying plaice and soles—at worst, cod or mackerel—were inwoven with her most sacred memories of the coming Sabbath; it is probable she thought Friday was short for frying-day.

With a sob she turned back, hurrying as if to escape the tug of temptation.

'Bloomah! Where are you off to?'

It was the alarmed cry of a classmate. Bloomah took to her heels, her face a fiery mass of shame and grief.

Towards midday Becky's fish, nicely browned and sprigged with parsley, stood cooling on the great blue willow-pattern dish, and Becky's neuralgia abated, perhaps from the mental relief of the spectacle.

When the clock struck twelve, Bloomah was allowed to scamper off to school in the desperate hope of saving the afternoon attendance.

The London sky was of lead, and the London pavement of mud, but her heart was aglow with hope. As she reached the familiar street a certain strangeness in its aspect struck her. People stood at the doors gossiping and excited, as though no Sabbath pots were a-cooking; straggling groups possessed the roadway, impeding her advance, and as she got nearer to the school the crowd thickened, the roadway became impassable, a gesticulating mob blocked the iron gate.

Poor Bloomah paused in her breathless career ready to cry at this malicious fate fighting against her, and for the first time allowing herself time to speculate on what was up. All around her she became aware of weeping and wailing and shrieking and wringing of hands.

The throng was chiefly composed of Russian and Roumanian women of the latest immigration, as she could tell by the pious wigs hiding their tresses. Those in the front were pressed against the bars of the locked gate, shrieking through them, shaking them with passion.

Although Bloomah's knowledge of Yiddish was slight—as became a scion of an old English family—she could make out their elemental ejaculations.

'You murderers!'

'Give me my Rachel!'

'They are destroying our daughters as Pharaoh destroyed our sons.'

'Give me back my children, and I'll go back to Russia.'

'They are worse than the Russians, the poisoners!'

'O God of Abraham, how shall I live without my Leah?'

On the other side of the bars the children—released for the dinner-interval—were clamouring equally, shouting, weeping, trying to get to their mothers. Some howled, with their sleeves rolled up, to exhibit the upper arm.

'See,' the women cried, 'the red marks! Oh, the poisoners!'

A light began to break upon Bloomah's brain. Evidently the School Board had suddenly sent down compulsory vaccinators.

'I won't die,' moaned a plump golden-haired girl. 'I'm too young to die yet.'

'My little lamb is dying!' A woman near Bloomah, with auburn wisps showing under her black wig, wrung her hands. 'I hear her talk—always, always about the red mark. Now they have given it her. She is poisoned—my little apple.'

'Your little carrot is all right,' said Bloomah testily. 'They've only vaccinated her.'

The woman caught at the only word she understood. 'Vaccinate, vaccinate!' she repeated. Then, relapsing into jargon and raising her hands heavenward: 'A sudden death upon them all!'

Bloomah turned despairingly in search of a wigless woman. One stood at her elbow.

'Can't you explain to her that the doctors mean no harm?' Bloomah asked.

'Oh, don't they, indeed? Just you read this!' She flourished a handbill, English on one side, Yiddish on the other.

Bloomah read the English version, not without agitation:

'Mothers, look after your little ones! The School Tyrants are plotting to inject filthy vaccine into their innocent veins. Keep them away rather than let them be poisoned to enrich the doctors.'

There followed statistics to appal even Bloomah. What wonder if the refugees from lands of persecution—lands in which anything might happen—believed they had fallen from the frying-pan into the fire; if the rumour that executioners with instruments had entered the school-buildings had run like wildfire through the quarter, enflaming Oriental imagination to semi-madness.

While Bloomah was reading, a head-shawled woman fainted, and the din and frenzy grew.

'But I was vaccinated when a baby, and I'm all right,' murmured Bloomah, half to reassure herself.

'My arm! I'm poisoned!' And another pupil flew frantically towards the gate.

The women outside replied with a dull roar of rage, and hurled themselves furiously against the lock.

A window on the playground was raised with a sharp snap, and the head-mistress appeared, shouting alternately at the children and the parents; but she was neither heard nor understood, and a Polish crone shook an answering fist.

'You old maid—childless, pitiless!'

Shrill whistles sounded and resounded from every side, and soon a posse of eight policemen were battling with the besiegers, trying to push themselves between them and the gate. A fat and genial officer worked his way past Bloomah, his truncheon ready for action.

'Don't hurt the poor women,' Bloomah pleaded. 'They think their children are being poisoned.'

'I know, missie. What can you do with such greenhorns? Why don't they stop in their own country? I've just been vaccinated myself, and it's no joke to get my arm knocked about like this!'

'Then show them the red marks, and that will quiet them.'

The policeman laughed. A sleeveless policeman! It would destroy all the dignity and prestige of the force.

'Then I'll show them mine,' said Bloomah resolutely. 'Mine are old and not very showy, but perhaps they'll do. Lift me up, please—I mean on your unvaccinated arm.'

Overcome by her earnestness the policeman hoisted her on his burly shoulder. The apparent arrest made a diversion; all eyes turned towards her.

'You Narronim!' (fools), she shrieked, desperately mustering her scraps of Yiddish. 'Your children are safe. Ich bin vaccinated. Look!' She rolled up her sleeve. 'Der policeman ist vaccinated. Look—if I tap him he winces. See!'

'Hold on, missie!' The policeman grimaced.

'The King ist vaccinated,' went on Bloomah, 'and the Queen, and the Prince of Wales, yes, even the Teachers themselves. There are no devils inside there. This paper'—she held up the bill—'is lies and falsehood.' She tore it into fragments.

'No; it is true as the Law of Moses,' retorted a man in the mob.

'As the Law of Moses!' echoed the women hoarsely.

Bloomah had an inspiration. 'The Law of Moses! Pooh! Don't you know this is written by the Meshummodim?'

The crowd looked blank, fell silent. If, indeed, the handbill was written by apostates, what could it hold but Satan's lies?

Bloomah profited by her moment of triumph. 'Go home, you Narronim!' she cried pityingly from her perch. And then, veering round towards the children behind the bars: 'Shut up, you squalling sillies!' she cried. 'As for you, Golda Benjamin, I'm ashamed of you—a girl of your age! Put your sleeve down, cry-baby!'

Bloomah would have carried the day had not her harangue distracted the police from observing another party of rioters—women, assisted by husbands hastily summoned from stall and barrow, who were battering at a side gate. And at this very instant they burst it open, and with a great cry poured into the playground, screaming and searching for their progeny.

The police darted round to the new battlefield, expecting an attack upon doors and windows, and Bloomah was hastily set down in the seething throng and carried with it in the wake of the police, who could not prevent it flooding through the broken side gate.

The large playground became a pandemonium of parents, children, police, and teachers all shouting and gesticulating. But there was no riot. The law could not prevent mothers and fathers from snatching their offspring to their bosoms and making off overjoyed. The children who had not the luck to be kidnapped escaped of themselves, some panic-stricken, some merely mischievous, and in a few minutes the school was empty.

The School Management Committee sat formally to consider this unprecedented episode. It was decided to cancel the attendance for the day. Red marks, black marks—all fell into equality; the very ciphers were reduced to their native nothingness. The school-week was made to end on the Thursday.

Next Monday morning saw Bloomah at her desk, happiest of a radiant sisterhood. On the wall shone the Banner.

THE BEARER OF BURDENS

I

When her Fanny did at last marry, Natalya—as everybody called the old clo'-woman—was not over-pleased at the bargain. Natalya had imagined beforehand that for a matronly daughter of twenty-three, almost past the marrying age, any wedding would be a profitable transaction. But when a husband actually presented himself, all the old dealer's critical maternity was set a-bristle. Henry Elkman, she insisted, had not a true Jewish air. There was in the very cut of his clothes a subtle suggestion of going to the races.

It was futile of Fanny to insist that Henry had never gone to the races, that his duties as bookkeeper of S. Cohn's Clothing Emporium prevented him from going to the races, and that the cut of his clothes was intended to give tone to his own establishment.

'Ah, yes, he does not take thee to the races,' she insisted in Yiddish. 'But all these young men with check suits and flowers in their buttonholes bet and gamble and go to the bad, and their wives and children fall back on their old mothers for support.'

'I shall not fall back on thee,' Fanny retorted angrily.

'And on whom else? A pretty daughter! Would you fall back on a stranger? Or perhaps you are thinking of the Board of Guardians!' And a shudder of humiliation traversed her meagre frame. For at sixty she was already meagre, had already the appearance of the venerable grandmother she was now to become, save that her hair, being only a pious wig, remained rigidly young and black. Life had always gone hard with her. Since her husband's death, when Fanny was a child, she had scraped together a scanty livelihood by selling odds and ends for a mite more than she gave for them. At the back doors of villas she haggled with miserly mistresses, gentlewoman and old-clo' woman linked by their common love of a bargain.

Natalya would sniff contemptuously at the muddle of ancient finery on the floor and spurn it with her foot. 'How can I sell that?' she would inquire. 'Last time I gave you too much—I lost by you.' And having wrung the price down to the lowest penny, she would pay it in clanking silver and copper from a grimy leather bag she wore hidden in her bosom; then, cramming the goods hastily into the maw of her sack, she would stagger joyously away. The men's garments she would modestly sell to a second-hand shop, but the women's she cleaned and turned and transmogrified and sold in Petticoat Lane of a Sunday morning; scavenger, earth-worm, and alchemist, she was a humble agent in the great economic process by which cast-off clothes renew their youth and freshness, and having set in their original sphere rise endlessly on other social horizons.

Of English she had, when she began, only enough to bargain with; but in one year of forced intercourse with English folk after her husband's death she learnt more than in her quarter of a century of residence in the Spitalfields Ghetto.

Fanny's function had been to keep house and prepare the evening meal, but the old clo'-woman's objection to her marriage was not selfish. She was quite ready to light her own fire and broil her own bloater after the day's tramp. Fanny had, indeed, offered to have her live in the elegant two-roomed cottage near King's Cross which Henry was furnishing. She could sleep in a convertible bureau in the parlour. But the old woman's independent spirit and her mistrust of her son-in-law made her prefer the humble Ghetto garret. Against all reasoning, she continued to feel something antipathetic in Henry's clothes and even in his occupation—perhaps it was really the subconscious antagonism of the old clo' and the new, subtly symbolic of the old generation and the smart new world springing up to tread it down. Henry himself was secretly pleased at her refusal. In the first ardours of courtship he had consented to swallow even the Polish crone who had strangely mothered his buxom British Fanny, but for his own part he had a responsive horror of old clo'; felt himself of the great English world of fashion and taste, intimately linked with the burly Britons whose girths he recorded from his high stool at his glass-environed desk, and in touch even with the lion comique, the details of whose cheap but stylish evening dress he entered with a proud flourish.

II

The years went by, and it looked as if the old woman's instinct were awry. Henry did not go to the races, nor did Fanny have to fall back on her mother-in-law for the maintenance of herself and her two children, Becky and Joseph. On the contrary, she doubled her position in the social scale by taking a four-roomed house in the Holloway Road. Its proximity to the Clothing Emporium enabled Henry to come home for lunch. But, alas! Fanny was not allowed many years of enjoyment of these grandeurs and comforts. The one-roomed grave took her, leaving the four-roomed house incredibly large and empty. Even Natalya's Ghetto garret, which Fanny had not shared for seven years, seemed cold and vacant to the poor mother. A new loneliness fell upon her, not mitigated by ever rarer visits to her grandchildren. Devoid of the link of her daughter, the house seemed immeasurably aloof from her in the social scale. Henry was frigid and the little ones went with marked reluctance to this stern, forbidding old woman who questioned them as to their prayers and smelt of red-herrings. She ceased to go to the house.

And then at last all her smouldering distrust of Henry Elkman found overwhelming justification.

Before the year of mourning was up, before he was entitled to cease saying the Kaddish (funeral hymn) for her darling Fanny, the wretch, she heard, was married again. And married—villainy upon villainy, horror upon horror—to a Christian girl, a heathen abomination. Natalya was wrestling with her over-full sack when she got the news from a gossiping lady client, and she was boring holes for the passage of string to tie up its mouth. She turned the knife viciously, as if it were in Henry Elkman's heart.

She did not know the details of the piquant, tender courtship between him and the pretty assistant at the great drapery store that neighboured the Holloway Clothing Emporium, any more than she understood the gradual process which had sapped Henry's instinct of racial isolation, or how he had passed from admiration of British ways into entire abandonment of Jewish. She was spared, too, the knowledge that latterly her own Fanny had slid with him into the facile paths of impiety; that they had ridden for a breath of country air on Sabbath afternoons. They had been considerate enough to hide that from her. To the old clo'-woman's crude mind, Henry Elkman existed as a monster of ready-made wickedness, and she believed even that he had been married in church and baptized, despite that her informant tried to console her with the assurance that the knot had been tied in a Registrar's office.

'May he be cursed with the boils of Pharaoh!' she cried in her picturesque jargon. 'May his fine clothes fall from his flesh and his flesh from his bones! May my Fanny's outraged soul plead against him at the Judgment Bar! And she—this heathen female—may her death be sudden!' And she drew the ends of the string tightly together, as though round the female's neck.

'Hush, you old witch!' cried the gossip, revolted; 'and what would become of your own grandchildren?'

'They cannot be worse off than they are now, with a heathen in the house. All their Judaism will become corrupted. She may even baptize them. Oh, Father in Heaven!'

The thought weighed upon her. She pictured the innocent Becky and Joseph kissing crucifixes. At the best there would be no kosher food in the house any more. How could this stranger understand the mysteries of purging meat, of separating meat-plates from butter-plates?

At last she could bear the weight no longer. She took the Elkman house in her rounds, and, bent under her sack, knocked at the familiar door. It was lunch-time, and unfamiliar culinary smells seemed wafted along the passage. Her morbid imagination scented bacon. The orthodox amulet on the doorpost did not comfort her; it had been left there, forgotten, a mute symbol of the Jewish past.

A pleasant young woman with blue eyes and fresh-coloured cheeks opened the door.

The blood surged to Natalya's eyes, so that she could hardly see.

'Old clo',' she said mechanically.

'No, thank you,' replied the young woman. Her voice was sweet, but it sounded to Natalya like the voice of Lilith, stealer of new-born children. Her rosy cheek seemed smeared with seductive paint. In the background glistened the dual crockery of the erst pious kitchen which the new-comer profaned. And between Natalya and it, between Natalya and her grandchildren, this alien girlish figure seemed to stand barrier-wise. She could not cross the threshold without explanations.

'Is Mr. Elkman at home?' she asked.

'You know the name!' said the young woman, a little surprised.

'Yes, I have been here a good deal.' The old woman's sardonic accent was lost on the listener.

'I am sorry there is nothing this time,' she replied.

'Not even a pair of old shoes?'

'No.'

'But the dead woman's—? Are you, then, standing in them?'

The words were so fierce and unexpected, the crone's eyes blazed so weirdly, that the new wife recoiled with a little shriek.

'Henry!' she cried.

Fork in hand, he darted in from the living-room, but came to a sudden standstill.

'What do you want here?' he muttered.

'Fanny's shoes!' she cried.

'Who is it?' his wife's eyes demanded.

'A half-witted creature we deal with out of charity,' he gestured back. And he put her inside the room-door, whispering, 'Let me get rid of her.'

'So, that's your painted poppet,' hissed his mother-in-law in Yiddish.

'Painted?' he said angrily. 'Madge painted? She's just as natural as a rosy apple. She's a country girl, and her mother was a lady.'

'Her mother? Perhaps! But she? You see a glossy high hat marked sixteen and sixpence, and you think it's new. But I know what it's come from—a battered thing that has rolled in the gutter. Ah, how she could have bewitched you, when there are so many honest Jewesses without husbands!'

'I am sorry she doesn't please you; but, after all, it's my business, and not yours.'

'Not mine? After I gave you my Fanny, and she slaved for you and bore you children?'

'It's just for her children that I had to marry.'

'What? You had to marry a Christian for the sake of Fanny's children? Oh, God forgive you!'

'We are not in Poland now,' he said sulkily.

'Ah, I always said you were a sinner in Israel. My Fanny has been taken for your sins. A black death on your bones.'

'If you don't leave off cursing, I shall call a policeman.'

'Oh, lock me up, lock me up—instead of your shame. Let the whole world know that.'

'Go away, then. You have no right to come here and frighten Madge—my wife. She is in delicate health, as it is.'

'May she be an atonement for all of us! I have the right to come here as much as I please.'

'You have no right.'

'I have a right to the children. My blood is in their veins.'

'You have no right. The children are their father's.'

'Yes, their Father's in heaven,' and she raised her hand like an ancient prophetess, while the other supported her bag over her shoulder. 'The children are the children of Israel, and they must carry forward the yoke of the Law.'

'And what do you propose?' he said, with a scornful sniff.

'Give me the children. I will elevate them in the fear of the Lord. You go your own godless way, free of burdens—you and your Christian poppet. You no longer belong to us. Give me the children, and I'll go away.'

He looked at her quizzingly. 'You have been drinking, my good mother-in-law.'

'Ay, the waters of affliction. Give me the children.'

'But they won't go with you. They love their step-mother.'

'Love that painted jade? They, with Jewish blood warm in their veins, with the memory of their mother warm in their hearts? Impossible!'

He opened the door gently. 'Becky! Joe! No, don't you come, Madge, darling. It's all right. The old lady wants to say "Good-day" to the children.'

The two children tripped into the passage, with napkins tied round their chins, their mouths greasy, but the rest of their persons unfamiliarly speckless and tidy. They stood still at the sight of their grandmother, so stern and frowning. Henry shut the door carefully.

'My lambs!' Natalya cried, in her sweetest but harsh tones, 'Won't you come and kiss me?'

Becky, a mature person of seven, advanced courageously and surrendered her cheek to her grandmother.

'How are you, granny?' she said ceremoniously.

'And Joseph?' said Natalya, not replying. 'My heart and my crown, will he not come?'

The four-and-a-half year old Joseph stood dubiously, with his fist in his mouth.

'Bring him to me, Becky. Tell him I want you and him to come and live with me.'

Becky shrugged her precocious shoulders. 'He may. I won't,' she said laconically.

'Oh, Becky!' said the grandmother. 'Do you want to stay here and torture your poor mother?'

Becky stared. 'She's dead,' she said.

'Yes, but her soul lives and watches over you. Come, Joseph, apple of my eye, come with me.'

She beckoned enticingly, but the little boy, imagining the invitation was to enter her bag and be literally carried away therein, set up a terrific howl. Thereupon the pretty young woman emerged hastily, and the child, with a great sob of love and confidence, ran to her and nestled in her arms.

'Mamma, mamma,' he cried.

Henry looked at the old woman with a triumphant smile.

Natalya went hot and cold. It was not only that little Joseph had gone to this creature. It was not even that he had accepted her maternity. It was this word 'mamma' that stung. The word summed up all the blasphemous foreignness of the new domesticity. 'Mamma' was redolent of cold Christian houses in whose doorways the old clo'-woman sometimes heard it. Fanny had been 'mother'—the dear, homely, Jewish 'mother.' This 'mamma,' taught to the orphans, was like the haughty parade of Christian elegance across her grave.

'When mamma's shoes are to be sold, don't forget me,' Natalya hissed. 'I'll give you the best price in the market.'

Henry shuddered, but replied, half pushing her outside: 'Certainly, certainly. Good-afternoon.'

'I'll buy them at your own price—ah, I see them coming, coming into my bag.'

The door closed on her grotesque sibylline intensity, and Henry clasped his wife tremblingly to his bosom and pressed a long kiss upon her fragrant cherry lips.

Later on he explained that the crazy old clo'-woman was known to the children, as to everyone in the neighbourhood, as 'Granny.'

III

In the bearing of her first child the second Mrs. Elkman died. The rosy face became a white angelic mask, the dainty figure lay in statuesque severity, and a screaming, bald-headed atom of humanity was the compensation for this silence. Henry Elkman was overwhelmed by grief and superstition.

'For three things women die in childbirth,' kept humming in his brain from his ancient Hebrew lore. He did not remember what they were, except that one was the omission of the wife to throw into the fire the lump of dough from the Sabbath bread. But these neglects could not be visited on a Christian, he thought dully. The only distraction of his grief was the infant's pressing demand on his attention.

It was some days before the news penetrated to the old woman.

'It is his punishment,' she said with solemn satisfaction. 'Now my Fanny's spirit will rest.'

But she did not gloat over the decree of the God of Israel as she had imagined beforehand, nor did she call for the dead woman's old clo'. She was simply content—an unrighteous universe had been set straight again like a mended watch. But she did call, without her bag, to inquire if she could be of service in this tragic crisis.

'Out of my sight, you and your evil eye!' cried Henry as he banged the door in her face.

Natalya burst into tears, torn by a chaos of emotions. So she was still to be shut out.

IV

The next news that leaked into Natalya's wizened ear was as startling as Madge's death. Henry had married again. Doubtless with the same pretext of the children's needs he had taken unto himself a third wife, and again without the decencies of adequate delay. And this wife was a Jewess, as of yore. Henry had reverted matrimonially to the fold. Was it conscience, was it terror? Nobody knew. But everybody knew that the third Mrs. Elkman was a bouncing beauty of a good orthodox stock, that she brought with her fifty pounds in cash, besides bedding and house-linen accumulated by her parents without prevision that she would marry an old hand, already provided with these household elements.

The old clo'-woman's emotions were more mingled than ever. She felt vaguely that the Jewish minister should not so unquestioningly have accorded the scamp the privileges of the hymeneal canopy. Some lustral rite seemed necessary to purify him of his Christian conjunction. And the memory of Fanny was still outraged by this burying of her, so to speak, under layers of successive wives. On the other hand, the children would revert to Judaism, and they would have a Jewish mother, not a mamma, to care for them and to love them. The thought consoled her for being shut out of their lives, as she felt she must have been, even had Henry been friendlier. This third wife had alienated her from the household, had made her kinship practically remote. She had sunk to a sort of third cousin, or a mother-in-law twice removed.

The days went on, and again the Elkman household occupied the gossips, and news of it—second-hand, like everything that came to her—was picked up by Natalya on her rounds. Henry's third wife was, it transpired, a melancholy failure. Her temper was frightful, she beat her step-children, and—worst and rarest sin in the Jewish housewife—she drank. Henry was said to be in despair.

'Nebbich, the poor little children!' cried Natalya, horrified. Her brain began plotting how to interfere, but she could find no way.

The weeks passed, with gathering rumours of the iniquities of the third Mrs. Elkman, and then at last came the thunder-clap—Henry had disappeared without leaving a trace. The wicked wife and the innocent brats had the four-roomed home to themselves. The Clothing Emporium knew him no more. Some whispered suicide, others America. Benjamin Beckenstein, the cutter of the Emporium, who favoured the latter hypothesis reported a significant saying: 'I have lived with two angels; I can't live with a demon.'

'Ah, at last he sees my Fanny was an angel,' said Natalya, neglecting to draw the deduction anent America, and passing over the other angel. And she embroidered the theme. How indeed could a man who had known the blessing of a sober, God-fearing wife endure a drunkard and a child-beater? 'No wonder he killed himself!'

The gossips pointed out that the saying implied flight rather than suicide.

'You are right!' Natalya admitted illogically. 'Just what a coward and blackguard like that would do—leave the children at the mercy of the woman he couldn't face himself. How in Heaven's name will they live?'

'Oh, her father, the furrier, will have to look after them,' the gossips assured her. 'He gave her good money, you know, fifty pounds and the bedding. Ah, trust Elkman for that. He knew he wasn't leaving the children to starve.'

'I don't know so much,' said the old woman, shaking her bewigged head.

What was to be done? Suppose the furrier refused the burden. But Henry's flight, she felt, had removed her even farther from the Elkman household. If she went to spy out the land, she would now have to face the virago in possession. But no! on second thoughts it was this other woman whom Henry's flight had changed to a stranger. What had the wretch to do with the children? She was a mere intruder in the house. Out with her, or at least out with the children.

Yes, she would go boldly there and demand them. 'Poor Becky! Poor Joseph!' her heart wailed. 'You to be beaten and neglected after having known the love of a mother.' True, it would not be easy to support them. But a little more haggling, a little more tramping, a little more mending, and a little less gorging and gormandising! They would be at school during the day, so would not interfere with her rounds, and in the evening she could have them with her as she sat refurbishing the purchases of the day. Ah, what a blessed release from the burden of loneliness, heavier than the heaviest sack! It was well worth the price. And then at bedtime she would say the Hebrew night-prayer with them and tuck them up, just as she had once done with her Fanny.

But how if the woman refused to yield them up—as Natalya could fancy her refusing—out of sheer temper and devilry? What if, amply subsidized by her well-to-do parent, she wished to keep the little ones by her and revenge upon them their father's desertion, or hold them hostages for his return? Why, then, Natalya would use cunning—ay, and force, too—she would even kidnap them. Once in their grandmother's hands, the law would see to it that they did not go back to this stranger, this bibulous brute, whose rights over them were nil.

It was while buying up on a Sunday afternoon the sloughed vestments of a Jewish family in Holloway that her resolve came to a head. A cab would be necessary to carry her goods to her distant garret. What an opportunity for carrying off the children at the same time! The house was actually on her homeward route. The economy of it tickled her, made her overestimate the chances of capture. As she packed the motley, far-spreading heap into the symmetry of her sack, pressing and squeezing the clothes incredibly tighter and tighter till it seemed a magic sack that could swallow up even the Holloway Clothing Emporium, Natalya's brain revolved feverish fancy-pictures of the coming adventure.

Leaving the bag in the basement passage, she ran to fetch a cab. Usually the hiring of the vehicle occupied Natalya half an hour. She would harangue the Christian cabmen on the rank, pleading her poverty, and begging to be conveyed with her goods for a ridiculous sum. At first none of them would take notice of the old Jewish crone, but would read their papers in contemptuous indifference. But gradually, as they remained idly on the rank, the endless stream of persuasion would begin to percolate, and at last one would relent, half out of pity, and would end by bearing the sack gratuitously on his shoulder from the house to his cab. Often there were two sacks, quite filling the interior of a four-wheeler, and then Natalya would ride triumphantly beside her cabby on the box, the two already the best of friends. Things went ill if Natalya did not end by trading off something in the sacks against the fare—at a new profit.

But to-day she was too excited to strike more than a mediocre bargain. The cumbrous sack was hoisted into the cab. Natalya sprang in beside it, and in a resolute voice bade the driver draw up for a moment at the Elkman home.

V

The unwonted phenomenon of a cab brought Becky to the door ere her grandmother could jump out. She was still under ten, but prematurely developed in body as in mind. There was something unintentionally insolent in her precocity, in her habitual treatment of adults as equals; but now her face changed almost to a child's, and with a glad tearful cry of 'Oh, grandmother!' she sprang into the old woman's arms.

It was the compensation for little Joseph's 'mamma.' Tears ran down the old woman's cheeks as she hugged the strayed lamb to her breast.

A petulant infantile wail came from within, but neither noted it.

'Where is your step-mother, my poor angel?' Natalya asked in a half whisper.

Becky's forehead gloomed in an ugly frown. Her face became a woman's again. 'One o'clock the public-houses open on Sundays,' she snorted.

'Oh, my God!' cried Natalya, forgetting that the circumstance was favouring her project. 'A Jewish woman! You don't mean to say that she drinks in public-houses?'

'You don't suppose I would let her drink here,' said Becky. 'We have nice scenes, I can tell you. The only consolation is she's better-tempered when she's quite drunk.'

The infant's wail rang out more clamorously.

'Hush, you little beast!' Becky ejaculated, but she moved mechanically within, and her grandmother followed her.

All the ancient grandeur of the sitting-room seemed overclouded with shabbiness and untidiness. To Natalya everything looked and smelt like the things in her bag. And there in a stuffy cradle a baby wrinkled its red face with shrieking.

Becky had bent over it, and was soothing it ere its existence penetrated at all to the old woman's preoccupied brain. Its pipings had been like an unheeded wail of wind round some centre of tragic experience. Even when she realized the child's existence her brain groped for some seconds in search of its identity.

Ah, the baby whose birth had cost that painted poppet's life! So it still lived and howled in unwelcome reminder and perpetuation of that brief but shameful episode. 'Grow dumb like your mother,' she murmured resentfully. What a bequest of misery Henry Elkman had left behind him! Ah, how right she had been to suspect him from the very first!

'But where is my little Joseph?' she said aloud.

'He's playing somewhere in the street.'

'Ach, mein Gott! Playing, when he ought to be weeping like this child of shame. Go and fetch him at once!'

'What do you want him for?'

'I am going to take you both away—out of this misery. You'd like to come and live with me—eh, my lamb?'

'Rather—anything's better than this.'

Natalya caught her to her breast again.

'Go and fetch my Joseph! But quick, quick, before the public-house woman comes back!'

Becky flew out, and Natalya sank into a chair, breathless with emotion and fatigue. The baby in the cradle beside her howled more vigorously, and automatically her foot sought the rocker, and she heard herself singing:

'Sleep, little baby, sleep, Thy father shall be a Rabbi; Thy mother shall bring thee almonds; Blessings on thy little head.'

As the howling diminished, she realized with a shock that she was rocking this misbegotten infant—nay, singing to it a Jewish cradle-song full of inappropriate phrases. She withdrew her foot as though the rocker had grown suddenly red-hot. The yells broke out with fresh vehemence, and she angrily restored her foot to its old place. 'Nu, nu,' she cried, rocking violently, 'go to sleep.'

She stole a glance at it, when it grew stiller, and saw that the teat of its feeding-bottle was out of its mouth. 'There, there—suck!' she said, readjusting it. The baby opened its eyes and shot a smile at her, a wonderful, trustful smile from great blue eyes. Natalya trembled; those were the blue eyes that had supplanted the memory of Fanny's dark orbs, and the lips now sucking contentedly were the cherry lips of the painted poppet.

'Nebbich; the poor, deserted little orphan,' she apologized to herself. 'And this is how the new Jewish wife does her duty to her step-children. She might as well have been a Christian.' Then a remembrance that the Christian woman had seemingly been an unimpeachable step-mother confused her thoughts further. And while she was groping among them Becky returned, haling in Joseph, who in his turn haled in a kite with a long tail.

The boy, now a sturdy lad of seven, did not palpitate towards his grandmother with Becky's eagerness. Probably he felt the domestic position less. But he surrendered himself to her long hug. 'Did she beat him,' she murmured soothingly, 'beat my own little Joseph?'

'Don't waste time, granny,' Becky broke in petulantly, 'if we are going.'

'No, my dear. We'll go at once.' And, releasing the boy, Natalya partly undid the lower buttons of his waistcoat.

'You wear no four-corner fringes!' she exclaimed tragically. 'She neglects even to see to that. Ah, it will be a good deed to carry you from this godless home.'

'But I don't want to go with you,' he said sullenly, reminded of past inquisitorial worryings about prayers.

'You little fool!' said Becky. 'You are going—and in that cab.'

'In that cab?' he cried joyfully.

'Yes, my apple. And you will never be beaten again.'

'Oh, she don't hurt!' he said contemptuously. 'She hasn't even got a cane—like at school.'

'But shan't we take our things?' said Becky.

'No, only the things you stand in. They shan't have any excuse for taking you back. I'll find you plenty of clothes, as good as new.'

'And little Daisy?'

'Oh, is it a girl? Your stepmother will look after that. She can't complain of one burden.'

She hustled the children into the cab, where, with the sack and herself, they made a tightly-packed quartette.

'I say, I didn't bargain for extras inside,' grumbled the cabman.

'You can't reckon these children,' said Natalya, with confused legal recollections; 'they're both under seven.'

The cabman started. Becky stared out of the window. 'I wonder if we'll pass Mrs. Elkman,' she said, amused. Joseph busied himself with disentangling the tails of his kite.

But Natalya was too absorbed to notice their indifference to her. That poor little Daisy! The image of the baby swam vividly before her. What a terrible fate to be left in the hands of the public-house woman! Who knew what would happen to it? What if, in her drunken fury at the absence of Becky and Joseph, she did it a mischief? At the best the besotted creature would not take cordially to the task of bringing it up. It was no child of hers—had not even the appeal of pure Jewish blood. And there it lay, smiling, with its beautiful blue eyes. It had smiled trustfully on herself, not knowing she was to leave it to its fate. And now it was crying; she heard it crying above the rattle of the cab. But how could she charge herself with it—she, with her daily rounds to make? The other children were grown up, passed the day at school. No, it was impossible. And the child's cry went on in her imagination louder and louder.

She put her head out of the window. 'Turn back! Turn back! I've forgotten something.'

The cabman swore. 'D'ye think you've taken me by the week?'

'Threepence extra. Drive back.'

The cab turned round, the innocent horse got a stinging flip of the whip, and set off briskly.

'What have you forgotten, grandmother?' said Becky. 'It's very careless of you.'

The cab stopped at the door. Natalya looked round nervously, sprang out, and then uttered a cry of despair.

'Ach, we shut the door!' And the inaccessible baby took on a tenfold desirability.

'It's all right,' said Becky. 'Just turn the handle.'

Natalya obeyed and ran in. There was the baby, not crying, but sleeping peacefully. Natalya snatched it up frenziedly, and hurried the fresh-squalling bundle into the cab.

'Taking Daisy?' cried Becky. 'But she isn't yours!'

Natalya shut the cab-door with a silencing bang, and the vehicle turned again Ghettowards.

VI

The fact that Natalya had taken possession of the children could not be kept a secret, but the step-mother's family made no effort to regain them, and, indeed, the woman herself shortly went the way of all Henry Elkman's wives, though whether she, like the rest, had a successor, is unknown.

The sudden change from a lone old lady to a mater-familias was not, however, so charming as Natalya had imagined. The cost of putting Daisy out to nurse was a terrible tax, but this was nothing compared to the tax on her temper levied by her legitimate grandchildren, who began to grumble on the first night at the poverty and pokiness of the garret, and were thenceforward never without a lament for the good old times. They had, indeed, been thoroughly spoilt by the father and the irregular ménage. The Christian wife's influence had been refining but too temporary. It had been only long enough to wean Joseph from the religious burdens indoctrinated by Fanny, and thus to add to the grandmother's difficulties in coaxing him back to the yoke of piety.

The only sweet in Natalya's cup turned out to be the love of little Daisy, who grew ever more beautiful, gracious, and winning.

Natalya had never known so lovable a child. All Daisy did seemed to her perfect. For instant obedience and instant comprehension she declared her matchless.

One day, when Daisy was three, the child told the grandmother that in her momentary absence Becky had pulled Joseph's hair.

'Hush! You mustn't tell tales,' Natalya said reprovingly.

'Becky did not pull Joey's hair,' Daisy corrected herself instantly.

Much to the disgust of Becky, who wished to outgrow the Ghetto, even while she unconsciously manifested its worst heritages, Daisy picked up the Yiddish words and phrases, which, in spite of Becky's remonstrances, Natalya was too old to give up. This was not the only subject of dispute between Becky and the grandmother, whom she roundly accused of favouritism of Daisy, and she had not reached fifteen when, with an independence otherwise praiseworthy, she set up for herself on her earnings in the fur establishment of her second step-mother's father, lodging with a family who, she said, bored her less than her grandmother.

In another year or so, freed from the compulsory education of the School Board, Joseph joined her. And thus, by the unforeseen turns of Fortune's wheel, the old-clo' woman of seventy-five was left alone with the child of seven.

But this child was compensation for all she had undergone, for all the years of trudging and grubbing and patching and turning. Daisy threaded her needle for her at night when her keen eyes began to fail, and while she made the old clo' into new, Daisy read aloud her English story-books. Natalya took an absorbing interest in these nursery tales, heard for the first time in her second childhood. 'Jack the Giant-killer,' 'Aladdin,' 'Cinderella,' they were all delightful novelties. The favourite story of both was 'Little Red Riding-Hood,' with its refrain of 'Grandmother, what large eyes you've got!' That could be said with pointed fun; it seemed to be written especially for them. Often Daisy would look up suddenly and say: 'Grandmother, what a large mouth you've got!' 'All the better to bite you with,' grandmother would reply. And then there would be hugs and kisses.

But Friday night was the great night, the one night of the week on which Natalya could be stopped from working. Only religion was strong enough to achieve that. The two Sabbath candles in the copper candlesticks stood on the white tablecloth, and were lighted as soon as the welcome dusk announced the advent of the holy day, and they shed their pious illumination on her dish of fish and the ritually-twisted loaves. And after supper Natalya would sing the Hebrew grace at much leisurely length and with great unction. Then she would tell stories of her youth in Poland—comic tales mixed with tales of oppression and the memories of ancient wrong. And Daisy would weep and laugh and thrill. The fusion of races had indeed made her sensitive and intelligent beyond the common, and Natalya was not unjustified in planning out for her some illustrious future.

But after eighteen months of this delightful life Natalya's wonderful vitality began slowly to collapse. She earned less and less, and, amid her gratitude to God for having relieved her of the burden of Becky and Joseph, a secret fear entered her heart. Would she be taken away before Daisy became self-supporting? Nay, would she even be able to endure the burden till the end? What made things worse was that, owing to the increase of immigrants, her landlord now exacted an extra shilling a week for rent. When Daisy was asleep the old woman hung over the bed, praying for life, for strength.

It was a sultry summer, making the trudge from door to door, under the ever-swelling sack, almost intolerable. And a little thing occurred to bring home cruelly to Natalya the decline of all her resources, physical and financial. The children's country holiday was in the air at Daisy's Board School, throwing an aroma and a magic light over the droning class-room. Daisy was to go, was to have a fortnight with a cottager in Kent; but towards the expenses the child's parent or guardian was expected to contribute four shillings. Daisy might have gone free had she pleaded absolute poverty, but that would have meant investigation. From such humiliation Natalya shrank. She shrank even more from frightening the poor child by uncovering the skeleton of poverty. Most of all she shrank from depriving Daisy of all the rural delights on which the child's mind dwelt in fascinated anticipation. Natalya did not think much of the country herself, having been born in a poor Polish village, amid huts and pigs, but she would not disillusion Daisy.

By miles of extra trudging in the heat, and miracles of bargaining with bewildered housewives, Natalya raised the four shillings, and the unconscious Daisy glided off in the happy, noisy train, while on the platform Natalya waved her coloured handkerchief wet with tears.

That first night without the little sunshiny presence was terrible for the old-clo' woman. The last prop against decay and collapse seemed removed. But the next day a joyous postcard came from Daisy, which the greengrocer downstairs read to Natalya, and she was able to take up her sack again and go forth into the sweltering streets.

In the second week the child wrote a letter, saying that she had found a particular friend in an old lady, very kind and rich, who took her for drives in a chaise, and asked her many questions. This old lady seemed to have taken a fancy to her from the moment she saw her playing outside the cottage.

'Perhaps God has sent her to look after the child when I am gone,' thought Natalya, for the task of going down and up the stairs to get this letter read made her feel as if she would never go up and down them again.

Beaten at last, she took to her bed. Her next-room neighbour, the cobbler's wife, tended her and sent for the 'penny doctor.' But she would not have word written to Daisy or her holiday cut short. On the day Daisy was to come back she insisted, despite all advice and warning, in being up and dressed. She sent everybody away, and lay on her bed till she heard Daisy's footsteps, then she started to her feet, and drew herself up in pretentious good health. But the sound of other footsteps, and the entry of a spectacled, silver-haired old gentlewoman with the child, spoilt her intended hug. Daisy's new friend had passed from her memory, and she stared pathetically at the strange lady and the sunburnt child.

'Oh, grandmother, what great eyes you've got!' And Daisy ran laughingly towards her.

The usual repartee was wanting.

'And the room is not tidied up,' Natalya said reproachfully, and began dusting a chair for the visitor. But the old lady waved it aside.

'I have come to thank you for all you have done for my grandchild.'

'Your grandchild?' Natalya fell back on the bed.

'Yes. I have had inquiries made—it is quite certain. Daisy was even called after me. I am glad of that, at least.' Her voice faltered.

Natalya sat as bolt upright as years of bending under sacks would allow.

'And you have come to take her from me!' she shrieked.

Already Daisy's new ruddiness seemed to her the sign of life that belonged elsewhere.

'No, no, do not be alarmed. I have suffered enough from my selfishness. It was my bad temper drove my daughter from me.' She bowed her silver head till her form seemed as bent as Natalya's. 'What can I do to repair—to atone? Will you not come and live with me in the country, and let me care for you? I am not rich, but I can offer you every comfort.'

Natalya shook her head. 'I am a Jewess. I could not eat with you.'

'That's just what I told her, grandmother,' added Daisy eagerly.

'Then the child must remain with you at my expense,' said the old lady.

'But if she likes the country so—' murmured Natalya.

'I like you better, grandmother.' And Daisy laid her ruddied cheek to the withered cheek, which grew wet with ecstasy.

'She calls you "grandmother," not me,' said the old gentlewoman with a sob.

'Yes, and I wished her mother dead. God forgive me!'

Natalya burst into a passion of tears and rocked to and fro, holding Daisy tightly to her faintly pulsing heart.

'What did you say?' Daisy's grandmother flamed and blazed with her ancient anger. 'You wished my Madge dead?'

Natalya nodded her head. Her arms unloosed their hold of Daisy. 'Dead, dead, dead,' she repeated in a strange, crooning voice. Gradually a vacant look crept over her face, and she fell back again on the bed. She looked suddenly very old, despite her glossy black wig.

'She is ill!' Daisy shrieked.

The cobbler's wife ran in and helped to put her back between the sheets, and described volubly her obstinacy in leaving her bed. Natalya lived till near noon of the next day, and Daisy's real grandmother was with her still at the end, side by side with the Jewish death-watcher.

About eleven in the morning Natalya said: 'Light the candles, Daisy, the Sabbath is coming in.' Daisy spread a white tablecloth on the old wooden table, placed the copper candlesticks upon it, drew it to the bedside, and lighted the candles. They burned with curious unreality in the full August sunshine.

A holy peace overspread the old-clo' woman's face. Her dried-up lips mumbled the Hebrew prayer, welcoming the Sabbath eve. Gradually they grew rigid in death.

'Daisy,' said her grandmother, 'say the text I taught you.'

'"Come unto Me, all ye that labour and are heavy laden,"' sobbed the child obediently, '"and I will give you rest."'

THE LUFTMENSCH

I

Leopold Barstein, the sculptor, was sitting in his lonesome studio, brooding blackly over his dead illusions, when the postman brought him a letter in a large, straggling, unknown hand. It began 'Angel of God!'

He laughed bitterly. 'Just when I am at my most diabolical!' He did not at first read the letter, divining in it one of the many begging-letters which were the aftermath of his East-End Zionist period. But he turned over the page to see the name of the Orientally effusive scribe. It was 'Nehemiah Silvermann, Dentist and Restaurateur.' His laughter changed to a more genial note; his sense of humour was still saving. The figure of the restaurateur-dentist sprang to his imagination in marble on a pedestal. In one hand the figure held a cornucopia, in the other a pair of pincers. He read the letter.

'3A, THE MINORIES, E.

'ANGEL OF GOD,

'I have the honour now to ask Your very kind humane merciful cordial nobility to assist me by Your clement philanthropical liberal relief in my very hard troublesome sorrows and worries, on which I suffer violently. I lost all my fortune, and I am ruined by Russia. I am here at present without means and dental practice, and my restaurant is impeded with lack of a few frivolous pounds. I do not know really what to do in my actual very disgraceful mischief. I heard the people saying Your propitious magnanimous beneficent charities are everywhere exceedingly well renowned and considerably gracious. Thus I solicit and supplicate Your good very kind genteel clement humanity by my very humble quite instant request to support me by Your merciful aid, and please to respond me as soon as possible according to Your generous very philanthropy in my urgent extreme immense difficulty.

'Your obedient servant respectfully,
'NEHEMIAH SILVERMANN,
'Dentist and Restaurateur.'

Such a flood of language carried away the last remnants of Barstein's melancholia; he saw his imagined statue showering adjectives from its cornucopia. 'It is the cry of a dictionary in distress!' he murmured, re-reading the letter with unction.

It pleased his humour to reply in the baldest language. He asked for details of Silvermann's circumstances and sorrows. Had he applied to the Russo-Jewish Fund, which existed to help such refugees from persecution? Did he know Jacobs, the dentist of the neighbouring Mansel Place?

Jacobs had been one of Barstein's fellow-councillors in Zionism, a pragmatic inexhaustible debater in the small back room, and the voluble little man now loomed suddenly large as a possible authority upon his brother-dentist.

By return of post a second eruption descended upon the studio from the 'dictionary in distress.'

'3A, THE MINORIES, E.

'MOST HONOURABLE AND ANGELICAL MR. LEOPOLD BARSTEIN,

'I have the honour now to thank You for Your kind answer of my letter. I did not succeed here by my vital experience in the last of ten years. I got my livelihood a certain time by my dental practice so long there was not a hard violent competition, then I had never any efficacious relief, protection, then I have no relation, then we and the time are changeable too, then without money is impossible to perform any matter, if I had at present in my grieved desperate position £4 for my restaurant, then I were rescued. I do not earn anything, and I must despond at last, I perish here, in Russia I was ruined, please to aid me in Your merciful humanity by something, if I had £15 I could start off from here to go somewhere to look for my daily bread, and if I had £30 so I shall go to Jerusalem because I am convinced by my bitter and sour troubles and shocking tribulations here is nothing to do any more for me. I have not been in the Russo-Jewish fund and do not know it where it is, and if it is in the Jewish shelter of Leman Street so I have no protection, no introduction, no recommendation for it. Poverty has very seldom a few clement humane good people and little friends. The people say Jacobs the dentist of Mansel Place is not a good man, and so it is I tried it for he makes the impossible competition. I ask Your good genteel cordial nobility according to the universal good reputation of Your gracious goodness to reply me quick by some help now.

'Your obedient Servant respectfully,
'NEHEMIAH SILVERMANN,
'Dentist and Restaurateur.'

This letter threw a new but not reassuring light upon the situation. Instead of being a victim of the Russian troubles, a recent refugee from massacre and robbery, Nehemiah had already existed in London for ten years, and although he might originally have been ruined by Russia, he had survived his ruin by a decade. His ideas of his future seemed as hazy as his past. Four pounds would be a very present help; he could continue his London career. With fifteen pounds he was ready to start off anywhither. With thirty pounds he would end all his troubles in Jerusalem. Such nebulousness appeared to necessitate a personal visit, and the next day, finding himself in bad form, Barstein angrily bashed in a clay visage, clapped on his hat, and repaired to the Minories. But he looked in vain for either a dentist or a restaurant at No. 3A. It appeared a humble corner residence, trying to edge itself into the important street. At last, after wandering uncertainly up and down, he knocked at the shabby door. A frowsy woman with long earrings opened it staring, and said that the Silvermanns occupied two rooms on her second floor.

'What!' cried Barstein. 'Is he married?'

'I should hope so,' replied the landlady severely. 'He has eleven children at least.'

Barstein mounted the narrow carpetless stairs, and was received by Mrs. Silvermann and her brood with much consternation and ceremony. The family filled the whole front room and overflowed into the back, which appeared to be a sort of kitchen, for Mrs. Silvermann had rushed thence with tucked-up sleeves, and sounds of frying still proceeded from it. But Mr. Silvermann was not at home, the small, faded, bewigged creature told him apologetically. Barstein looked curiously round the room, half expecting indications of dentistry or dining. But he saw only a minimum of broken-down furniture, bottomless cane chairs, a wooden table and a cracked mirror, a hanging shelf heaped with ragged books, and a standing cupboard which obviously turned into a bedstead at night for half the family. But of a dentist's chair there was not even the ruins. His eyes wandered over the broken-backed books— some were indeed 'dictionaries in distress.' He noted a Russo-German and a German-English. Then the sounds of frying penetrated more keenly to his brain.

'You are the cook of the restaurant?' he inquired.

'Restaurant!' echoed the woman resentfully. 'Have I not enough cooking to do for my own family? And where shall I find money to keep a restaurant?'

'Your husband said—' murmured Barstein, as in guilty confusion.

A squalling from the overflow offspring in the kitchen drew off the mother for a moment, leaving him surrounded by an open-eyed juvenile mob. From the rear he heard smacks, loud whispers and whimperings. Then the poor woman reappeared, bearing what seemed a scrubbing-board. She placed it over one of the caneless chairs, and begged his Excellency to be seated. It was a half holiday at the school, she complained, otherwise her family would be less numerous.

'Where does your husband do his dentistry?' Barstein inquired, seating himself cautiously upon the board.

'Do I know?' said his wife. 'He goes out, he comes in.' At this moment, to Barstein's great satisfaction, he did come in.

'Holy angel!' he cried, rushing at the hem of Barstein's coat, and kissing it reverently. He was a gaunt, melancholy figure, elongated to over six feet, and still further exaggerated by a rusty top-hat of the tallest possible chimneypot, and a threadbare frockcoat of the longest possible tails. At his advent his wife, vastly relieved, shepherded her flock into the kitchen and closed the door, leaving Barstein alone with the long man, who seemed, as he stood gazing at his visitor, positively soaring heavenwards with rapture.

But Barstein inquired brutally: 'Where do you do your dentistry?'

'Never mind me,' replied Nehemiah ecstatically. 'Let me look on you!' And a more passionate worship came into his tranced gaze.

But Barstein, feeling duped, replied sternly: 'Where do you do your dentistry?'

The question seemed to take some moments penetrating through Nehemiah's rapt brain, but at last he replied pathetically: 'And where shall I find achers? In Russia I had my living of it. Here I have no friends.'

The homeliness of his vocabulary amused Barstein. Evidently the dictionary was his fount of inspiration. Without it Niagara was reduced to a trickle. He seemed indeed quite shy of speech, preferring to gaze with large liquid eyes.

'But you have managed to live here for ten years,' Barstein pointed out.

'You see how merciful God is!' Nehemiah rejoined eagerly. 'Never once has He deserted me and my children.'

'But what have you done?' inquired Barstein.

The first shade of reproach came into Nehemiah's eyes.

'Ask sooner what the Almighty has done,' he said.

Barstein felt rebuked. One does not like to lose one's character as a holy angel. 'But your restaurant?' he said. 'Where is that?'

'That is here.'

'Here!' echoed Barstein, staring round again.

'Where else? Here is a wide opening for a kosher restaurant. There are hundreds and hundreds of Greeners lodging all around—poor young men with only a bed or a corner of a room to sleep on. They know not where to go to eat, and my wife, God be thanked, is a knowing cook.'

'Oh, then, your restaurant is only an idea.'

'Naturally—a counsel that I have given myself.'

'But have you enough plates and dishes and tablecloths? Can you afford to buy the food, and to risk it's not being eaten?'

Nehemiah raised his hands to heaven.

'Not being eaten! With a family like mine!'

Barstein laughed in spite of himself. And he was softened by noting how sensitive and artistic were Nehemiah's outspread hands—they might well have wielded the forceps. 'Yes, I dare say that is what will happen,' he said. 'How can you keep a restaurant up two pairs of stairs where no passer-by will ever see it?'

As he spoke, however, he remembered staying in an hotel in Sicily which consisted entirely of one upper room. Perhaps in the Ghetto Sicilian fashions were paralleled.

'I do not fly so high as a restaurant in once,' Nehemiah explained. 'But here is this great empty room. What am I to do with it? At night of course most of us sleep on it, but by daylight it is a waste. Also I receive several Hebrew and Yiddish papers a week from my friends in Russia and America, and one of which I even buy here. When I have read them these likewise are a waste. Therefore have I given myself a counsel, if I would make here a reading-room they should come in the evenings, many young men who have only a bed or a room-corner to go to, and when once they have learnt to come here it will then be easy to make them to eat and drink. First I will give to them only coffee and cigarettes, but afterwards shall my wife cook them all the Delicatessen of Poland. When our custom will become too large we shall take over Bergman's great fashionable restaurant in the Whitechapel Road. He has already given me the option thereof; it is only two hundred pounds. And if your gentility—'

'But I cannot afford two hundred pounds,' interrupted Barstein, alarmed.

'No, no, it is the Almighty who will afford that,' said Nehemiah reassuringly. 'From you I ask nothing.'

'In that case,' replied Barstein drily, 'I must say I consider it an excellent plan. Your idea of building up from small foundations is most sensible—some of the young men may even have toothache—but I do not see where you need me—unless to supply a few papers.'

'Did I not say you were from heaven?' Nehemiah's eyes shone again. 'But I do not require the papers. It is enough for me that your holy feet have stood in my homestead. I thought you might send money. But to come with your own feet! Now I shall be able to tell I have spoken with him face to face!'

Barstein was touched. 'I think you will need a larger table for the reading-room,' he said.

The tall figure shook its tall hat. 'It is only gas that I need for my operations.'

'Gas!' repeated Barstein, astonished. 'Then you propose to continue your dentistry too.'

'It is for the restaurant I need the gas,' elucidated Nehemiah. 'Unless there shall be a cheerful shining here the young men will not come. But the penny gas is all I need.'

'Well, if it costs only a penny—' began Barstein.

'A penny in the slot,' corrected Nehemiah. 'But then there is the meter and the cost of the burners.' He calculated that four pounds would convert the room into a salon of light that would attract all the homeless moths of the neighbourhood.

So this was the four-pound solution, Barstein reflected with his first sense of solid foothold. After all Nehemiah had sustained his surprise visit fairly well—he was obviously no Croesus—and if four pounds would not only save this swarming family but radiate cheer to the whole neighbourhood—

He sprung open the sovereign-purse that hung on his watch-chain. It contained only three pounds ten. He rummaged his pockets for silver, finding only eight shillings.

'I'm afraid I haven't quite got it!' he murmured.

'As if I couldn't trust you!' cried Nehemiah reproachfully, and as he lifted his long coat-tails to trouser-pocket the money, Barstein saw that he had no waistcoat.

II

About six months later, when Barstein had utterly forgotten the episode, he received another letter whose phraseology instantly recalled everything.

'To the most Honourable Competent Authentical Illustrious Authority and Universal Celebrious Dignity of the very Famous Sculptor.

'3A, THE MINORIES, E.

'DEAR SIR,

'I have the honour and pleasure now to render the real and sincere gratitude of my very much obliged thanks for Your grand gracious clement sympathical propitious merciful liberal compassionable cordial nobility of your real humane generous benevolent genuine very kind magnanimous philanthropy, which afforded to me a great redemption of my very lamentable desperate necessitous need, wherein I am at present very poor indeed in my total ruination by the cruel cynical Russia, therein is every day a daily tyrannous massacre and assassinate, here is nothing to do any more for me previously, I shall rather go to Bursia than to Russia. I received from Your dear kind amiable amicable goodness recently £4 the same was for me a momental recreating aid in my actual very indigent paltry miserable calamitous situation wherein I gain now nothing and I only perish here. Even I cannot earn here my daily bread by my perfect scientifick Knowledge of diverse languages, I know the philological neology and archaiology, the best way is for me to go to another country to wit, to Bursia or Turkey. Thus, I solicit and supplicate Your charitable generosity by my very humble and instant request to make me go away from here as soon as possible according to Your humane kind merciful clemency.

'Your obedient Servant respectfully,
'NEHEMIAH SILVERMANN,
'Dentist and Professor of Languages.'

So an Academy of Languages had evolved from the gas, not a restaurant. Anyhow the dictionary was in distress again. Emigration appeared now the only salvation.

But where in the world was Bursia? Possibly Persia was meant. But why Persia? Wherein lay the attraction of that exotic land, and whatever would Mrs. Silvermann and her overflowing progeny do in Persia? Nehemiah's original suggestion of Jerusalem had been much more intelligible. Perhaps it persisted still under the head of Turkey. Not least characteristic Barstein found Nehemiah's tenacious gloating over his ancient ruin at the hands of Russia.

For some days the sculptor went about weighed down by Nehemiah's misfortunes, and the necessity of finding time to journey to the Minories. But he had an absorbing piece of work, and before he could tear himself away from it a still more urgent shower of words fell upon him.

'3A, THE MINORIES, E.

'I have the honour now,' the new letter ran, 'to inquire about my decided and expecting departure. I must sue by my quite humble and very instant entreaty Your noble genteel cordial humanity in my very hard troublous and bitter and sour vexations and tribulations to effect for my poor position at least a private anonymous prompt collection as soon as possible according to Your clement magnanimous charitable mercy of £15 if not £25 among Your very estimable and respectfully good friends, in good order to go in another country even Bursia to get my livelihood by my dental practice or by my other scientifick and philological knowledge. The great competition is here in anything very vigorous. I have here no dental employment, no dental practice, no relations, no relief, no gain, no earning, no introduction, no protection, no recommendation, no money, no good friends, no good connecting acquaintance, in Russia I am ruined and I perish here, I am already desperate and despond entirely. I do not know what to do and what shall I do, do now in my actual urgent, extreme immense need. I am told by good many people, that the board of guardians is very seldom to rescue by aid the people, but very often is to find only faults, and vices and to make them guilty. I have nothing to do there, and in the russian jewish fund I found once Sir Asher Aaronsberg and he is not to me sympathical. I supply and solicit considerably Your kind humane clement mercy to answer me as soon as possible quick according to Your very gracious mercy.

'Your obedient Servant respectfully,
'NEHEMIAH SILVERMANN,
'Dentist and Professor of Languages.'

As soon as the light failed in his studio, Barstein summoned a hansom and sped to the Minories.

III

Nehemiah's voice bade him walk in, and turning the door-handle he saw the top-hatted figure sprawled in solitary gloom along a caneless chair, reading a newspaper by the twinkle of a rushlight. Nehemiah sprang up with a bark of joy, making his gigantic shadow bow to the visitor. From chimney-pot to coat-tail he stretched unchanged, and the same celestial rapture illumined his gaunt visage.

But Barstein drew back his own coat-tail from the attempted kiss.

'Where is the gas?' he asked drily.

'Alas, the company removed the meter.'

'But the gas-brackets?'

'What else had we to eat?' said Nehemiah simply.

Barstein in sudden suspicion raised his eyes to the ceiling. But a fragment of gaspipe certainly came through it. He could not, however, recall whether the pipe had been there before or not.

'So the young men would not come?' he said.

'Oh yes, they came, and they read, and they ate. Only they did not pay.'

'You should have made it a rule—cash down.'

Again a fine shade of rebuke and astonishment crossed his lean and melancholy visage.

'And could I oppress a brother-in-Israel? Where had those young men to turn but to me?'

Again Barstein felt his angelic reputation imperilled. He hastened to change the conversation.

'And why do you want to go to Bursia?' he said.

'Why shall I want to go to Bursia?' Nehemiah replied.

'You said so.' Barstein showed him the letter.

'Ah, I said I shall sooner go to Bursia than to Russia. Always Sir Asher Aaronsberg speaks of sending us back to Russia.'

'He would,' said Barstein grimly. 'But where is Bursia?'

Nehemiah shrugged his shoulders. 'Shall I know? My little Rebeccah was drawing a map thereof; she won a prize of five pounds with which we lived two months. A genial child is my Rebeccah.'

'Ah, then, the Almighty did send you something.'

'And do I not trust Him?' said Nehemiah fervently. 'Otherwise, burdened down as I am with a multitude of children—'

'You made your own burden,' Barstein could not help pointing out.

Again that look of pain, as if Nehemiah had caught sight of feet of clay beneath Barstein's shining boots.

'"Be fruitful and multiply and fill the earth,"' Nehemiah quoted in Hebrew. 'Is not that the very first commandment in the Bible?'

'Well, then, you want to go to Turkey,' said the sculptor evasively. 'I suppose you mean Palestine?'

'No, Turkey. It is to Turkey we Zionists should ought to go, there to work for Palestine. Are not many of the Sultan's own officials Jews? If we can make of them hot-hearted Zionists—'

It was an arresting conception, and Barstein found himself sitting on the table to discuss it. The reverence with which Nehemiah listened to his views was touching and disconcerting. Barstein felt humbled by the celestial figure he cut in Nehemiah's mental mirror. Yet he could not suspect the man of a glozing tongue, for of the leaders of Zionism Nehemiah spoke with, if possible, greater veneration, with an awe trembling on tears. His elongated figure grew even gaunter, his lean visage unearthlier, as he unfolded his plan for the conquest of Palestine, and Barstein's original impression of his simple sincerity was repeated and re-enforced.

Presently, however, it occurred to Barstein that Nehemiah himself would have scant opportunity of influential contact with Ottoman officials, and that the real question at issue was, how Nehemiah, his wife, and his 'at least eleven children,' were to be supported in Turkey. He mentioned the point.

Nehemiah waved it away. 'And cannot the Almighty support us in Turkey as well as in England?' he asked. 'Yes, even in Bursia itself the Guardian of Israel is not sleepy.'

It was then that the word 'Luftmensch' flew into Barstein's mind. Nehemiah was not an earth-man in gross contact with solidities. He was an air-man, floating on facile wings through the æther. True, he spoke of troublesome tribulations, but these were mainly dictionary distresses, felt most keenly in the rhapsody of literary composition. At worst they were mere clouds on the blue. They had nothing in common with the fogs which frequently veiled heaven from his own vision. Never for a moment had Nehemiah failed to remember the blue, never had he lost his radiant outlook. His very pessimism was merely optimism in disguise, since it was only a personal pessimism to be remedied by 'a few frivolous pounds,' by a new crumb from the hand of Providence, not that impersonal despair of the scheme of things which gave the thinker such black moments. How had Nehemiah lived during those first ten years in England? Who should say? But he had had the wild daring to uproot himself from his childhood's home and adventure himself upon an unknown shore, and there, by hook or crook, for better or for worse, through vicissitudes innumerable and crises beyond calculation, ever on the perilous verge of nothingness, he had scraped through the days and the weeks and the years, fearlessly contributing perhaps more important items to posterity than the dead stones, which were all he, the sculptor, bade fair to leave behind him. Welcoming each new child with feasting and psalmody, never for a moment had Nehemiah lost his robustious faith in life, his belief in God, man, or himself.

Yes, even deeper than his own self-respect was his respect for others. An impenetrable idealist, he lived surrounded by a radiant humanity, by men become as Gods. With no conscious hyperbole did he address one as 'Angel.' Intellect and goodness were his pole-stars. And what airy courage in his mundane affairs, what invincible resilience! He had once been a dentist, and he still considered himself one. Before he owned a tablecloth he deemed himself the proprietor of a restaurant. He enjoyed alike the pleasures of anticipation and of memory, and having nothing, glided ever buoyantly between two gilded horizons. The superficial might call him shiftless, but more profoundly envisaged, was he not rather an education in the art of living? Did he not incarnate the great Jewish gospel of the improvident lilies?

'You shall not go to Bursia,' said Barstein in a burst of artistic fervour. 'Thirteen people cannot possibly get there for fifteen pounds or even twenty-five pounds, and for such a sum you could start a small business here.'

Nehemiah stared at him. 'God's messenger!' was all he could gasp. Then the tall melancholy man raised his eyes to heaven, and uttered a Hebrew voluntary in which references to the ram whose horns were caught in the thicket to save Isaac's life were distinctly audible.

Barstein waited patiently till the pious lips were at rest.

'But what business do you think you—?' he began.

'Shall I presume dictation to the angel?' asked Nehemiah with wet shining eyes.

'I am thinking that perhaps we might find something in which your children could help you. How old is the eldest?'

'I will ask my wife. Salome!' he cried. The dismal creature trotted in.

'How old is Moshelé?' he asked.

'And don't you remember he was twelve last Tabernacles?'

Nehemiah threw up his long arms. 'Merciful Heaven! He must soon begin to learn his Parshah (confirmation portion). What will it be? Where is my Chumash (Pentateuch)?' Mrs. Silvermann drew it down from the row of ragged books, and Nehemiah, fluttering the pages and bending over the rushlight, became lost to the problem of his future.

Barstein addressed himself to the wife. 'What business do you think your husband could set up here?'

'Is he not a dentist?' she inquired in reply.

Barstein turned to the busy peering flutterer.

'Would you like to be a dentist again?'

'Ah, but how shall I find achers?'

'You put up a sign,' said Barstein. 'One of those cases of teeth. I daresay the landlady will permit you to put it up by the front door, especially if you take an extra room. I will buy you the instruments, furnish the room attractively. You will put in your newspapers—why, people will be glad to come as to a reading-room!' he added smiling.

Nehemiah addressed his wife. 'Did I not say he was a genteel archangel?' he cried ecstatically.

IV

Barstein was sitting outside a café in Rome sipping vermouth with Rozenoffski, the Russo-Jewish pianist, and Schneemann the Galician-Jewish painter, when he next heard from Nehemiah.

He was anxiously expecting an important letter, which he had instructed his studio-assistant to bring to him instantly. So when the man appeared, he seized with avidity upon the envelope in his hand. But the scrawling superscription at once dispelled his hope, and recalled the forgotten Luftmensch. He threw the letter impatiently on the table.

'Oh, you may read it,' his friends protested, misunderstanding.

'I can guess what it is,' he said grumpily. Here, in this classical atmosphere, in this southern sunshine, he felt out of sympathy with the gaunt godly Nehemiah, who had doubtless lapsed again into his truly troublesome tribulations. Not a penny more for the ne'er-do-well! Let his Providence look after him!

'Is she beautiful?' quizzed Schneemann.

Barstein roared with laughter. His irate mood was broken up. Nehemiah as a petticoated romance was too tickling.

'You shall read the letter,' he said.

Schneemann protested comically. 'No, no, that would be ungentlemanly—you read to us what the angel says.'

'It is I that am the angel,' Barstein laughed, as he tore open the letter. He read it aloud, breaking down in almost hysterical laughter at each eruption of adjectives from 'the dictionary in distress.' Rozenoffski and Schneemann rolled in similar spasms of mirth, and the Italians at the neighbouring tables, though entirely ignorant of the motive of the merriment, caught the contagion, and rocked and shrieked with the mad foreigners.

'3A, THE MINORIES, E.

'RIGHT HONOURABLE ANGELICAL MR. LEOPOLD BARSTEIN,

'I have now the honour to again solicit Your genteel genuine sympathical humane philanthropic kind cordial nobility to oblige me at present by Your merciful loan of gracious second and propitious favourable aidance in my actually poor indigent position in which I have no earn by my dental practice likewise no help, also no protection, no recommendation, no employment, and then the competition is here very violent. I was ruined by Russia, and I have nothing for the celebration of our Jewish new year. Consequentially upon your merciful archangelical donative I was able to make my livelihood by my dental practice even very difficult, but still I had my vital subsistence by it till up now, but not further for the little while, in consequence of it my circumstances are now in the urgent extreme immense need. Thus I implore Your competent, well famous good-hearted liberal magnanimous benevolent generosity to respond me in Your beneficent relief as soon as possible, according to Your kind grand clemence of Your good ingenuous genteel humanity. I wish You a happy new year.

'Your obedient servant respectfully,
'NEHEMIAH SILVERMANN,
'Dentist and Professor of Languages.'

But when the reading was finished, Schneemann's comment was unexpected.

'Rosh Hashanah so near?' he said.

A rush of Ghetto memories swamped the three artists as they tried to work out the date of the Jewish New Year, that solemn period of earthly trumpets and celestial judgments.

'Why, it must be to-day!' cried Rozenoffski suddenly. The trio looked at one another with rueful humour. Why, the Ghetto could not even realize such indifference to the heavenly tribunals so busily decreeing their life-or-death sentences!

Barstein raised his glass. 'Here's a happy new year, anyhow!' he said.

The three men clinked glasses.

Rozenoffski drew out a hundred-lire note.

'Send that to the poor devil,' he said.

'Oho!' laughed Schneemann. 'You still believe "Charity delivers from death!" Well, I must be saved too!' And he threw down another hundred-lire note.

To the acutely analytical Barstein it seemed as if an old superstitious thrill lay behind Schneemann's laughter as behind Rozenoffski's donation.

'You will only make the Luftmensch believe still more obstinately in his Providence,' he said, as he gathered up the New Year gifts. 'Again will he declare that he has been accorded a good writing and a good sealing by the Heavenly Tribunal!'

'Well, hasn't he?' laughed Schneemann.

'Perhaps he has,' said Rozenoffski musingly. 'Qui sa?'

THE TUG OF LOVE

When Elias Goldenberg, Belcovitch's head cutter, betrothed himself to Fanny Fersht, the prettiest of the machinists, the Ghetto blessed the match, always excepting Sugarman the Shadchan (whom love matches shocked), and Goldenberg's relatives (who considered Fanny flighty and fond of finery).

'That Fanny of yours was cut out for a rich man's wife,' insisted Goldenberg's aunt, shaking her pious wig.

'He who marries Fanny is rich,' retorted Elias.

'"Pawn your hide, but get a bride,"' quoted the old lady savagely.

As for the slighted marriage-broker, he remonstrated almost like a relative.

'But I didn't want a negotiated marriage,' Elias protested.

'A love marriage I could also have arranged for you,' replied Sugarman indignantly.

But Elias was quite content with his own arrangement, for Fanny's glance was melting and her touch transporting. To deck that soft warm hand with an engagement-ring, a month's wages had not seemed disproportionate, and Fanny flashed the diamond bewitchingly. It lit up the gloomy workshop with its signal of felicity. Even Belcovitch, bent over his press-iron, sometimes omitted to rebuke Fanny's badinage.

The course of true love seemed to run straight to the Canopy—Fanny had already worked the bridegroom's praying shawl—when suddenly a storm broke. At first the cloud was no bigger than a man's hand—in fact, it was a man's hand. Elias espied it groping for Fanny's in the dim space between the two machines. As Fanny's fingers fluttered towards it, her other hand still guiding the cloth under the throbbing needle, Elias felt the needle stabbing his heart up and down, through and through. The very finger that held his costly ring lay in this alien paw gratis.

The shameless minx! Ah, his relatives were right. He snapped the scissors savagely like a dragon's jaw.

'Fanny, what dost thou?' he gasped in Yiddish.

Fanny's face flamed; her guilty fingers flew back.

'I thought thou wast on the other side,' she breathed.

Elias snorted incredulously.

As soon as Sugarman heard of the breaking of the engagement he flew to Elias, his blue bandanna streaming from his coat-tail.

'If you had come to me,' he crowed, 'I should have found you a more reliable article. However, Heaven has given you a second helping. A well-built wage-earner like you can look as high as a greengrocer's daughter even.'

'I never wish to look upon a woman again,' Elias groaned.

'Schtuss!' said the great marriage-broker. 'Three days after the Fast of Atonement comes the Feast of Tabernacles. The Almighty, blessed be He, who created both light and darkness, has made obedient females as well as pleasure-seeking jades.' And he blew his nose emphatically into his bandanna.

'Yes; but she won't return me my ring,' Elias lamented.

'What!' Sugarman gasped. 'Then she considers herself still engaged to you.'

'Not at all. She laughs in my face.'

'And she has given you back your promise?'

'My promise—yes. The ring—no.'

'But on what ground?'

'She says I gave it to her.'

Sugarman clucked his tongue. 'Tututu! Better if we had followed our old custom, and the man had worn the engagement-ring, not the woman!'

'In the workshop,' Elias went on miserably, 'she flashes it in my eyes. Everybody makes mock. Oh, the Jezebel!'

'I should summons her!'

'It would only cost me more. Is it not true I gave her the ring?'

Sugarman mopped his brow. His vast experience was at fault. No maiden had ever refused to return his client's ring; rather had she flung it in the wooer's false teeth.

'This comes of your love matches!' he cried sternly. 'Next time there must be a proper contract.'

'Next time!' repeated Elias. 'Why how am I to afford a new ring? Fanny was ruinous in cups of chocolate and the pit of the Pavilion Theatre!'

'I should want my fee down!' said Sugarman sharply.

Elias shrugged his shoulders. 'If you bring me the ring.'

'I do not get old rings but new maidens,' Sugarman reminded him haughtily. 'However, as you are a customer—' and crying 'Five per cent. on the greengrocer's daughter,' he hurried away ere Elias had time to dissent from the bargain.

Donning his sealskin vest to overawe the Fershts, Sugarman ploughed his way up the dark staircase to their room. His attire was wasted on the family, for Fanny herself opened the door.

'Peace to you,' he cried. 'I have come on behalf of Elias Goldenberg.'

'It is useless. I will not have him.' And she was shutting the door. Her misconception, wilful or not, scattered all Sugarman's prepared diplomacies. 'He does not want you, he wants the ring,' he cried hastily.

Fanny indecorously put a finger to her nose. The diamond glittered mockingly on it. Then she turned away giggling. 'But look at this photograph!' panted Sugarman desperately through the closing door.

Surprise and curiosity brought her eyes back. She stared at the sheepish features of a frock-coated stranger.

'Four pounds a week all the year round, head cutter at S. Cohn's,' said Sugarman, pursuing this advantage. 'A good old English family; Benjamin Beckenstein is his name, and he is dying to step into Elias's shoes.'

'His feet are too large!' And she flicked the photograph floorwards with her bediamonded finger.

'But why waste the engagement-ring?' pleaded Sugarman, stooping to pick up the suitor.

'What an idea! A new man, a new ring!' And Fanny slammed the door.

'Impudence-face! Would you become a jewellery shop?' the baffled Shadchan shrieked through the woodwork.

He returned to Elias, brooding darkly.

'Well?' queried Elias.

'O, your love matches!' And Sugarman shook them away with shuddersome palms.

'Then she won't—'

'No, she won't. Ah, how blessed you are to escape from that daughter of Satan! The greengrocer's daughter now—'

'Speak me no more matches. I risk no more rings.'

'I will get you one on the hire system.'

'A maiden?'

'Guard your tongue! A ring, of course.'

Elias shook an obdurate head. 'No. I must have the old ring back.'

'That is impossible—unless you marry her to get it back. Stay! Why should I not arrange that for you?'

'Leave me in peace! Heaven has opened my eyes.'

'Then see how economical she is!' urged Sugarman. 'A maiden who sticks to a ring like that is not likely to be wasteful of your substance.'

'You have not seen her swallow "stuffed monkeys,"' said Elias grimly. 'Make an end! I have done with her.'

'No, you have not! You can still give yourself a counsel.' And Sugarman looked a conscious sphinx. 'You may yet get back the ring.'

'How?'

'Of course, I have the next disposal of it?' said Sugarman.

'Yes, yes. Go on.'

'To-morrow in the workshop pretend to steal loving glances all day long when she's not looking. When she catches you—'

'But she won't be looking!'

'Oh, yes, she will. When she catches you, you must blush.'

'But I can't blush at will,' Elias protested.

'I know it is hard. Well, look foolish. That will be easier for you.'

'But why shall I look foolish?'

'To make her think you are in love with her after all.'

'I should look foolish if I were.'

'Precisely. That is the idea. When she leaves the workshop in the evening follow her, and as she passes the cake-shop, sigh and ask her if she will not eat a "stuffed monkey" for the sake of peace-be-upon-him times.'

'But she won't.'

'Why not? She is still in love.'

'With stuffed monkeys,' said Elias cynically.

'With you, too.'

Elias blushed quite easily. 'How do you know?'

'I offered her another man, and she slammed the door in my face!'

'You—you offered—' Elias stuttered angrily.

'Only to test her,' said Sugarman soothingly. He continued: 'Now, when she has eaten the cake and drunk a cup of chocolate, too (for one must play high with such a ring at stake), you must walk on by her side, and when you come to a dark corner, take her hand and say "My treasure" or "My angel," or whatever nonsense you modern young men babble to your maidens—with the results you see!—and while she is drinking it all in like more chocolate, her fingers in yours, give a sudden tug, and off comes the ring!'

Elias gazed at him in admiration. 'You are as crafty as Jacob, our father.'

'Heaven has not denied everybody brains,' replied Sugarman modestly. 'Be careful to seize the left hand.'

The admiring Elias followed the scheme to the letter.

Even the blush he had boggled at came to his cheeks punctually whenever his sheep's-eyes met Fanny's. He was so surprised to find his face burning that he looked foolish into the bargain.

They dallied long in the cake-shop, Elias trying to summon up courage for the final feint. He would get a good grip on the ring finger. The tug-of-war should be brief.

Meantime the couple clinked chocolate cups, and smiled into each other's eyes.

'The good-for-nothing!' thought Elias hotly. 'She will make the same eyes at the next man.'

And he went on gorging her, every speculative 'stuffed monkey' increasing his nervous tension. Her white teeth, biting recklessly into the cake, made him itch to slap her rosy cheek. Confectionery palled at last, and Fanny led the way out. Elias followed, chattering with feverish gaiety. Gradually he drew up even with her.

They turned down the deserted Fishmonger's Alley, lit by one dull gas-lamp. Elias's limbs began to tremble with the excitement of the critical moment. He felt like a footpad. Hither and thither he peered—nobody was about. But—was he on the right side of her? 'The right is the left,' he told himself, trying to smile, but his pulses thumped, and in the tumult of heart and brain he was not sure he knew her right hand from her left. Fortunately he caught the glitter of the diamond in the gloom, and instinctively his robber hand closed upon it.

But as he felt the warm responsive clasp of those soft fingers, that ancient delicious thrill pierced every vein. Fool that he had been to doubt that dear hand! And it was wearing his ring still—she could not part with it! O blundering male ingrate!

'My treasure! My angel!' he murmured ecstatically.

THE YIDDISH 'HAMLET'

The little poet sat in the East-side café looking six feet high. Melchitsedek Pinchas—by dint of a five-pound note from Sir Asher Aaronsberg in acknowledgement of the dedication to him of the poet's 'Songs of Zion'—had carried his genius to the great new Jewry across the Atlantic. He had arrived in New York only that very March, and already a crowd of votaries hung upon his lips and paid for all that entered them. Again had the saying been verified that a prophet is nowhere without honour save in his own country. The play that had vainly plucked at the stage-doors of the Yiddish Theatres of Europe had already been accepted by the leading Yiddish theatre of New York. At least there were several Yiddish Theatres, each claiming this supreme position, but the poet felt that the production of his play at Goldwater's Theatre settled the question among them.

'It is the greatest play of the generation,' he told the young socialists and free-thinkers who sat around him this Friday evening imbibing chocolate. 'It will be translated into every tongue.' He had passed with a characteristic bound from satisfaction with the Ghetto triumph into cosmopolitan anticipations. 'See,' he added, 'my initials make M.P.—Master Playwright.'

'Also Mud Pusher,' murmured from the next table Ostrovsky, the socialist leader, who found himself almost deserted for the new lion. 'Who is this uncombed bunco-steerer?'

'He calls himself the "sweet singer in Israel,"' contemptuously replied Ostrovsky's remaining parasite.

'But look here, Pinchas,' interposed Benjamin Tuch, another of the displaced demigods, a politician with a delusion that he swayed Presidential elections by his prestige in Brooklyn. 'You said the other day that your initials made "Messianic Poet."'

'And don't they?' inquired the poet, his Dantesque, if dingy, face flushing spiritedly. 'You call yourself a leader, and you don't know your A B C!'

There was a laugh, and Benjamin Tuch scowled.

'They can't stand for everything,' he said.

'No—they can't stand for "Bowery Tough,"' admitted Pinchas; and the table roared again, partly at the rapidity with which this linguistic genius had picked up the local slang. 'But as our pious lunatics think there are many meanings in every letter of the Torah,' went on the pleased poet, 'so there are meanings innumerable in every letter of my name. If I am playwright as well as poet, was not Shakespeare both also?'

'You wouldn't class yourself with a low-down barnstormer like Shakespeare?' said Tuch sarcastically.

'My superiority to Shakespeare I leave to others to discover,' replied the poet seriously, and with unexpected modesty. 'I discovered it for myself in writing this very play; but I cannot expect the world to admit it till the play is produced.'

'How did you come to find it out yourself?' asked Witberg, the young violinist, who was never sure whether he was guying the poet or sitting at his feet.

'It happened most naturally—order me another cup of chocolate, Witberg. You see, when Iselmann was touring with his Yiddish troupe through Galicia, he had the idea of acquainting the Jewish masses with "Hamlet," and he asked me to make the Yiddish translation, as one great poet translating another—and some of those almond-cakes, Witberg! Well, I started on the job, and then of course the discovery was inevitable. The play, which I had not read since my youth, and then only in a mediocre Hebrew version, appeared unspeakably childish in places. Take, for example, the Ghost—these almond-cakes are as stale as sermons; command me a cream-tart, Witberg. What was I saying?'

'The Ghost,' murmured a dozen voices.

'Ah, yes—now, how can a ghost affect a modern audience which no longer believes in ghosts?'

'That is true.' The table was visibly stimulated, as though the chocolate had turned into champagne. The word 'modern' stirred the souls of these refugees from the old Ghettos like a trumpet; unbelief, if only in ghosts, was oxygen to the prisoners of a tradition of three thousand years. The poet perceived his moment. He laid a black-nailed finger impressively on the right side of his nose.

'I translated Shakespeare—yes, but into modern terms. The Ghost vanished—Hamlet's tragedy remained only the internal incapacity of the thinker for the lower activity of action.'

The men of action pricked up their ears.

'The higher activity, you mean,' corrected Ostrovsky.

'Thought,' said Benjamin Tuch, 'has no value till it is translated into action.'

'Exactly; you've got to work it up,' said Colonel Klopsky, who had large ranching and mining interests out West, and, with his florid personality, looked entirely out of place in these old haunts of his.

'Schtuss (nonsense)!' said the poet disrespectfully. 'Acts are only soldiers. Thought is the general.'

Witberg demurred. 'It isn't much use thinking about playing the violin, Pinchas.'

'My friend,' said the poet, 'the thinker in music is the man who writes your solos. His thoughts exist whether you play them or not—and independently of your false notes. But you performers are all alike—I have no doubt the leading man who plays my Hamlet will imagine his is the higher activity. But woe be to those fellows if they change a syllable!'

'Your Hamlet?' sneered Ostrovsky. 'Since when?'

'Since I re-created him for the modern world, without tinsel and pasteboard; since I conceived him in fire and bore him in agony; since—even the cream of this tart is sour—since I carried him to and fro in my pocket, as a young kangaroo is carried in the pouch of the mother.'

'Then Iselmann did not produce it?' asked the Heathen Journalist, who haunted the East Side for copy, and pronounced Pinchas 'Pin-cuss.'

'No, I changed his name to Eselmann, the Donkey-man. For I had hardly read him ten lines before he brayed out, "Where is the Ghost?" "The Ghost?" I said. "I have laid him. He cannot walk on the modern stage." Eselmann tore his hair. "But it is for the Ghost I had him translated. Our Yiddish audiences love a ghost." "They love your acting, too," I replied witheringly. "But I am not here to consider the tastes of the mob." Oh, I gave the Donkey-man a piece of my mind.'

'But he didn't take the piece!' jested Grunbitz, who in Poland had been a Badchan (marriage-jester), and was now a Zionist editor.

'Bah! These managers are all men-of-the-earth! Once, in my days of obscurity, I was made to put a besom into the piece, and it swept all my genius off the boards. Ah, the donkey-men! But I am glad Eselmann gave me my "Hamlet" back, for before giving it to Goldwater I made it even more subtle. No vulgar nonsense of fencing and poison at the end—a pure mental tragedy, for in life the soul alone counts. No—this cream is just as sour as the other—my play will be the internal tragedy of the thinker.'

'The internal tragedy of the thinker is indigestion,' laughed the ex-Badchan; 'you'd better be more careful with the cream-tarts.'

The Heathen Journalist broke through the laughter. 'Strikes me, Pin-cuss, you're giving us Hamlet without the Prince of Denmark.'

'Better than the Prince of Denmark without Hamlet,' retorted the poet, cramming cream-tart down his throat in great ugly mouthfuls; 'that is how he is usually played. In my version the Prince of Denmark indeed vanishes, for Hamlet is a Hebrew and the Prince of Palestine.'

'You have made him a Hebrew?' cried Mieses, a pimply young poet.

'If he is to be the ideal thinker, let him belong to the nation of thinkers,' said Pinchas. 'In fact, the play is virtually an autobiography.'

'And do you call it "Hamlet" still?' asked the Heathen Journalist, producing his notebook, for he began to see his way to a Sunday scoop.

'Why not? True, it is virtually a new work. But Shakespeare borrowed his story from an old play called "Hamlet," and treated it to suit himself; why, therefore, should I not treat Shakespeare as it suits me. The cat eats the rat, and the dog bites the cat.' He laughed his sniggering laugh. 'If I were to call it by another name, some learned fool would point out it was stolen from Shakespeare, whereas at present it challenges comparison.'

'But you discovered Shakespeare cannot sustain the comparison,' said Benjamin Tuch, winking at the company.

'Only as the mediæval astrologer is inferior to the astronomer of to-day,' the poet explained with placid modesty. 'The muddle-headedness of Shakespeare's ideas—which, incidentally, is the cause of the muddle of Hamlet's character—has given way to the clear vision of the modern. How could Shakespeare really describe the thinker? The Elizabethans could not think. They were like our rabbis.'

The unexpected digression into contemporary satire made the whole café laugh. Gradually other atoms had drifted toward the new magnet. From the remotest corners eyes strayed and ears were pricked up. Pinchas was indeed a figure of mark, with somebody else's frock-coat on his meagre person, his hair flowing like a dark cascade under a broad-brimmed dusky hat, and his sombre face aglow with genius and cocksureness.

'Why should you expect thought from a rabbi?' said Grunbitz. 'You don't expect truth from a tradesman. Besides, only youth thinks.'

'That is well said,' approved Pinchas. 'He who is ever thinking never grows old. I shall die young, like all whom the gods love. Waiter, give Mr. Grunbitz a cup of chocolate.'

'Thank you—but I don't care for any.'

'You cannot refuse—you will pain Witberg,' said the poet simply.

In the great city around them men jumped on and off electric cars, whizzed up and down lifts, hustled through lobbies, hulloed through telephones, tore open telegrams, dictated to clacking typists, filled life with sound and flurry, with the bustle of the markets and the chink of the eternal dollar; while here, serenely smoking and sipping, ruffled only by the breezes of argument, leisurely as the philosophers in the colonnades of Athens, the talkers of the Ghetto, earnest as their forefathers before the great folios of the Talmud, made an Oriental oasis amid the simoom whirl of the Occident. And the Heathen Journalist who had discovered it felt, as so often before, that here alone in this arid, mushroom New York was antiquity, was restfulness, was romanticism; here was the Latin Quarter of the city of the Goths.

Encouraged by the Master's good humour, young Mieses timidly exhibited his new verses. Pinchas read the manuscript aloud to the confusion of the blushing boy.

'But it is full of genius!' he cried in genuine astonishment. 'I might have written it myself, except that it is so unequal—a mixture of diamonds and paste, like all Hebrew literature.' He indicated with flawless taste the good lines, not knowing they were one and all unconscious reproductions from the English masterpieces Mieses had borrowed from the library in the Educational Alliance. The acolytes listened respectfully, and the beardless, blotchy-faced Mieses began to take importance in their eyes and to betray the importance he held in his own.

'Perhaps I, too, shall write a play one day,' he said. 'My "M," too, makes "Master."'

'It may be that you are destined to wear my mantle,' said Pinchas graciously.

Mieses looked involuntarily at the ill-fitting frock-coat.

Pinchas rose. 'And now, Mieses, you must give me a car-fare. I have to go and talk to the manager about rehearsals. One must superintend the actors one's self—these pumpkin-heads are capable of any crime, even of altering one's best phrases.'

Radsikoff smiled. He had sat still in his corner, this most prolific of Ghetto dramatists, his big, furrowed forehead supported on his fist, a huge, odorous cigar in his mouth.

'I suppose Goldwater plays "Hamlet,"' he said.

'We have not discussed it yet,' said Pinchas airily.

Radsikoff smiled again. 'Oh, he'll pull through—so long as Mrs. Goldwater doesn't play "Ophelia."'

'She play "Ophelia"! She would not dream of such a thing. She is a saucy soubrette; she belongs to vaudeville.'

'All right. I have warned you.'

'You don't think there is really a danger!' Pinchas was pale and shaking.

'The Yiddish stage is so moral. Husbands and wives, unfortunately, live and play together,' said the old dramatist drily.

'I'll drown her truly before I let her play my "Ophelia,"' said the poet venomously.

Radsikoff shrugged his shoulders and dropped into American. 'Well, it's up to you.'

'The minx!' Pinchas shook his fist at the air. 'But I'll manage her. If the worst comes to the worst, I'll make love to her.'

The poet's sublime confidence in his charms was too much even for his admirers. The mental juxtaposition of the seedy poet and the piquant actress in her frills and furbelows set the whole café rocking with laughter. Pinchas took it as a tribute to his ingenious method of drawing the soubrette-serpent's fangs. He grinned placidly.

'And when is your play coming on?' asked Radsikoff.

'After Passover,' replied Pinchas, beginning to button his frock-coat against the outer cold. If only to oust this 'Ophelia,' he must be at the theatre instanter.

'Has Goldwater given you a contract?'

'I am a poet, not a lawyer,' said Pinchas proudly. 'Parchments are for Philistines; honest men build on the word.'

'After all, it comes to the same thing—with Goldwater,' said Radsikoff drily. 'But he's no worse than the others; I've never yet found the contract any manager couldn't slip out of. I've never yet met the playwright that the manager couldn't dodge.' Radsikoff, indeed, divided his time between devising plays and devising contracts. Every experience but suggested fresh clauses. He regarded Pinchas with commiseration rather than jealousy. 'I shall come to your first night,' he added.

'It will be a tribute which the audience will appreciate,' said Pinchas. 'I am thinking that if I had one of these aromatic cigars I too might offer a burnt-offering unto the Lord.'

There was general laughter at the blasphemy, for the Sabbath, with its privation of fire, had long since begun.

'Try taking instead of thinking,' laughed the playwright, pushing forward his case. 'Action is greater than Thought.'

'No, no, no!' Pinchas protested, as he fumbled for the finest cigar. 'Wait till you see my play—you must all come—I will send you all boxes. Then you will learn that Thought is greater than Action—that Thought is the greatest thing in the world.'

II

Sucking voluptuously at Radsikoff's cigar, Pinchas plunged from the steam-heated, cheerful café into the raw, unlovely street, still hummocked with an ancient, uncleared snowfall. He did not take the horse-car which runs in this quarter; he was reserving the five cents for a spirituous nightcap. His journey was slow, for a side street that he had to pass through was, like nearly all the side streets of the great city, an abomination of desolation, a tempestuous sea of frozen, dirty snow, impassable by all save pedestrians, and scarcely by them. Pinchas was glad of his cane; an alpenstock would not have been superfluous. But the theatre with its brilliantly-lighted lobby and flamboyant posters restored his spirits; the curtain was already up, and a packed mass filled the house from roof to floor. Rebuffed by the janitors, Pinchas haughtily asked for Goldwater. Goldwater was on the stage, and could not see him. But nothing could down the poet, whose head seemed to swell till it touched the gallery. This great theatre was his, this mighty audience his to melt and fire.

'I will await him in a box,' he said.

'There's no room,' said the usher.

Pinchas threw up his head. 'I am the author of "Hamlet"!'

The usher winced as at a blow. All his life he had heard vaguely of 'Hamlet'—as a great play that was acted on Broadway. And now here was the author himself! All the instinctive snobbery of the Ghetto toward the grand world was excited. And yet this seedy figure conflicted painfully with his ideas of the uptown type. But perhaps all dramatists were alike. Pinchas was bowed forward.

In another instant the theatre was in an uproar. A man in a comfortable fauteuil had been asked to accommodate the distinguished stranger and had refused.

'I pay my dollar—what for shall I go?'

'But it is the author of "Hamlet"!'

'My money is as good as his.'

'But he doesn't pay.'

'And I shall give my good seat to a Schnorrer!'

'Sh! sh!' from all parts of the house, like water livening, not killing, a flame. From every side came expostulations in Yiddish and American. This was a free republic; the author of 'Hamlet' was no better than anybody else. Goldwater, on the stage, glared at the little poet.

At last a compromise was found. A chair was placed at the back of a packed box. American boxes are constructed for publicity, not privacy, but the other dozen occupants bulked between him and the house. He could see, but he could not be seen. Sullen and mortified he listened contemptuously to the play.

It was, indeed, a strange farrago, this romantic drama with which the vast audience had replaced the Sabbath pieties, the home-keeping ritual of the Ghetto, in their swift transformation to American life. Confined entirely to Jewish characters, it had borrowed much from the heroes and heroines of the Western world, remaining psychologically true only in its minor characters, which were conceived and rendered with wonderful realism by the gifted actors. And this naturalism was shot through with streaks of pure fantasy, so that kangaroos suddenly bounded on in a masque for the edification of a Russian tyrant. But comedy and fantasy alike were subordinated to horror and tragedy: these refugees from the brutality of Russia and Rumania, these inheritors of the wailing melodies of a persecuted synagogue, craved morbidly for gruesomeness and gore. The 'happy endings' of Broadway would have spelled bankruptcy here. Players and audience made a large family party—the unfailing result of a stable stock company with the parts always cast in the same mould. And it was almost an impromptu performance. Pinchas, from his proximity to the stage, could hear every word from the prompter's box, which rose in the centre of the footlights. The Yiddish prompter did not wait till the players 'dried up'; it was his rôle to read the whole play ahead of them. 'Then you are the woman who murdered my mother,' he would gabble. And the actor, hearing, invented immediately the fit attitude and emphasis, spinning out with elocutionary slowness and passion the raw material supplied to him. No mechanical crossing and recrossing the stage, no punctilious tuition by your stage-manager—all was inspiration and fire. But to Pinchas this hearing of the play twice over—once raw and once cooked—was maddening.

'The lazy-bones!' he murmured. 'Not thus shall they treat my lines. Every syllable must be engraved upon their hearts, or I forbid the curtain to go up. Not that it matters with this fool-dramatist's words; they are ink-vomit, not literature.'

Another feature of the dialogue jarred upon his literary instinct. Incongruously blended with the Yiddish were elementary American expressions—the first the immigrants would pick up. 'All right,' 'Sure!' 'Yes, sir,' 'Say, how's the boss?' 'Good-bye.' 'Not a cent.' 'Take the elevated.' 'Yup.' 'Nup.' 'That's one on you!' 'Rubber-neck!' A continuous fusillade of such phrases stimulated and flattered the audience, pleased to find themselves on such easy terms with the new language. But to Pinchas the idea of peppering his pure Yiddish with such locutions was odious. The Prince of Palestine talking with a twang—how could he permit such an outrage upon his Hebrew Hamlet?

Hardly had the curtain fallen on the act than he darted through the iron door that led from the rear of the box to the stage, jostling the cursing carpenters, and pushed aside by the perspiring principals, on whom the curtain was rising and re-rising in a continuous roar. At last he found himself in the little bureau and dressing-room in which Goldwater was angrily changing his trousers. Kloot, the actor-manager's factotum, a big-nosed insolent youth, sat on the table beside the telephone, a peaked cap on his head, his legs swinging.

'Son of a witch! You come and disturb all my house. What do you want?' cried Goldwater.

'I want to talk to you about rehearsals.'

'I told you I would let you know when rehearsals began.'

'But you forgot to take my address.'

'As if I don't know where to find you!'

Kloot grinned. 'Pinchas gets drinks from all the café,' he put in.

'They drink to the health of "Hamlet,"' said Pinchas proudly.

'All right; Kloot's gotten your address. Good-evening.'

'But when will it be? I must know.'

'We can't fix it to a day. There's plenty of money in this piece yet.'

'Money—bah! But merit?'

'You fellows are as jealous as the devil.'

'Me jealous of kangaroos! In Central Park you see giraffes—and tortoises too. Central Park has more talent than this scribbler of yours.'

'I doubt if there's a bigger peacock than here,' murmured Goldwater.

'I'll write you about rehearsals,' said Kloot, winking at Goldwater.

'But I must know weeks ahead—I may go lecturing. The great continent calls for me. In Chicago, in Cincinnati—'

'Go, by all means,' said Goldwater. 'We can do without you.'

'Do without me? A nice mess you will make of it! I must teach you how to say every line.'

'Teach me?' Goldwater could hardly believe his ears.

Pinchas wavered. 'I—I mean the company. I will show them the accent—the gesture. I'm a great stage-manager as well as a great poet. There shall be no more prompter.'

'Indeed!' Goldwater raised the eyebrow he was pencilling. 'And how are you going to get on without a prompter?'

'Very simple—a month's rehearsals.'

Goldwater turned an apoplectic hue deeper than his rouge.

Kloot broke in impishly: 'It is very good of you to give us a month of your valuable time.'

But Goldwater was too irate for irony. 'A month!' he gasped at last. 'I could put on six melodramas in a month.'

'But "Hamlet" is not a melodrama!' said Pinchas, shocked.

'Quite so; there is not half the scenery. It's the scenery that takes time rehearsing, not the scenes.'

The poet was now as purple as the player. 'You would profane my divine work by gabbling through it with your pack of parrots!'

'Here, just you come off your perch!' said Kloot. 'You've written the piece; we do the rest.' Kloot, though only nineteen and at a few dollars a week, had a fine, careless equality not only with the whole world, but even with his employer. He was now, to his amaze, confronted by a superior.

'Silence, impudent-face! You are not talking to Radsikoff. I am a Poet, and I demand my rights.'

Kloot was silent from sheer surprise.

Goldwater was similarly impressed. 'What rights?' he observed more mildly. 'You've had your twenty dollars. And that was too much.'

'Too much! Twenty dollars for the masterpiece of the twentieth century!'

'In the twenty-first century you shall have twenty-one dollars,' said Kloot, recovering.

'Make mock as you please,' replied the poet superbly. 'I shall be living in the fifty-first century even. Poets never die—though, alas! they have to live. Twenty dollars too much, indeed! It is not a dollar a century for the run of the play.'

'Very well,' said Goldwater grimly. 'Give them back. We return your play.'

This time it was the poet that was disconcerted. 'No, no, Goldwater—I must not disappoint my printer. I have promised him the twenty dollars to print my Hebrew "Selections from Nietzsche."'

'You take your manuscript and give me my money,' said Goldwater implacably.

'Exchange would be a robbery. I will not rob you. Keep your bargain. See, here is the printer's letter.' He dragged from a tail-pocket a mass of motley manuscripts and yellow letters, and laid them beside the telephone as if to search among them.

Goldwater waved a repudiating hand.

'Be not a fool-man, Goldwater.' The poet's carneying forefinger was laid on his nose. 'I and you are the only two people in New York who serve the poetic drama—I by writing, you by producing.'

Goldwater still shook his head, albeit a whit appeased by the flattery.

Kloot replied for him: 'Your manuscript shall be returned to you by the first dustcart.'

Pinchas disregarded the youth. 'But I am willing you shall have only a fortnight's rehearsals. I believe in you, Goldwater. I have always said, "The only genius on the Yiddish stage is Goldwater." Klostermann—bah! He produces not so badly, but act? My grandmother's hen has a better stage presence. And there is Davidoff—a voice like a frog and a walk like a spider. And these charlatans I only heard of when I came to New York. But you, Goldwater—your fame has blown across the Atlantic, over the Carpathians. I journeyed from Cracow expressly to collaborate with you.'

'Then why do you spoil it all?' asked the mollified manager.

'It is my anxiety that Europe shall not be disappointed in you. Let us talk of the cast.'

'It is so early yet.'

'"The early bird catches the worm."'

'But all our worms are caught,' grinned Kloot. 'We keep our talent pinned on the premises.'

'I know, I know,' said Pinchas, paling. He saw Mrs. Goldwater tripping on saucily as Ophelia.

'But we don't give all our talent to one play,' the manager reminded him.

'No, of course not,' said Pinchas, with a breath of hope.

'We have to use all our people by turns. We divide our forces. With myself as Hamlet you will have a cast that should satisfy any author.'

'Do I not know it?' cried Pinchas. 'Were you but to say your lines, leaving all the others to be read by the prompter, the house would be spellbound, like Moses when he saw the burning bush.'

'That being so,' said Goldwater, 'you couldn't expect to have my wife in the same cast.'

'No, indeed,' said Pinchas enthusiastically. 'Two such tragic geniuses would confuse and distract, like the sun and the moon shining together.'

Goldwater coughed. 'But Ophelia is really a small part,' he murmured.

'It is,' Pinchas acquiesced. 'Your wife's tragic powers could only be displayed in "Hamlet" if, like another equally celebrated actress, she appeared as the Prince of Palestine himself.'

'Heaven forbid my wife should so lower herself!' said Goldwater. 'A decent Jewish housewife cannot appear in breeches.'

'That is what makes it impossible,' assented Pinchas. 'And there is no other part worthy of Mrs. Goldwater.'

[Illustration: "You compare my wife to a Kangaroo!"]

'It may be she would sacrifice herself,' said the manager musingly.

'And who am I that I should ask her to sacrifice herself?' replied the poet modestly.

'Fanny won't sacrifice Ophelia,' Kloot observed drily to his chief.

'You hear?' said Goldwater, as quick as lightning. 'My wife will not sacrifice Ophelia by leaving her to a minor player. She thinks only of the play. It is very noble of her.'

'But she has worked so hard,' pleaded the poet desperately, 'she needs a rest.'

'My wife never spares herself.'

Pinchas lost his head. 'But she might spare Ophelia,' he groaned.

'What do you mean?' cried Goldwater gruffly. 'My wife will honour you by playing Ophelia. That is ended.' He waved the make-up brush in his hand.

'No, it is not ended,' said Pinchas desperately. 'Your wife is a comic actress—'

'You just admitted she was tragic—'

'It is heartbreaking to see her in tragedy,' said Pinchas, burning his boats. 'She skips and jumps. Rather would I give Ophelia to one of your kangaroos!'

'You low-down monkey!' Goldwater almost flung his brush into the poet's face. 'You compare my wife to a kangaroo! Take your filthy manuscript and begone where the pepper grows.'

'Well, Fanny would be rather funny as Ophelia,' put in Kloot pacifyingly.

'And to make your wife ridiculous as Ophelia,' added Pinchas eagerly, 'you would rob the world of your Hamlet!'

'I can get plenty of Hamlets. Any scribbler can translate Shakespeare.'

'Perhaps, but who can surpass Shakespeare? Who can make him intelligible to the modern soul?'

'Mr. Goldwater,' cried the call-boy, with the patness of a reply.

The irate manager bustled out, not sorry to escape with his dignity and so cheap a masterpiece. Kloot was left, with swinging legs, dominating the situation. In idle curiosity and with the simplicity of perfectly bad manners, he took up the poet's papers and letters and perused them. As there were scraps of verse amid the mass, Pinchas let him read on unrebuked.

'You will talk to him, Kloot,' he pleaded at last. 'You will save Ophelia?'

The big-nosed youth looked up from his impertinent inquisition. 'Rely on me, if I have to play her myself.'

'But that will be still worse,' said Pinchas seriously.

Kloot grinned. 'How do you know? You've never seen me act?'

The poet laid his finger beseechingly on his nose. 'You will not spoil my play, you will get me a maidenly Ophelia? I and you are the only two men in New York who understand how to cast a play.'

'You leave it to me,' said Kloot; 'I have a wife of my own.'

'What!' shrieked Pinchas.

'Don't be alarmed—I'll coach her. She's just the age for the part. Mrs. Goldwater might be her mother.'

'But can she make the audience cry?'

'You bet; a regular onion of an Ophelia.'

'But I must see her rehearse, then I can decide.'

'Of course.'

'And you will seek me in the café when rehearsals begin?'

'That goes without saying.'

The poet looked cunning. 'But don't you say without going.'

'How can we rehearse without you? You shouldn't have worried the boss. We'll call you, even if it's the middle of the night.'

The poet jumped at Kloot's hand and kissed it.

'Protector of poets!' he cried ecstatically. 'And you will see that they do not mutilate my play; you will not suffer a single hair of my poesy to be harmed?'

'Not a hair shall be cut,' said Kloot solemnly.

Pinchas kissed his hand again. 'Ah, I and you are the only two men in New York who understand how to treat poesy.'

'Sure!' Kloot snatched his hand away. 'Good-bye.'

Pinchas lingered, gathering up his papers. 'And you will see it is not adulterated with American. In Zion they do not say "Sure" or "Lend me a nickel."'

'I guess not,' said Kloot. 'Good-bye.'

'All the same, you might lend me a nickel for car-fare.'

Kloot thought his departure cheap at five cents. He handed it over.

The poet went. An instant afterwards the door reopened and his head reappeared, the nose adorned with a pleading forefinger.

'You promise me all this?'

'Haven't I promised?'

'But swear to me.'

'Will you go—if I swear?'

'Yup,' said Pinchas, airing his American.

'And you won't come back till rehearsals begin?'

'Nup.'

'Then I swear—on my father's and mother's life!'

Pinchas departed gleefully, not knowing that Kloot was an orphan.

III

On the very verge of Passover, Pinchas, lying in bed at noon with a cigarette in his mouth, was reading his morning paper by candle-light; for he tenanted one of those innumerable dark rooms which should make New York the photographer's paradise. The yellow glow illumined his prophetic and unshaven countenance, agitated by grimaces and sniffs, as he critically perused the paragraphs whose Hebrew letters served as the channel for the mongrel Yiddish and American dialect, in which 'congressman,' 'sweater,' and such-like crudities of to-day had all the outer Oriental robing of the Old Testament. Suddenly a strange gurgle spluttered through the cigarette smoke. He read the announcement again.

The Yiddish 'Hamlet' was to be the Passover production at Goldwater's Theatre. The author was the world-renowned poet Melchitsedek Pinchas, and the music was by Ignatz Levitsky, the world-famous composer.

'World-famous composer, indeed!' cried Pinchas to his garret walls. 'Who ever heard of Ignatz Levitsky? And who wants his music? The tragedy of a thinker needs no caterwauling of violins. Does Goldwater imagine I have written a melodrama? At most will I permit an overture—or the cymbals shall clash as I take my call.'

He leaped out of bed. Even greater than his irritation at this intrusion of Levitsky was his joyful indignation at the imminence of his play. The dogs! The liars! The first night was almost at hand, and no sign had been vouchsafed to him. He had been true to his promise; he had kept away from the theatre. But Goldwater! But Kloot! Ah, the godless gambler with his parents' lives! With such ghouls hovering around the Hebrew 'Hamlet,' who could say how the masterpiece had been mangled? Line upon line had probably been cut; nay, who knew that a whole scene had not been shorn away, perhaps to give more time for that miserable music!

He flung himself into his clothes and, taking his cane, hurried off to the theatre, breathless and breakfastless. Orchestral music vibrated through the lobby and almost killed his pleasure in the placards of the Yiddish 'Hamlet.' He gave but a moment to absorbing the great capital letters of his name; a dash at a swinging-door, and he faced a glowing, crowded stage at the end of a gloomy hall. Goldwater, limelit, occupied the centre of the boards. Hamlet trod the battlements of the tower of David, and gazed on the cupolas and minarets of Jerusalem.

With a raucous cry, half anger, half ecstasy, Pinchas galloped toward the fiddling and banging orchestra. A harmless sweeper in his path was herself swept aside. But her fallen broom tripped up the runner. He fell with an echoing clamour, to which his clattering cane contributed, and clouds of dust arose and gathered where erst had stood a poet.

Goldwater stopped dead. 'Can't you sweep quietly?' he thundered terribly through the music.

Ignatz Levitsky tapped his baton, and the orchestra paused.

'It is I, the author!' said Pinchas, struggling up through clouds like some pagan deity.

Hamlet's face grew as inky as his cloak. 'And what do you want?'

'What do I want?' repeated Pinchas, in sheer amaze.

Kloot, in his peaked cap, emerged from the wings munching a sandwich.

'Sure, there's Shakespeare!' he said. 'I've just been round to the café to find you. Got this sandwich there.'

'But this—this isn't the first rehearsal,' stammered Pinchas, a jot appeased.

'The first dress-rehearsal,' Kloot replied reassuringly. 'We don't trouble authors with the rough work. They stroll in and put on the polish. Won't you come on the stage?'

Unable to repress a grin of happiness, Pinchas stumbled through the dim parterre, barking his shins at almost every step. Arrived at the orchestra, he found himself confronted by a chasm. He wheeled to the left, to where the stage-box, shrouded in brown holland, loomed ghostly.

'No,' said Kloot, 'that door's got stuck. You must come round by the stage-door.'

Pinchas retraced his footsteps, barking the smooth remainder of his shins. He allowed himself a palpitating pause before the lobby posters. His blood chilled. Not only was Ignatz Levitsky starred in equal type, but another name stood out larger than either:

Ophelia .. .. .. Fanny Goldwater.

His wrath reflaming, he hurried round to the stage-door. He pushed it open, but a gruff voice inquired his business, and a burly figure blocked his way.

'I am the author,' he said with quiet dignity.

'Authors ain't admitted,' was the simple reply.

'But Goldwater awaits me,' the poet protested.

'I guess not. Mr. Kloot's orders. Can't have authors monkeying around here.' As he spoke Goldwater's voice rose from the neighbouring stage in an operatic melody, and reduced Pinchas's brain to chaos. A despairing sense of strange plots and treasons swept over him. He ran back to the lobby. The doors had been bolted. He beat against them with his cane and his fists and his toes till a tall policeman persuaded him that home was better than a martyr's cell.

Life remained an unintelligible nightmare for poor Pinchas till the first night—and the third act—of the Yiddish 'Hamlet.' He had reconciled himself to his extrusion from rehearsals. 'They fear I fire Ophelia,' he told the café.

But a final blow awaited him. No ticket reached him for the première; the boxes he had promised the café did not materialize, and the necessity of avoiding that haunt of the invited cost him several meals. But that he himself should be refused when he tried to pass in 'on his face'—that authors should be admitted neither at the stage door nor at the public door—this had not occurred to him as within the possibilities of even theatrical humanity.

'Pigs! Pigs! Pigs!' he shrieked into the box office. 'You and Goldwater and Kloot! Pigs! Pigs! Pigs! I have indeed cast my pearls before swine. But I will not be beholden to them—I will buy a ticket.'

'We're sold out,' said the box-office man, adding recklessly: 'Get a move on you; other people want to buy seats.'

'You can't keep me out! It's conspiracy!' He darted within, but was hustled as rapidly without. He ran back to the stage-door, and hurled himself against the burly figure. He rebounded from it into the side-walk, and the stage-door closed upon his humiliation. He was left cursing in choice Hebrew. It was like the maledictions in Deuteronomy, only brought up to date by dynamite explosions and automobile accidents. Wearying of the waste of an extensive vocabulary upon a blank door, Pinchas returned to the front. The lobby was deserted save for a few strangers; his play had begun. And he—he, the god who moved all this machinery—he, whose divine fire was warming all that great house, must pace out here in the cold and dark, not even permitted to loiter in the corridors! But for the rumblings of applause that reached him he could hardly have endured the situation.

Suddenly an idea struck him. He hied to the nearest drug-store, and entering the telephone cabinet rang up Goldwater.

'Hello, there!' came the voice of Kloot. 'Who are you?'

Pinchas had a vivid vision of the big-nosed youth, in his peaked cap, sitting on the table by the telephone, swinging his legs; but he replied craftily, in a disguised voice: 'You, Goldwater?'

'No; Goldwater's on the stage.'

Pinchas groaned. But at that very instant Goldwater's voice returned to the bureau, ejaculating complacently: 'They're loving it, Kloot; they're swallowing it like ice-cream soda.'

Pinchas tingled with pleasure, but all Kloot replied was: 'You're wanted on the 'phone.'

'Hello!' called Goldwater.

'Hello!' replied Pinchas in his natural voice. 'May a sudden death smite you! May the curtain fall on a gibbering epileptic!'

'Can't hear!' said Goldwater. 'Speak plainer.'

'I will speak plainer, swine-head! Never shall a work of mine defile itself in your dirty dollar-factory. I spit on you!' He spat viciously into the telephone disk. 'Your father was a Meshummad (apostate), and your mother—'

But Goldwater had cut off the connection. Pinchas finished for his own satisfaction: 'An Irish fire-woman.'

'That was worth ten cents,' he muttered, as he strode out into the night. And patrolling the front of the theatre again, or leaning on his cane as on a sword, he was warmed by the thought that his venom had pierced through all the actor-manager's defences.

At last a change came over the nightmare. Striding from the envied, illuminated Within appeared the Heathen Journalist, note-book in hand. At sight of the author he shied. 'Must skedaddle, Pin-cuss,' he said apologetically, 'if we're to get anything into to-morrow's paper. Your people are so durned slow—nearly eleven, and only two acts over. You'll have to brisk 'em up a bit. Good-bye.'

He shook the poet's hand and was off. With an inspiration Pinchas gave chase. He caught the Journalist just boarding a car.

'Got your theatre ticket?' he panted.

'What for?'

'Give it me.'

The Journalist fumbled in his waistcoat pocket, and threw him a crumpled fragment. 'What in thunder—' he began. And then, to Pinchas's relief, the car removed the querist.

For the moment the poet was feeling only the indignity of the position, and the Heathen Journalist as trumpeter of his wrongs and avenger of the Muses had not occurred to him. He smoothed out the magic scrap, and was inside the suffocating, close-packed theatre before the disconcerted janitor could meet the new situation. Pinchas found the vacated journalistic chair in the stage-box; he was installed therein before the managerial minions arrived on ejection bent.

'This is my house!' screamed Pinchas. 'I stay here! Let me be—swine, serpents, Behemoth!'

'Sh!' came in a shower from every quarter. 'Sit down there! Turn him out!' The curtain was going up; Pinchas was saved.

But only for more gruesome torture. The third act began. Hamlet collogued with the Queen. The poet pricked up his ears. Whose language was this? Certainly not Shakespeare's or his superior's. Angels and ministers of grace defend him! this was only the illiterate jargon of the hack playwright, with its peppering of the phrases of Hester Street. 'You have too many dead flies on you,' Hamlet's mother told him. 'You'll get left.' But the nightmare thickened. Hamlet and his mother opened their mouths and sang. Their songs were light and gay, and held encore verses to reward the enthusiastic. The actors, like the audience, were leisurely; here midnight and the closure were not synonymous. When there were no more encore verses, Ignatz Levitsky would turn to the audience and bow in acknowledgment of the compliment. Pinchas's eyes were orbs straining at their sockets; froth gathered on his lips.

Mrs. Goldwater bounded on, fantastically mad, her songs set to comic airs. The great house received her in the same comic spirit. Instead of rue and rosemary she carried a rustling green Lulov—the palm-branch of the Feast of Tabernacles—and shook it piously toward every corner of the compass. At each shake the audience rolled about in spasms of merriment. A moment later a white gliding figure, moving to the measure of the cake-walk, keyed up the laughter to hysteria. It was the Ghost appearing to frighten Ophelia. His sepulchral bass notes mingled with her terror-stricken soprano.

This was the last straw. The Ghost—the Ghost that he had laid forever, the Ghost that made melodrama of this tragedy of the thinker—was risen again, and cake-walking!

Unperceived in the general convulsion and cachinnation, Pinchas leaped to his feet, and, seeing scarlet, bounded through the iron door and made for the stage. But a hand was extended in the nick of time—the hand he had kissed—and Pinchas was drawn back by the collar.

'You don't take your call yet,' said the unruffled Kloot.

'Let me go! I must speak to the people. They must learn the truth. They think me, Melchitsedek Pinchas, guilty of this tohu-bohu! My sun will set. I shall be laughed at from the Hudson to the Jordan.'

'Hush! Hush! You are interrupting the poesy.'

'Who has drawn and quartered my play? Speak!'

'I've only arranged it for the stage,' said Kloot, unabashed.

'You!' gasped the poet.

'You said I and you are the only two men who understand how to treat poesy.'

'You understand push-carts, not poesy!' hissed the poet. 'You conspire to keep me out of the theatre—I will summons you!'

'We had to keep all authors out. Suppose Shakespeare had turned up and complained of you.'

'Shakespeare would have been only too grateful.'

'Hush! The boss is going on.'

From the opposite wing Hamlet was indeed advancing. Pinchas made a wild plunge forward, but Kloot's grasp on his collar was still carefully firm.

'Who's mutilating the poesy now?' Kloot frowned angrily from under his peaked cap. 'You'll spoil the scene.'

'Peace, liar! You promised me your wife for Ophelia!'

Kloot's frown relaxed into a smile. 'Sure! The first wife I get you shall have.'

Pinchas gnashed his teeth. Goldwater's voice rose in a joyous roulade.

'I think you owe me a car-fare,' said Kloot soothingly.

Pinchas waved the rejoinder aside with his cane. 'Why does Hamlet sing?' he demanded fiercely.

'Because it's Passover,' said Kloot. 'You are a "greener" in New York, otherwise you would know that it is a tradition to have musical plays on Passover. Our audiences wouldn't stand for any other. You're such an unreasonable cuss! Why else did we take your "Hamlet" for a Passover play?'

'But "Hamlet" isn't a musical play.'

'Yes, it is! How about Ophelia's songs? That was what decided us. Of course they needed eking out.'

'But "Hamlet" is a tragedy!' gasped Pinchas.

'Sure!' said Kloot cheerfully. 'They all die at the end. Our audiences would go away miserable if they didn't. You wait till they're dead, then you shall take your call.'

'Take my call, for your play!'

'There's quite a lot of your lines left, if you listen carefully. Only you don't understand stage technique. Oh, I'm not grumbling; we're quite satisfied. The idea of adapting "Hamlet" for the Yiddish stage is yours, and it's worth every cent we paid.'

A storm of applause gave point to the speaker's words, and removed the last partition between the poet's great mind and momentary madness. What! here was that ape of a Goldwater positively wallowing in admiration, while he, the mighty poet, had been cast into outer darkness and his work mocked and crucified! He put forth all his might, like Samson amid the Philistines, and leaving his coat-collar in Kloot's hand, he plunged into the circle of light. Goldwater's amazed face turned to meet him.

'Cutter of lines!' The poet's cane slashed across Hamlet's right cheek near the right eye. 'Perverter of poesy!' It slashed across the left cheek near the left eye.

The Prince of Palestine received each swish with a yell of pain and fear, and the ever-ready Kloot dropped the curtain on the tragic scene.

Such hubbub and hullabaloo as rose on both sides of the curtain! Yet in the end the poet escaped scot-free. Goldwater was a coward, Kloot a sage. The same prudence that had led Kloot to exclude authors, saved him from magnifying their importance by police squabbles. Besides, a clever lawyer might prove the exclusion illegal. What was done was done. The dignity of the hero of a hundred dramas was best served by private beefsteaks and a rumoured version, irrefutable save in a court of law. It was bad enough that the Heathen Journalist should supply so graphic a picture of the midnight melodrama, coloured even more highly than Goldwater's eyes. Kloot had been glad that the Journalist had left before the episode; but when he saw the account he wished the scribe had stayed.

'He won't play Hamlet with that pair of shiners,' Pinchas prophesied early the next morning to the supping café.

Radsikoff beamed and refilled Pinchas's glass with champagne. He had carried out his promise of assisting at the première, and was now paying for the poet's supper.

'You're the first playwright Goldwater hasn't managed to dodge,' he chuckled.

'Ah!' said the poet meditatively. 'Action is greater than Thought. Action is the greatest thing in the world.'

THE CONVERTS

I

As he sat on his hard stool in the whitewashed workshop on the Bowery, clumsily pasting the flamboyant portrait on the boxes of the 'Yvonne Rupert cigar,' he wondered dully—after the first flush of joy at getting a job after weeks of hunger—at the strange fate that had again brought him into connection, however remote, with stageland. For even to Elkan Mandle, with his Ghetto purview, Yvonne Rupert's fame, both as a 'Parisian' star and the queen of American advertisers, had penetrated. Ever since she had summoned a Jewish florist for not paying her for the hundred and eleven bouquets with which a single week's engagement in vaudeville had enabled her to supply him, the journals had continued to paragraph her amusing, self-puffing adventures.

Not that there was much similarity between the New York star and his little actress of the humble Yiddish Theatre in London, save for that aureole of fluffy hair, which belonged rather to the genus than the individual. But as the great Yvonne's highly-coloured charms went on repeating themselves from every box-cover he manipulated (at seventy-five cents a hundred), the face of his own Gittel grew more and more vivid, till at last the whole splendid, shameful past began to rise up from its desolate tomb.

He even lived through that prologue in the Ghetto garret, when, as benevolent master-tailor receiving the highest class work from S. Cohn's in the Holloway Road, he was called upstairs to assist the penniless Polish immigrants.

There she sat, the witching she-devil, perched on the rickety table just contributed to the home, a piquant, dark-eyed, yet golden-haired, mite of eleven, calm and comparatively spruce amid the wailing litter of parents and children.

'Settle this among yourselves,' she seemed to be saying. 'When the chairs are here I will sit on them; when the table is laid I will draw to; when the pious philanthropist provides the fire I will purr on the hearth.'

Ah, he had come forward as the pious philanthropist—pious enough then, Heaven knew. Why had Satan thrown such lures in the way of the reputable employer, the treasurer of 'The Gates of Mercy' Synagogue, with children of his own, and the best wife in the world? Did he not pray every day to be delivered from the Satan Mekatrig? Had he not meant it for the best when he took her into his workshop? It was only when, at the age of sixteen, Gittel Goldstein left the whirring machine-room for the more lucrative and laurelled position of heroine of Goldwater's London Yiddish Theatre that he had discovered how this whimsical, coquettish creature had insinuated herself into his very being.

Ah, madness, madness! that flight with her to America with all his savings, that desertion of his wife and children! But what delicious delirium that one year in New York, prodigal, reckless, ere, with the disappearance of his funds, she, too, disappeared. And now, here he was—after nigh seven apathetic years, in which the need of getting a living was the only spur to living on—glad to take a woman's place when female labour struck for five cents more a hundred. The old bitter tears came up to his eyes, blurring the cheerless scene, the shabby men and unlovely women with their red paste-pots, the medley of bare and coloured boxes, the long shelf of twine-balls. And as he wept, the vain salt drops moistened the pictures of Yvonne Rupert.

II

She became an obsession, this Franco-American singer and dancer, as he sat pasting and pasting, caressing her pictured face with sticky fingers. There were brief intervals of freedom from her image when he was 'edging' and 'backing,' or when he was lining the boxes with the plain paper; but Yvonne came twice on every box—once in large on the inside, once in small on the outside, with a gummed projection to be stuck down after the cigars were in. He fell to recalling what he had read of her—the convent education that had kept her chaste and distinguished beneath all her stage deviltry, the long Lenten fasts she endured (as brought to light by the fishmonger's bill she disputed in open court), the crucifix concealed upon her otherwise not too reticent person, the adorable French accent with which she enraptured the dudes, the palatial private car in which she traversed the States, with its little chapel giving on the bathroom; the swashbuckling Marquis de St. Roquière, who had crossed the Channel after her, and the maid he had once kidnapped in mistake for the mistress; the diamond necklace presented by the Rajah of Singapuri, stolen at a soirée in San Francisco, and found afterwards as single stones in a low 'hock-shop' in New Orleans.

And despite all this glitter of imposing images a subconscious thought was forcing itself more and more clearly to the surface of his mind. That aureole of golden hair, those piquant dark eyes! The Yvonne the cheap illustrated papers had made him familiar with had lacked this revelation of colour! But no, the idea was insane!

This scintillating celebrity his lost Gittel!

Bah! Misery had made him childish. Goldwater had, indeed, blossomed out since the days of his hired hall in Spitalfields, but his fame remained exclusively Yiddish and East-side. But Gittel!

How could that obscure rush-light of the London Ghetto Theatre have blazed into the Star of Paris and New York?

This Lent-keeping demoiselle the little Polish Jewess who had munched Passover cake at his table in the far-off happy days! This gilded idol the impecunious Gittel he had caressed!

'You ever seen this Yvonne Rupert?' he inquired of his neighbour, a pock-marked, spectacled young woman, who, as record-breaker of the establishment, had refused to join the strike of the mere hundred-and-fifty a day.

The young woman swiftly drew a knife from the wooden pail beside her, and deftly scraped at a rough hinge as she replied: 'No, but I guess she's the actress who gets all the flowers, and won't pay for 'em.'

He saw she had mixed up the two lawsuits, but the description seemed to hit off his Gittel to the life. Yes, Gittel had always got all the flowers of life, and dodged paying. Ah, she had always been diabolically clever, unscrupulously ambitious! Who could put bounds to her achievement? She had used him and thrown him away—without a word, without a regret. She had washed her hands of him as light-heartedly as he washed his of the dirty, sticky day's paste. What other 'pious philanthropist' had she found to replace him? Whither had she fled? Why not to Paris that her theatric gifts might receive training?

This chic, this witchery, with which reputation credited her—had not Gittel possessed it all? Had not her heroines enchanted the Ghetto?

Oh, but this was a wild day-dream, insubstantial as the smoke-wreaths of the Yvonne Rupert cigar!

III

But the obsession persisted. In his miserable attic off Hester Street—that recalled the attic he had found her in, though it was many stories nearer the sky—he warmed himself with Gittel's image, smiling, light-darting, voluptuous. Night and sleep surrendered him to grotesque combinations—Gittel Goldstein smoking cigarettes in a bath-room, Yvonne Rupert playing Yiddish heroines in a little chapel.

In the clear morning these absurdities were forgotten in the realized absurdity of the initial identification. But a forenoon at the pasting-desk brought back the haunting thought. At noon he morbidly expended his lunch-dime on an 'Yvonne Rupert' cigar, and smoked it with a semi-insane feeling that he was repossessing his Gittel. Certainly it was delicious.

He wandered into the box-making room, where the man who tended the witty nail-driving machine was seated on a stack of Mexican cedar-wood, eating from a package of sausage and scrapple that sent sobering whiffs to the reckless smoker.

'You ever seen this Yvonne Rupert?' he asked wistfully.

'Might as well ask if I'd smoked her cigar!' grumbled the nailer through his mouthfuls.

'But there's a gallery at Webster and Dixie's.'

'Su-er!'

'I guess I'll go some day, just for curiosity.'

But the great Yvonne, he found, was flaming in her provincial orbit. So he must needs wait.

Meantime, on a Saturday night, with a dirty two-dollar bill in his pocket, and jingling some odd cents, he lounged into the restaurant where the young Russian bloods assembled who wrote for the Yiddish Labour papers, and 'knew it all.' He would draw them out about Yvonne Rupert. He established himself near a table at which long-haired, long-fingered Freethinkers were drinking chocolate and discussing Lassalle.

'Ah, but the way he jumped on a table when only a schoolboy to protest against the master's injustice to one of his schoolfellows! How the divine fire flamed in him!'

They talked on, these clamorous sceptics, amplifying the Lassalle legend, broidering it with Messianic myths, with the same fantastic Oriental invention that had illuminated the plain Pentateuch with imaginative vignettes, and transfiguring the dry abstractions of Socialism with the same passionate personalization. He listened impatiently. He had never been caught by Socialism, even at his hungriest. He had once been an employer himself, and his point of view survived.

They talked of the woman through whom Lassalle had met his death. One of them had seen her on the American stage—a bouncing burlesque actress.

'Like Yvonne Rupert?' he ventured to interpose.

'Yvonne Rupert?' They laughed. 'Ah, if Yvonne had only had such a snap!' cried Melchitsedek Pinchas. 'To have jilted Lassalle and been died for! What an advertisement!'

'It would have been on the bill,' agreed the table.

He asked if they thought Yvonne Rupert clever.

'Off the stage! There's nothing to her on,' said Pinchas.

The table roared as if this were a good joke. 'I dare say she would play my Ophelia as well as Mrs. Goldwater,' Pinchas added zestfully.

'They say she has a Yiddish accent,' Elkan ventured again.

The table roared louder. 'I have heard of Yiddish-Deutsch,' cried Pinchas, 'never of Yiddish-Français!'

Elkan Mandle was frozen. By his disappointment he knew that he had been hoping to meet Gittel again—that his resentment was dead.

IV

But the hope would not die. He studied the theatrical announcements, and when Yvonne Rupert once again flashed upon New York he set out to see her. But it struck him that the remote seat he could afford—for it would not do to spend a week's wage on the mere chance—would be too far off for precise identification, especially as she would probably be theatrically transmogrified. No, a wiser as well as a more economical plan would be to meet her at the stage-door, as he used to meet Gittel. He would hang about till she came.

It was a long ride to the Variety Theatre, and, the weather being sloppy, there was not even standing-room in the car, every foot of which, as it plunged and heaved ship-like through the watery night, was a suffocating jam of human beings, wedged on the seats, or clinging tightly to the overhead straps, or swarming like stuck flies on the fore and hind platforms, the squeeze and smell intensified by the shovings and writhings of damp passengers getting in and out, or by the desperate wriggling of the poor patient collector of fares boring his way through the very thick of the soldered mass. Elkan alighted with a headache, glad even of the cold rain that sprinkled his forehead. The shining carriages at the door of the theatre filled him for once with a bitter revolt. But he dared not insinuate himself among the white-wrapped, scented women and elegant cloaked men, though he itched to enter the portico and study the pictures of Yvonne Rupert, of which he caught a glimpse. He found his way instead to the stage-door, and took up a position that afforded him a complete view of the comers and goers, if only partial shelter from the rain.

But the leaden hours passed without her, with endless fevers of expectation, heats followed by chills. The performers came and went, mostly on foot, and strange nondescript men and women passed too through the jealously-guarded door.

He was drenched to the skin with accumulated drippings ere a smart brougham drove up, a smart groom opened an umbrella, and a smart—an unimaginably smart—Gittel Goldstein alighted.

Yes, the incredible was true!

Beneath that coquettish veil, under the aureole of hair, gleamed the piquant eyes he had kissed so often.

He remained petrified an instant, dazed and staring. She passed through the door the groom held open. The doorkeeper, from his pigeon-hole, handed her some letters. Yes, he knew every trick of the shoulders, every turn of the neck. She stood surveying the envelopes. As the groom let the door swing back and turned away, he rushed forward and pushed it open again.

'Gittel!' he cried chokingly. 'Gittel!'

She turned with a quick jerk of the head, and in her flushed, startled face he read consciousness if not recognition. The reek of her old cherry-blossom smote from her costlier garments, kindling a thousand passionate memories.

'Knowest thou me not?' he cried in Yiddish.

In a flash her face, doubly veiled, was a haughty stare.

'Who is zis person?' she asked the doorkeeper in her charming French-English.

He reverted to English.

'I am Elkan, your own Elkan!'

Ah, the jostle of sweet and bitter memories. So near, so near again! The same warm seductive witch. He strove to take her daintily-gloved hand.

She shrank back shudderingly and thrust open the door that led to the dressing-rooms beside the stage.

'Ze man is mad, lunatic!' And she disappeared with that delicious shrug of the shoulders that had captivated the States.

Insensate fury overcame him. What! This creature who owed all this glory to his dragging her away from the London Ghetto Theatre, this heartless, brazen minx who had been glad to nestle in his arms, was to mock him like this, was to elude him again! He made a dash after her; the doorkeeper darted from his little room, but was hurled aside in a swift, mad tussle, and Elkan, after a blind, blood-red instant, found himself blinking and dripping in the centre of the stage, facing a great roaring audience, tier upon tier. Then he became aware of a pair of eccentric comedians whose scene he had interrupted, and who had not sufficient presence of mind to work him into it, so that the audience which had laughed at his headlong entrance now laughed the louder over its own mistake.

But its delightful moment of sensational suspense was brief. In a twinkling the doorkeeper's vengeful hands were on the intruder's collar.

'I want Yvonne Rupert!' shrieked Elkan struggling. 'She is mine—mine! She loved me once!'

A vaster wave of laughter swept back to him as he was hauled off, to be handed over to a policeman on a charge of brawling and assaulting the doorkeeper.

V

As he lay in his cell he chewed the cud of revenge. Yes, let them take him before the magistrate; it was not he that was afraid of justice. He would expose her, the false Catholic, the she-cat! A pretty convert! Another man would have preferred to blackmail her, he told himself with righteous indignation, especially in such straits of poverty. But he—the thought had scarcely crossed his mind. He had not even thought of her helping him, only of the joy of meeting her again.

In the chill morning, after a sleepless night, he had a panic-stricken sense of his insignificance under the crushing weight of law and order. All the strength born of bitterness oozed out as he stood before the magistrate rigidly and heard the charge preferred. He had a despairing vision of Yvonne Rupert, mocking, inaccessible, even before he was asked his occupation.

'In a cigar-box factory,' he replied curtly.

'Ah, you make cigar-boxes?'

'No, not exactly. I paste.'

'Paste what?'

He hesitated. 'Pictures of Yvonne Rupert on the boxes.'

'Ah! Then it is the "Yvonne Rupert" cigar?'

'Yes.' He had divined the court's complacent misinterpretation ere he saw its smile; the facile theory that brooding so much over her fascinating picture had unhinged his brain. From that moment a hardness came over his heart. He shut his lips grimly. What was the use of talking? Whatever he said would be discredited on this impish theory. And, even without it, how incredible his story, how irrelevant to the charge of assaulting the doorkeeper!

'I was drunk,' was all he would say. He was committed for trial, and, having no one to bail him out, lingered in a common cell with other reprobates till the van brought him to the Law Court, and he came up to justice in an elevator under the rebuking folds of the Stars and Stripes. A fortnight's more confinement was all that was meted out to him, but he had already had time enough to reflect that he had given Yvonne Rupert one of the best advertisements of her life. It would have enhanced the prisoner's bitterness had he known, as the knowing world outside knew, that he was a poor devil in Yvonne Rupert's pay, and that New York was chuckling over the original and ingenious dodge by which she had again asserted her sovereignty as an advertiser—delicious, immense!

VI

Short as his term of imprisonment was it coincided, much to his own surprise, with the Jewish Penitential period, and the Day of Atonement came in the middle. A wealthy Jewish philanthropist had organized a prison prayer-service, and Elkan eagerly grasped at the break in the monotony. Several of the prisoners who posed as Jews with this same motive were detected and reprimanded; but Elkan felt, with the new grim sense of humour that meditation on Yvonne Rupert and the world she fooled was developing in him, that he was as little of a Jew as any of them. This elopement to America had meant a violent break with his whole religious past. Not once had he seen the inside of an American synagogue. Gittel had had no use for synagogues.

He entered the improvised prayer-room with this ironic sense of coming back to Judaism by the Christian prison door. But the service shook him terribly. He forgot even to be amused by the one successful impostor who had landed himself in an unforeseen deprivation of rations during the whole fast day. The passionate outcries of the old-fashioned Chazan, the solemn peals and tremolo notes of the cornet, which had once been merely æsthetic effects to the reputable master-cutter, were now surcharged with doom and chastisement. The very sight of the Hebrew books and scrolls touched a thousand memories of home and innocence.

Ah, God, how he had sinned!

'Forgive us now, pardon us now, atone for us now!' he cried, smiting his breast and rocking to and fro.

His poor deserted wife and children! How terrible for Haigitcha to wake up one morning and find him gone! As terrible as for him to wake up one morning and find Gittel gone. Ah, God had indeed paid him in kind! Eye for eye, tooth for tooth.

The philanthropist himself preached the sermon. God could never forgive sins till the sinner had first straightened out the human wrongs.

Ah, true, true! If he could only find his family again. If he could try by love and immeasurable devotion to atone for the past. Then again life would have a meaning and an aim. Poor, poor Haigitcha! How he would weep over her and cherish her. And his children! They must be grown up. Yankely must be quite a young man. Yes, he would be seventeen by now. And Rachel, that pretty, clinging cherub!

In all those years he had not dared to let his thoughts pause upon them. His past lay like a misty dream behind those thousand leagues of ocean. But now it started up in all the colours of daylight, warm, appealing. Yes, he would go back to his dear ones who must still crave his love and guidance; he would plead and be forgiven, and end his days piously at the sacred hearth of duty.

'Forgive us now, pardon us now, atone for us now!'

If only he could get back to old England.

He appealed to the philanthropist, and lied amid all his contrition. It was desperation at the severance from his wife and children that had driven him to drink, lust of gold that had spurred him across the Atlantic. Now a wiser and sadder man, he would be content with a modicum and the wife of his bosom.

VII

He arrived at last, with a few charity coins in his pocket, in the familiar Spitalfields alley, guarded by the three iron posts over which he remembered his Yankely leaping. His heart was full of tears and memories. Ah, there was the butcher's shop still underneath the old apartment, with the tin labels stuck in the kosher meat, and there was Gideon, the fat, genial butcher, flourishing his great carving-knife as of yore, though without that ancient smile of brotherly recognition. Gideon's frigidity chilled him; it was an inauspicious omen, a symptom of things altered, irrevocable.

'Does Mrs. Mandle still live here?' he asked with a horrible heart-sinking.

'Yes, first floor,' said Gideon, staring.

Ah, how his heart leapt up again! Haigitcha, his dear Haigitcha! He went up the ever-open dusty staircase jostling against a spruce, handsome young fellow who was hurrying down. He looked back with a sudden conviction that it was his son. His heart swelled with pride and affection; but ere he could cry 'Yankely' the young fellow was gone. He heard the whirr of machines. Yes, she had kept on the workshop, the wonderful creature, though crippled by his loss and the want of capital. Doubtless S. Cohn's kind-hearted firm had helped her to tide over the crisis. Ah, what a blackguard he had been! And she had brought up the children unaided. Dear Haigitcha! What madness had driven him from her side? But he would make amends—yes, he would make amends. He would slip again into his own niche, take up the old burdens and the old delights—perhaps even be again treasurer of 'The Gates of Mercy.'

He knocked at the door. Haigitcha herself opened it.

He wanted to cry her name, but the word stuck in his throat. For this was not his Haigitcha; this was a new creature, cold, stern, tragic, prematurely aged, framed in the sombre shadows of the staircase. And in her eyes was neither rapture nor remembrance.

'What is it?' she asked.

'I am Elkan; don't you know me?'

She stared with a little gasp, and a heaving of the flat breasts. Then she said icily: 'And what do you want?'

'I am come back,' he muttered hoarsely in Yiddish.

'And where is Gittel?' she answered in the same idiom.

The needles of the whirring machines seemed piercing through his brain. So London knew that Gittel had been the companion of his flight! He hung his head.

'I was only with her one year,' he whispered.

'Then go back to thy dung-heap!' She shut the door.

He thrust his foot in desperately ere it banged to. 'Haigitcha!' he shrieked. 'Let me come in. Forgive me, forgive me!'

It was a tug-of-war. He forced open the door; he had a vision of surprised 'hands' stopping their machines, of a beautiful, startled girl holding the ends of a half-laid tablecloth—his Rachel, oh, his Rachel!

'Open the window, one of you!' panted Haigitcha, her shoulders still straining against the door. 'Call a policeman—the man is drunk!'

He staggered back, his pressure relaxed, the door slammed. This repetition of his 'Yvonne Rupert' experience sobered him effectually. What right, indeed, had he to force himself upon this woman, upon these children, to whom he was dead? So might a suicide hope to win back his place in the old life. Life had gone on without him—had no need of him. Ah, what a punishment God had prepared for him! Closed doors to the past, closed doors everywhere.

And this terrible sense of exclusion had not now the same palliative of righteous resentment. With Yvonne Rupert, the splendid-flaming, vicious ingrate, he had felt himself the sinned against. But before this wife-widow, this dutiful, hard-working, tragic creature, he had nothing but self-contempt. He tottered downstairs. How should he even get his bread—he whose ill-fame was doubtless the gossip of the Ghetto? If he could only get hold of Gideon's carving-knife!

VIII

But he did not commit suicide, nor did he starve. There is always one last refuge for the failures of the Ghetto, and Elkan's easy experience with the Jewish philanthropist had prepared the way for dealings with the Christian.

To-day the Rev. Moses Elkan, 'the converted Jew,' preaches eloquently to his blind brethren who never come to hear him. For he has 'found the light.' Exeter Hall's exposition of the Jewish prophecies has opened his eyes, and though his foes have been those of his own household, yet, remembering the terrible text, 'He that loveth son or daughter more than Me is not worthy of Me,' he has taken up his cross and followed after Christ alone.

And even if the good souls for whose thousands of pounds he is the annual interest should discover his true past—through this tale-bearer or another—is there not but the more joy over the sinner that repenteth?

Duties neglected, deadly sins trailing in the actual world their unchangeable irreversible consequences— all this is irrelevant. He has 'found the light.'

And so, while Haigitcha walks in darkness, Yvonne prays in her chapel and Elkan preaches in his church.

HOLY WEDLOCK

I

When Schneemann, the artist, returned from Rome to his native village in Galicia, he found it humming with gossip concerning his paternal grandmother, universally known as the Bube Yenta. It would seem that the giddy old thing hobbled home from synagogue conversing with Yossel Mandelstein, the hunchback, and sometimes even offered the unshapely septuagenarian her snuffbox as he passed the door of her cottage. More than one village censor managed to acquaint the artist with the flirtation ere he had found energy to walk the muddy mile to her dwelling. Even his own mother came out strongly in disapproval of the ancient dame; perhaps the remembrance of how fanatically her mother-in-law had disapproved of her married head for not being shrouded in a pious wig lent zest to her tongue. The artist controlled his facial muscles, having learnt tolerance and Bohemianism in the Eternal City.

'Old blood will have its way,' he said blandly.

'Yes, old blood's way is sometimes worse than young blood's,' said Frau Schneemann, unsmiling. 'You must not forget that Yossel is still a bachelor.'

'Yes, and therefore a sinner in Israel—I remember,' quoth the artist with a twinkle. How all this would amuse his bachelor friends, Leopold Barstein and Rozenoffski the pianist!

'Make not mock. 'Tis high time you, too, should lead a maiden under the Canopy.'

'I am so shy—there are few so forward as grandmother.'

'Heaven be thanked!' said his mother fervently. 'When I refused to cover my tresses she spoke as if I were a brazen Epicurean, but I had rather have died than carry on so shamelessly with a man to whom I was not betrothed.'

'Perhaps they are betrothed.'

'We betrothed to Yossel! May his name be blotted out!'

'Why, what is wrong with Yossel? Moses Mendelssohn himself had a hump.'

'Who speaks of humps? Have you forgotten we are of Rabbinic family?'

Her son had quite forgotten it, as he had forgotten so much of this naïve life to which he was paying a holiday visit.

'Ah yes,' he murmured. 'But Yossel is pious—surely?' A vision of the psalm-droners and prayer-shriekers in the little synagogue, among whom the hunchback had been conspicuous, surged up vividly.

'He may shake himself from dawn-service to night-service, he will never shake off his father, the innkeeper,' said Frau Schneemann hotly. 'If I were in your grandmother's place I would be weaving my shroud, not thinking of young men.'

'But she's thinking of old men, you said.'

'Compared with her he is young—she is eighty-four, he is only seventy-five.'

'Well, they won't be married long,' he laughed.

Frau Schneemann laid her hand on his mouth.

'Heaven forbid the omen,' she cried. ''Tis bringing a Bilbul (scandal) upon a respectable family.'

'I will go and talk to her,' he said gravely. 'Indeed, I ought to have gone to see her days ago.' And as he trudged to the other end of the village towards the cottage where the lively old lady lived in self-sufficient solitude, he was full of the contrast between his mother's mental world and his own. People live in their own minds, and not in streets or fields, he philosophized.

II

Through her diamond-paned window he saw the wrinkled, white-capped old creature spinning peacefully at the rustic chimney-corner, a pure cloistral crone. It seemed profane to connect such a figure with flirtation—this was surely the very virgin of senility. What a fine picture she made too! Why had he never thought of painting her? Yes, such a picture of 'The Spinster' would be distinctly interesting. And he would put in the Kesubah, the marriage certificate that hung over the mantelpiece, in ironical reminder of her days of bloom. He unlatched the door—he had never been used to knock at grannie's door, and the childish instinct came back to him.

'Guten Abend,' he said.

She adjusted a pair of horn spectacles, and peered at him.

'Guten Abend,' she murmured.

'You don't remember me—Vroomkely.' He used the old childish diminutive of Abraham, though he had almost forgotten he owned the name in full.

'Vroomkely,' she gasped, almost overturning her wheel as she sprang to hug him in her skinny arms. He had a painful sense that she had shrunk back almost to childish dimensions. Her hands seemed trembling as much with decay as with emotion. She hastened to produce from the well-known cupboard home-made Kuchen and other dainties of his youth, with no sense of the tragedy that lay in his no longer being tempted by them.

'And how goes your trade?' she said. 'They say you have never been slack. They must build many houses in Rome.' Her notion that he was a house-painter he hardly cared to contradict, especially as picture-painting was contrary to the Mosaic dispensation.

'Oh, I haven't been only in Rome,' he said evasively. 'I have been in many lands.'

Fire came into her eyes, and flashed through the big spectacles. 'You have been to Palestine?' she cried.

'No, only as far as Egypt. Why?'

'I thought you might have brought me a clod of Palestine earth to put in my grave.' The fire died out of her spectacles, she sighed, and took a consolatory pinch of snuff.

'Don't talk of graves—you will live to be a hundred and more,' he cried. But he was thinking how ridiculous gossip was. It spared neither age nor sexlessness, not even this shrivelled ancient who was meditating on her latter end. Suddenly he became aware of a shadow darkening the doorway. At the same instant the fire leapt back into his grandmother's glasses. Instinctively, almost before he turned his head, he knew it was the hero of the romance.

Yossel Mandelstein looked even less of a hero than the artist had remembered. There had been something wistful and pathetic in the hunchback's expression, some hint of inner eager fire, but this—if he had not merely imagined it—seemed to have died of age and hopelessness. He used crutches, too, to help himself along with, so that he seemed less the hunchback of yore than the conventional contortion of time, and but for the familiar earlocks pendent on either side of the fur cap, but for the great hooked nose and the small chin hidden in the big beard, the artist might have doubted if this was indeed the Yossel he had sometimes mocked at in the crude cruelty of boyhood.

Yossel, propped on his crutches, was pulling out a mouldering black-covered book from under his greasy caftan. 'I have brought you back your Chovoth Halvovoth,' he said.

In the vivid presence of the actual romance the artist could not suppress the smile he had kept back at the mere shadowy recital. In Rome he himself had not infrequently called on young ladies by way of returning books to them. It was true that the books he returned were not Hebrew treatises, but he smiled again to think that the name of Yossel's volume signified 'the duties of the heart.' The Bube Yenta received the book with thanks, and a moment of embarrassment ensued, only slightly mitigated by the offer of the snuffbox. Yossel took a pinch, but his eyes seemed roving in amaze, less over the stranger than over the bespread table, as though he might unaccountably have overlooked some sacred festival. That two are company and three none seemed at this point a proverb to be heeded, and without waiting to renew the hero's acquaintance, the artist escaped from the idyllic cottage. Let the lover profit by the pastry for which he himself was too old.

So the gossips spoke the truth, he thought, his amusement not unblended with a touch of his mother's indignation. Surely, if his grandmother wished to cultivate a grand passion, she might have chosen a more sightly object of devotion. Not that there was much to be said for Yossel's taste either. When after seventy-five years of celibacy the fascinations of the other sex began to tell upon him, he might at least have succumbed to a less matriarchal form of femininity. But perhaps his grandmother had fascinations of another order. Perhaps she had money. He put the question to his mother.

'Certainly she has money,' said his mother vindictively. 'She has thousands of Gulden in her stocking. Twenty years ago she could have had her pick of a dozen well-to-do widowers, yet now that she has one foot in the grave, madness has entered her soul, and she has cast her eye upon this pauper.'

'But I thought his father left him his inn,' said the artist.

'His inn—yes. His sense—no. Yossel ruined himself long ago paying too much attention to the Talmud instead of his business. He was always a Schlemihl.'

'But can one pay too much attention to the Talmud? That is a strange saying for a Rabbi's daughter.'

'King Solomon tells us there is a time for everything,' returned the Rabbi's daughter. 'Yossel neglected what the wise King said, and so now he comes trying to wheedle your poor grandmother out of her money. If he wanted to marry, why didn't he marry before eighteen, as the Talmud prescribes?'

'He seems to do everything at the wrong time,' laughed her son. 'Do you suppose, by the way, that King Solomon made all his thousand marriages before he was eighteen?'

'Make not mock of holy things,' replied his mother angrily.

The monetary explanation of the romance, he found, was the popular one in the village. It did not, however, exculpate the grandame from the charge of forwardness, since if she wished to contract another marriage it could have been arranged legitimately by the Shadchan, and then the poor marriage-broker, who got little enough to do in this God-forsaken village, might have made a few Gulden out of it.

Beneath all his artistic perception of the humours of the thing, Schneemann found himself prosaically sharing the general disapprobation of the marriage. Really, when one came to think of it, it was ridiculous that he should have a new grandfather thrust upon him. And such a grandfather! Perhaps the Bube was, indeed, losing her reason. Or was it he himself who was losing his reason, taking seriously this parochial scandal, and believing that because a doddering hunchback of seventy-five had borrowed an ethical treatise from an octogenarian a marriage must be on the tapis? Yet, on more than one occasion, he came upon circumstances which seemed to justify the popular supposition. There could be no doubt, for example, that when at the conclusion of the synagogue service the feminine stream from the women's gallery poured out to mingle with the issuing males, these two atoms drifted together with unnatural celerity. It appeared to be established beyond question that on the preceding Feast of Tabernacles the Bube had lent and practically abandoned to the hunchback's use the ritual palm-branch he was too poor to afford. Of course this might only have been gratitude, inasmuch as a fortnight earlier on the solemn New Year Day when, by an untimely decree, the grandmother lay ill abed, Yossel had obtained possession of the Shofar, and leaving the synagogue had gone to blow it to her. He had blown the holy horn—with due regard to the proprieties—in the downstairs room of her cottage so that she above had heard it, and having heard it could breakfast. It was a performance that charity reasonably required for a disabled fellow-creature, and yet what medieval knight had found a more delicate way of trumpeting his mistress's charms? Besides, how had Yossel known that the heroine was ill? His eye must have roved over the women's gallery, and disentangled her absence even from the huddled mass of weeping and swaying womanhood.

One day came the crowning item of evidence. The grandmother had actually asked the village postman to oblige her by delivering a brown parcel at Yossel's lodgings. The postman was not a Child of the Covenant, but Yossel's landlady was, and within an hour all Jewry knew that Yenta had sent Yossel a phylacteries-bag—the very symbol of love offered by a maiden to her bridegroom. Could shameless passion further go?

III

The artist, at least, determined it should go no further. He put on his hat, and went to find Yossel Mandelstein. But Yossel was not to be found so easily, and the artist's resolution strengthened with each false scent. Yossel was ultimately run to earth, or rather to Heaven, in the Beth Hamedrash, where he was shaking himself studiously over a Babylonian folio, in company with a motley assemblage of youths and greybeards equally careless of the demands of life. The dusky home of holy learning seemed an awkward place in which to broach the subject of love. In a whisper he besought the oscillating student to come outside. Yossel started up in agitation.

'Ah, your grandmother is dying,' he divined, with what seemed a lover's inaccuracy. 'I will come and pray at once.'

'No, no, she is not dying,' said Schneemann hastily, adding in a grim murmur, 'unless of love.'

'Oh, then, it is not about your grandmother?'

'No—that is to say, yes.' It seemed more difficult than ever to plunge into the delicate subject. To refer plumply to the courtship would, especially if it were not true, compromise his grandmother and, incidentally, her family. Yet, on the other hand, he longed to know what lay behind all this philandering, which in any case had been compromising her, and he felt it his duty as his grandmother's protector and the representative of the family to ask Yossel straight out whether his intentions were honourable.

He remembered scenes in novels and plays in which undesirable suitors were tackled by champions of convention—scenes in which they were even bought off and started in new lands. Would not Yossel go to a new land, and how much would he want over and above his fare? He led the way without.

'You have lived here all your life, Yossel, have you not?' he said, when they were in the village street.

'Where else shall a man live?' answered Yossel.

'But have you never had any curiosity to see other parts? Would you not like to go and see Vienna?'

A little gleam passed over Yossel's dingy face. 'No, not Vienna—it is an unholy place—but Prague! Prague where there is a great Rabbi and the old, old underground synagogue that God has preserved throughout the generations.'

'Well, why not go and see it?' suggested the artist.

Yossel stared. 'Is it for that you tore me away from my Talmud?'

'N—no, not exactly for that,' stammered Schneemann. 'Only seeing you glued to it gave me the idea what a pity it was that you should not travel and sit at the feet of great Rabbis?'

'But how shall I travel to them? My crutches cannot walk so far as Prague.'

'Oh, I'd lend you the money to ride,' said the artist lightly.

'But I could never repay it.'

'You can repay me in Heaven. You can give me a little bit of your Gan Iden' (Paradise).

Yossel shook his head. 'And after I had the fare, how should I live? Here I make a few Gulden by writing letters for people to their relatives in America; in Prague everybody is very learned; they don't need a scribe. Besides, if I cannot die in Palestine I might as well die where I was born.'

'But why can't you die in Palestine?' cried the artist with a new burst of hope. 'You shall die in Palestine, I promise you.'

The gleam in Yossel's face became a great flame of joy. 'I shall die in Palestine?' he asked ecstatically.

'As sure as I live! I will pay your fare the whole way, second-class.'

For a moment the dazzling sunshine continued on Yossel's face, then a cloud began to pass across it.

'But how can I take your money? I am not a Schnorrer.'

Schneemann did not find the question easy to answer. The more so as Yossel's eagerness to go and die in Palestine seemed to show that there was no reason for packing him off. However, he told himself that one must make assurance doubly sure and that, even if it was all empty gossip, still he had stumbled upon a way of making an old man happy.

'There is no reason why you should take my money,' he said with an artistic inspiration, 'but there is every reason why I should buy to myself the Mitzvah (good deed) of sending you to Jerusalem. You see, I have so few good deeds to my credit.'

'So I have heard,' replied Yossel placidly. 'A very wicked life it is said you lead at Rome.'

'Most true,' said the artist cheerfully.

'It is said also that you break the Second Commandment by making representations of things that are on sea and land.'

'I would the critics admitted as much,' murmured the artist.

'Your grandmother does not understand. She thinks you paint houses—which is not forbidden. But I don't undeceive her—it would pain her too much.' The lover-like sentiment brought back the artist's alarm.

'When will you be ready to start?' he said.

Yossel pondered. 'But to die in Palestine one must live in Palestine,' he said. 'I cannot be certain that God would take my soul the moment I set foot on the holy soil.'

The artist reflected a moment, but scarcely felt rich enough to guarantee that Yossel should live in Palestine, especially if he were an unconscionably long time a-dying. A happy thought came to him. 'But there is the Chalukah,' he reminded Yossel.

'But that is charity.'

'No—it is not charity, it is a sort of university endowment. It is just to support such old students as you that these sums are sent from all the world over. The prayers and studies of our old men in Jerusalem are a redemption to all Israel. And yours would be to me in particular.'

'True, true,' said Yossel eagerly; 'and life is very cheap there, I have always heard.'

'Then it is a bargain,' slipped unwarily from the artist's tongue. But Yossel replied simply:

'May the blessings of the Eternal be upon you for ever and for ever, and by the merit of my prayers in Jerusalem may your sins be forgiven.'

The artist was moved. Surely, he thought, struggling between tears and laughter, no undesirable lover had ever thus been got rid of by the head of the family. Not to speak of an undesirable grandfather.

IV

The news that Yossel was leaving the village bound for the Holy Land, produced a sensation which quite obscured his former notoriety as an aspirant to wedlock. Indeed, those who discussed the new situation most avidly forgot how convinced they had been that marriage and not death was the hunchback's goal. How Yossel had found money for the great adventure was not the least interesting ingredient in the cup of gossip. It was even whispered that the grandmother herself had been tapped. Her skittish advances had been taken seriously by Yossel. He had boldly proposed to lead her under the Canopy, but at this point, it was said, the old lady had drawn back—she who had led him so far was not to be thus led. Women are changeable, it is known, and even when they are old they do not change. But Yossel had stood up for his rights; he had demanded compensation. And his fare to Palestine was a concession for his injured affections. It was not many days before the artist met persons who had actually overheard the bargaining between the Bube and the hunchback.

Meantime Yossel's departure was drawing nigh, and all those who had relatives in Palestine besieged him from miles around, plying him with messages, benedictions, and even packages for their kinsfolk. And conversely, there was scarcely a Jewish inhabitant who had not begged for clods of Palestine earth or bottles of Jordan water. So great indeed were the demands that their supply would have constituted a distinct invasion of the sovereign rights of the Sultan, and dried up the Jordan.

With his grandmother's future thus off his mind, the artist had settled down to making a picture of the ruined castle which he commanded from his bedroom window. But when the through ticket for Jerusalem came from the agent at Vienna, and he had brazenly endured Yossel's blessings for the same, his artistic instinct demanded to see how the Bube was taking her hero's desertion. As he lifted the latch he heard her voice giving orders, and the door opened, not on the peaceful scene he expected of the spinster at her ingle nook, but of a bustling and apparently rejuvenated old lady supervising a packing menial. The greatest shock of all was that this menial proved to be Yossel himself squatted on the floor, his crutches beside him. Almost as in guilty confusion the hunchback hastily closed the sheet containing a huddle of articles, and tied it into a bundle before the artist's chaotic sense of its contents could change into clarity. But instantly a flash of explanation came to him.

'Aha, grandmother,' he said, 'I see you too are sending presents to Palestine.'

The grandmother took snuff uneasily. 'Yes, it is going to the Land of Israel,' she said.

As the artist lifted his eyes from the two amorphous heaps on the floor—Yossel and his bundle—he became aware of a blank in the familiar interior.

'Why, where is the spinning-wheel?' he cried.

'I have given it to the widow Rubenstein—I shall spin no more.'

'And I thought of painting you as a spinster!' he murmured dolefully. Then a white patch in the darkened wood over the mantelpiece caught his eye. 'Why, your marriage certificate is gone too!'

'Yes, I have taken it down.'

'To give to the widow Rubenstein?'

'What an idea!' said his grandmother seriously. 'It is in the bundle.'

'You are sending it away to Palestine?'

The grandmother fumbled with her spectacles, and removing them with trembling fingers blinked downwards at the bundle. Yossel snatched up his crutches, and propped himself manfully upon them.

'Your grandmother goes with me,' he explained decisively.

'What!' the artist gasped.

The grandmother's eyes met his unflinchingly; they had drawn fire from Yossel's. 'And why should I not go to Palestine too?' she said.

'But you are so old!'

'The more reason I should make haste if I am to be luckier than Moses our Master.' She readjusted her spectacles firmly.

'But the journey is so hard.'

'Yossel has wisdom; he will find the way while alive as easily as others will roll thither after death.'

'You'll be dead before you get there,' said the artist brutally.

'Ah, no! God will not let me die before I touch the holy soil!'

'You, too, want to die in Palestine?' cried the amazed artist.

'And where else shall a daughter of Israel desire to die? Ah, I forgot—your mother was an Epicurean with godless tresses; she did not bring you up in the true love of our land. But every day for seventy years and more have I prayed the prayer that my eyes should behold the return of the Divine Glory to Zion. That mercy I no longer expect in my own days, inasmuch as the Sultan hardens his heart and will not give us back our land, not though Moses our Master appears to him every night, and beats him with his rod. But at least my eyes shall behold the land of Israel.'

'Amen!' said Yossel, still propped assertively on his crutches. The grandson turned upon the interrupter. 'But you can't take her with you?'

'Why not?' said Yossel calmly.

Schneemann found himself expatiating upon the responsibility of looking after such an old woman; it seemed too absurd to talk of the scandal. That was left for the grandmother to emphasize.

'Would you have me arrive alone in Palestine?' she interposed impatiently. 'Think of the talk it would make in Jerusalem! And should I even be permitted to land? They say the Sultan's soldiers stand at the landing-place like the angels at the gates of Paradise with swords that turn every way. But Yossel is cunning in the customs of the heathen; he will explain to the soldiers that he is an Austrian subject, and that I am his Frau.'

'What! Pass you off as his Frau!'

'Who speaks of passing off? He could say I was his sister, as Abraham our Father said of Sarah. But that was a sin in the sight of Heaven, and therefore as our sages explain—'

'It is simpler to be married,' Yossel interrupted.

'Married!' echoed the artist angrily.

'The witnesses are coming to my lodging this afternoon,' Yossel continued calmly. 'Dovidel and Yitzkoly from the Beth Hamedrash.'

'They think they are only coming to a farewell glass of brandy,' chuckled the grandmother. 'But they will find themselves at a secret wedding.'

'And to-morrow we shall depart publicly for Trieste,' Yossel wound up calmly.

'But this is too absurd!' the artist broke in. 'I forbid this marriage!'

A violent expression of amazement overspread the ancient dame's face, and the tone of the far-away years came into her voice. 'Silence, Vroomkely, or I'll smack your face. Do you forget you are talking to your grandmother?'

'I think Mr. Mandelstein forgets it,' the artist retorted, turning upon the heroic hunchback. 'Do you mean to say you are going to marry my grandmother?'

'And why not?' asked Yossel. 'Is there a greater lover of God in all Galicia?'

'Hush, Yossel, I am a great sinner.' But her old face was radiant. She turned to her grandson. 'Don't be angry with Yossel—all the fault is mine. He did not ask me to go with him to Palestine; it was I that asked him.'

'Do you mean that you asked him to marry you?'

'It is the same thing. There is no other way. How different would it have been had there been any other woman here who wanted to die in Palestine! But the women nowadays have no fear of Heaven; they wear their hair unshorn—they—'

'Yes, yes. So you asked Yossel to marry you.'

'Asked? Prayed, as one prays upon Atonement Day. For two years I prayed to him, but he always refused.'

'Then why—?' began the artist.

'Yossel is so proud. It is his only sin.'

'Oh, Yenta!' protested Yossel flushing, 'I am a very sinful man.'

'Yes, but your sin is all in a lump,' the Bube replied. 'Your iniquity is like your ugliness—some people have it scattered all over, but you have it all heaped up. And the heap is called pride.'

'Never mind his pride,' put in the artist impatiently. 'Why did he not go on refusing you?'

'I am coming to that. Only you were always so impatient, Vroomkely. When I was cutting you a piece of Kuchen, you would snatch greedily at the crumbs as they fell. You see Yossel is not made of the same clay as you and I. By an oversight the Almighty sent an angel into the world instead of a man, but seeing His mistake at the last moment, the All-High broke his wings short and left him a hunchback. But when Yossel's father made a match for him with Leah, the rich corn-factor's daughter, the silly girl, when she was introduced to the bridegroom, could see only the hump, and scandalously refused to carry out the contract. And Yossel is so proud that ever since that day he curled himself up into his hump, and nursed a hatred for all women.'

'How can you say that, Yenta?' Yossel broke in again.

'Why else did you refuse my money?' the Bube retorted. 'Twice, ten, twenty times I asked him to go to Palestine with me. But obstinate as a pig he keeps grunting "I can't—I've got no money." Sooner than I should pay his fare he'd have seen us both die here.'

The artist collapsed upon the bundle; astonishment, anger, and self-ridicule made an emotion too strong to stand under. So this was all his Machiavellian scheming had achieved—to bring about the very marriage it was meant to avert! He had dug a pit and fallen into it himself. All this would indeed amuse Rozenoffski and Leopold Barstein. He laughed bitterly.

'Nay, it was no laughing matter,' said the Bube indignantly. 'For I know well how Yossel longed to go with me to die in Jerusalem. And at last the All-High sent him the fare, and he was able to come to me and invite me to go with him.'

Here the artist became aware that Yossel's eyes and lips were signalling silence to him. As if, forsooth, one published one's good deeds! He had yet to learn on whose behalf the hunchback was signalling.

'So! You came into a fortune?' he asked Yossel gravely.

Yossel looked the picture of misery. The Bube unconsciously cut through the situation. 'A wicked man gave it to him,' she explained, 'to pray away his sins in Jerusalem.'

'Indeed!' murmured the artist. 'Anyone you know?'

'Heaven has spared her the pain of knowing him,' ambiguously interpolated her anxious protector.

'I don't even know his name,' added the Bube. 'Yossel keeps it hidden.'

'One must not shame a fellow-man,' Yossel urged. 'The sin of that is equal to the sin of shedding blood.'

The grandmother nodded her head approvingly. 'It is enough that the All-High knows his name. But for such an Epicurean much praying will be necessary. It will be a long work. And your first prayer, Yossel, must be that you shall not die very soon, else the labourer will not be worthy of his hire.'

Yossel took her yellow withered hand as in a lover's clasp. 'Be at peace, Yenta! He will be redeemed if only by your merits. Are we not one?'

ELIJAH'S GOBLET

I

Aaron Ben Amram removed from the great ritual dish the roasted shankbone of lamb (symbolic residuum of the Paschal Sacrifice) and the roasted egg (representative of the ancient festival-offering in the Temple), and while his wife and children held up the dish, which now contained only the bitter herbs and unleavened cakes, he recited the Chaldaic prelude to the Seder—the long domestic ceremonial of the Passover Evening.

'This is the bread of affliction which our fathers ate in the land of Egypt. Let all who are hungry come in and eat; let all who require come in and celebrate the Passover. This year here, next year in the land of Israel! This year slaves, next year sons of freedom!'

But the Polish physician showed nothing of the slave. White-bearded, clad in a long white robe and a white skullcap, and throned on white pillows, he made rather a royal figure, indeed for this night of nights conceived of himself as 'King' and his wife as 'Queen.'

But 'Queen' Golda, despite her silk gown and flowery cap, did not share her consort's majestic mood, still less the rosy happiness of the children who sat round this fascinating board. Her heart was full of a whispering fear that not all the brave melodies of the father nor all the quaint family choruses could drown. All very well for the little ones to be unconscious of the hovering shadow, but how could her husband have forgotten the horrors of the Blood Accusation in the very year he had led her under the Canopy?

And surely he knew as well as she that the dreadful legend was gathering again, that the slowly-growing Jew-hatred had reached a point at which it must find expression, that the Pritzim (nobles) in their great houses, and the peasants behind their high palings, alike sulked under the burden of debts. Indeed, had not the Passover Market hummed with the old, old story of a lost Christian child? Not murdered yet, thank God, nor even a corpse. But still, if a boy should be found with signs of violence upon him at this season of the Paschal Sacrifice, when the Greek Church brooded on the Crucifixion! O God of Abraham, guard us from these fiends unchained!

But the first part of the elaborate ritual, pleasantly punctuated with cups of raisin wine, passed peacefully by, and the evening meal, mercifully set in the middle, was reached, to the children's vast content. They made wry, humorous mouths, each jest endeared by annual repetition, over the horseradish that typified the bitterness of the Egyptian bondage, and ecstatic grimaces over the soft, sweet mixture of almonds, raisins, apples, and cinnamon, vaguely suggestive of the bondsmen's mortar; they relished the eggs sliced into salt water, and then—the symbols all duly swallowed—settled down with more prosaic satisfaction to the merely edible meats and fishes, though even to these the special Passover plates and dishes and the purified knives and forks lent a new relish.

By this time Golda was sufficiently cheered up to meditate her annual theft of the Afkuman, that segment of Passover cake under Aaron's pillow, morsels of which, distributed to each as the final food to be tasted that night, replaced the final mouthful of the Paschal Lamb in the ancient Palestinian meal.

II

But Elijah's goblet stood in the centre of the table untasted. Every time the ritual cup-drinking came round, the children had glanced at the great silver goblet placed for the Prophet of Redemption. Alas! the brimming raisin wine remained ever at the same level.

They found consolation in the thought that the great moment was still to come—the moment of the third cup, when, mother throwing open the door, father would rise, holding the goblet on high, and sonorously salute an unseen visitor.

True, in other years, though they had almost heard the rush of wings, the great shining cup had remained full, and when it was replaced on the white cloth, a vague resentment as at a spurned hospitality had stirred in each youthful breast. But many reasons could be found to exculpate Elijah—not omitting their own sins—and now, when Ben Amram nodded to his wife to open the door, expectation stood on tip-toe, credulous as ever, and the young hearts beat tattoo.

But the mother's heart was palpitating with another emotion. A faint clamour in the Polish quarter at the back, as she replaced the samovar in the kitchen, had recalled all her alarms, and she merely threw open the door of the room. But Ben Amram was not absent-minded enough to be beguiled by her air of obedient alacrity. Besides, he could see the shut street-door through the strip of passage. He gestured towards it.

Now she feigned laziness. 'Oh, never mind.'

'David, open the street-door.'

The eldest boy sprang up joyously. It would have been too bad of mother to keep Elijah on the doorstep.

'No, no, David!' Golda stopped him. 'It is too heavy; he could not undo the bolts and bars.'

'You have barred it?' Ben Amram asked.

'And why not? In this season you know how the heathen go mad like street-dogs.'

'Pooh! They will not bite us.'

'But, Aaron! You heard about the lost Christian child!'

'I have saved many a Christian child, Golda.'

'They will not remember that.'

'But I must remember the ritual.' And he made a movement.

'No, no, Aaron! Listen!'

The shrill noises seemed to have veered round towards the front of the house. He shrugged his shoulders. 'I hear only the goats bleating.'

She clung to him as he made for the door. 'For the sake of our children!'

'Do not be so childish yourself, my crown!'

'But I am not childish. Hark!'

He smiled calmly. 'The door must be opened.'

Her fears lent her scepticism. 'It is you that are childish. You know no Prophet of Redemption will come through the door.'

He caressed his venerable beard. 'Who knows?'

'I know. It is a Destroyer, not a Redeemer of Israel, who will come. Listen! Ah, God of Abraham! Do you not hear?'

Unmistakably the howl of a riotous mob was approaching, mingled with the reedy strains of an accordion.

'Down with the Zhits! Death to the dirty Jews!'

'God in heaven!' She released her husband, and ran towards the children with a gesture as of seeking to gather them all in her arms. Then, hearing the bolts shot back, she turned with a scream. 'Are you mad, Aaron?'

But he, holding her back with his gaze, threw wide the door with his left hand, while his right upheld Elijah's goblet, and over the ululation of the unseen mob and the shrill spasms of music rose his Hebrew welcome to the visitor: 'Baruch habaa!'

Hardly had the greeting left his lips when a wild flying figure in a rich furred coat dashed round the corner and almost into his arms, half-spilling the wine.

'In God's name, Reb Aaron!' panted the refugee, and fell half-dead across the threshold.

The physician dragged him hastily within, and slammed the door, just as two moujiks—drunken leaders of the chase—lurched past. The mother, who had sprung forward at the sound of the fall, frenziedly shot the bolts, and in another instant the hue and cry tore past the house and dwindled in the distance.

Ben Amram raised the white bloody face, and put Elijah's goblet to the lips. The strange visitor drained it to the dregs, the clustered children looking on dazedly. As the head fell back, it caught the light from the festive candles of the Passover board. The face was bare of hair; even the side curls were gone.

'Maimon the Meshummad!' cried the mother, shuddering back. 'You have saved the Apostate.'

'Did I not say the door must be opened?' replied Ben Amram gently. Then a smile of humour twitched his lips, and he smoothed his white beard. 'Maimon is the only Jew abroad to-night, and how were the poor drunken peasants to know he was baptized?'

Despite their thrill of horror at the traitor, David and his brothers and sisters were secretly pleased to see Elijah's goblet empty at last.

III

Next morning the Passover liturgy rang jubilantly through the vast, crowded synagogue. No violence had been reported, despite the passage of a noisy mob. The Ghetto, then, was not to be laid waste with fire and sword, and the worshippers within the moss-grown, turreted quadrangle drew free breath, and sent it out in great shouts of rhythmic prayer, as they swayed in their fringed shawls, with quivering hands of supplication. The Ark of the Law at one end of the great building, overbrooded by the Ten Commandments and the perpetual light, stood open to mark a supreme moment of devotion. Ben Amram had been given the honour of uncurtaining the shrine, and its richly clad scrolls of all sizes, with their silver bells and pointers, stood revealed in solemn splendour.

Through the ornate grating of their gallery the gaily-clad women looked down on the rocking figures, while the grace-notes of the cantor on his central daïs, and the harmoniously interjected 'poms' of his male ministrants flew up to their ears, as though they were indeed angels on high. Suddenly, over the blended passion of cantor and congregation, an ominous sound broke from without—the complex clatter of cavalry, the curt ring of military orders. The swaying figures turned suddenly as under another wind, the women's eyes grew astare and ablaze with terror. The great doors flew open, and—oh, awful, incredible sight—a squadron of Cossacks rode slowly in, two abreast, with a heavy thud of hoofs on the sacred floor, and a rattle of ponderous sabres. Their black conical caps and long beards, their great side-buttoned coats, and pockets stuffed with protrusive cartridges, their prancing horses, their leaded knouts, struck a blood-curdling discord amid the prayerful, white-wrapped figures. The rumble of worship ceased, the cantor, suddenly isolated, was heard soaring ecstatically; then he, too, turned his head uneasily and his roulade died in his throat.

'Halt!' the officer cried. The moving column froze. Its bristling length stretched from the central platform, blocking the aisle, and the courtyard echoed with the clanging hoofs of its rear, which backed into the school and the poor-house. The Shamash (beadle) was seen to front the flamboyant invaders.

'Why does your Excellency intrude upon our prayers to God?'

The congregation felt its dignity return. Who would have suspected Red Judah of such courage—such apt speech? Why, the very Rabbi was petrified; the elders of the Kahal stood dumb. Ben Amram himself, their spokesman to the Government, whose praying-shawl was embroidered with a silver band, and whose coat was satin, remained immovable between the pillars of the Ark, staring stonily at the brave beadle.

'First of all, for the boy's blood!'

The words rang out with military precision, and the speaker's horse pawed clangorously, as if impatient for the charge. The men grew death-pale, the women wrung their hands.

'Ai, vai!' they moaned. 'Woe! woe!'

'What boy? What blood?' said the Shamash, undaunted.

'Don't palter, you rascal! You know well that a Christian child has disappeared.'

The aged Rabbi, stimulated by the Shamash, uplifted a quavering voice.

'The child will be found of a surety—if, indeed, it is lost,' he added with bitter sarcasm. 'And surely your Excellency cannot require the boy's blood at our hands ere your Excellency knows it is indeed spilt.'

'You misunderstand me, old dog—or rather you pretend to, old fox. The boy's blood is here—it is kept in this very synagogue—and I have come for it.'

The Shamash laughed explosively. 'Oh, Excellency!'

The synagogue, hysterically tense, caught the contagion of glad relief. It rang with strange laughter.

'There is no blood in this synagogue, Excellency,' said the Rabbi, his eyes a-twinkle, 'save what runs in living veins.'

'We shall see. Produce that bottle beneath the Ark.'

'That!' The Shamash grinned—almost indecorously. 'That is the Consecration wine—red as my beard,' quoth he.

'Ha! ha! the red Consecration wine!' repeated the synagogue in a happy buzz, and from the women's gallery came the same glad murmur of mutual explanation.

'We shall see,' repeated the officer, with iron imperturbability, and the happy hum died into a cold heart-faintness, fraught with an almost incredulous apprehension of some devilish treachery, some mock discovery that would give the Ghetto over to the frenzies of fanatical creditors, nay, to the vengeance of the law.

The officer's voice rose again. 'Let no one leave the synagogue—man, woman, or child. Kill anyone who attempts to escape.'

The screams of fainting women answered him from above, but impassively he urged his horse along the aisle that led to the Ark; its noisy hoofs trampled over every heart. Springing from his saddle he opened the little cupboard beneath the scrolls, and drew out a bottle, hideously red.

'Consecration wine, eh?' he said grimly.

'What else, Excellency?' stoutly replied the Shamash, who had followed him.

A savage laugh broke from the officer's lips. 'Drink me a mouthful!'

As the Shamash took the bottle, with a fearless shrug of the shoulders, every eye strained painfully towards him, save in the women's gallery, where many covered their faces with their hands. Every breath was held.

Keeping the same amused incredulous face, Red Judah gulped down a draught. But as the liquid met his palate a horrible distortion overcame his smile, his hands flew heavenwards. Dropping the bottle, and with a hoarse cry, 'Mercy, O God!' he fell before the Ark, foaming at the mouth. The red fluid spread in a vivid pool.

'Hear, O Israel!' A raucous cry of horror rose from all around, and was echoed more shrilly from above. Almighty Father! The Jew-haters had worked their fiendish trick. Now the men were become as the women, shrieking, wringing their hands, crying, 'Ai, vai!' 'Gewalt!' The Rabbi shook as with palsy. 'Satan! Satan!' chattered through his teeth.

But Ben Amram had moved at last, and was stooping over the scarlet stain.

'A soldier should know blood, Excellency!' the physician said quietly.

The officer's face relaxed into a faint smile.

'A soldier knows wine too,' he said, sniffing. And, indeed, the spicy reek of the Consecration wine was bewildering the nearer bystanders.

'Your Excellency frightened poor Judah into a fit,' said the physician, raising the beadle's head by its long red beard.

His Excellency shrugged his shoulders, sprang to his saddle, and cried a retreat. The Cossacks, unable to turn in the aisle, backed cumbrously with a manifold thudding and rearing and clanking, but ere the congregation had finished rubbing their eyes, the last conical hat and leaded knout had vanished, and only the tarry reek of their boots was left in proof of their actual passage. A deep silence hung for a moment like a heavy cloud, then it broke in a torrent of ejaculations.

But Ben Amram's voice rang through the din. 'Brethren!' He rose from wiping the frothing lips of the stricken creature, and his face had the fiery gloom of a seer's, and the din died under his uplifted palm. 'Brethren, the Lord hath saved us!'

'Blessed be the name of the Lord for ever and ever!' The Rabbi began the phrase, and the congregation caught it up in thunder.

'But hearken how. Last night at the Seder, as I opened the door for Elijah, there entered Maimon the Meshummad! 'Twas he quaffed Elijah's cup!'

There was a rumble of imprecations.

'A pretty Elijah!' cried the Rabbi.

'Nay, but God sends the Prophet of Redemption in strange guise,' the physician said. 'Listen! Maimon was pursued by a drunken mob, ignorant he was a deserter from our camp. When he found how I had saved him and dressed his bleeding face, when he saw the spread Passover table, his child-soul came back to him, and in a burst of tears he confessed the diabolical plot against our community, hatched through his instrumentality by some desperate debtors; how, having raised the cry of a lost child, they were to have its blood found beneath our Holy Ark as in some mystic atonement. And while you all lolled joyously at the Seder table, a bottle of blood lay here instead of the Consecration wine, like a bomb waiting to burst and destroy us all.'

A shudder of awe traversed the synagogue.

'But the Guardian of Israel, who permits us to sleep on Passover night without night-prayer, neither slumbers nor sleeps. Maimon had bribed the Shamash to let him enter the synagogue and replace the Consecration wine.'

'Red Judah!' It was like the growl of ten thousand tigers. Some even precipitated themselves upon the writhing wretch.

'Back! back!' cried Ben Amram. 'The Almighty has smitten him.'

'"Vengeance is mine, saith the Lord,"' quoted the Rabbi solemnly.

'Hallelujah!' shouted a frenzied female voice, and 'Hallelujah!' the men responded in thunder.

'Red Judah had no true belief in the God of Israel,' the physician went on.

'May he be an atonement for us all!' interrupted the Cantor.

'Amen!' growled the congregation.

'For a hundred roubles and the promise of personal immunity Red Judah allowed Maimon the Meshummad to change the bottles while all Israel sat at the Seder. It was because the mob saw the Meshummad stealing out of the synagogue that they fell upon him for a pious Jew. Behold, brethren, how the Almighty weaves His threads together. After the repentant sinner had confessed all to me, and explained how the Cossacks were to be sent to catch all the community assembled helpless in synagogue, I deemed it best merely to get the bottles changed back again. The false bottle contained only bullock's blood, but it would have sufficed to madden the multitude. Since it is I who have the blessed privilege of supplying the Consecration wine it was easy enough to give Maimon another bottle, and armed with this he roused the Shamash in the dawn, pretending he had now obtained true human blood. A rouble easily procured him the keys again, and when he brought me back the bullock's blood, I awaited the sequel in peace.'

'Praise ye the Lord, for He is good,' sang the Cantor, carried away.

'For His mercy endureth for ever,' replied the congregation instinctively.

'I did not foresee the Shamash would put himself so brazenly forward to hide his guilt, or that he would be asked to drink. But when the Epikouros (atheist) put the bottle to his lips, expecting to taste blood, and found instead good red wine, doubtless he felt at once that the God of Israel was truly in heaven, that He had wrought a miracle and changed the blood back to wine.'

'And such a miracle God wrought verily,' cried the Rabbi, grasping the physician's hand, while the synagogue resounded with cries of 'May thy strength increase,' and the gallery heaved frantically with blessings and congratulations.

'What wonder,' the physician wound up, as he bent again over the ghastly head, with its pious ringlets writhing like red snakes, 'that he fell stricken by dread of the Almighty's wrath!'

And while men were bearing the convulsive form without, the Cantor began to recite the Grace after Redemption. And then the happy hymns rolled out, and the choristers cried 'Pom!' and a breath of jubilant hope passed through the synagogue. The mighty hand and the outstretched arm which had redeemed Israel from the Egyptian bondage were still hovering over them, nor would the Prophet Elijah for ever delay to announce the ultimate Messiah.

THE HIRELINGS

I

Crowded as was the steamer with cultured Americans invading Europe, few knew that Rozenoffski was on board, or even that Rozenoffski was a pianist. The name, casually seen on the passengers' list, conveyed nothing but a strong Russian and a vaguer Semitic flavour, and the mere outward man, despite a leonine head, was of insignificant port and somewhat shuffling gait, and drew scarcely a second glance.

He would not have had it otherwise, he told himself, as he paced the almost deserted deck after dinner—it was a blessing to escape from the perpetual adulation of music-sick matrons and schoolgirls—but every wounded fibre in him was yearning for consolation after his American failure.

Not that his fellow-passengers were aware of his failure; he had not put himself to the vulgar tests. His American expedition had followed the lines recommended to him by friendly connoisseurs—to come before the great public, if at all, only after being launched by great hostesses at small parties; to which end he had provided himself with unimpeachable introductions to unexceptionable ladies from irresistible personalities—a German Grand Duke, a Bulgarian Ambassador, Countesses, both French and Italian, and even a Belgian princess. But to his boundless amazement—for he had always heard that Americans were wax before titles—not one of the social leaders had been of the faintest assistance to him, not even the owner of the Chicago Palace, to whom he had been recommended by the Belgian princess. He had penetrated through one or two esoteric doors, only to find himself outside them again. Not once had he been asked to play. It was some weeks before it even dawned upon the minor prophet of European music-rooms that he was being shut out, still longer before it permeated to his brain that he had been shut out as a Jew!

Those barbarous Americans, so far behind Europe after all! Had they not even discovered that art levels all ranks and races? Poor bourgeois money-mongers with their mushroom civilization. It was not even as if he were really a Jew. Did they imagine he wore phylacteries or earlocks, or what? His few childish years in the Russian Pale—what were they to the long years of European art and European culture? And even if in Rome or Paris he had foregathered with Jews like Schneemann or Leopold Barstein, it was to the artist in them he had gravitated, not the Jew. Did these Yankee ignoramuses suppose he did not share their aversion from the gaberdine or the three brass balls? Oh the narrow-souled anti-Semites!

The deck-steward stacked the chairs, piled up the forgotten rugs and novels, tidying the deck for the night, but still the embittered musician tramped to and fro under the silent stars. Only from the smoking-room where the amateur auctioneer was still hilariously selling the numbers for a sweepstake, came sounds in discord with the solemnity of sky and sea, and the artist was newly jarred at this vulgar gaiety flung in the face of the spacious and starry mystery of the night. And these jocose, heavy-jowled, smoke-soused gamblers were the Americans whose drawing-rooms he would contaminate! He recalled the only party to which he had been asked—'To meet the Bright Lights'—and which to his amazement turned out to be a quasi-public entertainment with the guests seated in rows in a hall, and himself— with the other Bright Lights—planted on a platform and made to perform without a fee. The mean vulgarians! But perhaps it was better they had left him untainted with their dollars—better, comparatively poor though he was, that America should have meant pure loss to him. He had at least kept the spiritual satisfaction of despising the despiser, the dignity of righteous resentment, the artist's pride in the profitless. And this riot of ugliness and diamonds and third-rate celebrities was the fashionable society to which, forsooth, the Jew could not be permitted access!

The aroma of an expensive cigar wafted towards him, and the face between whose prominent teeth it was stuck loomed vividly in the glare of an electric light. Rozenoffski recognised those teeth. He had seen countless pictures and caricatures of them, for did they not almost hold the globe in their grip? This, then was the notorious multi-millionaire, 'the Napoleon in dollars,' as a wit had summed him up; and the first sight of Andrew P. Wilhammer almost consoled the player for his poverty. Who, even for an imperial income, would bear the burden of those grotesque teeth, protruding like a sample of wares in a dentist's showcase? But as the teeth came nearer and the great rubicund face bore down upon him, the prominence of the notorious incisors affected him less than their carnivorous capacity—he felt himself almost swallowed up by this monstrous beast of prey, so admirably equated to our small day of large things, to that environment in which he, poor degenerate artist, was but a little singing-bird. The long-forgotten word Rishus came suddenly into his mind—was not the man's anti-Semitism as obtruded as his teeth?—Rishus, that wicked malice, which to a persecuted people had become almost a synonym for Christianity. He had left the thought behind him, as he had left the Hebrew word, while he went sailing up into the rosy ether of success, and Rishus had sunk into the mere panic-word of the Ghetto's stunted brood, shrinking and quivering before phantasms, sinuously gliding through a misunderstood world, if it was not, indeed, rather a word conveniently cloaking from themselves a multitude of their own sins. But now, as incarnated in this millionaire mammoth, the shadowy word took on a sudden solidity, to which his teeth gave the necessary tearing and rending significance.

Yes, in very sooth—he remembered it suddenly—was it not this man's wife on whom he had built his main hopes? Was she not the leader of musical America, to whom the Belgian princess had given him the scented and crested note of introduction which was to open to him all doors and all ears? Was it not in her marvellous marble music-room—one of the boasts of Chicago—that he had mentally seen himself enthroned as the lord of the feast? And instead of these Olympian visions, lo! a typewritten note to clench his fist over—a note from a secretary regretting that the state of Mrs. Wilhammer's health forbade the pleasure of receiving a maestro with such credentials. Rishus—Rishus indubitable!

II

Turning with morbid interest to look after the retreating millionaire, he found him in converse with a feminine figure at the open door of a deck-cabin. Could this be the great She, the arbitress of art? He moved nearer. Why, this was but a girl—nay, unless his instinct was at fault, a Jewish girl—a glorious young Jewess, of that radiant red-haired type which the Russian Pale occasionally flowered with. What was she doing with this Christian Colossus? He tried vainly to see her left hand; the mere possibility that she might be Mrs. Wilhammer shocked his Semitic instinct. Wilhammer disappeared within—the relation was obviously intimate—but the girl still stood at the door, a brooding magical figure.

Almost a sense of brotherhood moved him to speak to her, but he conquered the abnormal and incorrect impulse, contenting himself to walk past her with a side-glance, while at the end of the deck-promenade, instead of returning on his footsteps, he even arched his path round to the windy side. After some minutes of buffeting he returned chilled to his prior pacing ground. She was still there, but had moved under the same electric light which had illuminated Wilhammer's face, and she was reading a letter. As his walk carried him past her, he was startled to see tears rolling down those radiant cheeks. A slight exclamation came involuntarily from him; the girl, even more startled to be caught thus, relaxed her grip of the letter—a puff of wind hastened to whirl it aloft. Rozenoffski grasped at it desperately, but it eluded him, and then descending sailed sternwards. He gave chase, stumbling over belated chairs and deck-quoits, but at last it was safe in his clutch, and as he handed it to the agitated owner whom he found at his elbow, he noted with a thrill that the characters were cursive Hebrew.

'How can I zank you, sir!' Her Teutonic-touched American gave him the courage to reply gallantly in German:

'By letting me help you more seriously.'

'Ach, mein Herr'—she jumped responsively into German—'it was for joy I was crying, not sorrow.' As her American was Germanic, so was her German like the Yiddish of his remote youth, and this, adding to the sweetness of her voice, dissolved the musician's heart within his breast. He noted now with satisfaction that her fingers were bare of rings.

'Then I am rejoiced too,' he ventured to reply.

She smiled pathetically, and began to walk back towards her cabin. 'With us Jews,' she said, 'tears and laughter are very close.'

'Us Jews!' He winced a little. It was so long since he had been thus classed to his face by a stranger. But perhaps he had misinterpreted her phrase; it was her way of referring to her race, not necessarily to his.

'It is a beautiful night,' he murmured uneasily. But he only opened wider the flood-gates of race-feeling.

'Yes,' she replied simply, 'and such a heaven of stars is beginning to arise over the night of Israel. Is it not wonderful—the transformation of our people? When I left Russia as a girl—so young,' she interpolated with a sad smile, 'that I had not even been married—I left a priest-ridden, paralysed people, a cringing, cowering, contorted people—I shall never forget the panic in our synagogue when a troop of Cossacks rode in with a bogus blood-accusation. Now it is a people alive with ideas and volitions; the young generation dreams noble dreams, and, what is stranger, dies to execute them. Our Bund is the soul of the Russian revolution; our self-defence bands are bringing back the days of Judas Maccabæus. In the olden times of massacre our people fled to the synagogues to pray; now they march to the fight like men.'

They had arrived at her door, and she ended suddenly. The musician, fascinated, feared she was about to fade away within.

'But Jews can't fight!' he cried, half-incredulous, half to arrest her.

'Not fight!' She held up the Hebrew letter. 'They have scouts, ambulance corps, orderlies, surgeons, everything—my cousin David Ben Amram, who is little more than a boy, was told off to defend a large three-story house inhabited by the families of factory-labourers who were at work when the pogrom broke out. The poor frenzied women and children had barricaded themselves within at the first rumour, and hidden themselves in cellars and attics. My cousin had to climb to their defence over the neighbouring tiles and through a window in the roof. Soon the house was besieged by police, troops, and hooligans in devilish league. With his one Browning revolver David held them all at bay, firing from every window of the house in turn, so as to give the besiegers an impression of a large defensive force. At last his cartridges were exhausted—to procure cartridges is the greatest difficulty of our self-defence corps—they began battering in the big front-door. David, seeing further resistance was useless, calmly drew back the bolts, to the mob's amaze, and, as it poured in, he cried: 'Back! back! They have bombs!' and rushed into the street, as if to escape the explosion. The others followed wildly, and in the panic David ran down a dark alley, and disappeared in search of a new post of defence. Though the door stood open, and the cowering inhabitants were at their mercy, the assailants, afraid to enter, remained for over an hour at a safe distance firing at the house, till it was riddled with bullets. They counted nearly two hundred the next day, embedded in the walls or strewn about the rooms. And not a thing had been stolen—not a hooligan had dared enter. But David is only a type of the young generation—there are hundreds of Davids equally ready to take the field against Goliath. And shall I not rejoice, shall I not exult even unto tears?' Her eyes glowed, and the musician was kindled to equal fire. It seemed to him less a girl who was speaking than Truth and Purity and some dead muse of his own. 'The Pale that I left,' she went on, 'was truly a prison. But now—now it will be the forging-place of a regenerated people! Oh, I am counting the days till I can be back!'

'You are going back to Russia!' he gasped.

He had the sensation of cold steel passing through his heart. The pogroms, which had been as remote to him as the squabbles of savages in Central Africa, became suddenly vivid and near. And even vivider and nearer that greater danger—the heroic Cousin David!

'How can I live away from Russia at such a moment?' she answered quietly. 'Who or what needs me in America?'

'But to be massacred!' he cried incoherently.

She smiled radiantly. 'To live and die with my own people.'

The fire in his veins seemed upleaping in a sublime jet; he was like to crying, 'Thy people shall be my people,' but all he found himself saying was, 'You must not, you must not; what can a girl like you do?'

A bell rang sharply from the cabin.

'I must go to my mistress. Gute Nacht, mein Herr!'

His flame sank to sudden ashes. Only Mrs. Wilhammer's hireling!

III

The wind freshened towards the middle of the night, and Rozenoffski, rocking in his berth, cursed his encounter with the red-haired romanticist who had stirred up such a pother in his brain that he had not been able to fall asleep while the water was still calm. Not that he suffered physically from the sea; he was merely afraid of it. The shuddering and groaning of the ship found an echo in his soul. He could not shake off the conviction that he was doomed to drown. At intervals, during the tedious night, he found forgetfulness in translating into sound his sense of the mystic, masterless waste in which the continents swim like islands, but music was soon swallowed up in terror.

'No,' he sighed, with a touch of self-mockery. 'When I am safe on shore again, I shall weave my symphony of the sea.'

Sleep came at last, but only to perturb him with a Jewish Joan of Arc who—turned Admiral—recaptured Zion from her battleship, to the sound of Psalms droned by his dead grandfather. And, though he did not see her the next day, and was, indeed, rather glad not to meet a lady's maid in the unromantic daylight, the restlessness she had engendered remained, replacing the settled bitterness which was all he had brought back from America. In the afternoon this restlessness drove him to the piano in the deserted dining-hall, and his fever sought to work itself off in a fury of practice. But the inner turbulence persisted, and the new thoughts clung round the old music. He was playing Schumann's Fantasiestücke, but through the stormy passion of In der Nacht he saw the red hair of the heroic Jewess, and into the wistful, questioning Warum insinuated itself not the world-question, but the Jewish question—the sad, unending Jewish question—surging up again and again in every part of the globe, as Schumann's theme in every part of the piano—the same haunting musical figure, never the same notes exactly, yet essentially always the same, the wistful, questioning Warum. Why all this ceaseless sorrow, this footsore wandering, this rootless life, this eternal curse?

Suddenly he became aware that he was no longer alone—forms were seated at the tables on the fixed dining-chairs, though there was no meal but his music; and as he played on, with swift side-peeps, other fellow-passengers entered into his consciousness, some standing about, others hovering on the stairs, and still others stealing in on reverent tip-toe and taking favourable seats. His breast filled with bitter satisfaction.

So they had to come, the arrogant Americans; they had to swarm like rats to the pied piper. He could draw them at will, the haughty heathen—draw them by the magic of his finger-touch on pieces of ivory. Lo, they were coming, more and more of them! Through the corner of his eye he espied the figures drifting in from the corridors, peering in spellbound at the doors.

With a great crash on the keys, he shook off his morbid mood, and plunged into Scarlatti's Sonata in A, his fingers frolicking all over the board, bent on a dominating exhibition of technique. As he stopped, there was a storm of hand-clapping. Rozenoffski gave a masterly start of surprise, and turned his leonine head in dazed bewilderment. Was he not then alone? 'Gott im Himmel!' he murmured, and, furiously banging down the piano-lid, stalked from these presumptuous mortals who had jarred the artist's soliloquy.

But the next afternoon found him again at the public piano, devoting all the magic of his genius to charming a contemptible Christendom. He gave them Beethoven and Bach, Paradies and Tschaikowski, unrolled to them the vast treasures of his art and memory. And very soon, lo! the Christian rats were pattering back again, only more wisely and cautiously. They came crawling from every part of the ship's compass. Newcomers were warned whisperingly to keep from applause. In vain. An enraptured greenhorn shouted 'Encore!' The musician awoke from his trance, stared dreamily at the Philistines; then, as the presence of listeners registered itself upon his expressive countenance, he rose again—but this time as more in sorrow than in anger—and stalked sublimely up the swarming stairs.

It became a tradition to post guards at the doors to warn all comers as to the habits of the great unknown, who could only beat his music out if he imagined himself unheard. Scouts watched his afternoon advance upon the piano in an empty hall, and the word was passed to the little army of music-lovers. Silently the rats gathered, scurrying in on noiseless paws, stealing into the chairs, swarming about the doorways, pricking up their ears in the corridors. And through the awful hush rose the master's silvery notes in rapturous self-oblivion till the day began to wane, and the stewards to appear with the tea-cups.

And the larger his audience grew, the fiercer grew his resentment against this complacent Christendom which took so much from the Jew and gave so little. 'Shylocks!' he would mutter between his clenched teeth as he played—'Shylocks all!'

IV

With no less punctuality did Rozenoffski pace the silent deck each night in the hope of again meeting the red-haired Jewess. He had soon recovered from her menial office; indeed, the paradox of her position in so anti-Semitic a household quickened his interest in her. He wondered if she ever listened to his playing, or had realized that she had entertained an angel unawares.

But three nights passed without glimpse of her. Nor was her mistress more visible. The Wilhammers kept royally to themselves in their palatial suite, though the husband sometimes deigned to parade his fangs in the smoking-room, where with the luck of the rich he won heavily in the pools. It was not till the penultimate night of the voyage that Rozenoffski caught his second glimpse of his red-haired muse. He had started his nocturnal pacing much earlier than usual, for the inevitable concert on behalf of marine charities had sucked the loungers from their steamer-chairs. He had himself, of course, been approached by the programme-organizer, a bouncing actress from 'Frisco, with an irresistible air, but he had defeated her hopelessly with the mysterious sarcasm: 'To meet the Bright Lights?' And his reward was to have the deck and the heavens almost to himself, and presently to find the stars outgleamed by a girl's hair. Yes, there she was, gazing pensively forth from the cabin window. He guessed the mistress was out for once—presumably at the concert. His heart beat faster as he came to a standstill, yet the reminder that she was a lady's maid brought an involuntary note of condescension into his voice.

'I hope Mrs. Wilhammer hasn't been keeping you too imprisoned?' he said.

She smiled faintly. 'Not so close as Neptune has kept her.'

'Ill?' he said, with a shade of malicious satisfaction.

'It is curious and even consoling to see the limitations of Croesus,' she replied. 'But she is lucky—she just recovered in time.'

'In time for what?'

'Can't you hear?'

Indeed, the shrill notes of an amateur soprano had been rending the air throughout, but they had scarcely penetrated through his exaltation. He now shuddered.

'Do you mean it is she singing?'

The girl laughed outright. 'She sing! No, no, she is a sensitive receiver. She receives; she gives out nothing. She exploits her soul as her husband exploits the globe. There isn't a sensation or an emotion she denies herself—unless it is painful. It was to escape the concert that she has left her couch—and sought refuge in a friend's cabin. You see, here sound travels straight from the dining-hall, and a false note, she says, gives her nerve-ache.'

'Then she can't return till the close of the concert,' he said eagerly. 'Won't you come outside and walk a bit under this beautiful moon?'

She came out without a word, with the simplicity of a comrade.

'Yes, it is a beautiful night,' she said, 'and very soon I shall be in Russia.'

'But is Mrs. Wilhammer going to Russia, then?' he asked, with a sudden thought, wondering that it had never occurred to him before.

'Of course not! I only joined her for this voyage. I have to work my passage, you see, and Providence, on the eve of sailing, robbed Mrs. Wilhammer of her maid.'

'Oh!' he murmured in relief. His red-haired muse was going back to her social pedestal. 'But you must have found it humiliating,' he said.

'Humiliating?' She laughed cheerfully. 'Why more than manicuring her?'

The muse shivered again on the pedestal.

'Manicuring?' he echoed in dismay.

'Sure!' she laughed in American. 'When, after a course of starvation and medicine at Berne University, I found I had to get a new degree for America....'

'You are a doctor?' he interrupted.

'And, therefore, peculiarly serviceable as a ship-maid.'

She smiled again, and her smile in the moonlight reminded him of a rippling passage of Chopin. Prosaic enough, however, was what she went on to tell him of her struggle for life by day and for learning by night. 'Of course, I could only attend the night medical school. I lived by lining cloaks with fur; my bed was the corner of a room inhabited by a whole family. A would-be graduate could not be seen with bundles; for fetching and carrying the work my good landlady extorted twenty cents to the dollar. When the fur season was slack I cooked in a restaurant, worked a typewriter, became a "hello girl"—at a telephone, you know—reported murder cases—anything, everything.'

'Manicuring,' he recalled tenderly.

'Manicuring,' she repeated smilingly. 'And you ask me if it is humiliating to wait upon an artistic sea-sick lady!'

'Artistic!' he sneered. His heart was full of pity and indignation.

'As surely as sea-sick!' she rejoined laughingly. 'Why are you prejudiced against her?'

He flushed. 'Prej-prejudiced?' he stammered. 'Why should I be prejudiced? From all I hear it's she that's prejudiced. It's a wonder she took a Jewess into her service.'

'Where's the wonder? Don't the Southerners have negro servants?' she asked quietly.

His flush deepened. 'You compare Jews to negroes!'

'I apologize to the negroes. The blacks have at least Liberia. There is a black President, a black Parliament. We have nothing, nothing!'

'We!' Again that ambiguous plural. But he still instinctively evaded co-classification.

'Nothing?' he retorted. 'I should have said everything. Every gift of genius that Nature can shower from her cornucopia.'

'Jewish geniuses!' Her voice had a stinging inflection. 'Don't talk to me of our geniuses; it is they that have betrayed us. Every other people has its great men; but our great men—they belong to every other people. The world absorbs our sap, and damns us for our putrid remains. Our best must pipe alien tunes and dance to the measures of the heathen. They build and paint; they write and legislate. But never a song of Israel do they fashion, nor a picture of Israel, nor a law of Israel, nor a temple of Israel. Bah! What are they but hirelings?'

Again the passion of her patriotism uplifted and enkindled him. Yes, it was true. He, too, was but a hireling. But he would become a Master; he would go back—back to the Ghetto, and this noble Jewess should be his mate. Thank God he had kept himself free for her. But ere he could pour out his soul, the bouncing San Franciscan actress appeared suddenly at his elbow, risking a last desperate assault, discharging a pathetic tale of a comedian with a cold. Rozenoffski repelled the attack savagely, but before he could exhaust the enemy's volubility his red-haired companion had given him a friendly nod and smile, and retreated into her shrine of duty.

V

He spent a sleepless but happy night, planning out their future together; her redemption from her hireling status, their joint work for their people. He was no longer afraid of the sea. He was afraid of nothing—not even of the pogroms that awaited them in Russia. Russia itself became dear to him again—the beautiful land of his boyhood, whose birds and whispering leaves and waters had made his earliest music.

But dearer than all resurged his Jewish memories. When he went almost mechanically to the piano on the last afternoon, all these slumbering forces wakened in him found vent in a rhapsody of synagogue melody to which he abandoned himself, for once forgetting his audience. When gradually he became aware of the incongruity, it did but intensify his inspiration. Let the heathen rats wallow in Hebrew music! But soon all self-consciousness passed away again, drowned in his deeper self.

It was a strange fantasia that poured itself through his obedient fingers; it held the wistful chants of ancient ritual, the festival roulades and plaintive yearnings of melodious cantors, the sing-song augmentation of Talmud-students oscillating in airless study-houses, the long, melancholy drone of Psalm-singers in darkening Sabbath twilights, the rustle of palm-branches and sobbings of penitence, the long-drawn notes of the ram's horn pealing through the Terrible Days, the passionate proclamation of the Unity, storming the gates of heaven. And fused with these merely physical memories, there flowed into the music the peace of Sabbath evenings and shining candles, the love and wonder of childhood's faith, the fantasy of Rabbinic legend, the weirdness of penitential prayers in raw winter dawns, the holy joy of the promised Zion, when God would wipe away the tears from all faces.

There were tears to be wiped from his own face when he ended, and he wiped them brazenly, unresentful of the frenzied approval of the audience, which now let itself go, out of stored-up gratitude, and because this must be the last performance. All his vanity, his artistic posing, was swallowed up in utter sincerity. He did not shut the piano; he sat brooding a moment or two in tender reverie. Suddenly he perceived his red-haired muse at his side. Ah, she had discovered him at last, knew him simultaneously for the genius and the patriot, was come to pour out her soul at his feet. But why was she mute? Why was she tendering this scented letter? Was it because she could not trust herself to speak before the crowd? He tore open the delicate envelope. Himmel! what was this? Would the maestro honour Mrs. Wilhammer by taking tea in her cabin?

He stared dazedly at the girl, who remained respectful and silent.

'Did you not hear what I was playing?' he murmured.

'Oh yes—a synagogue medley,' she replied quietly. 'They publish it on the East Side, nicht wahr?'

'East Side?' He was outraged. 'I know nothing of East Side.' Her absolute unconsciousness of his spiritual tumult, her stolidity before this spectacle of his triumphant genius, her matter-of-fact acceptance of his racial affinity, her refusal to be impressed by the heroism of a Hebrew pianoforte solo, all she said and did not say, jarred upon his quivering nerves, chilled his high emotion. 'Will you say I shall have much pleasure?' he added coldly.

The red-haired maid nodded and was gone. Rozenoffski went mechanically to his cabin, scarcely seeing the worshippers he plodded through; presently he became aware that he was changing his linen, brushing his best frock-coat, thrilling with pleasurable excitement.

Anon he was tapping at the well-known door. A voice—of another sweetness—cried 'Come!' and instantly he had the sensation that his touch on the handle had launched upon him, as by some elaborate electric contrivance, a tall and beautiful American, a rustling tea-gown, a shimmer of rings, a reek of patchouli, and a flood of compliment.

'So delightful of you to come—I know you men of genius are farouches—it was awfully insolent of me, I know, but you have forgiven me, haven't you?'

'The pleasure is mine, gracious lady,' he murmured in German.

'Ach, so you are a German,' she replied in the same tongue. 'I thought no American or Englishman could have so much divine fire. You see, mein Herr, I do not even know your name—only your genius. Every afternoon I have lain here, lapped in your music, but I might never have had the courage to thank you had you not played that marvellous thing just now—such delicious heartbreak, such adorable gaiety, and now and then the thunder of the gods! I'm afraid you'll think me very ignorant—it wasn't Grieg, was it?'

He looked uncomfortable. 'Nothing so good, I fear—a mere impromptu of my own.'

'Your own!' She clapped her jewelled hands in girlish delight. 'Oh, where can I get it?'

'East Side,' some mocking demon tried to reply; but he crushed her down, and replied uneasily: 'You can't get it. It just came to me this afternoon. It came—and it has gone.'

'What a pity!' But she was visibly impressed by this fecundity and riotous extravagance of genius. 'I do hope you will try to remember it.'

'Impossible—it was just a mood.'

'And to think of all the other moods I seem to have missed! Why have I not heard you in America?'

He grew red. 'I—I haven't been playing there,' he murmured. 'You see, I'm not much known outside a few European circles.' Then, summoning up all his courage, he threw down his name 'Rozenoffski' like a bomb, and the red of his cheeks changed to the pallor of apprehension. But no explosion followed, save of enthusiasm. Evidently, the episode so lurid to his own memory, had left no impress on hers.

'Oh, but America must know you, Herr Rozenoffski. You must promise me to come back in the fall, give me the glory of launching you.' And, seeing the cloud on his face, she cried: 'You must, you must, you must!' clapping her hands at each 'must.'

He hesitated, distracted between rapture and anxiety lest she should remember.

'You have never heard of me, of course,' she persisted humbly; 'but positively everybody has played at my house in Chicago.'

'Ach so!' he muttered. Had he perhaps misinterpreted and magnified the attitude of these Americans? Was it possible that Mrs. Wilhammer had really been too ill to see him? She looked frail and feverish behind all her brilliant beauty. Or had she not even seen his letter? had her secretary presumed to guard her from Semitic invaders? Or was she deliberately choosing to forget and forgive his Jewishness? In any case, best let sleeping dogs lie. He was being sought; it would be the silliest of social blunders to recall that he had already been rejected.

'It is years since Chicago had a real musical sensation,' pleaded the temptress.

'I'm afraid my engagements will not permit me to return this autumn,' he replied tactfully.

'Do you take sugar?' she retorted unexpectedly; then, as she handed him his cup, she smiled archly into his eyes. 'You can't shake me off, you know; I shall follow you about Europe—to all your concerts.'

When he left her—after inscribing his autograph, his permanent Munich address, and the earliest possible date for his Chicago concert, in a dainty diary brought in by her red-haired maid—his whole being was swelling, expanding. He had burst the coils of this narrow tribalism that had suddenly retwined itself round him; he had got back again from the fusty conventicles and the sunless Ghettos— back to spacious salons and radiant hostesses and the great free life of art. He drew deep breaths of sea-air as he paced the deck, strewn so thickly with pleasant passengers to whom he felt drawn in a renewed sense of the human brotherhood. Rishus, forsooth!

SAMOOBORONA

I

Milovka was to be the next place reddened on the map of Holy Russia. The news of the projected Jewish massacre in this little Polish town travelled to the Samooborona (Self-Defence) Headquarters in Southern Russia through the indiscretion of a village pope who had had a drop of blood too much. It appeared that Milovka, though remote from the great centres of disturbance, had begun to seethe with political activity, and even to publish a newspaper, so that it was necessary to show by a first-class massacre that true Russian men were still loyal to God and the Czar. Milovka lay off the pogrom route, and had not of itself caught the contagion; careful injection of the virus was necessary. Moreover, the town was two-thirds Jewish, and consequently harder to fever with the lust of Jewish blood. But in revenge the pogrom would be easier; the Jewish quarter formed a practically separate town; no asking of dvorniks (janitors) to point out the Jewish apartments, no arming one's self with photographs of the victims; one had but to run amuck among these low wooden houses, the humblest of which doubtless oozed with inexhaustible subterranean wealth.

David Ben Amram was hurriedly despatched to Milovka to organize a local self-defence corps. He carried as many pistols as could be stowed away in a violin-case, which, with a music-roll holding cartridges, was an obtrusive feature of his luggage. The winter was just beginning, but mildly. The sun shone over the broad plains, and as David's train carried him towards Milovka, his heart swelled with thoughts of the Maccabean deeds to be wrought there by a regenerated Young Israel. But the journey was long. Towards the end he got into conversation with an old Russian peasant who, so far from sharing in the general political effervescence, made a long lament over the good old days of serfdom. 'Then, one had not to think—one ate and drank. Now, it is all toil and trouble.'

'But you were whipped at your lord's pleasure,' David reminded him.

'He was a nobleman,' retorted the peasant with dignity.

David fell silent. The Jew, too, had grown to kiss the rod. But it was not even a nobleman's rod; any moujik, any hooligan, could wield it. But, thank Heaven, this breed of Jew was passing away—killed by the pogroms. It was their one virtue.

At the station he hired a ramshackle droshky, and told his Jewish driver to take him to the best inn. Seated astride the old-fashioned bench of the vehicle, and grasping his violin-case like a loving musician, as they jolted over the rough roads, he broached the subject of the Jewish massacres.

'Bê!' commented the driver, shrugging his shoulders. 'We are in Goluth (exile)!' He spoke with resignation, but not with apprehension, and David perceived at once that Milovka would not be easy to arouse. As every man thought every other man mortal, so Milovka regarded the massacres as a terrible reality—for other towns. It was no longer even shocked; Kishineff had been a horror almost beyond belief, but Jew-massacres had since become part of the natural order, which babes were born into.

II

The landlord shook his head.

'All our rooms are full.'

David, still hugging his violin-case, looked at the dirty, mustard-smeared tablecloth on the long table, and at the host's brats playing on the floor. If this was the best, what in Heaven's name awaited him elsewhere?

'For how long?' he asked.

The landlord shrugged his shoulders like the driver. 'Am I the All-knowing?'

He wore a black velvet cap, but not with the apex that would have professed piety. Its square cut indicated to the younger generation that he was a man of the world, in touch with the times; to the old its material and hue afforded sufficient guarantee of ritual orthodoxy. He was a true host, the friend of all who eat and drink.

'But how many rooms have you?' inquired David.

'And how many shall I have but one?' protested the landlord.

'Only one room!' David turned upon the driver. 'And you said this was the best inn! I suppose it's your brother-in-law's.'

'And what do I make out of it, if it is?' answered the driver. 'You see he can't take you.'

'Then why did you bring me?'

'Because there is no room anywhere else either.'

'What!' David stared.

'Law of Moses!' corroborated the landlord good-humouredly, 'you've just come at the recruiting. The young men have flocked here from all the neighbouring villages to draw their numbers. There are heathen peasants in all the Jewish inns—eating kosher,' he added with a chuckle.

David frowned. But he reflected instantly that if this was so, the pogrom would probably be postponed till the Christian conscripts had been packed off to their regiments or the lucky ones back to their villages. He would have time, therefore, to organize his Jewish corps. Yes, he reflected in grim amusement, Russia and he would be recruiting simultaneously. Still, where was he to sleep?

'You can have the lezhanka,' said the host, following his thoughts.

David looked ruefully at the high stove. Well, there were worse beds in winter than the top of a stove. And perhaps to bestow himself and his violin in such very public quarters would be the safest way of diverting police attention. 'Conspirators, please copy,' he thought, with a smile. Anyhow, he was very tired. He could refresh himself here; the day was yet young; time enough to find a better lodging.

'Bring in the luggage,' he said resignedly.

'Tea?' said the host, hovering over the samovar.

'Haven't you a drop of vodka?'

The landlord held up hands of horror. 'Monopolka?' (monopoly), he cried.

'Haven't they left any Jewish licenses?' asked David.

'Not unless one mixed holy water with the vodka, like the baptized Benjamin,' said the landlord with grim humour. He added hastily: 'But his inn is even fuller than mine, four beds in the room.'

It appeared that the dinner was already over, and David could obtain nothing but half-warmed remains. However, hunger and hope gave sauce to the miserable meal, and he profited by the absence of custom to pump the landlord anent the leading citizens.

'But you will not get violin lessons from any of them,' his host warned him. 'Tinowitz the corn-factor has daughters who are said to read Christian story-books, but is it likely he will risk their falling in love with a young man whose hair and clothes are cut like a Christian's? Not that I share his prejudices, of course. I have seen the great world, and understand that it is possible to carry a handkerchief on the Sabbath and still be a good man.'

'I haven't come to give lessons in music,' said David bluntly, 'but in shooting.'

'Shooting?' The landlord stared. 'Aren't you a Jew, then, sir? I beg your pardon.' His voice had suddenly taken on the same ring as when he addressed the Poritz (Polish nobleman). His oleaginous familiarity was gone.

'Salachti!' (I have forgiven), said David in Hebrew, and laughed at the man's bemused visage. 'Don't you think, considering what has been happening, it is high time the Jews of Milovka learned to shoot?'

The landlord looked involuntarily round the room for a possible spy. 'Guard your tongue!' he murmured, terror-stricken.

David laughed on. 'You, my friend, shall be my first pupil.'

'God forbid! And I must beg you to find other lodgings.'

David smiled grimly at this first response to his mission. 'I dare say I shall find another stove,' he said cheerfully—at which the landlord, who had never in his life taken such a decisive step, began to think he had gone too far. 'You will take the advice of a man who knows the world,' he said in a tone of compromise, 'and throw all those crazy notions into the river where you cast your sins at New Year. A young, fine-looking man like you! Why, I can find you a Shidduch (marriage) that will keep you in clover the rest of your life.'

'Ha! ha! ha! How do you know I'm not married?'

'Married men don't go shooting so lightheartedly. Come, let me take you in hand; my commission is a very small percentage of the dowry.'

'Ah, so you're a regular Shadchan' (marriage-broker).

'And how else should I live? Do you think I get fat on this inn? But people stay here from all towns around; I get to know a great circle of marriageable parties. I can show you a much larger stock than the ordinary Shadchan.'

'But I am so link' (irreligious).

'Nu! Let your ear-locks grow—the dowry grows with them.' Mine host had quite recovered his greasy familiarity.

'I can't wait for my locks to grow,' said David, with a sudden thought. 'But if you care to introduce me to Tinowitz, you will not fail to profit by it, if the thing turns out well.'

The landlord rubbed his hands. 'Now you speak like a sage.'

III

Tinowitz read the landlord's Hebrew note, and surveyed the suitor disapprovingly. And disapproval did not improve his face—a face in whose grotesque features David read a possible explanation of his surplus stock of daughters.

'I cannot say I am very taken with you,' the corn-factor said. 'Nor is it possible to give you my youngest daughter. I have other plans. Even the eldest—'

David waved his hand. 'I told my landlord as much. Am I a Talmud-sage that I should thus aspire? Forgive and forget my Chutzpah (impudence)!'

'But the eldest—perhaps—with a smaller dowry—'

'To tell the truth, Panie Tinowitz, it was the landlord who turned my head with false hopes. I came here not to promote marriages, but to prevent funerals!'

The corn-factor gasped, 'Funerals!'

'A pogrom is threatened—'

'Open not your mouth to Satan!' reprimanded Tinowitz, growing livid.

'If you prefer silence and slaughter—' said David, with a shrug.

'It is impossible—here!'

'And why not here, as well as in the six hundred and thirty-eight other towns?'

'In those towns there must have been bad blood; here Jew and Russian live together like brothers.'

'Cain and Abel were brothers. There were many peaceful years while Cain tilled the ground and Abel pastured his sheep.'

The Biblical reference was more convincing to Tinowitz than a wilderness of arguments.

'Then, what do you propose?' came from his white lips.

'To form a branch of the Samooborona. You must first summon a meeting of householders.'

'What for?'

'For a general committee—and for the expenses.'

'But how can we hold a meeting? The police—'

'There's the synagogue.'

'Profane the synagogue!'

'Did not the Jews always fly to the synagogue when there was danger?'

'Yes, but to pray.'

'We will pray by pistol.'

'Guard your tongue!'

'Guard your daughters.'

'The Uppermost will guard them.'

'The Uppermost guards them through me, as He feeds them through you. For the last time I ask you, will you or will you not summon me a meeting of householders?'

'You rush like a wild horse. I thank Heaven you will not be my son-in-law.'

Tinowitz ended by demanding time to think it over. David was to call the next day.

When, after a sleepless night on the stove, he betook himself to the corn-factor's house, he found it barred and shuttered. The neighbours reported that Tinowitz had gone off on sudden business, taking his wife and daughters with him for a little jaunt.

IV

The flight of Tinowitz brought two compensations, however. David was promoted from the stove to the bedroom. For the lodger he replaced had likewise departed hurriedly, and when it transpired that the landlord had betrothed this young man to the second of the Tinowitz girls, David divined that the corn-factor had made sure of a son-in-law. His other compensation was to find in the remaining bed a strapping young Jew named Ezekiel Leven, who had come up from an outlying village for the military lottery, and who proved to be a carl after his own heart. Half the night the young heroes planned the deeds of derringdo they might do for their people. Ezekiel Leven was indeed an ideal lieutenant, for he belonged to one of the rare farming colonies, and was already handy with his gun. He had even some kinsfolk in Milovka, and by their aid the Rabbi and a few householders were hurriedly prevailed upon to assemble in the bedroom on a business declared important. Ezekiel himself must, unfortunately, be away at the drawing, but he promised to hasten back to the meeting.

Each member strolled in casually, ordered a glass of tea, and drifted upstairs. The landlord, uneasily sniffing peril and profit, and dismally apprehending pistol lessons, left the inn to his wife, and stole up likewise to the fateful bedroom. Here, after protesting fearfully that they would ruin him by this conspiratorial meeting, he added that he was not out of sympathy with the times, and volunteered to stand sentinel. Accordingly, he was posted at the ragged window-curtain, where, with excess of caution, he signalled whenever he saw a Christian, in uniform or no. At every signal David's oratory ceased as suddenly as if it had been turned off at the main, and the gaberdined figures, distributed over the two beds and the one chair, gripped one another nervously. But David was used to oratory under difficulties. He lived on the same terms with the police as the most desperate criminals, and a foreigner who should have witnessed the secret meetings at which tactics were discussed, arms distributed, scouts despatched, and night-watches posted, would have imagined him engaged in a rebellion instead of in an attempt to strengthen the forces of law and order.

He had come to Milovka, he explained, to warn them that the Black Hundreds were soon to be loosed upon the Jewish quarter. But no longer must the Jew go like a lamb to the shambles. Too long, when smitten, had he turned the other cheek, only to get it smitten too. They must defend themselves. He was there to form a branch of the Samooborona. Browning revolvers must be purchased. The wood-choppers must be organized as a column of axe-bearers. There would be needed also an ambulance corps, with bandages, dressings, etc.

The shudder at the first mention of the pogrom was not so violent as that which followed the mention of bandages. Each man felt warm blood trickling down his limbs. To what end, then, had he escaped the conscription? The landlord at the window wiped the cold beads off his brow, and was surprised to find his hand not scarlet.

'Brethren,' Koski the timber-merchant burst out, 'this is a Haman in disguise. To hold firearms is the surest way of provoking—'

'I don't say you shall hold firearms!' David interrupted. 'It is your young men who must defend the town. But the Kahal (congregation) must pay the expenses—say, ten thousand roubles to start with.'

'Ten thousand roubles for a few pistols!' cried Mendel the horse-dealer. 'It is a swindle.'

David flushed. 'We have to buy three pistols for every one we get safely into the town. But one revolver may save ten thousand roubles of property, not to mention your life.'

'It will end our lives, not save them!' persisted the timber-merchant. 'This is a plot to destroy us!'

A growl of assent burst from the others.

'My friends,' said David quietly. 'A plot to destroy you has already been hatched; the question is, are you going to be destroyed like rats or like men?'

'Pooh!' said the horse-dealer. 'This is not the first time we have been threatened, if not with death, at least with extra taxes; but we have always sent Shtadlonim (ambassadors). We will make a collection, and the president of the Kahal shall go at once to the Governor, and present it to him'—here Mendel winked—'to enable him to take measures against the pogrom.'

'The Governor is in the plot,' said David.

'He can be bought out,' said the timber-merchant.

'Pogroms are more profitable than presents,' rejoined David drily. 'Let us rather prepare bombs.' A fresh shudder traversed the beds and the chairs, and agitated the window-curtain.

'Bombs! Presents!' burst forth the old Rabbi. 'These are godless instruments. We are in the hands of the Holy One—blessed be He! The Shomer (Guardian) of Israel neither slumbereth nor sleepeth.'

'Neither does the Shochet (slaughterer) of Israel,' said David savagely.

'Hush! Epicurean!' came from every quarter at this grim jest; for the Shomer and the Shochet are the official twain of ritual butchery.

The landlord, seeing how the tide was turning, added, 'Brazen Marshallik (buffoon)!'

'I will appoint a day of fasting and prayer,' concluded the Rabbi solemnly.

A breath of reassurance wafted through the room. 'And I, Rabbi,' said Gütels the grocer, 'will supply the synagogue with candles to equal in length the graves of all your predecessors.'

'May thy strength increase, Gütels!' came the universal gratitude, and the landlord at the window-curtain drew a great sigh of relief.

'Still, gentlemen,' he said, 'if I may intrude my humble opinion—Reb Mendel's advice is also good. God is, of course, our only protection. But there can be no harm in getting, lehavdil (not to compare them), the Governor's protection too.'

'True, true.' And the faces grew still cheerier.

'In God's name, wake up!' David burst forth. 'In Samooborona lies your only salvation. Give the money to us, not to the Governor. We can meet and practise in your Talmud-Torah Hall!'

'The holy hall of study!' gasped the Rabbi. 'Given over to unlawful meetings!'

'The hooligans will meet there, if you don't,' said David grimly. 'Don't you see it is the safest place for us? The police associate it only with learned weaklings.'

'Hush, Haman!' said the timber-merchant, and rose to go. David's voice changed to passion; memories of things he had seen came over him as in a red mist: an old man scalped with a sharp ladle; a white-hot poker driven through a woman's eye; a baby's skull ground under a True Russian's heel. 'Bourgeois!' he thundered, 'I will save you despite yourselves.' The landlord signalled in a frenzy, but David continued recklessly, 'Will you never learn manli—'

They flung themselves upon him in a panic, and held him hand-gagged and struggling upon the bed.

Suddenly a new figure burst into the room. There was a blood-freezing instant in which all gave themselves up for lost. Their grip on David relaxed. Then the mist cleared, and they saw it was only Ezekiel Leven.

'Blessed art thou who comest!' cried David, jumping to his feet. 'You and I, Ezekiel, will save Milovka.'

'Alas!' Ezekiel groaned. 'I drew a low number—I go to fight for Russia.'

V

Fifteen thousand roubles were soon collected for the Governor, but even before they were presented to him the Rabbi, in mortal terror of that firebrand of a David, had rushed to inquire whether Self-Defence was legal, and might the Talmud-Torah Hall be legitimately used for drilling. Sharp came an order that Jews found with firearms or in conclave for non-religious purposes should be summarily shot. And so, when the Shtadlonim arrived with the fifteen thousand roubles, the Governor was able to point out severely that if a pogrom did occur they would have only themselves to blame. The Jews of Milovka had begun to carry pistols like revolutionaries; they planned illegal assemblies in halls; was it to be wondered at if the League of True Russians grew restive? However, he would do his best with these inadequate roubles to have extra precautions taken, but let them root out the evil weeds that had sprung up in their midst, else even his authority might be overborne by the righteous indignation of the loyal children of the Little Father. Tremblingly the Ambassadors crept back with their empty money-bags.

Poor David now found it impossible to get anybody to a meeting. His landlord had forbidden any more gatherings in the inn, and his original audience would have called as a deputation upon David to beg him to withdraw from the town, but that might have been considered a conspirative meeting. So one of the Ambassadors was sent to inform the landlord instead.

'Don't you think I've already ordered him off my premises?'

'But he is still here!'

'Alas! He threatens to shoot me—or anybody who massers (informs),' said the poor landlord.

The Ambassador shivered.

'As if I would betray a brother-in-Israel!' added the landlord reproachfully.

'No, no—of course not,' said the Ambassador. 'These fellows are best left alone; they wear fuses under their waistcoats instead of Tsitsith (ritual fringes). Let us hope, however, a sudden death may rid us of him.'

'Amen,' said the landlord fervently.

Not that David had any reason for clinging to so squalid a hostel. But his blood was up, and he took a malicious pleasure in inflicting his perilous presence upon his prudential host.

Reduced now to buttonholing individuals, he consoled himself with the thought that the population was best tackled by units. One fool or coward was enough to infect or betray a whole gathering.

Still intent on the sinews of war, he sallied out after breakfast, and approached Erbstein the Banker. Erbstein held up his hands. 'But I've just given a thousand roubles to guard us from a pogrom!'

'That was for the Governor. Give me only a hundred for Self-Defence.'

The Banker puffed tranquilly at his big cigar. 'But our rights are bound to come in the end. We can only get them gradually. Full rights now are nonsense—impossible. It is bad tactics to ask for what you cannot get. Only in common with Russia can our emancipation—'

'I am not talking of our rights, but of our lives.' David grew impatient.

Being a Banker, Erbstein never listened, though he invariably replied. His success in finance had made him an authority upon religion and politics.

'Trust the Octobrists,' he said cheerily.

'I'd rather trust our revolvers.'

The Banker's cigar fell from his mouth.

'An anarchist! like my nephew Simon!'

David began to realize the limitations of the financial intellect. He saw that to get ideas into Bankers' brains is even more difficult than to get cheques from their pockets. Still, there was that promising scapegrace Simon! He hurried out on his scent, and ran him to earth in a cosy house near the town gate. Simon practised law, it appeared, and his surname was Rubensky.

The young barrister, informed of his uncle's accusation of anarchism, laughed contemptuously. 'Bourgeois! Every idea that makes no money he calls anarchy. As a matter of fact, I'm the exact opposite of an anarchist: I'm a socialist. I belong to the P.P.S. We're not even revolutionary like the S.R.'s.'

'I'm afraid I'm a great ignoramus,' said David. 'I don't even know what all these letters stand for.'

Simon Rubensky looked pityingly as at a bourgeois.

'S.R.'s are the silly Social Revolutionists; I belong to the Polish Party of Socialism.'

'Ah!' said David, with an air of comprehension. 'And I belong to the Jewish Party of Self-Defence! I hope you'll join it too.'

The young lawyer shook his head. 'A separate Jewish party! No, no! That would be putting back the clock of history. The non-isolation of the Jew is an unconditional historic necessity. Our emancipation must be worked out in common with Russia's.'

'Oh, then you agree with your uncle!'

'With that bourgeois! Never! But we are Poles of the Mosaic Faith—Jewish Poles, not Polish Jews.'

'The hooligans are murdering both impartially.'

'And the Intellectuals equally,' rejoined Simon.

'But the Intellectuals will triumph over the Reactionaries,' said David passionately, 'and then both will trample on the Jews. Didn't the Hungarian Jews join Kossuth? And yet after Hungary's freedom was won—'

Simon's wife and sister here entered the room, and he introduced David smilingly as a Ghetto reactionary. The young women—sober-clad students from a Swiss University—opened wide shocked eyes.

'So young, too!' Simon's wife murmured wonderingly.

'Would you have me stand by and see our people murdered?'

'Certainly,' she said, 'rather than see the Zeitgeist set back. The unconditional historic necessity will carry us on of itself towards a better social state.'

'There you go with your Marx and your Hegel!' cried Simon's sister. 'I object to your historic materialism. With Fichte, I assert—'

'She is an S.R.,' Simon interrupted her to explain.

'Ah,' said David. 'Not a P.P.S. like you and your wife.'

'Simon, did you tell him I was a P.P.S.?' inquired his wife indignantly.

'No, no, of course not. A Ghetto reactionary does not understand modern politics. My wife is an S.D., I regret to say.'

'But I have heard of Social Democrats!' said David triumphantly.

Simon's sister sniffed. 'Of course! Because they are a bourgeois party—risking nothing, waiting passively till the Revolution drops into their hands.'

'The name of bourgeois would be better applied to those who include the landed peasants among their forces,' said Simon's wife angrily.

'If I might venture to suggest,' said David soothingly, 'all these differences would be immaterial if you joined the Samooborona. I could make excellent use of you ladies in the ambulance department.'

'Outrageous!' cried Simon angrily. 'Our place is shoulder to shoulder with our fellow-Poles.'

Simon's sister intervened gently. Perhaps the mention of ambulances had awakened sympathy in her S.R. soul. 'You ought to look among your own Party,' she said.

'My Party?'

'The Ghetto reactionaries—Zionists, Territorialists, Itoists, or whatever they call themselves nowadays.'

'Are there any here?' cried David eagerly.

'One heard of nothing else,' cried Simon bitterly. 'Fortunately, when the police found they weren't really emigrating to Zion or Uganda, the meetings were stopped.'

David eagerly took down names. Simon particularly recommended two young men, Grodsky and Lerkoff, who had at least the grace of Socialism.

But Grodsky, David found, had his own panacea. 'Only the S.S.'s,' he said, 'can save Israel.'

'What are S.S.'s?' David asked.

'Socialistes Sionistes.'

'But can't there be Socialism outside Zion?'

'Of course. We have evolved from Zionism. The unconditional historic necessity is for a land, but not for a particular land. Our Minsk members already call themselves S.T.'s—Socialist Territorialists.'

'But while awaiting your territory, there are the hooligans,' David reminded him. 'Simon Rubensky thought you would be a good man for the self-defence corps.'

'Join Rubensky! A P.P.S.! Never will I associate with a bourgeois like that!'

'He isn't joining.'

The S.S. hesitated. 'I must consult my fellow-members. I must write to headquarters.'

'Letters do not travel very quickly or safely nowadays.'

'But Party Discipline is everything,' urged Grodsky.

David left him, and hunted up Lerkoff, who proved to be a doctor.

'I want to get together a Samooborona branch,' he explained. 'Herr Grodsky has half promised—'

'That bourgeois!' cried Lerkoff in disgust. 'We can have nothing to do with traitors like that!'

'Why are they traitors?' David asked.

'All Territorialists are traitors. We Poali Zion must jealously guard the sacred flame of Socialism and Nationality, since only in Palestine can our social problem be solved.'

'Why only in Palestine?' inquired David mildly.

The P.Z. glared. 'Palestine is an unconditional historic necessity. The attempt to form a Jewish State elsewhere can only result in failure and disappointment. Do you not see how the folk-instinct leads them to Palestine? No less than four thousand have gone there this year.'

'And a hundred and fifty thousand to America. How about that folk-instinct?'

'Oh, these are the mere bourgeois. I see you are an Americanist Assimilator.'

'I am no more an A.A. than I am a Z.Z.,' said David tartly, adding with a smile, 'if there is such a thing as a Z.Z.'

'Would to Heaven there were not!' said Lerkoff fervently. 'It is these miserable Zioni-Zionists, with their incapacity for political concepts, who—'

Milovka, amid all its medievalism, possessed a few incongruous telephones, and one of these now started ringing violently in Dr. Lerkoff's study.

'Ah!' he exclaimed, 'talk of the devil. There is a man who combines all the worst qualities of the Z.Z.'s and the Mizrachi. He also imagines he has a throat disease due to swallowing flecks of the furs he deals in.' After which harangue he collogued amiably with his patient, and said he would come instantly.

'Hasn't he the disease, then?' asked David.

'He has no disease except too much vanity and too much money.'

'While you cure him of the first, I should like to try my hand at the second,' said David laughingly.

'Oh, I'll introduce you, if you let me off.'

'You I don't ask for money, but your medical services would be invaluable. Milovka is in danger.'

'Milovka to the deuce!' cried Lerkoff. 'Our future lies not in Russia.'

'I talk of our present. Do let me appoint you army surgeon.'

'Next year—in Jerusalem!' replied the doctor airily.

VI

Lerkoff asked David to wait in another room while he saw Herr Cantberg professionally. There was an Ark with scrolls of the Law in the room, betiding a piety and a purse beyond the normal. Presently Lerkoff reappeared chuckling.

'He knows all about you, you infamous rascal,' he said.

'You have told him?'

'He told me; he always knows everything. You are a baptized police spy, posing as a P.P.S. I suppose he's heard of your visit to Herr Rubensky.'

'But I shall undeceive him!'

'Not if you want his money. Such a blow to his vanity would cost you dear. Go in; I did not tell him you were the young man he was telling me of. I must fly.' The P. Z shook David's hand. 'Don't forget he's the bourgeois type of Zionist; his object is not to create the future, but to resurrect the dead past.'

'And mine is to keep alive the living present. Won't you—?' But the doctor was gone.

The Mizrachi Z.Z. proved unexpectedly small in stature and owl-like in expression; but his 'Be seated, sir—be seated; what can I do for you?' had the grand manner. It evoked a resentful chord in David.

'It is something I propose to do for you,' he said bluntly. 'Milovka is in danger.'

'It is, indeed,' said the M.Z.Z. 'When men like Dr. Lerkoff (in whose company I was sorry to see you) command a hearing, it is in deadly danger. An excellent physician, but you know the Talmudical saying: "Hell awaits even the best of physicians." And he calls himself a Zionist! Bah! he's more dangerous than that young renegade spy who dubs himself P.P.S.'

'But he seems very zealous for Zion,' said David uneasily.

Herr Cantberg shook his head dolefully. 'He'd introduce vaccination and serum-insertions instead of the grand old laws. As if any human arrangement could equal the wisdom of Sinai! And he actually scoffs at the Restoration of the Sacrifices!'

'But do you propose to restore them?' David was astonished.

The owl's eyes shone. 'What have we sacrificed ourselves for, all these centuries, if not for the Sacrifices? What has sanctified and illumined the long night of our Exile except a vision of the High Priest in his jewelled breastplate officiating again at the altar of our Holy Temple? Now at last the vision begins to take shape, the hope of Israel begins to shine again. Like a rosy cloud, like a crescent moon, like a star in the desert, like a lighthouse over lonely seas—'

The telephone impolitely interrupted him. His fine frenzy disregarded the ringing, but it jangled his metaphors. 'But, alas! our people do not see clearly!' he broke off. 'False prophets, colossally vain—may their names be blotted out!—confuse the foolish crowd. But the wheat is being sifted from the chaff, the fine flour from the bran, the edible herbs from the evil weeds, and soon my people will see again that only I—'

The telephone insisted on a hearing. Having refused to buy furs at the price it demanded, he resumed: 'Territorialist traitors mislead the masses, but in so far as they may bring relief to our unhappy people, I wish them Godspeed.'

'But what relief can they bring?' put in David impatiently. 'Without Self-Defence—'

'Most true. They will but kill off a few hundred people with fever and famine on some savage shore. But let them; it will all be to the glory of Zionism—'

'How so?' David asked, amazed.

'It will show that the godless ideals of materialists can never be realized, that only in its old home can Israel again be a nation. Then will come the moment for Me to arise—'

'But the English came from Denmark. And they're nation enough!'

The owl blinked angrily. 'We are the Chosen People—no historic parallel applies to us. As the dove returned to the ark, as the swallow returns to the lands of the spring, as the tide returns to the sands, as the stars—'

'Yes, yes, I know,' said David; 'but where is there room in Palestine for the Russian Jews?'

'Where was there room in the Temple for the millions who came up at Passover?' retorted Herr Cantberg crushingly.

The telephone here interposed, offering the furs cheaper.

'A godless Bundist!' the owl explained between the deals.

'A Bundist!' David pricked up his ears. From the bravest revolutionary party in Russia he could surely cull a recruit or two. 'Who is he?'

The owl tried to look noble, producing only a twinkle of cunning. 'Oh, I can't betray him; after all, he's a brother-in-Israel. Not that he behaves as such, opposing our candidate for the Duma! Three hundred and thirteen roubles,' he told the telephone sternly. 'Not a kopeck more. Eh? What? He's rung off, the blood-sucker!' He rang him up again. David made a note of the number.

'But what have you Zionists to do with the Parliament in Russia?' he inquired of the owl.

But the owl was haggling with the telephone. 'Three hundred and fifteen! What! Do you want to skin me, like your martins and sables?'

'You are busy,' interposed David, fretting at the waste of his day. 'I shall take the liberty of calling again.'

A telephone-book soon betrayed the Bundist's shop, and David hurried off to enlist him. The shopkeeper proved, however, so corpulent and bovine that David's heart sank. But he began bluntly: 'I know you're a Bundist.'

'A what?' said the fur-dealer.

David smiled. 'Oh, you needn't pretend with me; I'm a fighter myself.' He let a revolver peep out of his hip-pocket.

'Help! Gewalt!' cried the fur-dealer.

A beardless youth came running out of the back room. David laughed. 'Herr Cantberg told me that you were a Bundist,' he explained to the shopkeeper. 'And I came to meet a kindred spirit. But I was warned Herr Cantberg is always wrong. Good-morning.'

'Stop!' cried the youth. 'Go in, Reb Yitzchok; let me deal with this fire-eater.' And as the corpulent man retired with an improbable alacrity, he continued gravely: 'This time Herr Cantberg was not more than a hundred versts from the truth.'

David smiled. 'You are the Bundist.'

'Hush! Here I am the son-in-law. I study Talmud and eat Kest (free food). What news from Warsaw?'

'I want both you and your father-in-law,' said David evasively—'his money and your muscles.'

'He gives no money to the Cause, save unwillingly what I squeeze out of Cantberg.' The youth permitted himself his first smile. 'When he deals with that bourgeois at the telephone, I always egg him on to stand out for more and more, and my profit is half the extra roubles we extort. But as for myself, my life, of course, is at the disposal of headquarters.'

David was moved by this refreshing simplicity. He felt a little embarrassment in explaining that headquarters to him meant Samooborona, not Bund. The youth's countenance changed completely.

'Defend the Jews!' he cried contemptuously. 'What have we to do with the Jewish bourgeoisie?'

'The Bund is exclusively Jewish, is it not?'

'Merely because we found the rest of the Revolutionary body too clumsy for words. It was always getting caught, its printing-presses exhumed, its leaders buried. So we split off, the better to help our fellow-working-men. But we are a Labour party, not a Jewish party. We have the whole Russian Revolution on our shoulders; how can we throw away our lives for the capitalists of the Milovka Ghetto? Then there are the elections at hand—I have to work for the Left. Ah, here come some of our bourgeois; ask them, if you like. I will keep my father-in-law out of the shop.'

Two men in close confabulation strolled in, a third disconnected, but on their heels. With five Jews the concourse soon became a congress.

One of the couple turned out to be a Progressive Pole. He mistook David for a Zionist, and denounced him for a foreigner.

'We of the P.P.P.,' he said, 'will peacefully acquire equal rights with our fellow-Poles—nay, we shall be allowed to become Poles ourselves. But you Zionists are less citizens than strangers, and if you were logical, you would all—'

'Where's your own logic?' interrupted the disconnected man. 'Why don't you join the P.P.N. at once?'

The Progressive Pole frowned. 'The Nationalists! They are anti-Semites. I'd as soon join the League of True Russian Men.'

'And do you trust the P.P.P.?' his companion asked him. 'I tell you, Nathan, that only in the Progressive Democratic Party, with its belief in the equality of all nationalities—'

'If you want a Party free from anti-Semites,' David intervened desperately, 'you must join the Samoo—'

'I fear you will get no recruits here,' interrupted the Bundist, not unkindly. He added with a sneer: 'These gentlemen of the P.P.P. and the P.P.N. and the P.P.D. are all good Poles.'

'Good Poles!' echoed David no less bitterly. 'And the Poles voted en bloc to keep every Jewish candidate out of the Duma.'

'Even so we must be better Poles than they,' sublimely replied the member of the P.P.P. 'We are joining even the Clerical Parties of the Right for the good of our country. And now that the Party of National Concentration—'

'Go to the Labour Parties,' advised the P.D. 'There you may perchance find sturdy young men with the necessary Ghetto taint.' Of the four great Labour Parties, he proceeded to recommend the P.S.D. as the most promising for David's purposes. 'Not the Bolshewiki faction,' he added, 'but the Menshewiki. Recruits might also be found in the Proletariat or the P.P.S.—'

'No, I've tried the P.P.S.,' said David. 'But at any rate, gentlemen, since you must all see that the defence of our own lives is no undesirable object, a little contribution to our funds—'

A violent chorus of protest broke out. It was scarcely credible that only four men were speaking. All explained elaborately that they had their own Party Funds, and what a tax it was to run their candidates for the Duma, not to mention their Party Organ.

'You see,' said the Bundist, 'your only chance lies with the men of no Party, who have only their own bourgeois pleasures.'

'Are there such?' asked David eagerly.

A universal laugh greeted this inquiry.

'Alas, too many!' everybody told him. 'Our people are such individualists.'

'But where are these individualists?' cried David desperately.

As if in answer, the bovine proprietor, encouraged by the laughter, crept in again.

'You still here!' he murmured to David, taken aback.

'Yes, but if you'll give me a subscription for Jewish Self-Defence—'

'Jewish Emancipation!' cried the fur-dealer. 'Why didn't you say so at first?' He put his hand in his pocket. 'That's my Party—or rather the National Group in it, the Anti-Zionist faction.'

The stern Bundist laughed. 'No, he doesn't mean he's a J.E. even of the other faction.'

His father-in-law took his hand out of his pocket.

David cast a rebuking glance at the Bundist. 'Why did you interfere? Perhaps my way may prove the shortest to Jewish Emancipation.'

His hearers smiled a superior smile, and the fur-dealer shook his head. 'I belong also to the Promotion of Education Party—I am for peaceful methods,' he announced.

'So I perceived,' said David drily.

To be rid of him, the Bundist gave him the address of a man who kept aloof from Polish politics—a bourgeois cousin of his, Belchevski by name, who might just as well be killed off in the Samooborona.

But even Belchevski turned out to be a Territorialist. David imprudently told him he had seen his fellow-Territorialist Grodsky, who had half promised—

'Associate with a brainless, bumptious platform-screamer!' he screamed. 'He's worse than the hysterical Zionists. It is a territory we need, not Socialism.'

'I agree. But even more do we need Self-Defence.'

'The only Self-Defence is to leave Russia for a land of our own.'

'Five and a quarter million of us? Why, if two ships—one from Libau for the north, and one from Odessa for the south—sailed away every week, each bearing two thousand passengers, it would take over a quarter of a century. And by that time a new generation of us would have grown up.'

The Territorialist looked uneasy.

'Besides,' David continued, 'what new country could receive us at the rate of two hundred thousand a year? It would be a cemetery, not a country.'

The Territorialist smiled disdainfully. 'Why didn't you say at first you were a bourgeois? The unconditional historic necessity which has created the I.T.O. may drive at what pace it will; enough that as soon as our autonomous land is ready to receive us, I intend to be in the first shipload.'

'Have you this land, then?'

'Not yet. We've only had time to draw up the Constitution. No Socialism as that idiot Grodsky imagines. But Democracy. Hereditary privileges will be abol—'

'But what land is there?'

'Surely there are virgin lands.'

'Even the virgin lands are betrothed!' said David. 'And if there was one still without a lord and master, it would probably be a very ugly and sickly virgin. And, anyhow, it will be a long wooing. So in the meantime let me teach you to fire a pistol.'

'With all my heart—but merely to shoot wild beasts.'

'That is all I am asking for,' said David grimly.

Encouraged by this semi-success, David boldly called upon a tea-merchant quite unknown to him, and asked for a subscription to buy revolvers.

The tea-merchant, who was a small stout man, with a black cap of dubious cut, protested vehemently against such materialistic measures. Let them put their trust in Cultur! To talk Hebrew—therein lay Israel's real salvation. Let little children once again lisp in the language of Isaiah and Hosea—that was true Zionism.

'Then don't you want the Holy Land?' asked the astonished David.

'Merely as a centre of Cultur. Merely as a University where Herbert Spencer may be studied in the tongue of the Psalmist. All the rest is bourgeois Zionism. Political Zionism? Economic Zionism? Pah! Mere tawdry imitations of heathen politics!'

'Then you agree with the Chovevi Zionists!'

'Not at all. Zion is less a place than a state of mind. We want Culture—not Agriculture; we want the evolutionary efflorescence of Israel's inner personality—'

David fled, only to stumble upon a Nationalist who declared that Zionism was a caricature of true Nationalism, and Territorialism a cheap philanthropic substitute for it.

'Then why not join in the Self-Defence of our nation?' David asked.

'I will—when we are on our own soil. Your corps is a mere mockery of the military concept.'

David found no more comfort in his interview with the member of the L.A.E.R., who was convinced that only in the League for the Advancement of Equal Rights lay the Jew's true security. It was the one party whose success was sure, the only one based upon an unconditional historic necessity.

David's morning was not, however, to pass without the discovery of a man of no Party. And, strangely enough, he owed his find to the headache these innumerable Parties caused him. For, going into a chemist's shop for a powder, he was served by a red-bearded Jew whose genial face emboldened him to solicit a stock of bandages and antiseptics—in view of a possible pogrom.

'But the pogroms are over,' cried the chemist. 'They were but the expiring agonies of the old order. The reign of love is at hand, the brotherhood of man is beginning, and all races and creeds will henceforth live at peace under the new religion of science.'

David's headache rose again triumphant over the powder. Even a partisan would be easier to convince than this sort of seer.

'Why, a pogrom is planned for Milovka!'

'Impossible! Europe would not permit it. America would prohibit it. Did you not see the protest even in the Australian Parliament? Look on your calendar; we have reached the twentieth century, even according to the Christian calculation.'

David returned hopelessly to his inn.

Here he saw a burly Jew warming himself at the great stove. Before even ordering dinner, he made a last desperate attempt to save his morning.

'Me join a Jewish Self-Defence!' The burly Jew laughed loud and heartily. 'Why, I'm a True Believer!'

'A Meshummad!' David gasped. Modern as he was, the hereditary horror at the baptized apostate overcame him.

'Yes—I'm safe enough,' the Convert laughed. 'I've taken the cold-water cure. Besides, I'm the censor of Milovka!'

'Eh?' David looked like a trapped animal. The censor smiled on. 'Don't scowl at me like the other pious zanies. After all, you're an enlightened young man—a violinist, they tell me; you can't take your Judaism any more seriously than I take my baptism. Come—have a glass of vodka.'

'Then, you won't inform?' David breathed.

'Not unless you publish seditious Yiddish. Keep your pistols out of print. If my own skin is safe, that doesn't mean I'm made of stone like these Tartar devils. Landlord, the vodka. We'll drink confusion to them.'

'I—I have none,' stammered the landlord. 'I haven't the right.'

'There are no rights in Russia,' said the censor good-humouredly.

The landlord furtively produced a big bottle.

'But the idea of asking me to join the Self-Defence!' chuckled the burly Jew. 'You might as well ask me to play the violin!' he added with a wink.

David felt this was the first really sympathetic hearer he had met that morning.

VII

The vodka and a good three-course dinner (Plotki for fish, Lockschen for soup, and Zrazy for joint) brought David new courage, and again he sallied out to recruit.

This time he sought the market-place—a badly-paved square, bordered with small houses and congested with stalls and a grey, kaftaned crowd, amid which gleamed the blue blouses of the ungodly younger generation. He had hitherto addressed himself to the classes—he would hear the voice of the people.

On every side the voice babbled of the Duma—babbled happily, as though the word was a new religious charm or a witch's incantation. Crude political conversations broke out amid all the business of the mart. He had only to listen to know how he would be answered:

A blacksmith buying a new hammer stayed to argue with the vendor.

'We must put our trust in the Constitutional Democrats.'

'And why in the Cadets? Give me the Democrats.'

'Nay, we must put our trust only in the Czar.' (This came from the Rabbi's wife, who was cheapening fish at the next stall.)

'For shame, Rebbitzin! Put not your trust in Princes.'

The bystanders hushed down the text-quoter—a fuzzy-headed butcher-boy.

'Miserable Monarchists!' he sneered. 'We Jews will have no peace till the Republicans—'

'A Republic without Socialism!' interrupted a girl with a laundry basket. 'What good's that? Wait till the N.S.'s—'

'The D.R.'s are the only—' interrupted a phylactery-pedlar.

'And who but the Labour group promises equal rights to all nationalities?' interrupted a girl in spectacles. 'Trust the Trudowaja—'

'To the devil with the Labour Parties!' said an old-clo' man. 'Look how the Bundists have betrayed us. First they were bone of our bone; now it is they who by their recklessness provoke the pogroms.'

The blacksmith brought his hammer down upon the stall. 'There is only one party to trust, and that's the C.D.'s,' he repeated.

'Bourgeois!' simultaneously hissed the Republican youth and the Socialist lass.

'My children!' It was the bland voice of Moses the Shamash (beadle). 'Violence leads to naught. Even the Viborg Manifesto was a mistake. As a member of the Party of Peaceful Regeneration—'

'Peaceful Regeneration?' shouted the blacksmith. 'A Jew ally himself with the Reactionary Right, with the—!'

A Cossack galloped recklessly among the serried stalls. The Jews scattered before him like dogs. The member of the P.P.R. crawled under a barrow. Even the blacksmith froze up. David drew the moral when the Cossack had disappeared.

'Peaceful Regeneration!' he cried. 'There will be no Regeneration for you till you have the courage to leave Russian politics alone and to fight for yourselves.'

'Ah, you're a Maximalist,' said the beadle.

'No, I am only a Minimalist. I merely want the minimum—that we save our own lives.'

It was asking too little. The poor Russian Jews, like the rich Russian Jews, were largely occupied in saving the world, or, at least, Holy Russia. Crushed by such an excess of Christianity, David wandered round the market-place, looking into the bordering houses. In one of the darkest and dingiest sat a cobbler tapping at shoes, surrounded by sprawling children.

'Peace be to you,' called David.

'Peace have I always,' rejoined the cobbler cheerily.

David looked at the happy dirty children; he had seen their like torn limb from limb. 'But have you thought of the danger of a pogrom?' he said.

'I have heard whispers of it,' said the cobbler. 'But we Chassidim have no fear. Our wonder-rabbi, who has power over all the spheres, will utter a word, and—'

[Illustration: The Jews scattered before him like dogs.]

'A Tsaddik (wonder-rabbi) was killed in the last pogrom,' said David brutally. 'You must join a Self-Defence band.'

The cobbler ceased to tap. 'What! Go for a soldier! When the Rebbe caused me to draw a high number!'

'Our soldiering is not for Russia, but to save us from Russia. We must all join together!'

'Me join the Misnagdim!' cried the cobbler in horror. 'Never will I join with those who deny the Master-of-the-Name.'

David sighed. Suddenly he perceived a stalwart Jew lounging at a neighbouring door. He moved towards him, and broached the subject afresh. The lounger shook his head. 'You may persuade that foolish Chassid,' said he, 'but you cannot expect the rest of us to join with these heretics, these godless, dancing dervishes, who are capable even of saying the afternoon prayer in the evening!'

In the next house lived a Maskil (Intellectual), who looked up from his Hebrew newspaper to ask how he could be associated with a squad of young ignoramuses. His neighbour was a Karaite, drifted here from another community. The Karaite pointed out that Self-Defence was unnecessary in his case, as his sect was scarcely regarded by the authorities as Jewish. There were other motley Jews living round the market-place—a Lithuanian, who refused to co-operate with the Polish 'sweet-tooths,' and who was in turn stigmatized by a Pole as 'peel-barley,' in scarification of his reputedly stingy diet. A man from Odessa dismissed them both as 'cross-heads.' It was impossible to unite such mutually superior elements. Again weary and heart-sick, he returned towards the inn.

VIII

But his way was blocked by a turbulent stream of Jewish boys pouring out of the primary school. They seemed to range in years between eight and twelve, but even the youngest face wore a stamp of age, and though the air vibrated with the multiplex chatter which accompanies the exodus of cramped and muted pupils, the normal elements of joyousness, of horse-play, of individual freakishness, were absent. It was a common agitation that loosed all these little tongues and set all these little ears listening to the passionate harangues of ringleaders. Instead of hurrying home, the schoolboys lingered in knots round their favourite orators. A premature gravity furrowed all the childish foreheads.

With one of these orators David dimly felt familiar, and after listening for a few minutes to the lad's tirade against the 'autocracy of the school director' and the 'bureaucratic methods of the inspector,' it dawned upon him that the little demagogue was his own landlord's son.

'Hullo, Kalman!' he cried in surprise.

'Hullo, comrade!' replied the boy graciously.

'So you're a revolutionary, eh?' said David, smiling.

'All my class belongs to the Junior Bund,' replied the boy gravely.

'Then you're not so peaceful as papa!'

The lad's aplomb and dignity deserted him. He blushed furiously, and hung his head in shame of his Moderate parent.

'Never mind, Comrade Kalman,' said another boy, slapping his shoulder consolingly. 'We've all got some shady relative or another.'

A shrill burst of applause relieved the painful situation. Turning his head, David found all the childish eyes converged upon a single figure, a bulging-headed lad who had sprung into a sudden position of eminence—upon an egg-box. He was clothed in the blue blouse of Radicalism and irreligion, and the faint down upon his upper lip suggested that he must be nearing fifteen.

'Comrades!' he was crying. 'In my youth I myself was head boy at this school of yours, but even in those old days there was the same brutal autocracy. Your only remedy is a general strike. You must join the Syndical Anarchists.'

More shrill cheers greeted this fiery counsel. The members of the Junior Bund waved their satchels frenziedly. Only the landlord's son stood mute and frowning.

'You don't agree with him,' said David.

'No,' answered the little Bundist gravely. 'I follow Comrade Berl. But this fellow is popular because he was expelled from the Warsaw gymnasium as a suspect.'

'You must strike!' repeated the juvenile agitator. 'A strike is the only way of impressing the proletarian psychology. You must all swear to attend school no more till your demands are granted.'

'We swear!' came from all sides in a childish treble. But the frown on the brow of the landlord's son grew darker.

'It is well, comrades,' said the orator. 'Your success will be a lesson to your elders, too. Only by applying the Marxian philosophy of history can we upset the bourgeois Weltanschauung.'

The landlord's son reached the roof of the egg-box with one angry bound and stood beside the agitator. 'Marx is an old fogey!' he shouted. 'What's the good of a passive strike? Let us make a demonstration against the director; let us—'

'Who told you that?' sneered the orator. 'Comrade Berl or Comrade Schmerl?'

The boy missed the sarcasm of the rhyme. 'You know Schmerl's a mere milk-blooded "Attainer,"' he said angrily.

'Believe me,' was the soothing reply, 'even beyond the Five Freedoms the boycott is a better "Attainer" than the bomb.'

'Traitor! Bourgeois!' And a third boy jumped upon the egg-box. He had red hair and flaming eyes. 'If Russia is to be saved,' he shrieked, 'it will be neither by the Fivefold Formula of Freedom nor by the Fourfold Suffrage, but by the Integralists, who alone maintain the purity of the Social Revolutionary programme, as it was before the party degenerated into Maximalists and Mini—'

Here the egg-box collapsed under the weight of the three orators, and they sprawled in equal ignominy. But the storm was now launched. A score of the schoolboys burst into passionate abstract discussion. The unity necessary to the school strike was shattered into fragments.

David ploughed his way sadly through the mimetic mob of youngsters, who were yet not all apes and parrots, he reflected. Just as Jewry had always had its boy Rabbis, its infant phenomenons of the pulpit, prodigies of eloquence and holy learning, so it now had its precocious politicians and its premature sociologists. He was tempted for a moment to try his recruiting spells upon the juvenile Integralist, whose red hair reminded him of his girl cousin's, but it seemed cruel to add to the lad's risks. Besides, had not the boy already proclaimed—like his seniors—that Russia, not Jewry, was to be saved?

It was an hour of no custom when he got back to the inn, so that he was scarcely surprised to find host and hostess alike invisible. He sat down, and began to write a melancholy Report to Headquarters, but a mysterious and persistent knocking prevented any concentration upon his task. Presently he threw down his pen, and went to find out what was the matter. The noises drew him downwards.

The landlord, alarmed at the footsteps, blew out his light.

'It's only I,' said David.

The landlord relit the candle. David saw a cellar strewn with iron bars, instruments, boxes, and a confused heap of stones.

'Ah, hiding the vodka,' said David, with a smile.

'No, we are widening and fortifying the cellar—also provisioning the loft.'

'Samooborona?' said David.

'Precisely—and a far more effective form than yours, my young hot-head.'

'Perhaps you are right,' said David wearily. He went back to his Report. He was glad to think that the little Bundist had an extra chance. After all, he had achieved something, he would save some lives. Perhaps he would end by preaching the landlord's way—passive Samooborona was better than none.

IX

But the Report refused to write itself. It was too dismal to confess he had not collected a kopeck or one recruit. He picked up a greasy fragment of a Russian newspaper, and read with a grim smile that the Octobrists had excluded Jews from their meetings. That reminded him of Erbstein the Banker, who had bidden him put his trust in them. Would the Banker be more susceptible now, under this disillusionment? Alas! the question was, could a Banker be disillusioned? To be disillusioned is to admit having been mistaken, and Bankers, like Popes, were infallible.

David bethought himself instead of the owlish Mizrachi, his visit to whom had been left unfinished.

He threw down his pen, and repaired again to the house with the Ark and the telephone.

But as he reached Cantberg's door it opened suddenly, and a young man shot out.

'Never, father!' he was shrieking—'Never do I enter this house again.' And he banged the door upon the owl, and rushed into David's arms.

'I beg your pardon,' he said.

'It is my fault,' murmured David politely. 'I was just going to see your father.'

'You'll find him in a fiendish temper. He cannot argue without losing it.'

'I hope you've not had a serious difference.'

'He's such a bigoted Zionist—he cannot understand that Zionism is ein überwundener Standpunkt.'

'I know.'

'Ah!' said the young man eagerly. 'Then you can understand how I have suffered since I evolved from Zionism.'

'What are you now, if I may ask?'

'The only thing that a self-respecting Jew can be—a Sejmist, of course!'

'A Jewish Party?' asked David eagerly. After all the enthusiasm for Russian politics and world politics he was now pleased with even this loquacious form of Self-Defence.

'Come and have a glass of tea; I will tell you all about it,' said the young man, soothed by the prospect of airing his theories. 'We will go to Friedman's inn—the University Club, we call it, because the intellectuals generally drink there.'

'With pleasure,' said David, sniffing the chance of recruits. 'But before we talk of your Party I want to ask whether you can join me in a branch of the Samooborona.'

The young man's face grew overclouded.

'Our Party cannot join any other,' he said.

'But mine isn't a Party—a corps.'

'Not a Party?'

'No.'

'But you have a Committee?'

'Yes—but only—'

'And Branches?'

'Naturally, but simply—'

'And a Party-Chest?'

'The money is only—'

'And Conferences?'

'Of course, but merely—'

'And you read Referats—'

'Not unless—'

'Surely you are a Party!'

'I tell you no. I want all Parties.'

'I am sorry. But I'm too busy just now to consider anything else. Our Party-Day falls next week, and there's infinite work to be done.'

'Work!' cried David desperately. 'What work?'

'There will be many great speeches. I myself shall not speak beyond an hour, but that is merely impromptu in the debate. Our Referat-speakers need at least two hours apiece. We did not get through our last session till five in the morning. And there were scenes, I tell you!'

'But what is there to discuss?'

'What is there to discuss?' The Sejmist looked pityingly at David. 'The great question of the Duma elections, for one thing. To boycott or not to boycott. And if not, which candidates shall we support? Then there is the question of Jewish autonomy in the Russian Parliament—that is our great principle. Moreover, as a comparatively new Party, we have yet to thresh out our relations to all the existing Parties. With which shall we form blocs in the elections? While most are dangerous to the best interests of the Jewish people and opposed to the evolution of historic necessity, with some we may be able to co-operate here and there, where our work intersects.'

'What work?' David insisted again.

'Doesn't our name tell you? We are the Vozrozhdenie—the Resurrectionists—our work is an unconditional historic necessity springing from the evolution of—!'

The door of the inn arrested the Sejmist's harangue. As he pushed it open, a babel of other voices made continuance impossible. The noise came entirely from a party of four, huddled in a cloud of cigarette-smoke near the stove. In one of the four David recognised the tea-merchant of the morning, but the tea-merchant seemed to have no recollection of David. He was still expatiating upon the Individuality of Israel, which, it appeared, was an essence independent of place and time. He nodded, however, to the young Sejmist, observing ironically:

'Behold, the dreamer cometh!'

'I a dreamer, forsooth!' The young man was vexed to be derided before his new acquaintance. 'It is you Achad-Haamists who must wake up.'

The tea-merchant smiled with a superior air. 'The Vozrozhdenie would do well to study Achad-Haam's philosophy. Then they would understand that their strivings are bound to lead to self-constriction, not self-expression. You were saying that, too, weren't you, Witsky?'

Witsky, who was a young lawyer, demurred. 'What I said was,' he explained to the Sejmist, 'that in your search for territorial-proletariat practice you Sejmists have altogether lost the theory. Conversely the S.S.'s have sacrificed territorial practice to their territorial theory. In our party alone do you find the synthesis of the practical and the ideal. It alone—'

'May I ask whom you speak for?' intervened David.

'The newest Jewish Social Democratic Artisan Party of Russia!' replied Witsky proudly.

'Are you the newest?' inquired David drily.

'And the best. If we desire Palestine as the scene of our social regeneration, it is because the unconditional historic necessity—'

The Sejmist interrupted sadly: 'I see that our Conference will have to decide against relations with you.'

'Pooh! The S.D.A.'s will only be the stronger for isolation. Have we not of ourselves severed our relations with the D.K.'s? In the evolution of the forces of the people—'

'It is not right, Witsky, that you should mislead a stranger,' put in his sallow, spectacled neighbour. 'Or perhaps you misconceive the genetic moments of your own programme. What evolution is clearly leading to is a Jewish autonomous party in Parliament.'

'But we also say—' began the other two.

The sallow, spectacled man waved them down wearily. 'Who but the P.N.D.'s are the synthesis of the historic necessities? We subsume the Conservative elements of the Spojnia Narodowa National League and of the Party of Real Politics with the Reform elements of the Democratic League and the Progressive Democrats. Consequently—'

'But the true Polish Party—' began Witsky.

'The Kolo Polskie (Polish Ring) is half anti-Semitic,' began the Sejmist. The three were talking at once. Through the chaos a thin piping voice penetrated clearly. It came from the fourth member of the group—a clean-shaven ugly man, who had hitherto remained silently smoking.

'As a philosophic critic who sympathizes with all Parties,' he said, 'allow me to tell you, friend Witsky, that your programme needs unification: it starts as economic, and then becomes dualistic—first inductive, then deductive.'

'Moj Panie drogi (my dear sir),' intervened David, 'if you sympathize with all Parties, you will join a corps for the defence of them all.'

'You forget the philosophic critic equally disagrees with all Parties.'

David lost his temper at last. 'Gentlemen,' he shouted ironically, 'one may sit and make smoke-rings till the Messiah comes, but I assure you there is only one unconditional historic necessity, and that is Samooborona.'

And without drinking his tea—which, indeed, the Resurrectionist had forgotten to order—he dashed into the street.

X

He was but a youth, driven into action by hellish injustice. He had hitherto taken scant notice of all these Parties that had sprung up for the confusion of his people—these hybrid, kaleidoscopic combinations of Russian and Jewish politics—but as he fled from the philosophers through the now darkening streets, his every nerve quivering, it seemed to him as if the alphabet had only to be thrown about like dice to give always the name of some Party or other. He had a nightmare vision of bristling sects and pullulating factions, each with its Councils, Federations, Funds, Conferences, Party-Days, Agenda, Referats, Press-Organs, each differentiating itself with meticulous subtlety from all the other Parties, each defining with casuistic minuteness its relation to every contemporary problem, each equipped with inexhaustible polyglot orators speechifying through tumultuous nights.

Well, it could not be helped. In the terrible nebulous welter in which his people found themselves, it was not unnatural that each man should grope towards his separate ray of light. The Russian, too, was equally bewildered, and perhaps all this profusion of theories came in both from the same lack of tangibilities. Both peoples possessed nothing.

Perhaps, indeed, the ultimate salvation of the Jews lay in identifying themselves with Russia. But then, who could tell that the patriots who welcomed them to-day as co-workers would not reject them when the cause was won? Perhaps there was no hope outside preserving their own fullest identity. Poor bewildered Russian Jew, caught in the bewilderments both of the Russian and the Jew, and tangled up inextricably in the double confusion of interlacing coils!

The Parties, then, were perhaps inevitable; he must make his account with them. How if he formed a secret Samooborona Committee, composed equally of representatives of all Parties? But, then, how could he be sure of knowing them all? He might offend one by omitting or miscalling it; they formed and re-formed like clouds on the blue. A new Party, too, might spring up overnight. He might give deadly affront by ignoring this Jonah's gourd. Even as he thus mused, there came to him the voices of two young men, the one advocating a P.P.L.—a new Party of Popular Liberty—the other insisting that the new Volksgruppe of all anti-Zionist Parties was an unconditional historic necessity. He groaned.

It seemed to him as he stumbled blindly through the ill-paved alleys that a plague of doctors of philosophy had broken out over the Pale, doctrinaires spinning pure logic from their vitals, and fighting bitterly against the slightest deviation from the pattern of their webs. But the call upon Israel was for Action. Was it, he wondered with a flash of sympathy, that Israel was too great for Action; too sophisticated a people for so primitive and savage a function; too set in the moulds of an ancient scholastic civilization, so that, even when Action was attempted, it was turned and frozen into Philosophy? Or was it rather that eighteen centuries of poring over the Talmud had unfitted them for Action, not merely because the habit of applying the whole brain-force to religious minutiæ led to a similar intellectualization of contemporary problems—of the vast new material suddenly opened up to their sharpened brains—but also because many of these religious problems related only to the time when Israel and his Temple flourished in Palestine? The academic leisure and scrupulous discrimination that might be harmlessly devoted to the dead past had been imported into the burning present—into things that mattered for life or death.

Yes, the new generation chopped the logic of Zionism or Socialism, as the old argued over the ritual of burnt-offerings whose smoke had not risen since the year 70 of the Christian era, or over the decisions of Babylonian Geonim, no stone of whose city remained standing. The men of to-day had merely substituted for the world of the past the world of the future, and so there had arisen logically-perfect structures of Zionism without Zion, Jewish Socialism without a Jewish social order, Labour Parties without votes or Parliaments. The habit of actualities had been lost; what need of them when concepts provided as much intellectual stimulus? Would Israel never return to reality, never find solid ground under foot, never look eye to eye upon life?

But as the last patch of sunset faded out of the strip of wintry sky, David suddenly felt infinitely weary of reality; a great yearning came over him for that very unreality, that very 'dead past' in which pious Jewry still lived its happiest hours. Oh, to forget the Parties, the jangle of politics and philosophies, the tohu-bohu of his unhappy day! He must bathe his soul in an hour's peace; he would go back like a child to the familiar study-house of his youth, to the Beth Hamedrash where the greybeards pored over the great worm-eaten folios, and the youths rocked in their expository incantations. There lay the magic world of fantasy and legend that had been his people's true home, that had kept them sane and cheerful through eighteen centuries of tragedy—a watertight world into which no drop of outer reality could ever trickle. There lay Zion and the Jordan, the Temple and the Angels; there the Patriarchs yet hovered protectively over their people. Perhaps the Milovka study-house boasted even Cabbalists starving themselves into celestial visions and graduating for the Divine kiss. How infinitely restful after the Milovka market-place! No more, for that day at least, would he prate of Self-Defence and the horrible Modern.

He asked the way to the Beth Hamedrash. How fraternally the sages and the youths would greet him! They would inquire in the immemorial formula, 'What town comest thou from?' And when he told them, they would ask concerning its Rabbi and what news there was. And 'news,' David remembered with a tearful smile, meant 'new interpretations of texts.' Yes, this was all the 'news' that ever ruffled that peaceful world. Man lived only for the Holy Law; the world had been created merely that the Law might be studied; new lights upon its words and letters were the only things that could matter to a sensible soul. Time and again he had raged against the artificiality of this quietist cosmos, accusing it of his people's paralysis, but to-night every fibre of him yearned for this respite from the harsh reality. He rummaged his memory for 'news'—for theological ingeniosities, textual wire-drawings that might have escaped the lore of Milovka; and as one who draws nigh to a great haven, he opened the door of the Beth Hamedrash, and, murmuring 'Peace be to you,' dropped upon a bench before an open folio whose commentaries and super-commentaries twined themselves lovingly in infinite convolutions round its holy text. Immediately he was surrounded by a buzzing crowd of youths and ancients.

'Which Party are you of?' they clamoured eagerly.

XI

The pogrom arrived. But it arrived in a new form for which even David was unprepared. Perhaps in consequence of the Rabbi's warning to the Governor, Self-Defence was made ridiculous. No Machiavellian paraphernalia of agents provocateurs, no hooligans with false grey beards, masquerading as Jewish rioters or blasphemers. Artillery was calmly brought up against the Jewish quarter, as though Milovka were an enemy's town.

As the shells began to burst over the close-packed houses, David felt grimly that an economic Providence had saved him from wasting his time in training pistoliers.

The white-faced landlord, wringing his hands and saying his Vidui (death-bed confession), offered him and his violin-case a place in the cellar, but he preferred to climb to the roof, from which with the aid of a small glass, he had a clear view of the cordon drawn round the doomed quarter. A ricocheting cannon-ball crashed through the chimney-pots at his side, but he did not budge. His eyes were glued upon a figure he had espied amid the cannon.

It was Ezekiel Leven, his whilom lieutenant, with whom he had dreamed of Maccabean deeds. The new conscript, in the uniform of an artilleryman, was carefully taking sight with a Gatling gun.

'Poor Ezekiel!' David cried. 'Yours is the most humorous fate of all! But have you forgotten there is still one form of Samooborona left?' And with an ironic laugh he turned his pistol upon himself.

The great guns boomed on hour after hour. When the bombardment was over, the peace of the devil lay over the Ghetto of Milovka. Silent were all the fiery orators of all the letters of the alphabet; silent the Polish patriots and the lovers of Zion and the lovers of mankind; silent the bourgeois and the philosophers, the timber-merchants and the horse-dealers, the bankers and the Bundists; silent the Socialists and the Democrats; silent even the burly censor, and the careless Karaite and the cheerful Chassid; silent the landlord and his revolutionary infant in their fortified cellar; silent the Rabbi in his study, and the crowds in the market-place.

The same unconditional historic necessity had overtaken them all.

Israel Zangwill – A Short Biography

Israel Zangwill was born in London on 21st January 1864, to a family of Jewish immigrants from the Russian Empire. His father, Moses, was from modern-day Latvia, and his mother, Ellen Hannah Marks Zangwill, from modern-day Poland.

Zangwill was initially educated in Plymouth and Bristol. At age 9 he was enrolled into the Jews' Free School in Spitalfields in east London. The school was for the children of Jewish immigrants and added to its teaching, of both secular and religious matters, with supplies of clothing, food, and health care. Zangwill excelled here. He began to teach part-time at the school and eventually full time. Whilst teaching he also studied with the University of London and by 1884 had earned his BA with triple honours in philosophy, history, and the sciences.

He had already co-written a tale entitled 'The Premier and the Painter' when he resigned as a teacher owing to differences with the managers of the school. Zangwill now turned to journalism for his new career path, initiating Ariel, The London Puck, as well as working in various capacities for the London press.

His writing earned him the sobriquet "the Dickens of the Ghetto" primarily based on his much lauded novel 'Children of the Ghetto: A Study of a Peculiar People' in 1892 and its glimpse of the poverty-stricken life in London's Jewish quarter.

As a writer he was keen to reflect on his political and social outlooks. His simulation of Yiddish sentence structure in English aroused great interest. His mystery work, 'The Big Bow Mystery' (1892) was the first locked room mystery novel. Social satire flowed with 'The King of Schnorrers' (1894). A follow up to 'Children of the Ghetto' was 'Ghetto Tragedies' in 1894 and 'Dreamers of the Ghetto' in 1898 which included essays on famous Jews such as Baruch Spinoza, Heinrich Heine and Ferdinand Lassalle.

Zangwill was also involved with narrowly focused Jewish issues as an assimilationist, an early Zionist, and later a territorialist. In the early 1890s he had joined the Lovers of Zion movement in England. A few years later, in 1897, he took part in the "pilgrimage" of English Jews to Palestine. That same year he also joined Theodor Herzl (considered the father of modern political Zionism) in founding the World Zionist Organization and would take part in the first seven Zionist congresses. Zangwill was much admired as an orator and spoke movingly and eloquently on the issues he was passionate on.

In 1901 he had written that "Palestine is a country without a people; the Jews are a people without a country". On Herzl's visits to London, they worked closely together. In a debate at the Article Club in November 1901 however Zangwill was still mis-using the facts: "Palestine has but a small population of Arabs and fellahin and wandering, lawless, blackmailing Bedouin tribes." And made a direct plea to "restore the country without a people to the people without a country. For we have something to give as well as to get. We can sweep away the blackmailer—be he Pasha or Bedouin—we can make the wilderness blossom as the rose, and build up in the heart of the world a civilisation that may be a mediator and interpreter between the East and the West."

In 1902, Zangwill wrote that Palestine "remains at this moment an almost uninhabited, forsaken and ruined Turkish territory". But from this point on Zangwill began to see things differently which would, in 1905, result in his breakaway from Zionism.

Zangwill quit the established philosophy of Zionism when his plan for a homeland in Uganda was rejected and instead founded his own organisation; the Jewish Territorialist Organization. Its stated goal was to create a Jewish homeland in whatever territory in the world could be found for them. At that point in time suggestions were as varied as Canada, Australia, Mesopotamia, Argentina, Uganda and Cyrenaica.

Amongst the challenges in his life he found time to write poetry. He had translated a medieval Jewish poet in 1903 and his own volume 'Blind Children' in 1908 shows his promise in this new endeavour.

In 1908, Zangwill told a London court that he had been naive when he made his 1901 speech and had since recognised that the Arab population was twice that of the United States.

Zangwill was a supporter of both feminism and pacifism, but his greatest effect was as a writer who gained a wide audience with the idea of combining ethnicities into a single, American nation. The hero of 'The Melting Pot', proclaims: "America is God's Crucible, the great Melting-Pot where all the races of Europe are melting and reforming... Germans and Frenchmen, Irishmen and Englishmen, Jews and Russians – into the Crucible with you all! God is making the American."'

'The Melting Pot' made Zangwill's name as an admired playwright. The title itself was popularised as the phrase to use to describe American absorption of immigrants when it ran in the United States.

When the play opened in Washington D.C. on 5th October 1909, former President Theodore Roosevelt leaned over the edge of his box and shouted, "That's a great play, Mr. Zangwill, that's a great play." In a later letter in 1912 Roosevelt went further "That particular play I shall always count among the very strong and real influences upon my thought and my life."

'The Melting Pot' shone a spotlight on America's growth through the input of its new waves of immigrants. Zangwill was writing as "a Jew who no longer wanted to be a Jew. His real hope was for a world in which the entire lexicon of racial and religious difference is thrown away."

According to Ze'ev Jabotinsky, Zangwill told him in 1916 that, "If you wish to give a country to a people without a country, it is utter foolishness to allow it to be the country of two peoples. This can only cause trouble. The Jews will suffer and so will their neighbours. One of the two: a different place must be found either for the Jews or for their neighbours".

In 1917 he wrote "'Give the country without a people,' magnanimously pleaded Lord Shaftesbury, 'to the people without a country.' Alas, it was a misleading mistake. The country holds 600,000 Arabs."

With the end of World War I, and a more clearly defined idea of a Jewish settlement in Palestine, Zangwill once more returned to the Zionist effort and made efforts on behalf of the Balfour Declaration, proclaiming the right of a Jewish homeland in Palestine

In 1921 Zangwill wrote "If Lord Shaftesbury was literally inexact in describing Palestine as a country without a people, he was essentially correct, for there is no Arab people living in intimate fusion with the country, utilizing its resources and stamping it with a characteristic impress: there is at best an Arab encampment, the break-up of which would throw upon the Jews the actual manual labor of regeneration and prevent them from exploiting the fellahin, whose numbers and lower wages are moreover a considerable obstacle to the proposed immigration from Poland and other suffering centers".

Despite his advocacy on Jewish matters he would be disappointed to know that despite Israel now being established the quarrels of the Middle East continue to divide.

Israel Zangwill died on 1st August 1926 in Midhurst, West Sussex.

Israel Zangwill – A Concise Bibliography

The Bachelors' Club (1891)
The Old Maid's Club (1892)
Children of the Ghetto: A Study of a Peculiar People (1892)
Grandchildren of the Ghetto (1892)
The Big Bow Mystery (1892)
Merely Mary Ann (1893)
The King of Schnorrers (1894)
The Master (1895) (based on the life of George Wylie Hutchinson)
Without Prejudices (1896)
Dreamers of the Ghetto (1898)
Ghetto Tragedies, (1899)
"The Return to Palestine", New Liberal Review, (Dec. 1901)
Children of the Ghetto (1902)
"Providence, Palestine and the Rothschilds", The Speaker, vol. 4, no. 125 (22 February 1902)
Selected Religious Poems (1903) Translation of the Jewish Medieval Poet Solomon in Cabirol.
The Grey Wig: Stories and Novelettes (1903)
The Serio-Comic Governess (1904)
Merely Mary Ann (1904)
Ghetto Comedies, (1907)
Blind Children (1908) Poetry
The Melting Pot (1909)
Italian Fantasies (1910) Travel
Chosen Peoples, (1919)
The War For The World (1916)
The Principle of Nationalities (1917)
Chosen Peoples (1918)
Hands Off Russia: Speech by Mr. Israel Zangwill at the Albert Hall, February 8th, 1919. London: Workers'
Socialist Federation, n.d. (1919)
The Voice of Jerusalem. (1921)

Filmography

Children of the Ghetto (1915, based on the play Children of the Ghetto)
The Melting Pot (1915, based on the play The Melting Pot)
Merely Mary Ann (1916, based on the play Merely Mary Ann)
The Moment Before (1916, based on the play The Moment of Death)
Mary Ann (1918, based on the play Merely Mary Ann)
Nurse Marjorie (1920, based on the play Nurse Marjorie)
Merely Mary Ann (1920, based on the play Merely Mary Ann)
The Bachelor's Club (1921, based on the novel We Moderns)
We Moderns (1925, based on the play We Moderns)
Too Much Money (1926, based on the play Too Much Money)

Perfect Crime (1928, based on the novel The Big Bow Mystery)
Merely Mary Ann (1931, based on the play Merely Mary Ann)
The Crime Doctor (1934, based on the novel The Big Bow Mystery)
The Verdict (1946, based on the novel The Big Bow Mystery)